TETHER

Book One
The Tether Trilogy

ELIJAH STEELE

POLISHED KNOB PRESS

Unlock Your Happy Ending

polishedknobpress.com

For My Husband

Since Order first left our world a nightmare, you've reminded me that Chaos dares to raise its voice, dares to dream, dares to hope for something better. You stood when others would have fled—steadfast, unyielding, and true. This book endured because of your endless patience and unwavering support, and it is as much yours as mine, woven through with your faith, your friendship, and your love.

TABLE OF CONTENTS

Part I
LUST

July 3, 2026

"Lust is a pleasure bought with pains, a delight
hatched with disquiet, a content passed with
fear, and a sin finished with sorrow."

~ Demonax

"Could a greater miracle take place than for us
to look through each other's eyes for an
instant."

~ Henry David Thoreau

1
PRELUDE

WHISKEY DICK.

Dex never truly understood the term. Three bourbons in and he was now hard—and horny—as hell, evident by his failed attempt to contain the bulge in his jock, his erection spilling from the pouch and pinned down by the waistband.

At five-foot-eight, he carried himself like he took up more space—solid chest and thighs, thick arms veined from work, not vanity; Rugby had built his body, but his routine on the force had kept it honed. Black waves of hair, long on top and close-cropped at the sides, faded into a thick beard that softened the hard edges of his jaw. His face held an almost-magnetic force, somewhere between heat and gravity, a power amplified in the right light by the glow in his dark eyes.

This wasn't his scene anymore, but Eden was once his favorite club—dark and seedy without the pomp or pretension, filled with enough haze to make any sinner look like a saint and enough temptation to turn any saint into a sinner. Recent stress from work and a streak of horniness had brought him out tonight, and he was determined to relieve both.

He was on the prowl—eyes focused as he glanced around the dance floor, avoiding stares from men he wasn't interested in as he scanned the room. It wasn't their appearance that typically turned him off, but the desperation in their eyes as they all but begged for his attention. He didn't mind the occasional come-fuck-me eyes, especially if the glance was more playful than penetrating, but he was always creeped out by unnerving stares that lingered a little too long, and lips that were licked a bit too thirstily.

He preferred to hunt than to be hunted.

And just as Dex wondered if his own eyes carried the same desperation he despised, the spotlight swept across a stranger he'd never seen before. Dex knew he had been out of the club scene for a bit, but he'd not seen this man at the grocery store, the park, the gym, or even the coffee shop. If he were new to town, maybe Atlanta hadn't yet turned him bitter.

Charlie Denton hadn't planned on going to Eden. He'd told himself it was just a detour, harmless curiosity, just a stop before heading home for the night.

The place hit him the second he stepped inside—smoke, sweat, and a heat that had nothing to do with the hot July night. Music thumped low and relentless, a bassline that pressed into his ribs. Lights cut across the room in fractured colors, catching on bare shoulders, on leather harnesses, on skin slick with exertion and ecstasy. Men moved with an ease Charlie envied— hands on waists, mouths grazing necks, kisses on strangers' lips that bore the hunger of a long-lost love. He envied the casual intimacy of people who weren't afraid of being seen.

He ordered a bourbon, neat—stronger than he needed, but enough to steady him when part of him wanted to sprint for the exit. The first swallow burned, the second eased the tightness in his chest. By the third, the week-long itch he'd been carrying sharpened into hunger.

He remembered years ago, in a short stretch of being single after the ultimatum, when loneliness had driven him to the curtained-off booths in a seedy video store. He'd told himself it was boredom that led him inside, an accident when another man's mouth lingered beyond the other side of the gloryhole. But the memory never left. He'd replayed it too often for it to have meant nothing.

And now, standing here, drink in hand, surrounded by men who didn't hide what they wanted, that memory felt like a prophecy. He told himself it was still just curiosity, that he just wanted to see this world up-close instead of peering in from the outside. Dip a toe without diving—just the tip, maybe. But every swallow of bourbon betrayed the lie.

Charlie leaned against a column at the edge of the dance floor, letting the crowd surge around him. A man brushed past, hand grazing his chest, lingering long enough to make the offer clear. Another leaned close to be heard over the music, smile easy and unashamed. Charlie shook his head, muttering, "Not tonight." He tried to sound casual, but his pulse betrayed him. They moved on without offense, swallowed by the current of bodies.

And then he saw him. Dex.

It hit like a jolt to the spine—his partner on the force of twelve years, standing at the bar as if he belonged here. Charlie knew every line of that body, every gesture and habit, even the meaning of his stance. But here it looked different. Looser. Hungrier. His shoulders rippled as he leaned in, lips curving into the half-smile that had undone Charlie years ago and made him start questioning himself.

Charlie's throat tightened.

The jealousy surprised him—sharper than he'd imagined—but what struck first, hot and undeniable, was desire. In this light Dex looked like someone else entirely. Freer. Feral. Fuckable. Someone Charlie wanted to reach for in a way he'd never dared admit.

His hand tightened on the glass, bourbon sloshing at the rim.

Dex laughed at something, head tilting back just enough for the light to catch his profile. Then his eyes shifted—past Charlie, past the crowd—locking onto someone else.

Charlie followed his gaze to a man: older, broader, carrying the kind of quiet confidence that bent the room around him. The flicker in Dex's eyes, the way his smile sharpened, stabbed low in Charlie's gut.

Envy surged before he could stop it. He knew the look too well, and it confirmed the thing he'd been circling for years: his hunger for Dex was more than he'd ever wanted to admit. He slid against the wall, pressing into the shadows, watching.

Another man tried for his attention—this one bolder, hand brushing his thigh, mouth leaning close. Charlie turned, his voice sharp but kind: "Not interested."

The man smirked and moved on, unfazed.

Charlie's chest was tight, blood loud in his ears. The drink in his hand offered no comfort, its effects only impeding his departure. His eyes tracked Dex through the shifting bodies, unable to look away.

He'd come here for curiosity. But curiosity was gone now, stripped away by the bourbon, bass, and the sight of his work partner—the secret source of his urges—now chasing someone else. What was left was horniness, jealousy, and the bitter knowledge that he wanted nothing more than for Dex to notice him.

But Dex never looked his way.

Charlie stayed in the shadows, pushing away anyone who drifted too close, nursing his drink with a faint tremor in his hand, watching Dex cross the dance floor toward a man he wished was him.

The man in Dex's sight had the kind of body he craved: tall, bearded, broad-shouldered, with a chest and frame like a Norseman. Thick, strawberry-blond hair dusted across his pecs, down his stomach, and covered his forearms like prairie grass at sunset, glistening even through the fog of the smoke machine.

Completely drawn to him, Dex made his way across the distance for a closer inspection. A few men trying to flirt along the way impeded his progress, but Dex was kind, thanking them for the flattery, and he kept pushing his way through the sea of testosterone until he was shaking his ass directly in front of his target. Without being too obvious, Dex slid back little by little, just close enough for the man to make the next move.

They found each other in the rhythm, the man sliding behind, wrapping his arms loosely around

Dex's waist, pulling Dex close until he felt the man's heart pounding in his chest. From the first graze of skin, Dex knew—this wasn't going to be fast; it was going to be good.

They stayed like that for a while, gyrating and grinding to the drumming in the dark. Dex was lost in the man's arms, hair prickling as hands wandered playfully all over his chest and abdomen, an explorer seeking treasure.

If only he'd venture further south, Dex fantasized, cock pulsing at the thought.

Dex felt feral, leaning into the man's sweat-soaked, furry abdomen pressed against his back. Hands deserted their original quest and were now massaging his neck, gently kneading desires into Dex's skin, molding him like clay, his arms raised just enough for Dex to breathe in the intoxicating musk of his pits.

He couldn't take the suspense. Dex turned to meet the eyes of the man that had ensnared him in more than just his arms—striking blue, something the spotlight had failed to point out.

"New to Atlanta?" Dex asked.

"Not exactly..." the man's baritone voice carried a Southern drawl hidden beneath Ivy League polish, "...prodigal son returns home."

"I'm Dex."

"David," he replied, smiling, "a pleasure."

Dex winked, "Exactly what I am hoping."

David pulled him closer. Dex eye-level with the top of his chest, instinctively laid his head there as they danced. David's heartbeat accelerated, not from dancing but from danger. Dex felt it, too, equally unsure, equally afraid of the next step.

He kissed David's chest through sweaty fur—musky, salty, sweet with pheromones that spiked Dex's pulse. Spotting a shimmer on David's left nipple, he flicked it with his tongue, earning a soft purr.

Dex looked up to find David staring down in amused delight, a smile spreading. "What... what is it?"

"You're *fucking* adorable."

Dex blushed, caught off guard by the gentleness. "You're one to talk, handsome."

The spotlight found David once again, and his head glowed under it as he lowered it to meet Dex's. Their lips met in a soft first kiss. Dex's hand cupped David's neck, urging him not to stop. Their tongues danced in rhythm with their feet, fifteen minutes feeling like an hour as the music pulsed and the crowd dissolved into darkness.

"Woof," David growled, pulling away only to turn Dex around, pressing belly to back once again, lips trailing to Dex's neck and ears.

As David's arms tightened, Dex felt David's hard cock pressed firmly against the top of his ass. He let David know it didn't go unnoticed, grinding back against him as they danced. Unable to abstain from touching it any longer, he turned back around and brushed against the bulge in David's jeans purposely, teasingly.

He wanted to pull it out right there on the dance floor, but he felt David was far too modest to expose himself to a room full of eyes. Dex thought it a lost cause—that David was too prudish for any play at all—until David guided Dex's hand into the waistband of his Levi's.

It was rock hard long before Dex's fingers grazed it and seemed to swell even more in his grasp—just shy of eight inches with the perfect girth.

"You did that," David murmured, kissing him. "He's been at attention since our tongues first touched."

Dex smiled mischievously. Hand still wrapped tightly around David's cock, Dex led him into Eden's darkroom, found an empty stretch of wall, and pushed him against it. The air was ripe with sweat and sex, the floor sticky with secrets, walls lit only by flickering strobes and instinct. He sensed David's hesitation layered over eagerness, so he whispered in his ear, "Ignore everyone else— there's no one here except you and me."

Charlie had followed at a distance, telling himself he only needed to know. To see. The bourbon still hummed in his blood, but not enough to drown out the sick pulse of curiosity pulling him down the narrow hallway behind Dex and his conquest.

The darkroom at Eden was more suggestion than space—velvet black, corners swallowed whole, bodies moving like shadows against shadows. The smell hit first: sweat, cologne, sex. Then the chorus—low moans and whispers rang out with the wet rhythm of mouths at work, the buzz of zippers going in both directions, all punctuated by the unmistakable sounds of men railing or being railed in the obscurity.

Even in the low red spill of light, Charlie picked out Dex instantly: the slope of his shoulders, the way he leaned into someone else. Into the man from the dance floor who, despite the darkness, Charlie had to admit was rather stunning. He understood the pull.

Still, Charlie's gut twisted. The man he'd spent twelve years beside in a police cruiser—secretly lusting over most of them—was now on his knees for another man, lips closing around him with a hunger Charlie had only fantasized about.

He froze, caught between lunging forward and announce his presence and the raw desire to just watch. His hand drifted without thought, unbuttoning his jeans, slipping inside, fingers wrapping around himself. The first slow stroke stole his breath. Jealousy and arousal coiled together, indistinguishable.

Dex's head bobbed lower, the man's hands gripping his hair. The sounds were obscene and beautiful, echoing in the dark. Charlie stroked in time, unable to look away, betrayal and lust sparking until he couldn't tell which burned hotter.

Then—a touch. Not his own.

A hand found him in the dark, sure and steady. He startled, but before he could react, a mouth followed—wet heat enveloping him, slow and deliberate. Someone unseen, faceless in the dark, nursing him with the same rhythm Dex was giving his conquest.

Charlie bit back a moan, one hand braced against the wall, the other still stroking himself at the base as the stranger's mouth worked him. His eyes never left Dex.

Every time Dex's man groaned, every time Dex swallowed deeper, Charlie's arousal spiked, shame threading through it until he was dizzy. He was fucking a stranger's mouth in the dark while watching the man he truly wanted on his knees for someone else.

God help him—he couldn't stop.

July 4, 2026

“I'm down on my knees, I wanna take you there.
In the midnight hour, I can feel your power.
Just like a prayer, you know I'll take you
there.”

~ Madonna

2
ORATORIO

THE NIGHT BEFORE the world changed, Dex Truitt was on his knees.

Not in prayer. But in an act far more honest.

Heavy bass rumbled the darkroom floor beneath his knees, tempo pulsing like a metronome conducting the rhythm of his oratorio. David's thighs framed either side of Dex's head, muscles taut and quivering under his grip. Dex took his time, taking in the heavy musk—sweat mixed with a hint of sandalwood he could only guess was David's bodywash. He savored the way David's breath hitched each time he slowed, the way David's fingers knotted into his hair—respectful, obedient, asking without asking. Dex liked that— a man who knew how to let go without needing to dominate, holding tension and tenderness in the same space.

As his tongue circled the head, Dex wondered what David's cock looked like in the light. He traced its shape with a teasing flick he knew drove men wild, dipping into the slit to taste his prize of precum—the nectar of the god that stood before him.

Dex worked David's shaft with more intention, cupping his hairy, heavy hangers with one hand while stroking with his other, matching the rhythm of his mouth. David's breath grew shallow; his balls pulled up as his cock stiffened in Dex's throat.

A low purr built in David's abdomen—Dex felt it each time his forehead pressed into his stomach as he tried to take him deeper, hungry for the payoff. David's balls tightened further, the purr exploding into a feral growl that surely drew attention. Dex didn't care—he'd earned the salty, sweet release that shot forcefully down his throat... one, two, three heavy ropes pulsed until his throat and mouth were full. He slid David out just enough to swallow, then worked his head for the remnants until his mouth was full again.

Dex climbed to his feet, met David's gaze, and pressed a cum-filled kiss on his trembling lips. "You taste like... breakfast at your place in the morning."

"I don't usually..." David began, breath ragged.

"I know," Dex whispered. He didn't need him to finish. He'd felt it from the start—the hesitation, the ache for connection under the bravado. Dex always read people without trying. And though the room was dark, he stared deeply into David. "But—*this* is different, and you can't tell me you don't feel it."

"I don't know what *this* is," David responded, "but I can honestly say that you are definitely far different from any man I've met before."

Charlie zipped up quickly, the metallic purr loud in the hushed darkness. His breathing stayed uneven, pulse thrumming in his throat. The stranger who had just swallowed him hadn't spoken, hadn't even lingered—just melted back into the shadows, one more faceless silhouette among many.

For a moment Charlie lingered against the wall, the smell of men and sex heavy in the air. His legs trembled faintly, release tangled with adrenaline. Movement pulled Charlie's eye—Dex, hair mussed, with the man at his side—and his gut clenched.

He waited until they'd slipped beyond the threshold before stepping from the room, steadying himself with a shaky breath. Bass slammed up from the floorboards into his bones. Lights spun across sweat-slick bodies, leather straps, and mouths pressed together in ravenous abandon.

Charlie scanned the room, catching Dex and his companion just before they slipped through the main doors together and into the night.

His chest tightened, jealousy crawling up his throat like fire. Ridiculous, he knew. Jen was at home, probably flipping through bridal magazines she'd dog-eared years ago. She had said yes after breaking up with him once for dragging his feet. Three years later—still no date, no vows, just an unanswered promise like a question he couldn't bring himself to answer.

And here he was. In Eden. Watching Dex.

Dex didn't know he was here. Didn't know about the darkroom, the stranger's mouth, the way Charlie's eyes had clung to him from the shadows. Hell, Dex had no idea Charlie even looked at men this way. How could he? Charlie had worked so hard to build a wall of ridicule and slurs between them when they first partnered up, burying the truth under all that noise.

But the wall had cracks. And Dex, without even trying, kept finding them.

This jealousy, this anger—it was one-sided, private, absurd. Yet knowing that didn't make it any less real.

Fuck, he thought bitterly. *If Dex can have his fun, so can I.*

Petty, maybe, but the tightness in his chest loosened at the thought of letting go of the lies he'd spent his life telling himself. He let the crowd take him, bodies pressing in, heat clinging. He moved with them, hips falling into the rhythm of the bass, bourbon still warm enough in his blood to still feel its effects.

Then he saw him.

Shirtless, torso thick but solid, blond fur covering his chest and stomach, catching the strobes in flashes of gold. A black leather harness cut bold lines across him, snug against the blond thatch beneath. His beard was thick, blond shot darker near the jaw, framing a confident grin. His eyes—clear, electric, striking even in the chaos and fog—locked on Charlie's without blinking.

Charlie froze under his stare.

The man moved closer until the crowd blurred away, beard brushing Charlie's cheek as he leaned close. "Dancing or just watching?"

The graze of beard was new, strange, but it lit a fire under Charlie's skin.

"I—" his voice caught, but a hand was already on his hip, pulling him into rhythm. His body betrayed him, moving before his mind caught up.

It felt terrifyingly natural.

The man leaned closer, "I'm Ryan."

Charlie turned, lips nearly touching Ryan's ear, "I'm Charlie."

Bass, lights, heat—everything blurred into sensation. Ryan's smile disarmed him, and his eyes penetrated, staring so deeply it felt like he saw through Charlie's walls.

Then Ryan leaned in—mouth hovering close, a question without words—waiting without pushing.

Charlie froze, needs colliding with nerves at the thought of his first kiss with a man. His heart was pounding so loudly it nearly drowned out the music.

Then Charlie leaned in. Their mouths met in a rush of heat, hesitation burning into hunger. He'd always been told he kissed well, but he was used to women; instinct carried him where experience could not, and he found the act wasn't so different—even slightly better.

Ryan's beard brushed against him, rough and warm, ruggedness contrasted with the lush softness of lips. Charlie angled his head, deepening the kiss, and Ryan answered with a slow, coaxing drag of tongue, stealing his breath and stripping away the last of his nerves. His knees weakened, chest tightened, cock stiffened, stretching the limits of his jeans.

Ryan's hands slid up Charlie's arms, gripping the swell of his shoulders, tugging him closer. Charlie mirrored, hands rising into the thick fur of Ryan's chest, gripping the leather harness strapped across it. The sensation intoxicated him: warm coarse hair, smooth strap, steady ripple of muscle shifting underneath.

Charlie's body answered—heat surging low, cock leaking, chest rising in shallow, hungry pulls of breath. He pressed forward, bodies meeting in a hard line of muscle and warmth, kiss spilling wetter, hungrier.

Ryan finally pulled back, only far enough to breathe. His eyes searched Charlie's face, burning with surprise and desire.

"Holy fuck," he growled, voice rough and reverent. "That was hot."

Ryan's hands slid up Charlie's sides, pausing at his chest. He leaned in, murmuring against his ear: "Shirt off."

Charlie hesitated; years of habit and fear. But Ryan tugged at the hem, and something within him snapped loose. He yanked it over his head and tucked it through his belt.

Cool air kissed his skin before Ryan's lips and hands did. Fingers combed slowly through his chest hair.

"Fuck, you're gorgeous," Ryan said.

The words hit harder than Charlie expected.

Ryan groaned into his mouth, kissing deeper. Their bodies pressed together, fur against fur with only leather between them. Charlie's grip tightened—one fist around the strap, the other hand sliding to Ryan's flank.

Every scrape of beard, every drag of fur, every grind of hips—it was all new, all electric. His cock pressed hard against Ryan each time their hips collided.

Charlie laughed shakily, half a gasp. "You have me breathless."

Ryan's grin was wolfish. "Go ahead and catch your breath, but I can't promise I won't steal it again."

Then his mouth was back, fierce and hungry, beard scratching, tongue teasing. Charlie let himself be pulled under—every nerve lit, every denial gone.

Dex was gone with his stranger; and here, with Ryan, Charlie felt seen instead of just watching.

Ryan finally pulled back from the kiss, eyes dropping, grin spreading. "Jesus, you're leaking." He cupped the bulge, feeling dampness and heat soak through. A firm squeeze, then quick work of button and fly—denim tugged down just enough to free him. Charlie's cock slapped heavy and slick into Ryan's hand, head gleaming wet in the strobe.

Ryan didn't hesitate. Right there on the dance floor, he sank to his knees, harness creaking as he bent, mouth open, swallowing Charlie halfway in one practiced motion. The crowd surged around them, bass rattling, bodies glistening. Charlie surrendered for a moment—head tipped back, a raw groan tearing out as Ryan worked him slow and deep.

Then he felt the eyes. Dozens of them. Being watched pressed in on him, strangers' hungry stares crawling his skin. His body tensed. "No, stop," he pleaded, dragging Ryan up by the shoulders.

Ryan rose smoothly, lips wet, smirk unfazed. He leaned close, voice hot against Charlie's ear. "They're staring because you have a beautiful cock... and they're jealous I'm the one tasting it." He gave Charlie's shaft one last stroke, the precum oozing into his palm, before tucking him back into his jeans.

Charlie grabbed Ryan's wrist, pulling Ryan's palm to his lips, and licked at the viscous reward from it.

Without another word, Ryan threaded fingers through Charlie's and tugged him toward the coat check. Once Ryan showed the number, the attendant handed over a duffel. Ryan rummaged, pulled out a black jockstrap, and pressed it into Charlie's chest. "Let's go to the bathroom and get you into this."

Charlie hesitated—shame and thrill colliding—but Ryan's grin was relentless, coaxing. He followed.

In the cramped stall, Ryan pushed him against the door, stripped him quickly, then slid the jock into place. Before Charlie could catch his breath, Ryan was on his knees again, mouth wrapped back around him, hungry, devouring. Charlie braced himself on the metal walls, thighs trembling as Ryan's tongue worked.

Ryan pulled up after only a minute of teasing. "Sorry—you interrupted me earlier, so I wanted a longer go of it."

Charlie just laughed under his breath and kissed him.

Ryan stripped off his own pants, tucked them in his bag, and laid Charlie's clothes on top. "Let's drop this off and go dance."

"You drop that off. I'll grab us a couple waters."

Ryan found Charlie at the bar and downed the water he handed him. "Thanks, I needed that. You should finish yours, too—no pockets." He slapped his ass lightly.

They slid back to the floor near the deejay booth. Ryan's body fur glistened with sweat— something Charlie thought would repulse him, but it enthralled him instead. They kissed, pressed together, bodies slick, crowd roaring around them.

Even when Ryan turned with his ass pressed against him, Charlie was just as turned on holding him, fingers combing through fur. He kissed Ryan's shoulders and neck with a tenderness that surprised even him.

As their dancing turned erotic, Ryan's desire sharpened with every beat, every grind. He pulled Charlie close with a growl, "Come home with me."

Charlie shook his head, panic flashing in his eyes. "I can't. My fiancée—she's waiting at home."

Ryan's eyes narrowed, then softened. His hand slid down Charlie's chest, over the band of the jock. "Then let's go to the darkroom."

Charlie followed, pulse hammering with memory of his last experience within its abyss. At the threshold, Ryan snatched a foil packet from the container mounted by the door and tucked it into his teeth. Inside, darkness swallowed them, lit only by the dim red glow from the doorway. He pressed Charlie to the wall, freed his cock from the jock, tore the wrapper with his teeth, and rolled the condom on with deft hands.

"Don't worry, my ass is already pre-lubed," he murmured, turning to the wall, leaning forward into the perfect entry angle. "Just fuck me."

Charlie trembled, breath shaking, but lined up and slid in. Ryan groaned low as the heat and slickness welcomed him, Charlie's forehead falling to his shoulder in pure pleasure. His thrusts started tentative, careful, but Ryan's moans unlocked something feral. Ryan opened wider, urging him deeper, harder. Charlie gripped the harness, pulling him back, hips snapping until he lost himself in the rhythm. Release hit hard, a shudder ripping through him as he emptied his balls for the second time that night.

Ryan eased off him, slipped the rubber free, pinching it closed. "I want to taste you," he rasped, tipping his head back and pouring its contents down his throat.

Charlie was stunned, but something reckless slipped free. "I wanna taste too."

Ryan laughed, low and wild, kissing him deep, sharing the creamy saltiness still lingering on his tongue.

Panting, they slipped back out to the coat check. Ryan handed Charlie his clothes. "I know you have a fiancée but put my number in your phone... you never know when you'll need another release.

Reluctantly, Charlie opened his phone and handed it over. "Just don't make me regret it."

Ryan sent himself a message with Charlie's name, a chime sounding from his bag. "I promise you won't."

"And what about this?" Charlie tugged at the waistband of the jock he still wore.

"Keep it... so you can remember this moment." He gave Charlie one last lingering kiss, then turned back to the floor, leaving Charlie to dress alone.

Charlie closed his tab, smiled once more, and waved toward Ryan. But guilt over the life he betrayed built with every step toward his car, crashing over him in waves as he sat behind the wheel.

3

NOCTURNE

DAVID GRIPPED DEX'S hand tightly, afraid that letting it go would make him vanish—afraid that it was all in his head and Dex would cease to exist the moment he released him. He smiled, watching their arms swinging in unison as they walked down the sidewalk to his place.

Dex was a dream for him—dark features; a short, stocky build; thick beard and thicker legs; and a charm about him that wouldn't quit. He couldn't believe his luck—*so fucking adorable!*

"You live down the street?" Dex asked, trying to match the cadence of David's steps, his shorter legs desperately failing.

"Convenient, right?" David replied. "How about you—what part of the city?

"Midtown, south of Eighth Street," Dex said. "Convenient to the park."

"And you're sure you wanna come back to my place? We could always plan for another night."

"I don't want to pressure you and ruin an amazing night," Dex said, squeezing his hand, "but honestly, I am not ready for it to end. I want to say something else, but I'm afraid you'll think I am laying it on thick just to get laid."

"I am not that cynical, Dex," David smiled. "And no one promised you were getting laid anyway."

"Oh, really? That eight-inch weapon you're packing said something different earlier."

"God's cruel joke," David chuckled, "was giving me a dick just shy of that coveted mark."

"Something tells me that you've never received a single complaint."

"Enough about my dick—what were you going to say that was supposed to get you laid?"

"Just that I've dealt with a lot of loss in my life, seen a lot of death in my work—and tomorrow is never promised."

"Oof! That *is* laying it on thick. What do you do that brings so much death?"

"Promise not to run away?"

"Lemme guess. Funeral director?"

"No," Dex chuckled. "I'm a cop."

"Yeah, okay, mister public sex," David joked.

"It was just you and me, remember?" Dex replied. "Besides, you've got no evidence—it would never hold up in court."

David nearly bent over laughing, "You're schooling a lawyer on evidentiary support—and we could always pump your stomach for evidence."

"Pump my stomach all you want—you'd just prove your involvement in the crime."

"Touché."

They had already passed three apartment buildings as they walked south along Cheshire Bridge, David sensing Dex's hope that each was their destination as they approached.

"How much longer to your place?"

David guided Dex off Cheshire onto Liddell Drive, stopped, and pulled him close for another kiss. "Almost there, I promise. Just up ahead off Telfair."

David had told Dex that he was a lawyer, but that fact didn't quite register until they reached his townhouse. "Wow—okay, mister prodigal son. This place is nice! You do well for yourself."

"Did," David corrected as they climbed the stairs into the main living area. "Back in Boston, before family obligations brought me back home."

"A *Hah-vahd* boy, are you?" Dex teased in his best Boston accent.

David smiled, taking the bait. "Brown, actually. Not *smaht* enough for *Hah-vahd*. I joined a Boston firm after law school, and it's been home ever since."

"Family obligations?"

"Yep. My father passed on Memorial Day weekend."

"Sorry to hear that."

"Don't be," David said. "My dad was an abusive asshole all my life, and his drunk ass shouldn't have been driving. He hit a sandbar and was ejected from his boat—snapped his neck and died instantly."

Dex's heart sank. He hadn't expected that.

"My mom was hurt pretty badly," David continued, "but another boat saw it happen and pulled her to safety."

Dex hooked David by the belt loop and pulled him into his arms. The embrace was genuine. As David tightened his hold, the feelings flooded through. Dex often saw his sensitivity as a curse, but in that moment it let him glimpse all the pain David tried to hide.

He felt the weight of David's trauma: his drive to escape family, scars of a father's deep-rooted homophobia, and a mother's paralysis to stop the abuse. The story echoed in his own, making the connection even stronger.

"My family never accepted my sexuality either," Dex said, breaking the silence.

David pulled back eyes searching. "But I... I never... how did you know?"

"You said you'd never met anyone like me, remember?" Dex smiled, leaning in for another kiss. Not passionate like the one on the dance floor, but it was tender, weighted with past pain, present pleasure, and the possibility of a brighter future.

"Shall we go up to the bedroom?"

Dex ran his fingers through David's ginger beard, tugging until he lowered for a kiss. "Sure, but don't think that means you're getting lucky."

"An adorable man kissing me in my kitchen means that I already have," David countered, grabbing Dex's hand and leading him upstairs.

David could feel himself blushing. After too many bad one-night stands in his twenties, he vowed never to move this fast again. But Dex was right—*this* was (without a doubt) different, and so was Dex.

He gave Dex another tender kiss. "I don't want you to get the wrong impression of me."

"You forget that you already left an impression," Dex teased, "...in the back of my throat."

"Trust me, I won't forget that experience anytime soon."

David moved closer, slid his hands up Dex's sides, fingers slipping under his tight, black tank. He lifted it off in one fluid motion, freeing his hands to explore Dex's furry, muscular chest without restraint.

David lips and tongue teased from collar to ear as Dex's hands slid under his tee, tugging it off with equal ease, pausing only to let it pass between them.

"Even more striking in the light," Dex said, running his hands through David's chest hair.

David's mouth had already migrated to Dex's chest, tasting his sweat-slick skin. He flicked a nipple with his tongue while Dex fumbled with the button of his Levi's. Without pausing, David slid his fingers under the waistband of Dex's shorts, cupping his furry ass cheeks as he slid them to the floor.

Dex still fumbled with his Levi's, so David grabbed his wrist and leaned toward his ear. "I'll get them off, then I'll get you off."

"No," Dex insisted. "I don't want to get off yet."

"Fair enough," David agreed. "But let me at least give you a taste of my skills while getting a taste of you."

He released Dex's wrist and undid his own jeans, stripping fast, cock already standing stiff. Dex was hard too, though his hung downward with the weight—impossible not to notice.

"And you called *me* big boy?" David mused.

He stepped back to admire the full beauty of the man before him: fur blanketing a muscular chest, arms and shoulders nearly as broad at his own, ink covering both pecs, shoulders, and arms in a canvas of artwork with stories he longed to learn. Stomach fur blended into a full bush, trimmed just enough to maximize visual length—not that Dex needed help.

A mischievous tugged at Dex's mouth. "Like what you see?"

"More than that—I want and need it," David said, grabbing Dex's waist and tossing him on the bed with ease.

David positioned Dex on his back, coaxing him down onto the pillows. His hand slid from chest to abdomen until it reached the base of Dex's shaft.

Dex's cock was a masterpiece—one David could spend hours worshipping if given the chance. He started with his nose first, burying it deep in the glistening forest of hair at bush, groin, sack, and thighs, all steeped heavily in musk and sweat.

"Good to know there's some piggy hiding behind that polish," Dex said, breath catching as David's beard brushed his skin.

David inhaled deeply, savoring Dex's scent. "I have my moments."

Next came David's tongue, tracing a line from knee to navel before licking the entire nine inches of Dex's dick from tip to base.

Eagerness bubbled inside David as he pulled back the hood of Dex's dick—like unwrapping a gift. He plunged it past his lips, tongue circling inside the foreskin, tasting sweat, precum, and even the faint tang of piss. He wasn't one for watersports, but his cock twitched as if to defy that claim.

He worked Dex's shaft tenderly, mouth flooding with saliva as he swallowed most of the length. Precum mixed with spit, sweetening every motion.

Dex's balls were nearly as big as his own; David licked at them, eagerly tasting the intense saltiness as he gently sucked. Back at Dex's cock, he relished the girth—big enough to fill, not overwhelm. He made a fervid attempt to deepthroat, but out of practice, it was too great a challenge.

"Come here," Dex said, hand reaching.

David grabbed it, fingers intertwining eagerly, allowing Dex to pull him up to the head of the bed.

"That felt amazing," Dex assured, pulling him close for a kiss, "but I have other plans for my load."

Finally seeing David's body in the light was a revelation—no prying eyes, no distractions, just them. Dex had felt it even before the spotlight hit, something pulling him to turn at the exact moment, never guessing the connection would be this intense, this mutual.

His cock was as unapologetically handsome as the rest of him—veined and thick, promising stretch without sting. It rose from a tousled halo of copper-tinged curls that framed the base like a masterpiece. The shaft tapered into a pretty, pink head, smooth and plush like the crown of a ripe mushroom—flushed with arousal, angled with purpose. Beneath swung generous balls, heavy and furred, primal and untrimmed. All heat, heft, and hunger—too gorgeous not to worship.

But not now—having worshipped it earlier, Dex craved something else.

Dex's strength belied his stature. With a suggestive nudge and whispered desire, he flipped David onto his stomach. Kisses trailed down his neck and back, landing at the target he'd wanted since those Levi's fell to the floor: a muscular ass covered in reddish-blond hair.

It was damp—glistening with sweat from a night of dancing. As he ran his nose along David's hairy crack, the spiciness of sandalwood he'd experienced earlier mixed with David's natural sweet scent.

It tasted even better than it smelled. Soon his tongue circled the fleshy ridges of David's hole, then pressed inside—tender but eager.

"Fuuuuck!" they cried in unison, David in a baritone avowal of pure pleasure, Dex's more growl than grammar.

Dex worked David's hole with his tongue, David bucking with pleasure, pushing for him to go deeper.

"You taste amazing," Dex panted.

"And that feels amazing," David replied, squirming to reach something from the nightstand. He tossed it toward Dex. "I want to feel you inside me."

Dex grabbed lube that landed near his left hand, coated his shaft, and spread the rest over David's spit-slicked hole. "On your knees."

"Yes, sir," David said instinctively, obeying. He spread his knees wide, lowering his ass at the perfect height for easy entry. "It's been a while— be gentle."

"Gentle is my only mode at first," Dex reassured, smacking his dick playfully against David's hole a couple times before easing the head in with gentle pressure.

Once the tip slid in and he knew David wasn't in pain, Dex gripped his hips and thrust slowly, working deeper with a steady rhythm, drawing prayers, moans, and curses alike.

Confident that David was now accustomed to his cock, Dex pulled out, flipped him over so they were face to face, and reentered with ease as their lips met with a kiss.

It wasn't long before Dex reached the edge. He leaned to David's ear and told him he was close.

David grabbed his own cock, stroking in cadence with Dex's thrusts, working his head for more stimulation to meet the moment. "I'm getting close, too—fuck me harder. I want you deep. I want to feel your load when it releases."

"I'm almost there—kiss me."

The moment their lips and tongues touched, Dex flooded David's insides with one of his most intense loads in ages. Feeling it, David came too, shooting ropes across his chest and both their beards, cum pooling between them.

"You shoot massive loads," Dex said, pulling back to eye the mess. He eased out, then leaned forward to lap up the cum coating David.

"Come here," David said, pulling Dex close to lick his own load from Dex's beard.

Dex collapsed beside him. David chuckled, "That was awful—I didn't like that at all."

"Right?" Dex laughed. "Neither did I."

"Shower?"

"Fuck no. I want your scent on my beard as I fall asleep tonight—and when I wake in the morning."

“Good—’cause the piggy in me wants my scent on you too…” He buried his nose in Dex’s beard before kissing him—tender, then deep.

Dex shivered. “Let’s get under the covers.”

“So, you’re staying?” David asked, sliding back the covers.

Dex did the same. “You owe me breakfast, remember?”

“Okay, but I’m a terrible cook.”

Dex kissed him again, then turned on his side, back against David’s chest, pulling David’s arm around him. “I’ll cook.”

4
AUBADE

DAVID WAS ALREADY between Dex's cheeks when he woke, beard buried, tongue working his hole in slow, worshipful circles as if he had all the time in the world. Dex stirred, stretching into the sensation, one arm thrown above his head, legs widening in quiet, yielding invitation.

"Well, good morning," Dex grinned, voice still gravelly with sleep.

David answered with a moan, muffled against Dex's ass, the vibrations teasing deeper. His hands slid beneath Dex's thighs, spreading him open, anchoring him. Wet heat moved in slow rhythm, breaking only to breathe across slick flesh or drag his beard into the scent before diving back in.

Dex bit his lip. "Is this your way of asking for breakfast in bed?"

David surfaced, eyes gleaming. "More like an appetizer."

Soon they were tangled again, Dex rolling over and tugging David in for a kiss that tasted of sleep, skin, his own sweaty ass, and everything in between. Their hands roamed as if they hadn't already memorized each other the night before.

"Sorry if I was too forward this morning with my wandering tongue," David said. "The sun hit your ass like a spotlight, and I was jealous—my scent was on you all night, but yours wasn't on me."

"Are you serious? I've wanted you inside me since your dick was tickling my tonsils last night. Thank the Imodium I took before going out last night that I was clean enough for your spelunking trip."

"You want me inside you? This whole time I figured you were a top."

"I prefer the top bunk, but I'm very much vers," Dex assured. "Work's brutal—that's why I went out. Don't judge, but I was planning to find some sexy, dom daddy to rail me and fuck the stress away. Why do you think I took the Imodium? I didn't want any... *surprises*."

"Surprise!" David grinned, flashing quick jazz hands."

Dex chortled. "Not the surprise I meant—trust me, you were a welcome one."

"You sure I didn't rain on your ass-pounding parade?"

"I skipped the parade for the main event—absolutely no regrets. And I did find a sexy man to rail me. Your tongue felt amazing, but I want something bigger."

David lifted Dex from the bed, legs wrapped tightly around his hips, lips never parting. He carried him into the bathroom and set him down as the water hissed to life.

The shower was steam, heat, and hands. David pressed Dex to the tile, kissed along his spine, his shoulders, then down again. There wasn't much foreplay—David had already tongue-worshipped him in bed—so Dex didn't mind the pace. He arched as David pushed inside, slow and steady, one hand braced at Dex's hip, the other gripping the handrail for leverage. The thrusts were unhurried, reverent, like David meant to make the moment last forever.

Neither spoke—it wasn't needed. Every breath was shared; every motion answered like a call and response. When they came, it was nearly in sync—David pressed deep, Dex biting his right wrist to stifle the noise as his other hand stroked himself. Little effort was needed; the slight upward curve of David's cock found all the right spots. The orgasm came from David's talents more than his own, cum leaking out in short spurts as David thrusted.

Dex clenched down tight, holding David's dick hostage with his asshole, wanting every drop of his load inside.

"Woof." David's low growl rumbled in Dex's ear, sending shockwaves down his spine.

When the spasms eased, Dex released his still-hard prisoner, sliding him out inch by inch at a teasing pace, glancing down as David kegeled and bounced it with feigned machismo.

"Thank heavens for Imodium," Dex announced when he saw David's cock pristine.

David chuckled. "I don't want to sound crass, but you could've covered it and I'd still be smiling. Why do you think I moved us to the shower? Even Imodium fails sometimes."

"I know..." Dex said sheepishly. "I might've taken two."

"Geesh, you were hoping for a parade," David teased. He kissed Dex deeply, hand at his neck, gently coaxing him to turn as he pinned him against the glass.

"What are you up to, mister?"

"Just turning you around so you didn't miss the next float," David explained, spitting on his hand, coating his cock—his favorite lube—before sliding gently back in.

Dex moaned. The angle was different, deeper, each thrust more deliberate. David might have complained about being just shy of eight inches, but he hit places bigger cocks never had.

David held Dex's chest tight, mouth roaming neck and shoulders, biting playfully as his thrusts quickened. Dex heard the familiar purr build in David's chest, felt it vibrate louder until the growl alone sent him over the edge, hands free.

"Fuuuuuuck!" Dex rumbled as his load shot in ropes, glad his hood was pulled back so he could watch as he painted the glass below white.

Dex was still leaking, insides pulsing wildly as David's second load released inside him, the growl against his back crescendoing into a deep grunt.

Neither moved, warm water cascading from the rainfall shower above, failing to wash away the sensuality and sin it'd just witnessed.

"I couldn't let you leave later without a proper railing," David said as he eased out, finally breaking the silence with a grin curling his mouth. "I take my challenges seriously."

Dex turned, hand under the waterfall. "And apparently literally, Mr. Rain-on-My-Parade."

"I do what I can," David joked, crossing the spray for a kiss. He grabbed the loofah, adding body wash. "May I?"

Dex smiled warmly. "Not much I wouldn't let you do at this point—just leave the beard alone. I'm not ready to wash away your scent completely."

David pulled Dex from the falling water, lathering his entire body in slow circles from neck down. Dex caught the soft sandalwood notes, memories of the night before replaying behind closed eyelids as the fragrance hit his nose.

He kept his eyes closed, afraid that opening them would expose more than he already had. He felt vulnerable but protected. There was a gentle strength about David—someone who'd never hurt for pleasure just to witness pain, someone who'd stand for those he loved, but not to be crossed if provoked.

David dropped to his knees, surprising Dex when he gently sucked the foreskin of his now-flaccid cock. He slipped his tongue inside for the trapped remnants of his load. As if cradling real huevos, he cupped Dex's balls with gentle care, massaging softly, coaxing one last drop, craving one more taste.

Dex finally opened his eyes. "Still hungry?"

"Both for food and for you," David said, smiling up at Dex. "I can taste the bourbon in your jizz, you know—it gives it a sweetness I'll never tire of. Reminds me of our first kiss."

"Yeah," Dex admitted, "I might've had a few last night—it gave me the courage to approach you."

David snorted, lathering Dex's legs and ass, circling a soapy finger around his well-fucked hole.

"What?" Dex asked, biting his lip, holding back a moan as David toyed with his ass.

"Something tells me you don't need courage from a bottle," David said, rising to grab the spray nozzle anchored to the wall. He turned the valve for the hose and held the spray away from them until the cold water was replaced with warm, slowly and sensually rinsing the suds from Dex's tanned skin. "I see a lot of shorter guys overcompensate with arrogance, like they've something to prove. But you carry yourself with a confidence that doesn't need proving."

"I stopped proving my worth to people long ago. If they can't see it without help, they don't deserve to look."

"See—that's what I am talking about," David agreed. "That confidence—I never had it, not like you. I spent my childhood hiding who I was, and adulthood trying to be a heteronormalized, palatable version of gay. Thinking if I wasn't too gay, my father and family would accept me."

David spun Dex to rinse his backside. "When I came out in college, I diluted myself every time I returned home so my father wouldn't be uncomfortable. Then I realized he feared my sexuality more than I feared his disapproval. That's when I decided to come out at home too—not just the safe spaces."

"I'm sorry." Dex said quietly, unsure what else to offer.

He sensed how their recent communion and reprise had opened David up, so he let him talk while gently scrubbing his body, silently admiring how his blond-red body hair darkened to coppery-brown when wet.

With the same tenderness David had shown, Dex washed down his body, carefully avoiding the beard so his scent lingered there a bit longer.

When Dex dropped to his knees, eye-level with his cock for the second time in twelve hours, David teased, "Now why does this look so familiar?"

"Technically, this is my first time seeing it in this light," Dex pointed out. "And I've gotta say— it's a real showpiece."

It still hung heavy despite the double round, but the sudden attention made it rise to the occasion in full force.

"Thank you, I grew it myself," David said proudly, giving it another kegeled bounce.

Dex grinned, opened his mouth, and welcomed the grower—teasing with tongue for a couple minutes before lathering it with the loofah and giving it a playful smack. "We should hurry before I am tempted for another round—'cause clearly you're up for it."

"Agreed. Besides, someone promised to cook us breakfast."

"I did, didn't I?"

5
OVERTURE

DAVID COULDN'T STOP smiling at Dex, standing in his kitchen in a borrowed pair of pajama bottoms and his favorite *Stranger Things* tee. As he made coffee and set the table, he watched Dex move around with a familiarity even he didn't have yet. He'd only moved in a few weeks ago—after his mom no longer needed constant care, right before his father's funeral and their blowup—but Dex navigated it like he lived there.

"Scrambled or omelets," Dex asked, pulling eggs from the fridge, "Any preference?"

"Omelet sounds fantastic. Cheese in the drawer—I can chop veggies."

"I saw some sausage in the fridge—sound good?"

David slid beside him at the island, pulled a cutting board from the lower cabinet, then kissed the back of his neck. "Is your mind always on the sausage?"

"Not typically," Dex said, turning to return a true kiss. "But after that shower, my mind's definitely been on yours."

"Glad you liked it," David replied. "You gave it to me good last night, too, mister. It'd been a while."

Dex passed him a bell pepper. "Half an onion and half of this?"

"Yes, sir."

"Good boy," Dex teased. "Maybe I'll throw you another bone to later."

David panted playfully, tongue out.

"Mind if I show you the way I learned?" Dex offered after seeing his attempt to cut the onion.

"Please—I told you I am hopeless in the kitchen."

When Dex slid in front of him, David wrapped his arms at Dex's waist, lips lingering at his neck as he looked over his shoulder at the lesson.

Dex showed him how to hold the knife, curl in his fingertips so the knuckles would guide the blade instead of slicing his digits, and where to notch and slice for the perfect dice.

"Where'd you learn to cook?"

"My grandmother and mom. They taught to be a good, little housewife—and then judged me for wanting to please a man."

"Sounds like we *do* have some things in common," David said empathetically. "Do you still speak with them?"

"I yell at them all the time," Dex admitted, "but they're no longer on this Earth. My grandmother died six years ago, and my mother passed from complications from COVID—refused the vaccination and it killed her."

"I'm really sorry, Dex."

"Don't be. She was indoctrinated into right-wing fanaticism. She hated my father—who I never met—for cheating on her during her pregnancy, but she worshipped the ground the president walked on before her death... the irony was completely lost on her."

"Yikes," David said, tightening his grip on Dex.

"Enough about horrible families... have a seat, and I'll have breakfast done soon enough."

David kissed his neck again and headed to finish prepping the coffee now that it was brewed. "Cream, sugar?"

"Yes, and yes."

David finished the coffees, headed to the dining table, and glanced again at the man in his kitchen. A smile beamed across his face as he thought to himself, *I could definitely get used to this.*

Dex watched David stare out at a bird on the balcony outside, goofy smile and all. There was a warmth to his aura, a genuineness often lacking in the other guys in his past, and not what he expected when he shook his ass in front of him to get his attention the night before.

Heat still lingered on his neck from where David's lips had been, reminding him of the tenderness he'd been shown from the moment they met. He remembered what David told him last night at Eden, that he was unlike anyone he'd met before, but the truth was David was unlike anyone Dex had ever met. Admittedly, it scared him—not David, not the possibility for more, but the fact that he had tapped into David's emotions more easily than anyone else before... and he knew, without a doubt, what David was feeling.

Dex plated up and made his way to the table, placing one in front of David before taking a seat next to him. "I hope you like it."

"If it's like everything else with you so far, I am guessing it'll be the best omelet I've ever tasted," David assured.

"Now look who's laying it on thick."

"Too mushy?" David asked. "I promise I am not usually this cheesy."

"Nah, not too mushy," Dex answered while cutting his omelette. "I'd be lying if I said I wasn't reeling the whole time I was cooking."

"Same," admitted David. "My face hurts from smiling."

"I noticed. I kept thinking—I could get used to this."

After breakfast, Dex helped David clear the table and the two of them washed and put away the dishes.

"Not to go full lesbian on you," David snickered, "but I could get used to this, too."

"Speaking of—plans today?" Dex threw out the invitation casually, like it hadn't been dancing around in the back of his mind all morning. "My friend Casey's throwing a Fourth of July thing up at Lake Lanier. Burgers, beers, and fireworks over the water. Want to come?"

David raised an eyebrow over his second cup of coffee. "You're inviting me to meet your friends already?"

"Don't worry," Dex smirked. "They'll hate you."

That got the laugh he wanted, and forty minutes later, they were in David's car with the windows down, riding northbound toward the lake. They made a quick stop at a roadside gas station to pick up a couple six-packs of Corona—just enough to be polite and not show up empty handed. Neither of them wanted to overdrink and risk driving back buzzed later, but the gesture was more about contribution than consumption.

The house was a stunner. Lakefront, tucked just off Woodlake Drive, with a tiered deck that looked built for summer keggers. The moment they stepped into the crowd, Dex felt a subtle shift—eyes scanning, lingering.

Casey bounded over in a red romper and hugged Dex like he hadn't ghosted her Christmas party the year before.

"You actually came," she teased, though her voice was sincere. "And damn—your boy is hot. Trying to make me jealous?"

She turned to David with an exaggerated wink that made him blush.

"David, meet my best friend, Casey," Dex said.

Casey hugged David like they were already old friends. "Nice to meet you, David."

"Nice to meet you, too."

"I loved being Dex's fake girlfriend in college," Casey blurted, alcohol clearly fueling her. "Of course, once he came out, it was a bitch trying to find a guy who didn't think I'd turn them gay."

"You're impossible," Dex laughed. "Please excuse her—she's drunk."

"What closeted gay didn't have a beard, am I right?" David joked.

Another couple entered, and Casey excused herself, leaving them to fend off the crowd alone.

As introductions started, the usual questions came—how they met, how long they'd been together. They navigated the mild awkwardness, nothing they couldn't handle, especially once they grabbed beers to loosen up.

Then came the curveball.

David visibly stiffened, gaze locking on a man by the grill, laughing with another tending it— mid-thirties, deep tan, square jaw, casual patriotic tank and cargo shorts.

"Shit," David muttered.

"You okay?" Dex asked under his breath.

"I know that guy—Jason King. We went to high school together. He was... kind of a dick back then."

Before Dex could offer an out, Jason spotted David and lit up with genuine recognition.

"David? No way!"

David froze but managed a smile as Jason approached, beer in one hand, the other lifted in a gesture of goodwill. When David offered his, Jason faked a handshake and pulled him into a hug.

"Dude. I'm really sorry. I heard about your dad..." Jason released him and added, "He was a good guy."

"Thanks, he was," David said quietly, choking on the lie as left his mouth.

Jason nodded, then smirked at Dex. "So... who's this lucky fella?"

Dex offered his hand. "Dex."

"Jason. Nice to meet ya," he said, shaking it. He looked back at David with a lingering glance. "You look good—so good to see you, man. And I'm glad your mom's doing better."

"Good to see you, Jace."

Jason squeezed David's hand before heading back to the grill. It was... oddly sweet.

David exhaled. "Well. That was unexpected."

"More of a story there?" Dex teased.

"You could say that..." David said, blushing slightly.

"High school crush?"

"Nah… high school fuckbuddy," David admitted. "Well—playmate. It never got to the fucking part."

"Now this story I have to hear…"

"Not a lot to tell, to be honest." David took a chug of beer to stall having to tell it. "We were friends my freshman year—he was a sophomore. My dad forced me to try out for football to prove I was a man. That's when Jace and I became… friends."

"Locker room?"

"How'd you guess?"

"Let's get out of earshot." Dex grabbed his hand and led him down toward the lake. "I wanna hear the details."

David started as they walked, "I always took my time getting undressed so most of the boys would be done showering by the time I got in there. Jason lingered behind longer than the rest of the team one day. He was on the far-left side when I entered, so I went to the right. I had my eyes closed, washing my hair; when I opened them, he was standing right beside me, smiling."

"Wow—that's creepy."

"It startled me for sure, but it wasn't creepy," Dex explained. "He was kind of sweet—he said he'd tried to get my attention, but I didn't hear him over the water. He congratulated me on throws during practice, welcomed me to the team… and that's when I noticed his erection."

"Big boy?"

David smiled. "See… always thinking about the sausage."

"Yeah, yeah…"

"Smaller than me—maybe seven, but thicker."

"So, you just reached out and grabbed it? How did the playing start?"

"No. After seeing his erection, I got hard instantly," David explained. "He caught me off guard asking if he could touch it. I said yes—but only if I could touch his."

"And then what?"

"And then I got too nervous—didn't want someone to walk in. He invited me back to his place after practice." David took another chug of Corona. "I ate dinner with his family and stayed the night. We started off jerking ourselves while lying in bed together, then we stroked each other as we rubbed one another with our free hand. He got weird after he came, but he still held me that night as we slept."

"How long did this go on?"

"Until football season ended. Nearly every Friday I was at his house. First jerk sessions, then he asked if he could suck me after a few weeks. But he was always afraid of anal—said jerking and oral weren't gay, but taking a dick was, in his words, 'gross and gay as hell.'"

"Sounds real gay," Dex joked, sipping his beer. "I'm in."

"Last I heard, he was married with two kids—guess it was just a phase."

"Well, he was giving you the one-over back there. You think he quit dick for sure?"

"Why—you want a threesome?"

"Hardly," Dex scoffed. "But he's been at Casey's husband's side all night. I might have to tell her she's turned another gay."

"Stop!" David laughed "That's awful—you wouldn't!"

"I'm joking. I wouldn't have the heart."

They glanced back toward the grill where Jason and Casey's husband, Greg, were laughing, roughhousing, and they witnessed an ass-slap that lingered a bit too long.

David looked at Dex and laughed, "You might have to..."

The sun dipped lower. Fireflies flickered. The Margaritaville fireworks show kicked off just after nine, each boom echoing across the lake like distant thunder. Dex and David found a quiet spot at the railing, drinks in hand, fingers brushing but not quite intertwined.

The sky was alive with color. Golden comets burst overhead, trailing glitter like pollen in the humid air. The crowd on the deck hooted at the crescendo. Margaritaville's fireworks bloomed red, white, and blue—mirrored in the still surface of the lake below.

Dex leaned against the railing with a cold beer tucked between his hands. David stood beside him, fingers grazing the back of his waistband in rhythm with the music pulsing from the outdoor speakers. Heat from the day still clung to the boards beneath their feet, but a lake breeze gave momentary relief.

Then the light changed.

It wasn't another firework.

It bloomed behind the hills—farther north, too wide. A sudden, unnatural brightness lit the clouds—not sharp and colorful, but pale and pulsing. A light that didn't flicker or fade.

A murmur rippled through the guests.

"Is that part of the show?" someone asked.

But the light didn't end. It expanded, saturating the sky with a silvery-pink cast that grew more eerie by the second. Fireflies vanished. Dogs barked across the cove, then went silent. The bass cut out as someone fumbled with the remote.

Then, far above the treeline, streaks of green and violet shimmered across the atmosphere like oil on water.

"Is that the aurora borealis?" David asked.

"In Georgia?" Dex rasped, his voice catching. "No fucking way."

A second later, everyone's phones vibrated in eerie unison, chiming over the fireworks still bursting as eyes turned to screens—or to the fading phenomenon in the northeastern sky.

Dex glanced his screen and read aloud: "Emergency Alert. Nuclear detonation detected. Affected Mid-Atlantic metro regions include Baltimore, Boston, New York, Philadelphia, and Washington, D.C.

"Other affected regions include Southeast Florida, Montana, North Dakota, and Wyoming. Seek shelter immediately. Fallout risk—this is not a drill."

Gasps came in a cacophony. Someone screamed. A champagne flute shattered on the deck.

David grabbed Dex's hand and pulled him inside. People were already crowding around the living room television as Greg flipped through static before finding a live broadcast—chaotic, fragmented.

"...early reports of simultaneous detonations... Washington confirmed, words of New York City and Philadelphia... we urge everyone east of the Mississippi to—"

The screen glitched.

Dex stood frozen. The world tilted. Something primal, buried, told him with bone-deep certainty: nothing would ever be the same.

David's phone screen lit again—not an alert, a call. He stared blankly at the name on the screen: Mom.

He turned to Dex, voice low. "I've gotta go. I need to get back to the city. As mad as I still am with her, I need to check on my mother."

Dex's throat tightened. "Let me come with you."

David gently shook his head. "No. Stay here. It's safer. Besides... explaining everything to her with you there—it'd be too much."

There was no malice—just truth. Still, it stung.

Dex nodded slowly. "Okay. Give me your number, so I know you made it back safely."

David rattled it off. Dex typed it fast, sending a short message:

Hey. It's Dex. Stay safe. I mean it.

The signal struggled, then: *Message failed to send.*

"Shit," Dex muttered. He looked up—David was already at his car, headlights flashing as he unlocked the door and climbed inside.

Dex raised a half-wave, something unresolved settling over him, as David disappeared down the drive, taillights fading into darkness.

Dex stood there a long time, phone in hand, willing the message to send.

It never did.

July 5, 2026

"When you are sorrowful look again in your heart, and you shall see that in truth you are weeping for that which has been your delight."

~Kahlil Gibran, *The Prophet*

6
REQUIEM

DEX WAS THANKFUL for the ride back to Atlanta, though less than thrilled about the driver: his ex, Jake, whom he hadn't noticed at Casey's party until after David's sudden exodus.

Jake Hodges, a farm boy from Buford, looked born to bear weight—thick through the shoulders, broad in the chest, his muscled frame stretching the seams of a faded tee. Wavy black hair, cut close on the sides, crowned his head, intensifying his deep-set, puppy-dog brown eyes that always seemed to ask more than they said. His movements showed he was used to command, but his smile—when it came—was boyish and disarming.

Dex stared at his phone—the signal was back, but the message still failed no matter how many times he tried resending it. He tossed the phone to the floor in frustration. "I think I typed the number wrong—he rattled it off so fast I must've inverted a digit."

"I'm sure that's it," Jake said, supportive but cautious.

"What do you think happens to the world now? Do you think Atlanta is in danger?"

Jake was ex-military. After a few tours, he came home with an honorable discharge to help his mother care for his dying father. He wasn't book-smart, but far from dumb; he knew his shit when it came to bodybuilding, tactical warfare, and combat.

"It's not good, but I think Atlanta will be safe for now. Looks like they didn't hit any cities in the TVA or Southern Company grid zones, so no mass exodus into Atlanta for refuge."

"TVA?"

"The Tennessee Valley Authority," explained Jake.

"Got it. How'd you end up at the party?"

"Greg, Jason, and I all work together—Station Seventeen."

"When did you become a fireman? Last time I saw you, you were still a personal trainer."

"I still have my bootcamp class, but I cut down on days to fit around my firehouse shifts," Jake said.

"I gotta ask..." Dex pried. "Are Jason and Greg fucking? David and I were sure of it—small world, they went to the same high school and used to mess around."

"Oh, absolutely!" Jake leaned closer, his beguiling eyes locking on Dex, and whispered, "I've fucked both of them, too—but they don't know it."

Dex laughed loudly. "Do you think Casey knows?"

“From the vibes I’ve read, I think the three of them have fucked more than once.”

“No shit! Okay, Casey… you go, girl!”

“I should’ve taken Turner McDonald instead of I-85,” Jake muttered as they reached just north of the Perimeter, traffic already slowing. “How’s everyone on the force—still partners with Charlie?”

“Yeah—still a quasi-homophobic asshole, but he knows I can kick his ass, so he stays pretty quiet now.”

“Of all the partners they could’ve paired up,” Jake began, “they put a homo with a homophobe.”

“He’s gotten better—mind more open, less quick to judge. More afraid I’ll beat his ass than fuck it.”

A two-minute lull followed as Jake focused on the thickening traffic ahead, which soon brought them to a dead stop.

“But you would, right?” Jake asked, breaking the silence.

“Fuck it?”

“Yeah.”

“Oh, absolutely!” Dex admitted. “If only to prove a man can give him as much—if not more—pleasure as a woman.”

“Helps that he’s hot.”

“Definitely doesn’t hurt.”

Jake smirked at Dex's reply, but the moment passed quickly as they both stared at the sea of brake lights stretching down the interstate.

A low hum from the radio filled the silence—an emergency broadcast update: "...casualties in the Northeast are now estimated in the millions. Fallout projections suggest a southwest drift, but current models remain unstable. Officials urge all citizens to remain indoors and avoid non-essential travel."

Dex leaned his head against the window. "God, this feels like a dream I can't wake from."

Jake glanced sideways. "Nightmare, more like."

Dex gave a stifled laugh. "Yeah."

"Are you sure you're okay?"

"I keep thinking about him. I keep getting this weird feeling that something bad happened."

Jake didn't ask who. He already knew. He hadn't met David, but he'd seen them at the party and hadn't dared approach. As much as he had wanted to talk to Dex, he cared enough to give him space; but once David left, he took advantage of the absence and moved in. Though he didn't live in the city, he welcomed the request to drive Dex back into Atlanta—hoping for closure, never imagining he'd be at a loss for words.

After another fifteen minutes of inching forward, Jake finally broke the tension. "Listen... I'm sorry."

Dex turned to him. "For what?"

"For everything. For how things ended. For not having the balls to tell you why I pulled away."

Dex raised a brow but stayed quiet.

Jake tightened his grip on the wheel. "It wasn't because I didn't care. I did—still do. I just... couldn't handle how intense it got for me. And I knew I'd never be your whole world. Not the way you were becoming mine."

Dex didn't respond right away. He let the silence sit—heavy and unsaid. But the tension in his body softened, even if only a little.

By the time they reached the city limits, it was just before midnight. Atlanta's skyline loomed ahead—still lit, but strangely subdued. The streets were unusually still—no honking, no crowds, just the low hum of a city bracing for whatever came next.

Jake yawned and rubbed his neck when they pulled to a stop in the driveway. "Mind if I crash at your place? I don't feel like driving back to the lake, and traffic will be hell again."

Dex nodded. "Yeah, that's fine. Make yourself at home. I'll be back soon—I need to go check on someone first."

Jake didn't need to ask who.

Dex made the short trip to David's townhouse, unease mounting. The porch light was off. Windows dark. He knocked once. Then again, louder.

Nothing.

He pulled out his phone and tried calling the number. It went straight to a wrong-number recording, but he still texted:

You okay? Just checking in.

Hey... I'm worried. Call me.

Please. Just let me know you're safe.

All three sent. None delivered.

He stood on the steps longer than he should have, hoping a light might flicker on. But the place stayed silent—empty in a way Dex could feel in his core.

He returned to his apartment with a pit forming in his stomach.

The scent of garlic and rosemary greeted him before he even stepped inside. Jake was plating food in the kitchen, barefoot in gym shorts and a soft black tee, hair still damp from a recent shower.

"I made us a late dinner," he said with a proud smile. "Your favorite—rosemary and mushroom chicken. You had all the ingredients in the fridge, and I figured you could use something comforting."

Dex smiled despite the anxiety knotting his chest. "You remembered?"

"Of course. You taught me well." He carried both plates to the table, already set with flatware, flickering candles, and wineglasses brimming with a buttery chardonnay.

They ate in silence, the only sound was the news murmuring from the living room.

Jake broke the quiet. "Strange, isn't it? The world falling apart outside... and us in here, eating dinner like it's just another night."

Dex nodded, eyes unfocused. "Feels like we're pretending. Like if we just go through the motions, maybe it won't all crash down."

"I can turn off the news, if you want."

"Nah," Dex said, taking a small bite. It was delicious—the lessons had certainly paid off—but his appetite was knotted. "It's a reminder of the reality of what happened today. A reminder that nothing will be the same."

Jake pushed a mushroom around his plate, appetite also clenched. "I tried calling my mom again after I showered. Still nothing."

Dex lowered his head and sipped his wine. "Sometimes I forget what it's like to miss someone you've known your whole life."

"Oh, Dex, I'm so sorry, I—"

"It's okay, Jake," Dex cut in. "You have every right to worry about your mom without walking on eggshells around me."

Silence followed—not awkward, but heavy with what neither needed to say.

"Do you think we're safe here?" Jake asked finally.

"No," Dex said flatly. "But safer than most."

Jake gave a dry half-laugh and stood, reaching for Dex's plate. "Guess that's enough for tonight... you barely touched yours."

"I'm sorry, Jake. It was delicious, but my stomach's too full of dread to shove anything else into it. I've just got a bad feeling," Dex elaborated. "Something's wrong. Other than the crumbling world. I can feel it."

Jake's brow furrowed. "You really like this guy, huh?"

Dex nodded, drained his wine, and poured more. "It's more than that. I don't know. It felt... real. All the way down, not just surface stuff, potential for something great."

Jake carried the dishes to the sink, then returned and poured another glass to keep pace. "And you only just met yesterday?"

"I know what you're going to say... it's too soon to tell, that I don't know him well enough yet to make a judgment."

"That's not at all what I was going to say. I know what it's like to connect with someone that deeply, that quickly," Jake said. "I've been in your shoes. I'm no one to judge."

"You've been in more than just my shoes," Dex joked, trying to lighten the mood. He knew Jake knew. Jake had felt the same way after their first kiss, and he'd made those feelings no secret.

Jake reached across the table, brushing Dex's hands. "I'm here, okay?"

"I'm sorry I hurt you, Jake," Dex said, voice steady. "I'm sorry you never felt I wanted you as much as you wanted me—I did. But I lost my way, fell into a labyrinth of self-pity and doubt, angry at my own grief for a mother who didn't deserve my tears."

Jake just listened, unsure what to say.

"I felt completely alone when I lost her," Dex continued. "I think I pushed you away because I was angry—with her and with myself. I was so sure everyone I cared for would eventually hurt me."

Jake was silent, blindsided by Dex's honesty. Hell, Dex hadn't expected it either. He studied Jake's face, memorizing what was already etched deep: the familiarity, the warmth of his hand, the tenderness born not of infatuation but of love and shared history.

Maybe it was grief, fear, or just the need to feel something human—something real—but Dex stood, walked around the table, and pulled Jake up by the hand.

Jake didn't speak, just stood puzzled, his face asking: *what?*

Dex pulled him closer. They kissed—slow at first. Jake tasted of garlic, wine, and something aching to be remembered. Even after showering with Dex's soap, he somehow smelled just as Dex remembered—the unmistakable notes of sharp citrus and cedar.

"Your beard still smells the same. How is that possible?"

"I always kept a bottle of my beard oil in the back of the drawer with your trimmer... opened it out of habit after the shower and was just as surprised to see it as you are now to smell it."

Jake's hands slipped beneath Dex's shirt, dragging it upward. Dex helped peel it off, then tugged Jake's tee free. His body was as familiar as it was changed—still strong, lean from years of training, but softened at the edges. A little weight in the belly, fuller—not from laziness, but from firehouse casseroles and the comfort of no longer training for stage lights.

Dex's eyes traveled down his torso. What struck him more was the hair—Jake had always shaved bare for competitions, but his body was smooth and rigid like marble. Now, dark hair traced his pecs and stomach, thick at the center of his chest and feathering down in a trail toward the waistband of his shorts—and to the treasure below.

Jake caught him looking and smirked. "Like what you see?"

Dex stepped in, fingers grazing the coarse hair on Jake's chest, then sliding up to the back of his neck. He dragged his fingers through Jake's beard—longer than he remembered, full and dark, with a touch more salt at the chin. It suited him.

"Yeah," Dex murmured. "I do."

They kissed again, hungrier now. Jake dropped to his knees with quiet urgency, hands sliding up Dex's thighs as he leaned forward. He glanced up once, pupils blown wide, beard brushing Dex's belly. "I've wanted this since I saw you again."

Dex didn't answer. He just watched, breath held, as Jake mouthed him through his jeans, then unzipped and freed his cock—thick and heavy in his hand.

Jake took him slowly at first, tongue circling the head, eyes still locked upward. His mouth was hot and sure, practiced but playful—like he wasn't just sucking Dex's cock, he was remembering it and all its hotspots.

Dex let his head tip back, one hand resting lightly on Jake's crown, the other sliding to his shoulder.

Jake quickened his rhythm, taking him deeper, spit slicking the base as his hand gripped what he couldn't take. His beard scratched Dex's lower belly, grounding—familiar, real.

"Fuck," Dex muttered, voice rough.

Jake pulled back, licking the underside—slow, teasing—then rose to his feet, pressed a kiss to Dex's lips, and whispered, "You still taste like sin… and salvation."

They tumbled onto the bed in a tangle. Dex rolled Jake beneath him, kissed him deep, then paused to look—really look.

Jake lay back, his body on full display: dark hair covering his chest and stomach, thicker around his groin. His cock was hard, thick, flushed, with the same slight downward curve.

"You've changed," Dex said quietly, spreading his thighs as he knelt between them.

Jake gave a faint, amused smile. "Yeah. A little."

"Looks good on you."

Jake pulled him down by the neck. "Then come show me."

Dex grabbed a condom from the nightstand out of habit, knowing Jake's usual preferences for protection—but Jake caught his wrist to stop him.

"I want to feel you—no barriers," Jake said, spreading his legs and breathing deep.

Dex eased in slowly, one hand gripping Jake's thigh, the other brushing his side. Jake's breath hitched as he was filled, but he didn't look away—he watched Dex like he'd been waiting years for this moment.

They moved together slowly, bodies slick with sweat, as if both longed to return to a moment before the world collapsed—even if that moment was different for each.

Dex thrust deep and steady, every stroke pulling a soft gasp or groan from Jake. His hands roamed Dex's back, fingers digging in when Dex hit just right.

"God... Dex..." Jake moaned, lips brushing his ear as Dex leaned in. "Don't stop."

Dex grunted louder, hips pumping harder, skin slapping skin above the low murmur of the TV in the next room.

Jake clutched at him, voice catching, as a load shot from his cock hands-free, "Dex... fuck... Dex—"

Dex grunted louder, breath ragged, the sight of Jake's load driving his own release as he bred him. He leaned in with a labored whisper, "Fuck, David."

Jake stiffened beneath him.

Dex froze, the name still echoing in the silence.

He pulled out, chest heaving, and sat back against the headboard. "Shit."

Jake didn't speak right away. He rolled onto his side, away from Dex, and reached for the sheet.

"I didn't mean to—" Dex started.

"I know," Jake said softly. "You don't have to say it."

Dex sat in silence, fists clenched at his stupidity, pulse pounding.

The room collapsed into silence.

Jake stared up at the ceiling, chest rising and falling. A long moment passed before he spoke. "So... he's really under your skin, huh?"

Dex didn't answer—except with tears, his body trembling.

Jake turned to face him, searching. His voice cracked. "Can I hold you? Just... as a friend?"

Dex nodded through sobs.

Jake shifted closer, draping an arm over Dex's chest, his face settling into the crook of his neck. Dex's body was warm and comforting. Familiar enough to bring Jake's own tears.

They lay like that for a long time. Not lovers. Not strangers. Just two men who'd shared love and history—and now shared a moment that felt like the end of something they couldn't name.

"That shouldn't have happened," Dex said at last, breaking the silence.

"I know," Jake agreed. "But I won't lie—it's what I wanted."

A pause stretched before Jake whispered again. "I wish I hadn't ended things the way I did. You didn't deserve that. I was selfish, scared... I thought walking away was easier than admitting things."

Dex closed his eyes, the words piercing more than he expected.

"I see you now—stronger, harder around the edges, but still you. And I can't help thinking... maybe if I'd been braver, you wouldn't hurt the way you do tonight." His grip tightened. "I'm sorry, Dex. I really am.

Darkness hung heavy between them, as if the space was draped black, the silence palpable, like a requiem mourning what was.

The TV flickered in the dark, painting the room in red and blue. News anchors looked shaken, maps smeared with crimson fallout projections. Footage looped: burning skylines, panicked civilians, dust clouds swallowing neighborhoods whole.

"Do you think this is the end of America?" Jake whispered.

"America died the moment that asshat got elected his first term."

"You know what I mean."

Dex exhaled. "I don't know."

Neither moved. Outside, sirens wailed—long and lonely.

Jake's voice came again, softer. "If it is... I'm glad I'm here with you, even if it's just for tonight."

Dex stayed silent but squeezed Jake tighter, not needing words. He wasn't sure what tomorrow held. He turned his head, resting his cheek against Jake's hair, and heard the soft, familiar snore. "I'm glad you are, too."

Jake's eyes closed, but Dex remained awake, listening to him doze while thinking of David—staring at the ceiling, searching the dark, finally finding solace and sleep in the stillness.

Part II
LOVE

July 26, 2026

"Love is patient, love is kind. It does not envy, it does not boast, it is not proud. It does not dishonor others, it is not self-seeking, it is not easily angered, it keeps no record of wrongs. Love does not delight in evil but rejoices with the truth. It always protects, always trusts, always hopes, always perseveres."

~ 1 Corinthians 13:4-7

7
CHAOS

THEY APPEARED JUST before dawn on July Twenty-Sixth.

To the east, the hulking face of Stone Mountain loomed in darkness, a massive granite monolith asleep beneath fallout haze creeping slowly from the north. The air was still. The birds were silent. And then—without warning—the horizon buzzed with the hum of a low-flying squadron of Black Hawks.

Militarized utility trucks and armored personnel carriers surrounded the park under cover of night. By the time the sun was stretching from the horizon, the convoys were already moving into position. What had once been Georgia's most visited attraction—infamous for its Confederate carvings and laser shows—was now the staging ground for a coup. Black banners draped the carvings of Lee, Jackson, and Davis, each emblazoned with a white ouroboros encircled in barbed wire.

No press conferences. No democratic debate. Only silence and occupation.

By mid-morning, a line of armored vehicles cut off access to the park's western entrance, while personnel fanned out across the village green and camping areas, clearing civilians and taking inventory. The historic railroad depot became a command hub; and the antebellum museum, a temporary barracks. Observation posts rose on the mountain itself—sniper nests dug into the granite folds.

The first official message came via hijacked broadcast shortly after noon:

"This is Commander Thomas Gallows. Effective immediately, Stone Mountain Park and its surrounding regions are under our jurisdiction. Civilian access is prohibited. All municipal and state authorities are to stand down. The United States government no longer functions in its prior capacity. A new regime has been established."

Few believed it. Fewer understood it. Most were still processing the detonation alerts from two weeks before.

But things escalated.

Two days later, the governor was scheduled to address the state.

In a symbolic show of resilience, the remaining leadership insisted on broadcasting from the Capitol steps, flanked by surviving cabinet members and security forces. Thirty seconds into the live feed, the camera jolted. Screams echoed. A single shot cracked the air, then another, then chaos before the feed cut.

It was an overthrow, a message, a scare tactic.

Dex and Charlie sat in the patrol car parked on Spring, Dex jotting notes from the domestic disturbance call they'd just cleared. The radio buzzed with static and chatter—white noise—until he heard talk about the incident at the State Capitol.

"Are you fucking serious?" Charlie blurted. "They just killed the governor!"

Dex stopped writing and turned up the volume, but little less came over the radio. "You think they're the ones behind the bombs on the Fourth?"

"You really think they have that kind of resources and manpower?" Charlie asked.

"I don't know. They still haven't verified the source—some say Russia, others a BRICS coordinated effort."

"Think this is a local faction of that—or unrelated domestic terrorism?"

Dex just shrugged. He wasn't sure what to think anymore. Life since the pandemic had been a shitshow. A culture of cruelty had taken power and infiltrated the weak-minded—like his mother— changing who they once were. Bullying had become celebrated instead of censured. Up was down, down was up, and the world teemed with propagandized lies passed off as truth in the pursuit of power and greed.

"This reminds me of the riots on *Jan sixth*," Charlie said.

"Weren't you there?" Dex joked. "Seems like your crowd."

"Ouch." Charlie looked over at him, genuine hurt in his eyes. "I know I was a dumb shit for a while, but do you really think that little of me?"

"You voted for him in twenty-sixteen," Dex pointed out.

"Fair," admitted Charlie, "but I've told you many times about how big a mistake that was."

"Yeah, you have. I'm sorry," Dex said, resting a hand on his leg in a gesture of apology.

Charlie's leg tightened, but instead of commenting—or pushing it away like he typically would—he continued.

"I'm not the same person I was twelve years ago when we got partnered. You've taught my stubborn ass a lot. I've let go of a lot of old ideas and stereotypes because of you."

"It hasn't gone completely unnoticed," Dex conceded, quickly pulling his hand back after realizing it was still there.

"Thank you for noticing."

Then Dex noticed something else: an armored truck rolling down Spring and turning on Fifth— the first of many in a convoy advancing toward Georgia Tech. Once on campus, men and women in black uniforms—matching no known state or federal designation—spilled from the vehicles and got in formation.

"They're not National Guard," Charlie muttered, one hand on the wheel, the other near his holster.

"No," Dex said quietly. "They're absolutely not."

As Charlie eased the patrol car closer without drawing attention, Dex radioed dispatch and reported what they were witnessing.

Laura's recognizable voice—though slightly garbled—answered: "Go for Dispatch."

"Signal fifty-four in progress at the Fifth Avenue block of Georgia Tech. We're approaching with caution but recommend against deploying backup. Too many carrying heavy artillery—more officers could escalate the situation."

"Ten-four."

A black-clad enforcer stepped into the road ahead and raised a fist, signaling them to stop. Another flanked the driver's side, unslinging a weapon too advanced for standard law enforcement. It wasn't protocol or procedure.

Dex cracked the window. "APD. What's your jurisdiction?"

The enforcer didn't answer. He slammed the butt of his rifle against the glass—hard enough to make a point, but not hard enough to shatter it.

Dex closed the window.

Charlie braked and reached for his door handle, but the moment he opened it, a second enforcer lunged. Dex acted on instinct—drawing his weapon and firing twice. The first shot hit Kevlar. The second struck flesh.

The attacker on Charlie reeled backward, clutching his upper thigh.

Dex sprang from the cruiser, seizing the last rifleman—still rattled by his companion's injury—and forcing him to the ground in one swift motion. Dex kicked the weapon out of reach and zip-tied his hands and legs, keeping a knee pressed between his shoulder blades.

"Who are you?" Dex demanded, weapon still trained on him. "What agency are you with?"

"You'll find out soon enough, pig!"

On the other side of the car, Charlie was shaken—pale, his hands trembling as he zip-tied his wounded attacker.

Dex looked up just in time to see the rest of the militia—he didn't know what else to call them—charging toward the cruiser once they spotted the commotion. "Charlie! We've got to go!"

Charlie looked up, grabbed his assailant's weapon, and hopped into the driver's seat as Dex snatched the other firearm and dove into the passenger seat.

They'd had a handful of high-speed chases, but Dex had never seen Charlie handle the patrol car with such finesse. Charlie quickly backed away from the campus, swung the car around without a full stop, and sped toward the station.

"You just saved my ass!" Charlie shouted. "Holy shit... I was sure I was dead."

"Don't thank me yet," Dex said. "Something tells me this is just the beginning of survival."

They took Georgia Tech by siege, claiming it as their in-city headquarters. In the following days and weeks, the sprawling Midtown campus—thankfully mostly evacuated in the wake of the bombings—was repopulated—not with students, but with defectors and tactical staff.

Dormitories were converted into housing for high-clearance personnel. Classrooms became indoctrination halls and communications labs. Research facilities—especially those tied to biotech and data science—were repurposed for chemical development and surveillance tech. The rec center was transformed into a tactical training compound. The library tower became a facial-recognition command post.

Every entrance would be guarded, every window blacked out. What was once a hub of progress was now a compound of control.

Dex hoped the shower would wash away the feeling of unease that weighed heavily on him after the day's events, but it hadn't. He still sat in the locker room in just his towel when Charlie—still visibly on edge—entered and plopped down on the bench across from him, back toward Dex.

"Fucking crazy day, huh?" Charlie asked as he kicked off his shoes. "Cap'n says the terrorists infiltrated both the Capitol and the Fulton County Courthouse."

"And they've also taken over Georgia Tech—I saw amateur drone footage streaming live until it was shot down."

Charlie stood, stripped off his shirt, and dropped trou—standing naked before grabbing a towel from his locker and wrapping it around his waist. He walked the short distance to the showers, hung his towel on the hook, and stepped beneath a showerhead directly in Dex's line of sight.

Charlie was still a stupid asshole at times with his off-color jokes, but he'd changed since those rough first years as Dex's partner—especially lately. There was a time when Charlie avoided the locker room entirely if Dex was present. He'd claimed he didn't want a fag checking him out and fantasizing.

The straight guys with that mindset usually didn't have bodies worth fantasizing about—but Charlie did, and he'd crept into Dex's fantasies more often since he stopped avoiding the locker room.

Dex glanced across the space at his partner's drenched form under the cascading water, thick, black fur matted against his skin. If Charlie were gay, he'd be called an otter jock—muscles and fur alike.

As much as his inner voice told him to look away, Dex just sat and watched Charlie—lathering his hair and torso—his mind drifting back to that steamy morning with David in the shower, a moment that now felt like eons ago. He was hurt, frustrated, worried, and lost. There was still no word from David, and his townhouse remained as empty as Dex felt—no matter how many times he checked it.

"Drinks?" Charlie called out, voice raw, pulling Dex from his thoughts. "We're off for a couple days and I need to calm down. I hoped the shower would help, but it didn't—and I can't go home like this."

"Mine didn't help me either," Dex replied, finally pulling himself off the bench and grabbing fresh clothes. "You think it's safe, Charlie?

"You're right—who knows what these punks are capable of," Charlie agreed. "But I don't want to go home to an empty house, so let's just grab a drink somewhere away from Midtown or Downtown."

"Empty house?" Dex asked. For as long as he'd known him, Charlie had been with the same girl. "Where's Jen?"

"When the bombs came crashing down, so did my world," Charlie said as he lathered his junk—stroking a little too long before finally migrating to his balls.

"Jen and I were supposed to go to my family's place, but she said she was sick, stomach hurting too much to eat bad barbecue and stay up drinking all night."

Charlie rinsed, shut off the shower, and grabbed his towel. Drying off, he continued: "I told her I'd stay home and look after her, but she insisted that I go, said she'd never hear the end of it from my mom if she kept me from going... so I drove to the lake alone."

Dex, dressing and packing his bag, paused at the mention of the lake. "Lanier?"

"No, Altoona," Charlie said, rewrapping the towel at his waist as he returned to his locker. "When the shit hit the fan, I rushed back to the city to check on her."

The words stung—too close to David's rushed departure back to the city.

"There was a truck in the driveway when I arrived—one I knew well."

"Jen cheated on you?"

"With my fucking brother! The same asshole brother who lied to my mom and said he couldn't make it on the Fourth because of a construction job in Alabama. Clearly just wrecking a home, not building one."

"I'm sorry, Charlie. Why didn't you say anything?"

"Embarrassment?" Charlie admitted, pulling the towel from his waist and turning toward Dex.

Charlie most certainly had nothing to be embarrassed about. His damp bush glistened, practically an arrow pointing to the meat hanging below it.

Dex had only seen it from afar before, and it hadn't looked big then; clearly, Charlie was a grower. He wasn't sure why Charlie was so engorged, but he couldn't look away, rapidly committing the details to his mental spank bank.

Charlie was uncut—a surprise to Dex, who'd rarely seen an uncut cock on a white man. He'd never asked about Charlie's background and wondered but decided now wasn't the time to ask.

While Charlie wasn't fully erect by any means, Dex could tell both the girth and length would be decent at full potential. Dex, almost certain he was visibly drooling, was glad Charlie finally turned—breaking the spell.

It didn't take Charlie long to dress and gather his things—or maybe time just moved faster once he wasn't naked.

"Ready?" he asked, swinging his bag strap onto his shoulder.

"Ready," Dex said. "Hungry?"

"Starving."

Almost in unison, they both asked, "Mexican?"

"Perfect," Dex said. "There's a great little Mexican place near me, away from the busy part of Midtown."

Charlie left his truck at the station and Dex drove since he knew the spot. Dex was thankful that the restaurant was quiet—even the patio seats were empty. Less chance of drawing unnecessary attention.

Once the hostess seated them—Charlie requesting a back-corner table—he grinned, mischief lighting his eyes. "Let's do some shots!"

Tempted to drown his thoughts, Dex still groaned. "I'm not really a shot guy—they fuck me up too fast."

"That's the point, isn't it? I wanna forget the day we had," Charlie countered. "C'mon, don't be a pussy!"

"I thought you liked pussy," Dex joked.

"Shut up—you know what I mean. Just one, before the meal."

"Fine. Just one.

It wasn't just one. Another shot came before the food, then another after—plus the pitcher of margaritas. Dex was already tipsy.

When the fourth round of shots arrived, Dex turned it down, "I still have to drive."

"I still have to drive, too."

"Absolutely not. You are not driving, mister. The alcohol's hitting you harder—you've barely touched your food."

"Guess I was more thirsty than hungry," Charlie snorted.

"You can stay with me—I'm only a few blocks from here," Dex offered. "I'll drive you to the station for your truck in the morning.

"In that case," Charlie said, giving Dex a lingering, mischievous look before downing both shots, "I'm not driving after all."

8

CONFESSIONS

BY THE TIME they left, Charlie had to lean against Dex for balance, nearly toppling them both twice before reaching the vehicle.

"Don't you dare vomit in my Jeep," Dex said, unlocking the door and helping Charlie into the passenger seat.

"I won't," Charlie slurred, "I'm a classy bitch."

Though they were only a few blocks away, Charlie dozed off before they got to Dex's. Waking him wasn't hard—but getting him out of the car and up the porch steps was no picnic.

"Jesus, Charlie—you've got lead boots."

Charlie popped out of his stupor, flexed his chest and arms, and grinned. "All iron, baby!"

He stumbled, but Dex caught him before he went down, pulling him close enough that their faces landed inches apart.

"Thanks for saving my sweet ass today, partner," Charlie said, planting a kiss right on his lips.

Blood rushed south in a way it hadn't in weeks. Dex gently pushed Charlie back, just enough to avoid the embarrassment of him noticing the growing erection.

"That's what partners are for," Dex said, ignoring the kiss. "Now let's get inside."

Dex fumbled with the keys some until finally getting the door open, then guided Charlie to the sofa.

"Just crash here. I'll grab you some water."

Charlie dropped onto it with a sigh. "Thanks, man. I mean it."

Dex grabbed a blanket and pillow from the hallway closet on his way back to the sofa with a bottle of water, returning to find Charlie watching him with an unreadable expression.

"You ever think about it?" Charlie asked.

Dex raised an eyebrow. "Think about what?"

Charlie didn't answer—just grabbed the sizeable bulge at his crotch.

Dex froze.

"I saw you looking at me today," Charlie said. "Watching me in the shower. Staring at my meat by the lockers."

"Sorry. I was lost in thought." It wasn't a lie, but not the whole truth either.

"I didn't hate it." Charlie sat up, eyes glassy but sincere. "I've been an asshole, I know. But you're... you've always had my back—even when I didn't deserve it."

"Charlie—"

"I think I've always been scared. Scared to admit I was curious. Scared of how comfortable I felt around you despite all the machismo."

Dex stepped forward slowly. "You're drunk."

Charlie stood to meet him. "I'm not that drunk."

They stared at each other in the quiet, city static bleeding through the windows. Then Charlie kissed him—a real kiss. Hungry, not hesitant. Full of pent-up tension and something closer to grief than lust.

Dex's mind was still filled with thoughts of David, but it had been over two weeks since he'd felt another's touch. He responded in kind, pulling Charlie closer, backing him onto the sofa until they both sank into it—mouths locked, hands mapping fantasized terrain now charged with new meaning.

Dex came up for air briefly. "Charlie, are you sure this is okay?"

Charlie stared at him—then a sudden wave of nausea washed over his face. "Can I use your bathroom?"

"Of course. Down the hall, to the left."

Charlie slapped a hand over his mouth and bolted, the bathroom door slamming behind him.

Charlie spotted the shower first—faster than finding the toilet and struggling with the lid. Standing over the drain, he thought about what led him to this moment in the first place. He'd seen the way Dex watched him in the station shower earlier—it had admittedly turned him on. Maybe it was the brush with death, the reminder tomorrow isn't promised, that fueled his fear of missing out on a part of himself he'd only recently admitted.

Dex's reaction when he'd dropped his towel earlier had only stoked his curiosity further. Part of him had hoped Dex would pretend he hadn't showered and join him, but when he didn't, the urge for Dex only grew stronger, his dick now hardening at the thought of him.

Charlie's invitation for drinks had been in earnest—he needed liquid courage to follow through. He'd only meant to have enough to boost his bravado, but he had overdone it. His stomach's rejection of the surplus alcohol was proof.

A knock came from the other side of the door. "Everything okay in there?"

"Yeah, too much to drink." Worried Dex might think his nausea was related to it, he added, "I promise it had nothing to do with our kiss."

"Do you need anything?"

"I vomited on myself a little," Charlie admitted. "Mind if I rinse off in the shower?"

"Of course. Take your time. I'll grab you some clothes to wear when you get out."

Charlie seized the chance to reassure him it wasn't regret. "Who said I planned on wearing clothes?"

Dex stood outside the bathroom door in disbelief. The straight partner he'd secretly fantasized about for well over a decade had just kissed him—and was now openly flirting. He couldn't believe his ears. Maybe the detonations had catapulted them into an alternate reality. The last few weeks—especially today—felt like the whole world had shifted.

Even though Charlie had joked, Dex still fetched him a pair of shorts and a tank top, leaving them on the table across from the bathroom door. Pretending he hadn't heard Charlie's last comment, he called louder over the fan and shower, both of which had been turned on while he was away, "Clothes are on the table outside the door."

There wasn't a response from the other side, so Dex walked away and headed toward the kitchen. He wasn't a shot guy, but tonight he was and he needed something to calm the mix of fear, excitement, and lust. He tipped back whiskey straight from the bottle, letting the burn chase down his hesitation.

He returned to the sofa and glanced at his phone, instinctively opening the Messages thread with David. Maybe habit, maybe guilt—but mostly longing for a missed chance. That ache gave him resolve—he wouldn't miss this chance with Charlie.

An endless stack of failed, unsent messages filled his screen, but he sent another anyway. Failed again, its exclamatory icon mocking him, as if screaming for him to stop.

Charlie's stomach had settled from the vomiting, but now nerves took over, butterflies filling the space where the alcohol had been. It wasn't Dex—his attraction had started long ago, maybe from the beginning, even if he hadn't admitted to it. It was fear: that he'd lose his partner if things went wrong, if the attraction wasn't as mutual as anticipated. And with the world's future so uncertain, he couldn't afford to lose anything else.

He'd replayed this moment in his head more times than he cared to admit. Since the night at Eden, the chance hadn't come—until today, when Dex stared at him in the shower and gave him a clear sign of interest.

He noticed the convenient hose anchored on the wall. A few weeks ago, he might not have known its use. But after Eden, his urges had driven him to research. And after Jen left, he no longer feared anyone seeing his search history.

He'd even bought one for himself after he kicked Jen out. The first tries hadn't gone so well, but practice had helped. Now, afraid that Dex might be thinking he was stalling, he made quick work of it. He'd showered only hours before, but he re-scrubbed his intimate areas to make sure he was fresh and clean.

When Charlie turned off the water, a voice called out from the other side of the door:

"There are clean towels in the cabinet just outside of the shower, and there's a porcelain tumbler under the sink with a bunch of brand-new toothbrushes in it."

He wasn't surprised Dex was prepared for the occasional hook-up. A flicker of jealousy rose at the thought of men before him, but he pushed it away. It was now his turn; the other guys no longer mattered.

Charlie's reflection smiled back at him—a rare sight these last weeks. The shower had sobered him more than he'd planned, but he'd already made the hard move: kissed his partner of twelve years. A man who'd filled his thoughts for years—more so these last weeks.

He'd cheated too—with Ryan—but Jen's betrayal had been a blessing in disguise. Ending things with her was the catalyst into a lot of introspection and forced him to deal with some hard truths he'd hidden from everyone, even himself. Freedom from a dead relationship gave him a chance to figure out what might make him happy.

He lingered at the mirror, then bit the bullet and—even though he didn't exit it at that moment—opened the bathroom door.

Dex brushed his teeth at the kitchen sink with a spare toothbrush from his gym bag, changed into a cute jock and lounge pants, and paced the open space of his living room, dining area, and kitchen. He was standing by the fridge when Charlie shut off the shower.

"Thanks," Charlie called out, responding to his tips about the towel and toothbrush.

The anticipation was killing him. He tried sitting on the sofa, but his leg bounced restlessly. He stood again, positioning himself at the island with a direct view of the bathroom door.

When it finally opened, the shaft of light spilling from its frame revealed Charlie's shadow in the hall, the cast of his dick dancing on the floor as it swung like a pendulum between his legs.

Realizing he wasn't exiting the bathroom just yet, Dex broke the silence. "Feeling better?"

"Much!" Charlie called, still inside the bathroom and drying, evident by the shadow mirroring every movement with the towel. "Sorry about earlier—I'm a little embarrassed."

Dex heard him brushing his teeth. "Don't be."

The faucet turned off. Dex watched Charlie's shadow dry its mouth with the towel before moving across the floor, dick still swinging, and Charlie appearing in the threshold tagging along behind it.

The thoughts of David that haunted Dex earlier vanished, replaced by every single fantasy he'd ever had about his partner. He'd seen Charlie naked several times in the locker room, but there was something about seeing him in his house—smiling face, legs spread slightly, cock dangling heavily—that had Dex hard and dripping already.

"All these years of smelling you next to me in the patrol car," Charlie said, raising his left arm to sniff his pit. "Never thought one day I'd be smelling it on me."

"Woof," escaped Dex's mouth in a low growl.

"Like on the app," Charlie said, walking toward the island—surprising the hell out of Dex.

"How do you know about the apps?" Dex asked. "Have you been a secret fag this whole time?"

"Fag? I thought you hated that word."

"Only offensive when it comes from…" Dex cut off his own sentence, leaning in to kiss Charlie—slow, deep, sucking his bottom lip as he pulled away. "…a homophobe's lips."

"Woof." Charlie echoed him, ignoring the jab at his past. He smiled widely, looked down, then back up with a wink.

Dex's jaw dropped when he followed Charlie's gaze. "Well, you've definitely been keeping *that* a secret."

"It likes to play hide-and-seek."

"Looks like I found it."

Charlie's cock was hard and throbbing, the thick vein on top of it pulsing like a visual heartbeat. Dex wasn't fond of his own foreskin, but Charlie's was perfect—the head peeking just past his hood, not too loose, not too tight. Shaved around the base, bush kept full—or perhaps slightly trimmed—with a pair of hairy low-hangers dangling beneath.

"Are you going to make me stand here naked all by myself, or are you going to take off your clothes and join me?" Charlie asked between kisses.

"No one's stopping you from removing them…"

"Fair point." Charlie buried one hand in Dex's chest hair and slipped the other under his waistband, shoving his pants past his muscled ass.

Though his dick was fully contained by it, Dex was stretching the limits of his jock's pouch once again. Charlie spun him around to admire his ass, "You fill those out nicely, mister."

Charlie pulled Dex close, belly pressed to Dex's back, cock resting against his ass—only making it harder. Lips grazed his ear, tongue trailing tenderly to the nape, then slowly along his spine, inching southward to the furry patch above Dex's crack. Dex moaned as Charlie's tongue continued its path, finally finding the fleshy treasure it was seeking.

"Wasn't sure I could do that," Charlie confessed. "How'd I do?"

"Felt great—like you've had some practice," Dex praised, adding, "Not to ruin the moment, but... why the sudden change of teams?"

"I don't want to leave this moment, Dex—it's taken too long to get here," Charlie replied. "Can we revisit in the morning?"

He spun Dex around, kissing him with the same hunger as before his expeditious trip to the bathroom. Their tongues danced—switching between a passionate tango and a graceful waltz— as he peeled off Dex's jock, freeing him from its prison.

July 27, 2026

"What the caterpillar calls the end,
the rest of the world calls a butterfly."

~Lao Tzu

9
CHRYSALIS

DAVID'S FIRST BREATHS were labored, like gasps pulled from underwater, almost drowning. He clawed at the mask on his face, flinching as fluorescent lights overhead seared into his skull. His body felt stiff and uncooperative. Aside from the steady beeps from the monitors at his side— and the sterile air burning his nose—the room was empty.

He didn't know where he was.

Or who he was.

His name floated just beyond reach—like a dream you know you've just forgotten. He pushed himself upright, wincing at the pounding in his head and the ache in his abdomen. He lifted his left arm: an IV dripped something milky into his veins. A blue band imprinted with a Northside Medical logo circled his wrist.

A nurse bustled in, startling him. Her eyes flicked to the vitals monitor, then to David.

"Oh my God, you're awake!" she exclaimed, relief breaking over her face. She leaned into the hall. "Room three-thirty-seven is awake! Can we get him extubated?"

Within minutes, a team of nurses and nurse techs appeared in David's room and began removing the breathing tube from his throat. Despite being extremely gentle, the process hurt like hell; he gagged a bit as it slid out.

The team filtered out shortly after.

"Here you go, dear," the nurse said, offering some ice chips. "This will help you swallow. Try not to talk yet—it may take days before you voice is back, once we can give you warmer liquids."

David pointed to her clipboard, then to himself.

"Oh, you want to write?"

He nodded.

"I'll get you a message board. One moment."

She returned quickly with a whiteboard and a marker.

David scribbled a quick message and showed it to her: *Where am I?*

"Northside Medical, in Duluth. You were found unconscious two weeks ago—the night of the Fourth. Car accident. A drunk driver ran a stop sign into the passenger side of your vehicle. Mild head trauma. You've been in a coma since then."

What's my name?

"You don't remember your name?"

No.

"Your ID says your name is David Gibson, from Atlanta. Head injuries are known to cause temporary amnesia."

David's breath caught as he scrawled on the message board again.

I don't remember anything.

Charlie looked to Dex for guidance. He'd watched his share of gay porn since his sexcapades at Eden—Ryan had led him then, told him what to do—and since giving Jen the boot, but he still wasn't what to do now. Part of him wanted to take the lead, to explore Dex's body like a new toy. But another part was tired of leading. He ached to hand over control, to be the toy this time.

"Bedroom?" Dex suggested, like he'd read his thoughts.

"Lead the way." The words left his mouth almost of their own fruition, desire manifesting as submission. It surprised—and aroused—him.

Dex laced their fingers together and tugged him toward the bedroom; Charlie felt like he was floating above the floor. The lamps sparked to life with a flip of a switch, revealing a room that was larger than he expected. A king-size bed sat between the lamps on one wall; a sling waited on the opposite side.

Dex grabbed a remote from the wall and turned on the rope lights that ran behind the crown molding framing the ceiling. It lit the room in a warm white light at first, but with a quick button selection, the room's walls were now bathed in red.

"Interesting setup," Charlie said as Dex led him to the bed.

"Thanks. It's aided in some fun nights over the years," Dex replied.

"I bet."

At the foot of the bed, Dex left Charlie on one side while he crossed the to the opposite. "Help me with the duvet?"

Once the blanket was folded back onto itself a couple times at the footboard, Dex climbed onto his side and Charlie climbed onto his, meeting in the middle with a kiss.

"Just relax," Dex murmured, pushing gently on his chest.

Charlie didn't need much coaxing. He lay back, resting his head on the pillow, and watching Dex, anticipating every touch and kiss from him.

"You're more relaxed than I expected," Dex said. Dex straddled Charlie's hips and slid back until Charlie's erection pressed against his ass.

"I'm a ball of nerves, Dex. If you were anyone else, I'd be drenched in sweat—or not here at all. But I trust you with my life on the streets. Why wouldn't I trust you with it in the sheets."

Dex searched Charlie's eyes for truths and desires long hidden. No matter how hard he looked, he found no answers—especially to his question to *why now?*

He kissed Charlie's upper abs, burying his face in the fur that blanketed his partner's torso, pausing at each nipple before kissing tenderly along his neck.

Dex's lips and tongue traced the distance from Charlie's collarbone to his ear, eliciting soft moans that grew in volume as he drew closer to his destination, sucking playfully on the lobe.

He reached down for Charlie's right hand with his left, wove their fingers together, and lifted his arm behind his head to expose his pit, wasting no time burying his nose in its depths, lapping at the musk already tangled in the hair.

"Fuuuuck!" Charlie growled. "I saw that in porn and thought it was disgusting—but it feels fucking amazing. I didn't realize how sensitive that spot was."

"Your scent is amazing—sweet, light, sexy."

"May I?" Charlie asked, lifting Dex's right arm with his left.

"Go for it," Dex encouraged.

Charlie waited for the go-ahead before diving into Dex's pit, inhaling like he'd strapped on an oxygen mask and his life depended on it.

Dex felt Charlie's cock thicken against his ass as Charlie's tongue circled, bathing his pit with a virgin eagerness he hadn't felt in a while.

“Fuuuuck, you’re right. Your scent is intoxicating... sweet, musky, citrusy.”

“I put on some citrus oil after my shower at the station—it keeps the odor at bay,” Dex explained, coaxing Charlie back toward the pillow with a hand on his chest.

Dex kissed down Charlie’s abs, one by one, along his way to the prize, burying his nose in the bush with the same gusto Charlie had shown his pit.

“How big is this thing, anyway?”

“I usually say ‘big enough.’ Jen measured once—said it was nine.”

Dex only smiled, then opened his mouth and slowly worked Charlie’s dick down his throat, lips sliding closer to its cleanly-shaved base but never reaching.

“It’s definitely big enough,” Dex agreed, coming up for air.

“Wow, impressive,” Charlie said. “Jen hated giving head—probably for the best, since she sucked at sucking. She certainly didn’t have your throat skills.”

“Not many do,” Dex said proudly.

He teased him longer, tongue sliding inside his hood, circling his head, tracing along his frenulum until Charlie squirmed, then down his shaft to his balls, sucking gently, pausing often at the tip to taste the steady leak of precum. Dex lifted his balls, licking along his taint, tongue darting cautiously toward his hole.

Charlie chuckled. "Don't worry—I found your shower attachment."

"I wasn't worried," Dex lied with a laughed. "Just admittedly surprised that you knew what it was."

"Got one at home."

Dex paused, lifting his head.

Charlie smirked. "Let's just say I've had a lot of alone time since the Fourth—since walking in on my brother fucking Jen in our bed.

"It flipped a switch in my head, like waking from a coma. I decided to live in the moment instead of dwelling on the past. First week, I fucked at least a dozen women trying to prove my urges weren't real—only ended up resenting them. I realized it wasn't what I wanted, and my urges weren't going away. A few nights watching porn, I noticed I watched the men more than the women. That was the nail in the coffin.

"With Jen gone, I had the freedom to explore. Looked up some gay porn—my dick got harder, orgasms more intense than with straight porn. I bought some toys, the attachment, and even bought a harness because I thought the ones in the porn looked fucking hot."

"Wow, Charlie—so this has been brewing a while?" Dex asked.

"Years. But I never admitted it to myself until recently. Feels like I'm a butterfly finally emerging from its cocoon."

Dex abandoned Charlie's groin reluctantly, crawled up beside him, and looked into his eyes as he held him. A mischievous smirk curled the corner of his mouth, "So how long have you been fantasizing about this moment?"

Charlie blushed slightly but refused to answer—he kissed Dex hard instead to silence him. He kept his mouth busy, migrating to Dex's neck, collarbone, chest, then slowly down his body until he reached Dex's very attentive cock.

Dex's torso wasn't nearly as furry as Charlie's, but his natural, untrimmed bush marked the start of fur galore—bush, balls, legs, and ass all thick with black hair. Charlie buried his nose in the crease between thigh and dick, tickling him with the sensitivity. He licked one side, then the other, tongued his balls, then paused.

"Overwhelmed?" Dex asked, catching the hesitation.

"A little," Charlie admitted, "Only because I've never done it before."

"First—get out of your head," Dex urged. "No one expects you to be an expert on your first try. Men have the advantage—you've got a dick, so treat mine like it's yours. Think about what feels good, where you're sensitive, what others have done in the past that worked. I am guessing you've got plenty of experience receiving."

"Yeah, but we both know *bad* head exists."

"Touché—but that just means you know what *not* to do. Don't worry—Daddy's a good coach."

"Daddy?" Charlie looked up, one brow raised.

"Well, you're like a baby gay—someone's gotta show you the ropes."

"Guess it's a good thing I've got daddy issues then... Daddy Dex."

Charlie wrapped Dex's cock in his hand, stroking softly to draw back the foreskin. Dex expected a mouth but surprised instead when Charlie leaned in and sniffed.

"You're into smells," Dex pointed out.

"Oh, definitely... When I was younger, I thought maybe I was gay because I loved smelling my hands after touching my sweaty, musky dick—it made me rock hard." He chuckled. "Guess I was, turns out."

Instead of starting at the tip like Dex had, Charlie began at the base, kissing and licking up the shaft with eager tenderness until reaching the head. He slid it into his mouth slowly, softly, tongue circling its entirety. He lingered at the frenulum and tip, licking and sucking at the sweet spill of precum.

"Yours is as sweet as mine," Charlie said. "I used to think I was gay because I liked to taste mine."

"Turns out you were," Dex said playfully, without missing a beat.

"Yeah, yeah..."

10
CRESCENDO

WITHOUT MUCH WARNING, Charlie engulfed Dex's cock, taking almost the full length into his mouth; he pulled back, then engulfed it again, taking even more, repeating until his lips reached the base, withdrawing with strings of saliva webbing and coating Dex's dick.

"Jesus!" Dex called out. "There's no way that was your first time."

"So... I did good, Daddy?"

Dex smiled at the playfulness and played along. "Very good, son"

"Confession..." Charlie began, still stroking Dex's dick but sitting up to meet his eyes. "About a year ago, Jen and I split up for a few weeks—she gave me an ultimatum, pissed I hadn't proposed. She went to her mother's; about a week in, my balls were getting a little blue."

He stopped stroking but kept Dex's dick firmly in his grasp.

"One night after work I passed a seedy adult video store and pulled in—curious, maybe looking for relief. It was mostly men; I almost turned until I saw a woman eyeing me.

"She went to a booth and motioned to the adjoining one before stepping in, so I obeyed. I couldn't see her—just her lips—and heard her whisper through the gloryhole that she wanted to blow me.

"I was already hard, so I undid my pants and fed my dick through the hole, waiting for the glory— and boy did I get it. You said to pull from my own blowjob experiences; that one was one of the best I'd had. The technique I just used on you was part of that."

Charlie slid up along Dex's body and met his lips with a kiss.

"Wow, you have been keeping secrets from your partner."

"There's more..." Charlie continued, sliding into Dex's pit and resting his head on his chest.

Dex tightened his arm around Charlie. "I'm listening."

"It's a bit embarrassing, but I got off within minutes—the blowjob was *that* good. When I went to pull out, my dick was yanked back in. Still hard, I figured a repeat—then felt a condom rolled down the length. Next thing, I'm sliding into a lubed, hot hole. I lasted a little longer than with the blowjob, but not by much—the hole was tight, and I soon found out why. The condom slid off as I pulled out, so I quickly pulled my pants up and exited the booth.

"Outside, the woman who'd lured me in was chatting up another guy. I was confused until I realized I'd miscounted doors and hadn't gone to the adjacent booth. As I tried to slip out, the other door swung open and revealed a rugged, muscle-bound guy who gave me a knowing smile."

"And how did it make you feel—being blown by a man, fucking one?"

"I panicked—thought maybe I he'd given me something. Then I remembered the condom and stopped stressing. I've thought of that night often while whacking it—how different his ass felt from Jen's pussy."

"So, you're not a gay virgin after all."

"Another confession," Charlie said. "Part of me felt tricked out of a true first experience with a guy; the booth guy was my first time fucking a man…"

Dex just stared at Charlie and listened.

"…but not the last."

Dex's eyes widened; Charlie flushed. A long pause settled between them.

"I was at Eden the night you were," Charlie said finally. "The night before the bombs."

Dex gasped and sat up to look Charlie in the eyes. "Wait, what? Why didn't you say anything?"

"You were with someone."

"David," Dex said.

Charlie finally had a name. "Right… what happened to him, by the way?"

"I went home with him, and we spent an incredible night together—so incredible I invited him to join me on the Fourth for my friend's party at her house on Lanier," Dex explained. "After the alerts hit, his mom called and he panicked about her being alone. We'd gone to the party in his SUV, so when he rushed back to the city, Jake had to give me a ride home."

Charlie's expression shifted at "Jake," but he let it pass. "Listen, if you don't want to do this, I get it. I wouldn't want to ruin anything you might be building with David."

Dex climbed back on top of him—warm skin on skin—straddling his hips, eyes searching. "I didn't tell you about David because I wanted to stop," he said softly. "I told you because... you've actually been a welcome distraction."

"Just a distraction?"

Dex smirked. "An unexpected development, more accurate."

"He just ghosted you?"

"Not exactly," Dex started, explaining the quick number grab, the likely mistype, and the stream of undeliverable messages. David hadn't returned to his townhouse—maybe he'd stayed with his mother outside the city.

"What if something happened to him? An accident? Were you guys drinking?"

Dex hadn't even considered it; his mind reeled with accident scenarios like a movie projector. "We had a beer or two—lots of food. He was okay to drive."

"And Jake brought you home?" Charlie pressed, returning to the real pressure point. "That was nice of him."

"Yeah, I guess—" Charlie's voice cut out, "but left before I woke the next morning."

"He stayed the night?" Charlie asked, a jealous tinge in his tone.

"Traffic back to Atlanta was pretty bad, and he was tired," Dex replied, omitting the rest of what happened with Jake that night.

"You asked me earlier how long I'd been fantasizing about this moment..." Charlie's voice trailed off as he lifted his head to look at Dex. "I've lost count... a kiss in the patrol car, or maybe a blowjob if the kiss led there; pinning you against the locker, or you pinning me against the tile in the showers..."

"Why'd you wait until now?"

"Actually, it almost happened sooner. The day I went to that adult arcade, I had finally worked up the courage to invite you for a drink after work. Jen had left me, and Jake had left you—felt like fate. Then Jake showed up that day at the station wanting to talk, killing my chance."

"I had no idea."

"How could you? A week later Jen and I had made up—and so did you and Jake."

"Not for long. We split again a few weeks later—well, he left me," Dex replied. "And Jen's a stupid girl for fucking it up after you took her back."

"Well, Jake's a stupid boy—period. And Jen wasn't the only one who fucked up—but she doesn't know that."

"What do you mean?"

"That night at Eden I met someone," Charlie admitted. "We kissed, we danced; he made me put on one of his jocks; we danced and kissed more... and then I fucked him in the darkroom."

"And I thought I was a slut for hauling David in the darkroom—meanwhile, you lost your virginity in a video booth, and your second time was in a darkroom?" Dex teased, leaning in for a kiss.

"But it wasn't slutty—not really," Charlie corrected after pulling back from the kiss. "It was connected, intimate even despite the not-so-intimate place."

"If you'd already been with a man, why take so long to tell me?"

"There's more I should probably tell you..."

Dex raised his eyebrow and smiled. "Do tell."

"That night, when I realized that you were really into David and I didn't have a shot, I got a little jealous," Charlie admitted. "I watched you kissing; my craving for your kiss grew stronger the longer I watched. When you and David left the dance floor, I followed—not sure where you were headed. Then I saw you there, the red light on you just before you dropped to your knees.

"At first, I just watched through the dark, wishing it were your mouth on me—red light cutting through the shadows. Then I did more than watch: I pulled out my dick and started stroking, and a stranger in the shadows found my dick with his mouth.

"It startled me at first, but I just kept watching your mouth while feeling the stranger and started imagining it was you sucking me—your lips, your tongue, both working their magic. When David let out that low growl, it pushed me over the edge—I think he and I shot our loads in sync."

Dex felt Charlie's dick stiffen against his ass. "That's actually really fucking hot—knowing you were there watching and fantasizing—knowing, in a way, I made you come that night."

"I've craved you ever since," Charlie confessed, lifting his head and kissing him—tender first, then deeper.

Dex rolled his hips slowly, sliding their cocks against each other, both already hard and slick with anticipation. Charlie gasped into his mouth.

Without breaking the kiss, Dex reached down, guiding Charlie's wrists above his head, pinning them gently to the mattress as he kissed along his jaw and throat. Then, without a word, Dex shifted his weight, slid back, and flipped Charlie onto his stomach in one smooth, commanding motion. Charlie let out a surprised breath—half-laugh, half-moan—but didn't resist.

"Just relax," Dex murmured, voice low and steady. "Let Daddy take care of you."

Charlie turned his head, breath already quickening, muscles taut with anticipation. Dex paused to admire him—broad shoulders tapering to a trim waist, the soft curve of his ass rising invitingly from the sheets.

He slid between Charlie's thighs, hands spreading him open—then leaned in.

The first press of tongue drew a sharp gasp. Dex didn't rush—he lingered, licking long and slow, teasing the rim with flicks and swirls, savoring every twitch, every moan spilling from Charlie's lips.

Charlie's hips trembled, then pressed back against Dex's face.

"Oh my *God*," he breathed, voice breaking. "Dex…"

"I know," Dex murmured, barely audible between the licks. "Just let go."

He buried his face deeper, tongue pushing inward, fucking him with it with slow, steady pressure. One hand gripped Charlie's hip, the other slid up his spine—a grounding touch that kept him anchored.

Charlie panted now, helpless to do anything but feel. He arched, moaned, begged—softly, breathlessly—for more.

When Dex finally pulled away—lips slick and face flushed—Charlie whimpered at the loss. Reaching for the lube, Dex pulled him into a kiss, his tongue lingering intentionally to give Charlie a taste of himself.

"Is that what I taste like?" Charlie asked, surprised.

"Yeah," Dex said. "Fucking delicious."

"Wow. I can't wait to taste you."

Dex kissed Charlie again while slicking his fingers, then eased one inside. Charlie tensed for half a second—until Dex kissed the space between his shoulder blades.

"Still good?" he whispered.

Charlie nodded, eyes shut tight. "Yeah. Fuck, yeah."

Dex worked him open slowly, adding a second, then a third finger—stretching, coaxing, never rushing. By the time he withdrew and slicked his cock, Charlie was rocking his hips, desperate and ready.

Dex lined up behind him, one hand firm on his hip, the other guiding himself in.

The first push drew a gasp from them both— thick, tight, hot.

"Jesus, you feel *so* good," Dex groaned.

Charlie let out a sound between a moan and a sob. "Don't stop."

"I won't," Dex promised, voice raw.

He started slowly—deep, measured thrusts— giving Charlie time to adjust. Each stroke dragged a new sound from him, each breath heavier than the last.

"Fuck... Dex... oh God—"

"You're doing great," Dex murmured, gripping both hips now, pulling him back to meet each thrust.

The sound of their bodies meeting—skin on skin, slick and rhythmic—filled the room, underscored by Charlie's moans and Dex's low growls.

But Dex wanted more.

He pulled out gently, slid his hands under Charlie, and urged him to roll over.

"I want to see you," he said.

Charlie let Dex guide him, his legs falling open as Dex settled between them. Dex lined up again, pressed forward—sliding back in at a deeper, fuller angle, making Charlie cry out in surprise and pleasure.

Dex kissed him—hard, hungry—as he began to thrust again, grinding with a slow, deliberate rhythm.

Charlie wrapped his legs around Dex's waist, clinging, eyes wide and glassy.

"You okay?" Dex asked between kisses.

Charlie nodded quickly, mouth parting. "Yeah— God—*don't stop.*"

Dex kissed him again, pouring everything into it—lust, need, tenderness—then whispered against his lips: "I'm gonna come inside you."

Charlie moaned, back arching as Dex's pace quickened, breath ragged. The kiss deepened as their bodies tensed, sweat-slicked skin clinging in the best way.

Then Dex gasped, groaning into Charlie's mouth as he spilled deep inside, hips locked tight, his entire body shuddering with release.

Charlie clung to him, trembling, riding the waves—his own orgasm triggered moments after, trapped between their bodies.

They collapsed together, bodies tangled, hearts racing in sync.

Dex didn't move right away. He kissed Charlie's temple, his cheek, his mouth—slower now, softer.

"You're incredible," he murmured, still inside, still hard.

Charlie laughed breathlessly, eyes fluttering open. "You say that to all your unexpected developments?"

Dex grinned. "Only the ones who take cock like that their first try."

Charlie blushed, pulling Dex closer, kissing him, not ready to let go.

Everything felt electric, almost unreal. His skin tingled. His heart was hammering—not from exertion now, but from something warmer. Calmer. Foreign.

He hadn't known what to expect from his first time—awkwardness, maybe. Pain. A disconnect between fantasy and reality.

But this was *everything.*

Dex shifted, brushing the damp hair back from Charlie's forehead. He pressed a slow, grounding kiss there, another on his cheek, and finally one to his lips—lazy, unhurried, the kind that said: *I'm not going anywhere. Not yet.*

"You okay?" Dex asked softly, voice low, a little hoarse.

Charlie blinked up at him, dazed. "Yeah," he said, smiling, breath catching. "More than okay."

Dex smiled back and gently pulled out, making Charlie wince a little—but even that felt strangely intimate. Dex murmured an apology against his neck, then rolled to the side, grabbed the small towel near the bed, and wiped them both down before tugging the blankets around them.

Charlie turned instinctively into Dex's chest, curling close. Dex's arm wrapped around his back, palm wide and warm between his shoulder blades. Charlie finally exhaled, words spilling before he could stop them. "I didn't expect it to feel that good."

Dex chuckled, a low rumble against his cheek. "That's because most guys rush it. Or treat it like a transaction."

"Well," Charlie said, voice lighter, "you didn't rush it. It was perfect."

Dex pulled him in tighter. "Wasn't going to rush through things with you."

Charlie's cheeks flushed. He kept his face tucked into Dex's collarbone, not quite ready to meet his gaze.

"Daddy fucked you good?" Dex teased, fingertips tracing circles along Charlie's spine.

Charlie smiled into his skin. "Worth the wait."

Dex kissed the top of his head, a quiet laugh escaping. "Glad I could ruin you for anyone else."

"You might've," Charlie said, half-joking.

He finally looked up, searching Dex's face—expecting cocky satisfaction, maybe smug amusement.

But Dex just looked calm and open, thumb brushing softly along his jaw.

"Thank you," Charlie whispered.

"For what?"

"For not rushing. For making it feel…" He struggled for the word. "Safe. Intimate. Intense. And… hot as fuck."

Dex grinned. "Kinda my specialty."

Charlie laid his head back down, heart full in a way that had nothing to do with sex.

They drifted in and out of silence, fingers tangled, legs brushing under the sheets.

Eventually, Charlie whispered, "So what happens now?"

Dex didn't answer right away. He just pulled Charlie closer and kissed his head again.

"We sleep," he murmured. "And worry about that in the morning."

July 28, 2026

I don't love you as if you were salt-rose, topaz,
or arrow of carnations that propagate fire:
I love you as one loves certain obscure things,
secretly, between the shadow and the soul.

I love you as the plant that doesn't bloom but carries
the light of those flowers, hidden, within itself,
and thanks to your love the tight aroma that arose
from the earth lives dimly in my body.

I love you without knowing how, or when, or from where,
I love you directly without problems or pride:
I love you like this because
I don't know any other way to love,

except in this form in which I am not nor are you,
so close that your hand upon my chest is mine,
so close that your eyes close with my dreams.

~Pablo Neruda, *Sonnet XVII*

11
COALESCE

DEX WOKE UP well ahead of Charlie. He'd sobered up by the time they fell asleep, but Dex still wanted Charlie to sleep off any chance of a hangover. He climbed in the shower, still processing the events of the night with a sting of guilt—like he'd moved on from David far too quickly: first with Jake, now with Charlie.

It was just a one-night stand.

He clung to that thought as water rushed over him, willing it to replace the contradictory pull of David. But he couldn't ignore the invisible tether he'd forged with him—sudden, yes, but strong.

At the same time, Dex couldn't deny the weight of what he shared with Charlie—a connection twelve years in the making, slow-growing and quiet until last night made it real, blooming into something he'd only ever dared to imagine.

And Charlie was here—lying in his bed in the next room—while David had seemingly vanished, as if Dex had imagined him. Part of him wondered if maybe he had.

Unsure what the morning might bring, Dex took his time—thoroughly prepping, just in case another round of playtime was on the table. He'd just rinsed the last of the soap from his body when a knock sounded at the bathroom door.

"Mind if I come in and piss?" Charlie called.

"Come on in," Dex called back.

The door swung open, and Charlie strolled in—completely naked and clearly in a hurry, beelining for the toilet.

"Where do you think you're going?" Dex drawled, low and teasing. "Get that cute ass in here."

Charlie froze mid-step, then grinned. "Yes, sir." He trotted over like an eager pup—dick wagging—and slipped into the steam-filled shower.

The glass door clicked shut as he kissed Dex—wet, warm, unbothered. "Good morning, sexy," Charlie murmured. "Now can I pee? I'm *seriously* about to burst."

Charlie started to turn, but Dex caught his wrist and tugged him back. He took Charlie's chubbed cock and aimed it at himself.

"Go for it," Dex commanded, not caring that he'd already showered.

Charlie blinked. "Wait, seriously? That's... a thing?"

"Oh yeah," Dex said with a crooked grin. "Some guys are *really* into it; I just like it in the shower."

Charlie hesitated, then gave in—the need outweighing the nerves. With a sigh of relief, a warm stream arced and hit Dex just beneath the chest, liquid gold trickling down the ridges of his abs.

Dex pulled him closer until their bare bodies were flush, water and warmth mixing between them. Charlie's stream fountained upward between them as Dex leaned in for another kiss.

Their beards caught most of the spray, but a little splash kissed their lips before the falling water washed it away. Neither flinched. Charlie kissed deeper, hands gliding over Dex's slick back.

Then, without warning, Dex dropped to his knees.

Charlie's eyes widened as Dex angled his face up and let the stream hit him—over his chest, across his throat, onto his face. He opened his mouth, caught a little, let it pool, the playfully spit it against Charlie's thigh with a grin.

"Holy *fuck*," Charlie muttered, caught between arousal and disbelief.

Dex rose, rinsed quickly, and stepped into Charlie's arms again. Water cascaded down their bodies as they kissed once—slower, steamier, charged.

"I never thought that'd be so hot," Charlie admitted, pulling back just enough to meet his eyes. "Though... I think it had more to do with *you* than the act."

"So, you liked it?"

Charlie nodded, then ran a hand through Dex's hair. "You always this full throttle in the morning?"

"Only for guests with good aim." Dex smirked, re-lathered with the loofah for a quick touch-up, rinsed, then kissed Charlie before stepping toward the door.

"You're not going to shower with me?" Charlie asked, puppy eyed. "It's one of my favorite things."

"We definitely will," Dex said, leaning to look past Charlie at the attachment, "but I figured I'd give you some privacy."

Charlie looked back, following the line of sight, then smiled. "Got it."

"Take your time—I'll be in the bedroom when you're done."

The glass door clicked shut behind Dex, leaving Charlie alone in the shower.

He didn't move.

Steam curled around him like a veil, thick in the dim light, clinging to his skin as water poured over his shoulders in a steady, soothing stream. Palms to tile. Head down. Breath slow.

He stayed there, grounded in the heat, letting the silence settle.

His hole was slightly tender from last night, but not sore. Just a subtle, stretched ache—a phantom echo of Dex inside him. Not painful. Not raw. A pulse of memory tucked between his legs.

He shifted, rolling his hips, feeling the warmth of the attachment slide between his cheeks. No telling what the morning held. No promises had been made. But he liked being *ready*—the anticipation and intentionality. Despite the uncertainty in his head, his body felt open. Willing.

Images from the night before flickered in his mind—Dex's mouth, his hands, his voice low and steady. The way he'd touched him, read him, coaxing out moans and tremors Charlie hadn't known were there until Dex found them.

He smiled to himself—small, private.

It had been good. *Really* good.

What made it linger was the lack of pressure—Dex hadn't rushed or expected more than Charlie was ready to give. It made him want to give more.

Not to match Dex. Not to prove anything. Just because he wanted to.

He tilted his head back into the spray, rinsed once more, then turned off the water. The air outside the stream was cooler, but the heat still clung to his skin, something hot humming low in his chest.

He towel-dried quickly, wiped the water from his eyes with the back of his hand, and stepped into the fogged-up bathroom. His reflection was a blur in the mirror—softened by condensation, but clear enough to brush his teeth.

He cracked the door and padded out—still damp, cock hanging heavy—flushed with blood and curiosity.

The bedroom was dim, lit by gauzy morning light slipping between the blinds.

Dex was already on the bed. Face down. Legs spread. A pillow cradled his chest; arms folded beneath it. His ass—high, round, unabashedly presented—was aimed squarely at the door. Waiting. Wordless.

Charlie froze in the doorway, heart kicking hard against his ribs.

Dex didn't look back. Didn't speak.

He didn't have to.

Charlie crossed the room slowly, silently, like approaching an altar. He slid onto the bed behind Dex, knelt between his legs, and ran his hands up the backs of his thighs, over the round swell of his ass, spreading him just enough to reveal the pink, vulnerable center of him.

Dex let out a low breath. A hum.

Charlie dipped forward.

He slowly kissed the curve of each cheek, then the cleft between them. When his tongue made first contact, Dex shuddered—then pressed back in clear invitation.

Charlie worked him open with long, hungry licks. Not delicate. Not rough. Exploratory. Greedy. Lustful. Dex tasted clean—skin, musk, warmth, water, want—the kind of flavor that made Charlie crave more.

Dex moaned into the pillow, one leg sliding wider. His hips rolled back against Charlie's face as Charlie tongued him deeper, hungrier.

He'd eaten his fair share of women, but this was a first. Even so, he didn't feel tentative—he felt *hooked*. On the reaction. On the power. On the intimacy of having Dex spread open for him.

Eventually, Dex shifted slightly, looked back over his shoulder, voice wrecked. "Keep that up and I'm gonna come just from your tongue."

Charlie smirked, kissed the base of Dex's spine, and reached for the lube, conveniently placed on the tray at the foot of the bed. "I've got other plans."

Dex lowered his head again, exhaling hard into the mattress.

Charlie slicked himself, guided his cock to Dex's hole, and paused—pressing the tip without pushing. Letting the heat of it settle there. Letting tension build. Letting Dex blossom—then slowly easing inside.

Dex pushed back slightly. "Don't tease unless you plan to deliver."

"Oh, I plan to," Charlie said, voice low.

He leaned forward, one hand on Dex's lower back, the other guiding his cock. The head popped in, tight and slow. Dex groaned, arms flexing against the sheets.

"Fuck—yeah," Dex breathed.

Charlie eased forward, inch by inch, until fully inside. He stayed there, hips flush, letting himself feel it—how good it was to be buried in Dex. How wild that Dex had offered him this—*asked* for it, opened himself without a word.

He started to move—slow and deliberate. Deep strokes. Letting the tension unspool, letting Dex feel every inch. "You like that, Daddy?"

Dex met him thrust for thrust—panting, swearing, and pressing back with intent.

"Harder," he muttered. "Take it. It's yours."

Charlie groaned, pace quickening. He gripped Dex's hips, pulling him back into each thrust—skin against skin, the rhythm of their fuck frenzy echoing through the room.

He felt feral. Alive. As if everything he'd ever doubted about himself burned away in this moment.

When he came—deep inside, buried to the hilt with a choked-off growl—it wasn't just release. It was claiming. A bit of Dex. A bit of territory.

And more claiming himself. Embracing his truth.

He slumped forward onto Dex's back, breathing hard, lips brushing the curve of his shoulder.

Neither said anything right away.

Eventually, Dex turned his head, eyes glazed, mouth parted in a lazy grin.

"So," he rasped, "*that's* what curiosity looks—feels—like."

Charlie laughed against his skin, not bothering to pull out just yet. "Guess I'm a fast learner."

"I'll say!"

Charlie caught his breath, draped over Dex's slick back, orgasm still trembling in his thighs. Beneath him, Dex's shoulders rose with slow, deep breaths—*still* rock hard.

As he shifted, the weight of Dex's cock pressed against his leg. He reached down without thinking and wrapped a hand around it; it throbbed in his palm.

"Shit," he murmured. "You didn't get off."

Dex smiled into the mattress. "Didn't need to. Watching—feeling—you wreck me was more than worth it."

Charlie pressed a lazy kiss between his shoulder blades. "Still... feels unfair," he whispered.

He gave Dex a teasing squeeze, and Dex hissed softly.

"I think I know how to fix that," Charlie said, lips brushing his skin.

Dex turned his head slightly. "Yeah?"

Charlie looked toward the corner of the room where the sling stood in its black frame—leather straps suspended from a freestanding steel base, gleaming in the low light. A mirror was mounted above, tilted just so. Another on the adjacent wall, angled to reflect the side view. The whole setup looked deliberate. *Designed.* Intimidating and seductive.

Charlie's pulse quickened. "How does it work?"

Dex looked over his shoulder and smiled—slow and sure. "Like a charm."

Charlie met his eyes. "I want to feel you inside me again. *There.*"

Dex was already rising, moving with the kind of strength that felt like a promise. "Say no more."

Charlie barely had time to gasp before Dex scooped him up—one arm under his knees, the other around his back—and carried him across the room.

"Jesus," Charlie laughed, wrapping his arms around Dex's neck. "You're really going to *carry* me?"

Dex grinned. "I like watching you blush when I manhandle you."

"Can't say that I've minded you manhandling me."

Dex reached the sling and lowered Charlie carefully onto the leather hammock. He lifted Charlie's legs effortlessly into the stirrups— already angled and waiting—adjusted a few tension straps, then stepped back to admire.

"Comfortable?" he asked, voice thicker now.

"Yes, Daddy," Charlie chirped.

Charlie shifted in his leather cradle, testing the way the chains and straps supported him. Legs spread, ass exposed, back slightly elevated— completely vulnerable.

It felt *hot.*

He looked up. The mirror overhead reflected everything—the curve of his thighs, the gleam of sunlight across his skin, the sweat-damp fur on his stomach and chest, the flushed pink of nipples.

And then Dex, stepping between his legs, thick cock glistening with lube and aimed right at his hole.

"I can see it," Charlie said, eyes wide. "All of it."

Dex ran his hands slowly down Charlie's calves, hooking his fingers under the stirrups, and spread him a little more. "That's the point."

Charlie felt the heat of Dex's tip press against him—no warning now, just presence. He inhaled sharply as Dex eased in—slow, steady, filling—with the same tenderness and patience as last night.

The sling creaked; the steel frame shifting subtly with the motion. The springs added a gentle bounce to the rhythm, amplifying every movement.

Charlie looked up again and watched Dex disappear into him, watched his own body react—thighs quivering, fingers clenching the side straps, chest heaving.

"Fuck," he gasped. "This is insane."

"Yeah?" Dex grunted, thrusting deeper. "You like being on display?"

"I *love* watching you fuck me," Charlie groaned, hips lifting. "I love seeing it happen."

Dex leaned in and gripped the chains for leverage, grinding deep as the sling swayed. His body flexed above Charlie's, perfectly framed in the mirror—tattooed arms, sweat-sheened abs, eyes locked on the place they connected.

Charlie felt split open in the best way—no floor, no bed, no gravity. Just Dex, the sling, the constant motion of being taken—he'd marked his territory earlier in the bed and in the shower; now Dex was claiming his.

The frame jingled softly with the rhythm—metal on metal, chain on hook.

"Touch yourself," Dex coaxed. "I want to see you fall apart again."

Charlie obeyed, hand wrapping around his already-hard cock. It didn't take much—just a few strokes and the view above—to send him spiraling. He watched his face twist in ecstasy as his orgasm overtook him, cock pulsing, cum streaking across his belly.

Dex wasn't far behind.

He grabbed the straps at his sides and pulled the hammock, Charlie's twitching hole clenching in time with the momentum of the sling.

With a sharp thrust and a guttural growl, he spilled inside Charlie, hips grinding as deep as they could go. The sound he made was raw—almost a snarl—and Charlie felt every pulse fill him.

They stayed there for a minute. Two. Five.

Panting. Glowing. Wrecked.

Charlie looked up once more—at himself slack and satisfied, at Dex hovering above him, chest still rising and falling. He let his head drop back into the cradle of leather.

"Okay," he murmured. "I get why you like this thing."

Dex chuckled, wiping sweat from his brow. "You were fucking *made* for it."

Charlie reached for him, trying to pull him closer. "I'm starting to think you were made for fucking me."

Part III
SALVATION

December 24, 2025

"Knowledge of sin is the beginning of
salvation."

~ Epicurus

12
CATALYST

THE HUM OF the fluorescent lights pressed down on the silence of the lab, a mechanical heartbeat that had long ago woven itself into their rhythm. The biomed wing at Emory was nearly deserted at this hour, but six figures remained, scattered among the benches like players refusing to leave the stage.

The room smelled faintly of disinfectant and stale coffee. Evidence of their siege lay everywhere—papers stacked in untidy drifts, coded notes scrawled across whiteboards, pipette trays left to dry beside half-eaten cartons of noodles.

A poinsettia sat forgotten on the counter near the door, one of several decorations a facilities worker had delivered earlier in the week. No one had watered it. Its leaves curled, edges browning under the sterile lights.

Somewhere beyond these walls, families gathered under trees; candles flickered in churches; choirs lifted carols into the December night. It was Christmas Eve. And here they were— sleepless, hunched over machines— trying to give birth to something they hoped would matter more than any gift.

Asa Whitby stood at the central bench, palms flat against the polymer surface as he leaned into the monitor. Scrolling data flashed across his wire-rimmed glasses—numbers racing too quickly for anyone but him to track. He tapped the keyboard's edge with one finger, impatient, as if coaxing the machine to keep pace with his mind. His hair had gone silver earlier than it should have—not from age, but from grinding tension— and under the lab's hard light it gleamed almost like a halo. He had once been a clinician, long before research consumed him, and he still carried himself like someone who'd sat with the dying, with no illusions about how fragile people really were.

Across the bench, Derek Spaulding leaned back on his stool, twirling a capped vial between his fingers. He grinned at his reflection in the fluid—clear, ordinary, yet extraordinary. Derek was always too cavalier, too quick to pronounce victory, but brilliance clung to him like static. His twin, Emily, perched opposite—arms crossed, lips pressed tight in irritation. Where he saw fireworks, she saw kindling far too close to an open flame. Their arguments often filled the space between experiments—sharp-edged, unending— but that friction kept their work from toppling into chaos.

Gabriella Spencer hunched over her notebook, muttering as she checked handwritten data against printed logs. Her braids had fallen loose from the bun she'd tied at the start of her shift; one strand constantly brushed from her glasses. She was still in scrubs, a stethoscope half-buried in her satchel. She carried her patients into the lab— faces and names scribbled in margins—as though Corazamine wasn't just data but a chance to save the people she had already watched slip into silent compliance.

Priyanka Patel typed furiously, her laptop propped on a stack of journals, code and cross-referenced spreadsheets glowing on her screen. She always insisted on documentation—no matter how late the hour, no matter how many times Derek told her to relax. She had studied bioethics alongside neuroscience, and it showed in every sharp question she lobbed into the silence. Tonight, her eyes glittered with the same thrill as the others, but her fingers still moved with discipline. If history ever looked back on this moment, she wanted no cracks in the record.

Sanjay Khan stood a little apart, back against the wall, arms folded across his chest. He didn't fidget, didn't pace, didn't fill silence with talk. He just watched. Always watching. Before pivoting to neuroscience, he had been a systems engineer, and he still carried that stillness—a man who listened for the groan in the gears before a machine collapsed. His presence was a ballast. When he spoke, his words carried weight—rare and carefully chosen.

They weren't a natural team. Their disciplines barely aligned, their temperaments less so. They had fought as much as they'd collaborated. But over the last nine months—through long nights and repeated failure—they had become something more than colleagues. Not friends, not exactly—believers bound to the same fire. And tonight, as bells rang across the city announcing the arrival of midnight mass, they found themselves waiting on a birth of their own.

"Check the resonance values again," Asa said without looking up, his voice flat with fatigue but taut with anticipation.

Emily exhaled, almost a sigh. "I already ran them twice. The model's holding. No bleed, no false positives. The algorithm cross-mapped limbic resonance against control—there's clean separation."

"Too clean," Asa murmured, pushing his glasses up the bridge of his nose. "Run it again."

Derek groaned, rolling his eyes so hard Emily nearly smacked him. "He won't believe it until the numbers sing him a lullaby. Fine—one more pass."

He tapped a command into the console beside Asa, then flipped the tube upright between his palms. "But I'm telling you..." he said, holding the vial higher now, "this—Corazamine batch twelve—is it. No manic spikes. No burnout. Just resonance—balanced and stable."

Gabriella's head snapped up, her voice raw. "And you're absolutely certain?"

Derek's grin widened. "Certain enough that I'd dose myself tonight—if Priya would stop lecturing me about IRB approvals."

"Don't tempt me," Priyanka said dryly without looking up. "The paperwork alone would kill you faster than a failed compound."

The machine beeped softly, confirming the rerun. Emily leaned in, lips parting, then pressed them into a line. She turned the screen so Asa could see for himself.

The graph held steady. The spike smoothed into a plateau—no spirals, no collapse.

Asa exhaled slowly, bracing a hand on the bench. "Then we've done it."

Even Priyanka looked up this time. "If it holds past day three."

"It will," Sanjay said from the wall, voice low but certain. "Ninety-seven percent probability. That's not hope—that's success."

For a moment, none of them moved—six people frozen around a vial of clear liquid, as though waiting for it to glow. It didn't. It sat inert, ordinary, the same as the dozens that had failed before. But they knew. The weight of it pressed on the air between them until it felt heavier than the building around them.

Corazamine.

The compound that had consumed their lives, hollowed their nights, and stolen their families' patience. A neurochemical designed not only to unlock but to amplify—lighting up the mirror neurons that let humans resonate with each other. To drag empathy back from the cliff. To give humanity a fighting chance against itself.

Gabriella's voice was quiet. "It looks like nothing."

"Most miracles do," Emily said. "A child born in a manger once set fire to an empire."

"Let's just hope we're not crucified for the fire we're about to start," Derek added, a smile flickering at the edge of lips.

"Not this time," Asa said, voice steady. "Not this one." He let his palm hover above the vial without touching. "It's proof we don't have to surrender to what's happening—fear as policy, hatred as law. We can't legislate people back into their humanity. But maybe we can remind them how to feel it."

"Empathy as inoculation," Derek said. "A vaccine against cruelty."

Gabriella's eyes shone. "Do you think it could really stop it—the hatred, the propaganda, the wars?"

"Not stop," Asa said. "But blunt. Delay. Redirect. Give people time to see each other before the fear hardens."

He looked at each of them in turn—Derek's reckless brightness, Emily's wary precision, Gabriella's haunted urgency, Priyanka's razor gaze, Sanjay's calm. For a moment, he let himself believe that six people in a room could change the course of history.

Emily's voice cut in—sharp, pragmatic. "Or we manipulate. Let's call it what it is. This isn't teaching. It isn't leadership. It's dosing. What happens when a government makes it mandatory? Who decides how much empathy is enough? Who decides what people should feel?"

No one answered right away.

Sanjay's tone was measured. "Better empathy than fear."

"Is it?" Emily pressed. "Forced empathy isn't empathy—it's compliance wrapped in good intentions."

Derek groaned, throwing up his hands. "You could argue with gravity if you thought it'd irritate me."

"She's not wrong," Asa said quietly. "These questions will follow us—and they should. What we've built isn't just medicine. It's dangerous. But pretending fear is safer than connection—that's the lie already killing us."

Priyanka's fingers stilled on the keys. "If we do nothing, we're complicit, watching the collapse and congratulating ourselves on our ethics. I'd rather risk too much empathy than bury what's left of it."

Gabriella whispered, "What's the cost of waiting for a perfect cure while the world burns?"

The silence after was heavy. They didn't speak of their ghosts, but each carried them. Gabriella's patients who had given up. Priyanka's cousins beaten at a rally. Derek and Emily's father, who still refused to speak to Derek because he was gay. Asa's colleagues who had laughed him out of a conference for suggesting empathy could be enhanced. Sanjay's brother, who had enlisted and never returned. None of them said the names, but the names lived in the room like witnesses.

Through the glass wall of the lab, a string of colored bulbs blinked faintly in the hallway—the only sign the building remembered what night it was. Red and green reflections bled dimly on the polished floor, their cheer jarringly out of place against the lab's sterile white light. Gabriella noticed them first and smiled faintly. "Christmas lights," she murmured. "Strange we're here instead of anywhere else tonight."

"Where else would we be?" Derek said. "Some people celebrate the birth of a savior. We celebrate the resurrection of empathy."

"Careful," Priyanka warned, though her lips curved despite herself. "Blasphemy isn't a great look on Christmas Eve."

Derek raised his hands in mock surrender. "Three wise men and three wise women, gathered around a miracle. Tell me it's not poetic."

Asa didn't smile. "The difference is theirs was meant to last."

They returned to their tasks with diligence—double-checking logs, rerunning models, cataloguing every line. The ritual itself felt sacred. Each pipette rinse, each recorded value slowed as though history itself had been asked to hold still.

At last, Derek rummaged through a cabinet and pulled out a bottle of cheap sparkling wine. "Not champagne," he said with a grin, "but history is often toasted in humility."

They circled the bench, the vial resting at its center like a relic. Beakers, cups, whatever vessels they could find filled with fizzing liquid.

"What are we drinking to?" Gabriella asked, lifting hers.

"To a cure for cruelty," Derek offered.

"To hearts that remember how to love," Priyanka said.

"To the possibility of peace," Sanjay murmured.

Emily tapped hers reluctantly. "To hope... if it isn't already too late."

Finally, Asa raised his mug. His gaze swept over them—the vial, the poinsettia wilting in the corner, the faint glow of Christmas lights down the hall. "To Corazamine," he said softly. "Our nativity. May it remind us of who we are before we forget entirely."

The clink of plastic, glass, and ceramic echoed like a discordant bell, and they drank.

For half an hour, fatigue lifted. They teased Derek when he nearly dropped his beaker, laughed at Priyanka's insistence on logging the toast itself as "lab morale data." Emily even smiled once—though she rolled her eyes when Derek noticed. They laughed too loudly, spoke too freely, allowed themselves to imagine a future where their cure mattered.

Outside, the world sang carols to a holy birth. Inside, they believed they had brought forth one of their own. None of them saw the faint red light blinking on the secondary monitor, recording every word. None of them guessed their miracle had already been noticed.

For now, there was only the fragile glow of victory—six scientists in a lab on Christmas Eve, believing they had brought forth salvation to the world.

Part IV
DAMNATION

December 25, 2025

"What can an eternity of damnation matter to
someone who has felt, if only for a second,
the infinity of delight?"

~ Charles Baudelaire

13
GENESIS

BEFORE THE WORLD was told what to fear by Thomas Gallows, no one had heard his name—just another shadow among countless others. He stood on a rooftop across from Emory University's neuroscience wing, a cigarette pinched between two fingers, its ember casting a faint red glow against the dark. Gallows didn't smoke for pleasure—he smoked to still the tremor in his hand. To give weight to waiting. To remind himself that this quiet vantage was for the salvation of humanity—or so his narrow worldview insisted.

Below, fluorescent lights buzzed through the lab's windows, slicing the night into sterile squares. Inside, a research team was building their version of salvation. Corazamine, they called it: a synthetic neurochemical designed to trigger empathy. It heightened mirror neurons and activated the anterior insula. In theory, it made people feel—connect—more. Grief, joy, shame, tenderness... all amplified like the swell of a symphony.

Gallows drew on the cigarette, exhaled, and watched the smoke feather into the night. He thought of the word *empathy* with the same distaste he reserved for mildew. To him, it was rot dressed as virtue. Empathy weakened the authority, dissolved hierarchies, made nations porous.

Borders blurred. Armies hesitated. Laws softened. And this team of scientists—idealists locked in their sterile temple—believed they'd bottled a cure.

Gallows knew better. He had seen what came of compassion: weakness, division, revolt. And he would not allow it.

The rooftop felt like a pulpit; the city below, a congregation that did not yet know his name. He let the silence swell inside him like breath before a sermon. In Gallows' eyes, the world was already a fallen Eden, and he had been chosen not to restore it but to rebuild it on harder soil. If the meek had inherited the earth, they had already ruined it. What the world needed now was not shepherds—but executioners.

The first breach hadn't come with guns. It came with a man named Loring.

Gallows remembered their first meeting two months earlier, in an out-of-service campus café that reeked of burned beans and curdled milk. The young researcher had shown up with a stack of slides and a thesis-length defense of Corazamine. He was eager, disheveled—tie crooked, eyes darting with a mix of excitement and insecurity. Gallows hadn't had to say much. He let silence stretch, watching the man squirm until he filled it with his own doubts.

"They don't listen to me," Loring confessed, fingers trembling over the rim of his paper cup. "Spaulding thinks I'm reckless. Asa thinks I'm naïve. Spencer treats me like an intern. But I see it—what this can do. If we can make people feel again, maybe we can heal the fractures."

"You think fractures heal by reopening the wound?" Gallows asked softly.

Loring blinked, caught off guard. "It's not reopening—it's cleansing. Empathy could—"

"Empathy," Gallows interrupted, rolling the word like it soured on his tongue, "is the serpent. A whisper that makes men question authority. It has undone empires. Empathy made Rome falter, made kings bend, made armies hesitate. You want to sanctify it? No—you want to unleash it."

Loring looked down, shame flickering across his features. Gallows leaned in, lowering his voice to the cadence of confession. "You're not wrong to want recognition. You're not wrong to want to be heard. But you're worshiping a false idol. And idols fall. When it does, will you fall with it—or stand above the rubble?"

It was all Loring needed.

Within weeks, he was parroting Gallows' talking points in lab meetings, seeding doubt about the compound's safety, sliding hard drives across tables in dim corners. A single ember coaxed into flame.

But Gallows wasn't alone. He never pretended otherwise.

A month before that rooftop vigil over Emory, he'd been summoned to a warehouse outside Birmingham—a cavernous space that reeked of oil and smoke. The man waiting for him was Baron Vexley, a name known only in certain circles: former intelligence officer, defense contractor, once flagged for blacksite operations so brutal even the Pentagon balked. When he vanished from public record, no one asked questions. They should have.

Vexley greeted him with blueprints spread across a steel table— neural scans, intercepted transmissions, predictive models of population collapse. His voice was quiet, confident—the kind of tone that didn't need volume to command obedience.

"If you want to control a population," Vexley said, striking a match, "you don't need bullets. You teach them not to feel."

The words stayed with Gallows: empathy as contagion, compassion as disease. Corazamine wasn't salvation—it was an infection waiting to spread. Together, they sharpened that idea until it hardened into doctrine. In Vexley's view, revolutions weren't born from hunger or poverty but from the ability to feel them in others. Kill empathy, kill revolt. Gallows agreed.

Vexley laid out his vision with the cadence of scripture. "Our commandments," he said, ticking them off like verses. "One: The heart must be hardened. Two: Obedience must replace compassion. Three: Memory must serve power, not pity. Four: Fear must outlive hope." He tapped the blueprint with his finger. "This is not politics. It's faith. And faith, once embedded, doesn't need to argue—it dictates."

Gallows listened, enraptured. In Vexley he saw a tactician. In himself, something more: a prophet. The one who would stand before a broken world and preach deliverance from the disease of feeling. Vexley would build the structure. Gallows would carry the fire.

The Order did not begin as the Order. It began as a whisper—a coalition of outcasts and zealots huddled in smoke-choked backrooms. Military brass who despised civilian oversight. Judges longing for a return to harsher times. Survivalist broadcasters. Senators two rungs from irrelevance. Technocrats burned by Silicon Valley libertines. Some came for power. Others for vengeance. All agreed on one truth: empathy was dangerous.

The gatherings were strange at first—too many egos, too many agendas. Men sermonizing about patriotism. Women cloaking vengeance in legalese. Gallows preached fear. Vexley preached control. But the coalition needed something steadier—someone to translate paranoia into policy.

That someone was Regina.

She arrived one night in Atlanta, stepping from a government-plated sedan Gallows hadn't arranged. Tall. Severe. Her hair bound in a knot. She wore authority like an aura. Where Gallows inspired through paranoia and Vexley through precision, Regina radiated pure control.

She introduced herself simply: "Regina Roth, strategic operations."

Within an hour, she was reorganizing their chaos into a chain of command.

Gallows had bristled at first. He was used to being the voice in the room, the one who steered the silence until others revealed weakness. But Vexley only smiled. "Every church needs a spine," he said. "She's it."

Regina was ruthless—and Gallows found it fascinating. When one early recruit—a sheriff from Alabama—questioned their methods, she leaned close and whispered something in his ear. He left that night, pale and silent, and never returned. Two days later, he resigned without explanation. She never bragged about what she'd said. She didn't need to. From then on, Gallows kept her close. She became the voice that cut through noise—the blade trimming weakness from their cause.

Their early meetings drifted like dust across the country: an abandoned oil rig in the Gulf, a hunting lodge in Montana, basements beneath legitimate military compounds. They sat with weapons manufacturers tired of red tape. With governors who chafed under federal control. With media barons eager to monetize chaos. Each brought something—money, soldiers, airtime. Each left with doctrine: empathy is the enemy.

Gallows shaped the rhetoric. Vexley had the data. Regina had the discipline. But Gallows knew how to hold a room. He preached with the cadence of a revivalist, calling empathy a plague—a soft rot weakening the marrow of civilization. His words landed like scripture—because he spoke them with the zeal of a prophet.

"We must harden the human heart," he would say—and men who had never wept felt justified in their cruelty. Women who had clawed into power nodded like parishioners when he told them, "We must replace compassion with compliance."

Regina sat beside him, eyes sharp, cataloguing every flicker of doubt. Afterward, she would murmur what each man feared most—and what each woman needed promised. Gallows listened, learned, and adapted his sermons until no one left the room unconvinced. She had a talent for pressure points, for bending people without breaking them. He began to think of her not as a subordinate but as the necessary counterbalance to his fire. If he was prophet, she was priestess—binding their scripture to practice.

The gatherings began to take on the rhythm of ritual. Men removed their hats before Gallows spoke. Women took notes as if recording gospel. Maps unfurled like altar cloths. Commandments drafted, memorized, repeated. They called themselves patriots, but to Gallows it sounded like discipleship. And every disciple needed a savior.

On rooftops and in warehouses, their plan began to take shape. The scientists in Emory's glass tower thought they were crafting salvation, but Gallows knew the true gift would be inversion. Not amplification of empathy—but its burial. Not a cure for cruelty, but an inoculation against feeling.

The Order wasn't official—not yet. No banners. No broadcasts. Just darkness in hate-filled rooms, whispering that the future belonged not to those who cared, but to those who stopped caring. Gallows could feel it coalescing—this hunger for control disguised as patriotism. It was intoxicating.

And as Gallows stood once more on that rooftop, cigarette ember glowing like a watchfire, Regina joined him. She had a way of appearing without sound, as if conjured by his doubt.

"They believe they're giving birth tonight," she said, nodding at the lit windows of the lab below.

Gallows smirked. "Let them. Every birth needs a death to follow."

Her eyes narrowed, calculating. "Then we'll be the midwife."

He flicked the ash into the dark. "And the reaper."

Regina said nothing, but the corner of her mouth curled—the faintest acknowledgment of shared purpose.

The Order still had no name. But in that moment—on a rooftop overlooking the fragile miracle of Corazamine—they had already begun. The world would not remember this Christmas Eve for the quiet triumph inside Emory's walls. It would remember the shadows watching from above.

And it would remember the name Gallows.

Part V
ORDER

July 28, 2026

"When liberty destroys order, the hunger for
order will destroy liberty."

~ Will Durant

14
REVELATION

CHARLIE WAS STILL in the sling when Dex finally eased out of him—slow, careful, as though he didn't want to disturb the quiet hum of stillness between them.

The chains creaked softly as Dex's fingers brushed the curve of Charlie's thigh before offering a steadying hand. Charlie didn't take it right away. He just lay there, legs still spread, sweat and semen cooling on his chest, heart thudding somewhere between wrecked and weightless.

He turned his head, gaze locking with his reflection in the wall mirror—and then upward, to the angled panel overhead, still tilted perfectly above the sling. Dex stood framed between his legs, spent and panting, one hand resting loosely on the leather edge of the cradle as if reminding himself how to breathe.

"That was..." Charlie voice came out hoarse, "fucking insane."

Dex chuckled, raking a hand through his sweat-damp hair. "Yeah. It really was."

Charlie pushed himself upright slowly, wincing as gravity reclaimed him. Dex steadied him, letting Charlie lean against his chest for a moment as he slid free of the sling.

They stayed like that—skin to skin, heartbeat to heartbeat. No words, only breath. A silence that wasn't awkward or heavy. Just full.

Eventually Dex pressed a kiss to Charlie's temple. "Hungry?"

Charlie scoffed. "After *that?* I could eat a whole goddamn bear."

"You just ate a bear—licked the plate clean—don't you remember?" Dex smirked.

"You know what I mean."

"Gimme ten minutes and I'll bring you breakfast in bed."

Charlie reached down, grabbed Dex's cock—still damp, still half-hard despite everything—and growled low, "Woof."

Dex swatted his hand away. "Go sit your ass down until I decide you're ready for round three."

Charlie arched a brow. "I *am.*"

"Such an eager pup." Dex shot him a look—half threat, half promise—before turning toward the kitchen.

Despite Dex's promise, Charlie tugged on a loose tank from the floor moments later and padded after him, still bare below the waist. The apartment was bright now—curtains open, morning sun spilling in golden sheets across the worn wood floor.

Dex was already at the stove, humming low and tuneless, flipping something in a skillet. The scent of melting butter and vanilla wafted toward Charlie like an invisible rope, pulling him closer.

Charlie hopped onto the stool, folding his arms on the counter. "You're really cooking right now?"

Dex shrugged. "I love cooking."

Charlie leaned over, sniffing theatrically. "Wait—is that..."

Dex turned with a plate in hand. "Blueberry pancakes."

Charlie stared. "How the hell? Did I ever tell you that's my favorite?"

Dex set the plate in front of him. "Charlie, I've been your partner forever... I know you."

Charlie's eyes widened. "Apparently."

Halfway through breakfast, the TV—switched on by Dex for background noise—caught Charlie's eye. The muted screen flickered between maps and aerial drone footage. Not the usual loop of traffic updates and city council fluff. This was something else.

Dex grabbed the remote and turned up the volume.

> *"Eight coordinated supply drops appeared without public notice at the edges of Atlanta's perimeter..."*

Charlie froze mid-chew.

"Flatbed trucks carrying steel girders, composite mesh, and high-impact barriers were delivered to Buckhead, Cascade Heights, East Point, Druid Hills, West End, South River Industrial, North Druid Hills, and Decatur."

The broadcast cut to footage: cranes unloading panels, soldiers in unmarked gear, concrete pylons being driven into red Georgia clay.

Charlie stood and moved closer to the TV. "They're too evenly spaced for it to be random."

"They're building something," Dex said quietly.

Charlie leaned in closer, studying the map of the drop points on the screen before exhaling.

"A wall," they said in unison, reaching the same conclusion simultaneously.

By noon—despite having the day off—Charlie and Dex were showered, dressed, and out the door to investigate. Charlie wore some of Dex's clothes.

"I look like a kid in his dad's clothes," Charlie joked, holding out his arms to show the shirt's bagginess.

"Aren't you?" Dex smirked.

"It says medium—my size—but your back and shoulders stretched it so much it looks like I'm wearing a parachute," Charlie added.

They drove the perimeter in Dex's Jeep, staying just out of sight or blending with the unmarked vehicles. Each site was more fortified than the last by the time they reached it.

At Cascade Heights, they saw workers mounting drone turrets and sonic emitters along the upper edge of the barrier. The structure was *tactical.*

It was a prison wall.

Charlie leaned against the passenger door, watching a forklift hoist a mesh panel into place. "This is happening too fast."

Dex nodded. "That's how they get away with it."

"What the hell are they using to build this?"

Dex's voice was flat. "Prefab steel. Plasma welders. And fear."

Charlie glanced at him. "You're getting poetic."

"I'm getting angry."

Traffic along I-285 had already shifted. Every ramp leading in was marked for government use only—but not by city, state, or federal agencies. The same emblem as the trucks that overtook Georgia Tech.

One corridor—an eastbound carve-out of I-20—had been stripped of civilian access entirely. Dex pulled over by a condemned office building in Grant Park and climbed to the roof with Charlie in tow.

From the roof, they watched a military caravan push through the restricted corridor: six supply trucks, two APCs, and a surveillance drone hovering overhead like a mechanical carrion bird.

"They're feeding the beast," Dex murmured.

"And we're locked in with it."

Dex patted Charlie's shoulder, then grabbed his hand. "Let's go home."

"Home?"

"Well, my place. You're not driving to Stockbridge. Not only do I think they wouldn't let you return, but I don't think you'd even get out. We'll swing by the station and grab your truck."

Charlie nodded, glancing at the progress in just one day. "Feels like this wall is to keep us in."

The sun was setting by the time they reached the city, the fading light in the west mirroring the waning hope in Dex's core.

"Did you turn in the guns we took off those two men yesterday?" Charlie asked as they pulled into the station to grab his truck.

"I didn't—they're in the cruiser's trunk."

"Got the keys on you?"

"Of course. Why?"

"These people seem to be operating outside of the law. We have no idea what to expect from them, and we should be prepared for the worst," Charlie said, opening the passenger door. "Grab them while I get my truck—meet you at your place."

Dex nodded.

Charlie's words echoed in Dex's head as he went to the cruiser to pull the weapons from the trunk. He was right: no one knew who these people were or what they were capable of.

Back in the Jeep, Dex called Charlie. "Change of plans. Follow me. There's something I want to grab."

Fifteen minutes later, Dex pulled into the lot of a row of self-storage units on the east side of the city. Charlie parked beside him, frowning as Dex hopped out and keyed in a code at the rusted gate.

"What is this place?" Charlie asked, climbing out of his truck.

"My mom's old prep stash," Dex said. "She was a doomsday nut before it was cool. When I sold her house after she died, I couldn't stomach throwing it all out, so I shoved it in here. Figured it would collect dust." He shrugged as the gate rolled open. "Guess she was right. Just... not in the way she thought."

Inside the dim unit, stacked totes and shelves rose like aisles in a makeshift bunker. Buckets of rice and beans. Guns and boxes of ammo. A set of long-range walkie-talkies.

Charlie whistled low. "Jesus, Dex. This is half armory, half grocery store."

"Half a basement," Dex corrected, tugging the tarp off a row of Rubbermaid bins. "We can't haul all this. Most of it is bulk stuff anyway. But batteries, lanterns, camping gear—things we can use now.”

Together they picked through the stash, Dex’s flashlight catching the faded Sharpie labels on each bin. Dex grabbed solar chargers, propane canisters, a collapsible water filter. Charlie unearthed a pair of sleeping bags and laughed when Dex pulled out a portable crank radio.

“Your mom really was ready for the apocalypse.”

“Yeah. She just thought it’d come from the other side.” He shook his head, lips tight. “Never imagined her side would be the ones we’d need prepping against.”

They loaded the Jeep with the practical gear, leaving behind the pallets of dried beans and cracked wheat. On their way out, Dex pulled a few jars from a crate labeled *Pantry*—homemade preserves and marinara, a vacuum-sealed bag of dried pasta, even a couple bottles of red wine that had been wrapped in newspaper.

Back at Dex’s apartment, Charlie unpacked the haul while Dex set the jars on the counter. Charlie’s face broke into a grin when he saw the sauce jars and pasta. “If you have some ground beef or sausage and fresh bell peppers, you’re in luck. I learned some authentic Italian cooking from my uncle back in Jersey.”

Dex arched a brow. “You’ve been holding out on me.”

“Was waiting for an apocalypse,” Charlie teased.

"I keep my fridge and freezer fairly stocked. We live on coffee and donuts and cheap takeout when we're on duty. At home, cooking's my therapy."

"Great! You can be my sous chef," Charlie teased.

"So, you're Italian, then?" Dex asked. "I guess the uncut dick makes more sense."

"Italian and Greek on my mom's side. Appalachian redneck on my dad's," Charlie said with a faint smirk. "He died when I was fifteen. I think that's when the whole macho act kicked in—trying to fill shoes that were way too big. Mom shipped my brother and me up to Jersey to stay with our aunt and uncle that summer, but when I came back, it was all eyes on me. Be the man of the house. Carry the weight."

The kitchen buzzed with soft music and motion. Dex chopped herbs and peppers while Charlie browned sausage, their rhythm seamless—passing utensils, tasting sauce, flirty banter punctuated with stolen kisses. By the time the pasta was tossed and the wine poured, the air between them felt lighter, anchored in something domestic, something real.

While Charlie prepped the salad and pulled bread from the oven, Dex opened a bottle of red blend and set the table, lighting a candle more for mood than light. For a moment, it felt almost normal.

"You think we're safe here in the city?" Charlie asked after finishing his plate.

"I've been wondering that all day—if we'd be safer outside the city, if we could even leave if we wanted."

"Maybe we should ask the Sarg or Captain Ramirez when we go back in on Friday."

"Yeah, that's not a bad idea. Maybe he'll have some guidance. Maybe we should stop by before."

Elsewhere in the city, normal was being dismantled.

Towers in Brookhaven, College Park, and near Piedmont Park collapsed in sequence. Silent figures in black carried out controlled demolitions. Broadcast gear destroyed. Communication lines severed. Atlanta's voice was snuffed like a candle.

Dex and Charlie curled on the sofa with wine and a blanket. Charlie nuzzled into Dex's chest, one leg draped over his lap, while Dex absently toyed with his fingers. The television flickered with scenes from the perimeter they'd seen earlier.

"Can we turn off the news? Watch something else—take our minds off everything?" Charlie asked.

Dex squeezed his hand. "You read my mind. I just want to pretend the world outside hasn't changed while embracing what has changed inside these walls."

Dex scrolled through channels, searching for something mindless. "Alright then—what's your poison?"

Charlie leaned up to sip his wine. "Honestly? Surprise me."

Dex paused, hovered on a title. "Ever seen *To Wong Foo*?"

Charlie squinted. "Is that the drag one? With Patrick Swayze?"

"And Wesley Snipes, and John Leguizamo. Absolute gold," Dex said, pressing play. "It's like the Australian classic, *Priscilla*, but unapologetically American."

Charlie grinned. "Exactly what we need when America's collapsing."

The movie unfolded in glitter and sass, lipstick and middle-American resistance. They laughed harder than they had in a while, especially given the last few weeks. Dex quoted along with the iconic lines; Charlie clutched his side during the "little Latin boy in drag" scene.

Midway through, Charlie glanced at Dex. "You're kind of like Vita. A little butch, a little daddy, a lot of backbone."

Dex raised an eyebrow. "I'm flattered. But if anyone's fierce in this room, it's you—oversized shirt looking like an undercover otter superhero."

Charlie kissed his cheek. "Thanks for this."

Dex turned, caught Charlie's mouth in a slow, affirming kiss. "Anytime."

They shifted under the blanket, bodies pressed together, the movie casting warm light across their faces.

Halfway through, the screen froze—then black.

White text appeared: Two minutes.

A countdown ticked.

Charlie sat up. "Fuck—what does that mean?"

At zero, an emblem appeared: a coiled serpent wrapped in barbed wire.

A man's face filled the screen—stern, clean-shaven, precise. Dark suit, darker tie. Behind him, the same emblem in matte silver.

"This is Thomas Gallows," the man said. "Acting voice of the Order."

His tone was calm. Distant. As if announcing flight times at an airport not orchestrating a coup.

"As of this evening, your local communication centers have been decommissioned. Control has been restored. Panic has been neutralized."

The screen behind him shifted: drones sweeping highways, tanks rolling through other cities.

"Atlanta is not alone. Dallas, Denver, Nashville, Birmingham, Cincinnati, Phoenix, St. Louis, and many other cities have joined in the restoration of America."

He paused, letting the words settle.

"To protect you—and preserve the future—we have established a controlled perimeter around your city. This zone, known now as The Curtain, is your sanctuary."

Charlie blinked. "Sanctuary?"

"Inside The Curtain," Gallows continued, "you are safe. Resources will be gathered, rationed, and distributed. Professionals—doctors, engineers, educators, tradespeople—will be assigned roles according to skill and utility. Your contribution is mandatory."

Dex stiffened.

"All residential and commercial property, transportation, infrastructure, and supply networks within The Curtain are now under our stewardship. Ownership is obsolete. Your homes now belong to the community trust. Your vehicles to the collective transport network. Compliance is required."

Gallows leaned forward, his voice colder now. "Freedom is found in obedience. Peace preserved through control. Disruption will be corrected."

He smiled faintly, like the edge of his mouth had been programmed. "We are The Order. And we are already among you."

The screen went black.

Dex and Charlie sat in the silence that followed, Charlie clutching Dex tightly.

The echo of their fears now had a name.

The room was quiet again.

Not the kind of quiet that felt peaceful, but the kind that left a void. The broadcast had ended, but neither Dex nor Charlie had moved much since. A few words exchanged. A couple of soft glances. The weight of what had just unfolded still hung as charged as post-storm humidity.

Dex leaned against the kitchen counter, arms crossed tight across his chest, eyes fixed on the floor like it had something to say. Charlie stood at the dining-room window, the barely-lit skyline of the city softly reflected in the glass.

He finally turned. "I can't stop shaking."

Dex looked up, brow furrowed. "You cold?"

"No." Charlie grimaced. "Just... raw."

Dex stepped toward him—slowly. As if the distance required more than feet. As if it demanded surrender.

When they stood toe-to-toe, neither spoke.

Charlie traced the seam of Dex's shirt with one fingertip. "That speech... those words... it all feels surreal."

"I know," Dex murmured.

"But this—" Charlie's hand slid up, splaying across Dex's chest, over his heart. "This is still real, right?"

Dex covered Charlie's hand with his own and squeezed. "This is the only thing that feels real right now."

For a moment, they just stood—breathing, looking, remembering what whole felt like.

Then Dex whispered, "Come here," and led him down the hallway to the bedroom like the night before—only different now.

It wasn't about heat or hunger. It was about holding onto the safest thing—and letting go.

The nightstand lamp was already dimmed; the room brushed in golden amber. At the foot of the bed Charlie faced him, hands on Dex's chest again, pushing his shirt up slowly, like it meant something deeper. Dex raised his arms, letting Charlie undress him without a word. Then Charlie stripped—just as slow, just as deliberate.

They parted around the bed and met in the middle, bodies folding like pages finding their place in a story already being written.

Dex kissed him like time had stopped—like if he got it right, the world might unburn, the bombs might go undetonated, and the clock would return to the time before.

Charlie let out a small, shaky breath as their lips parted. "I need you to hear this," he said. "And I don't want you to say anything back. Not yet."

Dex paused, then nodded.

Charlie brushed a strand from Dex's brow. "I've had a lot of sex," he said softly. "So much of it was meaningless. So much of it armor—lies to protect myself from truth I was afraid to accept."

He paused, swallowed hard.

"But this... with you? This entire time I've left my guard down—no shield, no sword. It's the first time in a long time I'm not bracing for impact."

His eyes glistened.

"I don't want to just fuck tonight," he whispered. "I want to make love."

Dex's throat tightened. He didn't speak. Instead, he kissed Charlie again—tender, sure— hands cradling his jaw, as if holding the weight of the moment. His lips mapped the quiet between them, the ache, the promise.

Charlie exhaled into him, then guided them back, pulling Dex down until they were chest to chest, stomach to stomach, skin to skin.

There was no urgency—only a low, steady surge between them.

Dex's hands roamed Charlie's ribs, the curve of his waist, his lower back. Every inch he touched felt like an unspoken vow. Instead of telling, he showed.

When he finally entered him, it was with a tenderness that made Charlie gasp—less from the sensation than from the feeling of being seen. Known. A void filled.

They moved together in slow waves—rhythmic, harmonic, breathing in unison. Every push, every pull, every inch a conversation for which neither of them had the words. Unspoken truths that didn't go unfelt.

Charlie's fingers threaded through Dex's hair, clutched his neck, curled against his shoulder blades.

And Dex gave everything he had.

He kissed Charlie's chest, his throat, his cheek, his temple; pressed his forehead to Charlie's; moved inside him like he was writing something permanent—a love letter in motion: *I see you. I want you. I'm yours and you're mine.*

Charlie bit his bottom lip to keep from crying—not because it hurt, but because it didn't. He had never felt this safe—to be soft, vulnerable.

Neither broke eye contact.

Charlie whispered his name once. Just once. Then: *I love you,* swallowed by a kiss.

The words shattered something inside Dex in the best possible way.

When they came, it was quiet—shuddering— lips on lips, arms tight, mouths gasping each other's names like prayers.

Dex didn't move after.

He just held Charlie—still inside him, still wrapped around him—as if letting go would collapse everything outside those bedroom walls.

Charlie kissed his neck. "I know you're scared," he said. "So am I. But this—us—friends who make better lovers, is worth holding onto."

Dex exhaled—a soft sound, part pain, part peace. He didn't say *I love you.* He didn't need to. He kissed Charlie's chest once, then again, then again—until Charlie threaded fingers through his hair and closed his eyes.

They lay tangled in silence, in something unspoken and larger than them both. For the first time all day, the world felt far away.

July 29, 2026

"An exodus isn't about where you go but about
leaving a place to which you might never
return; it's about losing those you leave behind
and leaving those you lose along the way.

It is in leaving that we discover what chains
us; it is in loss that we learn what we carried
all along."

15
EXODUS

THE STORE WAS crowded in a way Dex hadn't seen since Atlanta's last ice storm. Despite picking up supplies from his mother's stash, Dex wanted to get a few more non-perishables out of caution.

Carts rattled too fast down narrow aisles, customers clutching doubles of things they didn't need—beans, batteries, bleach. A woman argued with the cashier over the two-pack limit on bottled water. Nobody met anyone else's eyes for long.

Dex and Charlie moved like partners on a call. Dex scanned shelves, calculating what would last and what would fit in the Jeep. Charlie hefted the heavy items, dropping them into the cart with the same efficiency he used to clear crowds. They didn't speak much, but their closeness said enough—shoulders brushing, a quick squeeze on the arm when they crossed.

"You're strangling it," Charlie murmured, nodding at Dex's white-knuckled grip on the cart.

Dex loosened his grip. "Feels like everything is going to get yanked out from under us."

"Not everything," Charlie said, his fingers lingering longer than necessary on Dex's forearm.

At the next aisle, a clerk restocking shelves gave them a wary look, eyes darting from Charlie to Dex. Dex felt the heat of being watched but didn't flinch. The world was already breaking—they weren't going to apologize for who they were. Charlie caught the clerk's eye, held it just long enough, and the man looked away.

They turned down the canned-goods aisle. Dex counted vegetables under his breath—the counting routine a centering habit he'd never lost. At the endcap, they nearly collided with a man backing out of the pharmacy row, a six-pack of beer hoisted like a trophy. He wore a precinct softball tee stretched over a sagging beer gut Dex recognized instantly.

O'Hara.

He clocked them, eyes flicking from the cart, to their closeness, to Dex's hand on the rail where Charlie's had just been. A slow grin spread—more gum than teeth.

"Well, if it isn't Starsky and Hutch," O'Hara said loud enough to turn heads at the register.

Charlie didn't look at Dex. He fixed O'Hara with the same quiet he used when breaching a room on a warrant. "Walk away," he warned.

O'Hara snorted. "Don't get righteous on me, Denton. I'm just surprised it took you this long to... come out as a two-for-one special. Christ, we were freezing our balls off on traffic detail while you were warming each other up in the—"

Charlie punched him.

It wasn't a haymaker. It was clean, close, fast— so fast Dex barely registered the step before

O'Hara's head snapped backward, the six pack hit the tile with a crash. The crack echoed under the thin fluorescent light; the bored teen behind the ammo counter gaped.

O'Hara staggered, hand to his nose, blood streaming. "What the hell—"

Charlie's voice stayed even. "That was for the last twelve years."

O'Hara's pressed the hem of his shirt to his nose, fingers trembling, beer guy exposed. "You just signed your own—"

"I told you to walk away," Charlie repeated, louder this time.

O'Hara did, muttering through spit and blood as he shouldered past them.

Dex exhaled slowly. Charlie watched him, the anger gone as quickly as it flashed.

"You didn't have to—" Dex started.

Charlie stepped into his space, not touching but unmistakably there. "I wanted to," he said. "Should've a long time ago."

Dex felt the prickle at his hairline. In a dented-can reflection, he saw them as anyone else might: two men, shoulders nearly touching, one with a blood on his knuckles that he hadn't wiped away. He reached without thinking, folded Charlie's hand in his, thumb dragging across reddened skin. Not a kiss, but enough to make two people at the register look away.

Charlie didn't.

He squeezed Dex's hand once—an anchor's tug—then pulled away with a tiny, private smile that said he'd wanted to be seen.

They finished fast after that—paid, loaded the Jeep, and fought the afternoon traffic back with a vigilance that made the city feel like a chessboard.

Dex didn't speak until they'd reached his drive. "He deserved worse."

Charlie wiped his knuckles with a damp paper towel once they got inside from their first load of groceries. "He'll get it. From the world."

"You shouldn't have to fight for me like that."

Charlie met his eyes. "I didn't fight for you," he said, the corner of his mouth lifting. "I fought for us. Besides, you could've just as easily kicked his ass."

They cooked because it felt like the only normal left. Dex chopped onions in sharp, steady strokes while Charlie sautéed the chicken, his spoon circling slow, as if each stir might hold time back.

"I shouldn't have let it get to me," Charlie said finally, eyes fixed on pan. "Him. Any of them."

"You hit him because he deserved it," Dex defended. "Not because he was right."

"That, too." Charlie gave a short laugh, pulled the chicken from the pan, and set the spoon across the rim. At the sink, he scrubbed his hands longer than needed, dried them, and left the towel slung over his shoulder. When he came back to the island, elbows braced, his voice softened. "That's not why he's stuck in my head."

"Then why?" Dex asked.

"Because I was him." Charlie admitted, glancing up at Dex. "Once upon a time."

Dex stopped mid-chop. "Charlie—"

"I know what I said back then," Charlie pressed on. "The jokes I let happen when you weren't around—hell, sometimes when you were. I could blame the culture, say it was easier to blend in and be one of the guys, that I was terrified someone would see me seeing you. All that's true. But it wasn't just that."

He paused, searching Dex's face. "I was cruel because it hurt. Because I hurt. Because I didn't know how to be what I was—and a part of me resented how fearless you seemed in being yourself. At the core of it, I was more terrified of losing you. What if I finally got up the courage and you shot me down, rejected me?"

Dex's eyes stung in a way that had nothing to do with the onions. He set the knife down, dragged the heel of his hand over his lashes, irritated at the weakness of tears he couldn't stop.

Charlie reached across the island, grabbed Dex's free hand, and took a breath. "Do you remember that warehouse off Boulevard? The one that reeked like fry oil and rat shit?"

"Which day?" Dex said, a smile tugging despite the tears.

"The second raid. We came in the side door and found the kid in the freezer. Everyone else had written him off—but you swore he was alive. You were right. His heart was just slowed too far to register. You always knew stuff like that—a sixth sense."

"You never guessed I was a witch, Charlie?"

"I probably should have guessed you were—you've had me under your spell for a while." Charlie tipped the chopped veggies into the pan and glanced at Dex with softened eyes. "That night I drove home and couldn't think about anything except how much I didn't want to lose you—ever. Not as a partner. Not as... anything. And the next morning I was an asshole to you in the locker room because the idea of anyone witnessing my true feelings for you made my skin feel inside-out."

Dex thought back, the memory unspooling with cruel clarity: the clang of lockers, a joke about "date night with your cat," landing harder than it should because Dex hadn't slept—and because Charlie's laugh had sounded like a door slamming.

As if reading him, Charlie added, "After that day in the locker room—after seeing how much I hurt you—I vowed to never do it again."

"You sure it wasn't my dick slapping you in the face?" Dex teased, recalling how he pinned Charlie to the floor in a naked tackle.

"I can't say that I didn't fantasize over that moment a few times while whacking it," Charlie admitted. "You honestly didn't think it was strange that I started going in first at crime scenes—just to protect you."

"I always figured you went in first to prove you were better," Dex said. "Like a pissing contest."

"It was a shield," Charlie said. "For you. Stupid, maybe. But it was love—I just didn't know the word for it then." He slid the chicken back into the pan and added the sauce. "I know it now."

The words—*I love you*—burned at the back of Dex's throat, aching to be freed, but doubt and the fear of saying them too soon locked his jaw. He let his lips speak instead, pressing a kiss against Charlie with the desperate hope that touch might carry the truth his voice couldn't.

The stove hissed as sauce bubbled over the edges of the pan, pulling them from their kiss. Dex reached behind Charlie, turned down the heat, and gave him another peck.

Charlie stood with his back to the stove for a moment, feeling the warmth, the smell of onion and garlic and teriyaki threading the room, the shape of Dex in his arms. He knew it wasn't fair to expect those words yet—but Charlie had felt it for years, long before Dex ever knew.

When the moment settled, Dex opened the drawer, pulled two forks without thinking, and handed one over. They ate straight from the pan—plates felt too formal, chairs felt too far apart, hunger too sharp to wait with no patience for ceremony. Dex speared a broccoli floret, held it out; Charlie leaned in and took it straight from the fork, eyes never leaving Dex's. The intimacy surprised them both—even after the night before—hunger in every sense.

"Worth it?" Dex asked softly.

"Punching O'Hara?" Charlie licked sauce from his bottom lip, then smirked. "I'll ice my hand and decide."

"I meant telling me."

"Worth it," Charlie said, smirk gone. "Just wish I'd said it sooner."

They didn't turn on the television. Night thickened at the windows as thunder rolled somewhere far over DeKalb; the power flickered twice, thought better of it, and held.

Dex fell asleep on the sofa, head in Charlie's lap, one wrist crossed over his sternum. Charlie draped a quilt over him and watched him breathe. Lines on Dex's face hadn't been there five years ago—a crease at the left temple from squinting, a freckle that had darkened near his brow. Charlie skimmed his fingers up and down Dex's forearm in slow, steady strokes, unconsciously matching the rhythm of Dex's breath. The word *lucky* circled his thoughts, fitting in a quiet way he'd never trusted before.

Then Dex jerked in his sleep.

The sound he made wasn't loud—small and sharp. Charlie set the remote aside, folded forward, hand to Dex's shoulder, the word *hey* forming in his mouth.

Dex's eyes opened too wide. For a second he was somewhere else—murky, sirens sounding, a hallway stinking of bleach and cordite and time running thin. He took one shuddering breath, then another, until Charlie's face came into focus.

"Hey," Charlie said softly. "Welcome back."

Dex swallowed. "You went in first," he said, voice raw. "I told you to hold, and you—" He shut his eyes, shaking his head. "—didn't come out."

Charlie tightened his grip on Dex's shoulder. "I'm here," he repeated. "I'm not going anywhere."

Dex exhaled like it hurt. He sat up, dragged both hands over his beard, and let them fall. A moment passed. Then he looked at Charlie carefully, like centering a sightline. "Promise me something?"

"Okay."

"No more going in first," Dex said. "No more playing shield. If we go, we go together—or we don't go."

Charlie held his gaze. It would have been easy to make a joke or deflect to training protocol. He didn't want easy. He nodded once. "Together," he said. "Now and every time after."

Something loosened in Dex's shoulders. He leaned forward until his forehead touched Charlie's temple, both breathing the same air. The kiss started there—forehead to temple to cheek— and wandered without agenda. Dex tasted like salt and worry; Charlie tasted like tiramisu and the last of the red they'd split with dinner.

It wasn't urgent. It didn't need to be. When Charlie grazed Dex's bottom lip with his teeth, Dex made a small, wanting sound, then stilled.

Charlie pulled back just enough to see him. "I want to make love to you," he said. "But I want you comfortable more than I want that. Tell me what you need."

Dex looked at his mouth, then his eyes. He nodded—yes—and hesitated—no—both at once. "I'm—I haven't—" He didn't finish.

"I know," Charlie said, easing the weight of it. "Come shower with me."

Steam bloomed against tile like a new weather system. The bathroom fogged fast, heat beading on mirror and glass. The sound of water amplified everything—the slip of feet, the low laugh when spray caught them in the face, the breath when warmth hit cold skin. They fit in the space the way they fit everywhere—adjusting without choreography, hip to hip, shoulder to sternum. Charlie soaped Dex's back slowly, mapping muscle and scar, the long curve of spine. Dex closed his eyes, letting the water rinse the raw places the day had left.

When Charlie turned him, Dex didn't look away. He set his palms at Charlie's waist, thumbs pressing lightly. The kiss this time was deeper, the water stitching the pause between breaths. Charlie talked him through every step: here's what I'm doing, tell me if you want less, say stop and I stop. Dex said *okay*—and meant it. Then said yes and meant that more.

It wasn't a scene to catalogue; it was a conversation slowed until words weren't needed. Charlie kept his hand at Dex's chest, feeling the climb and settle of each breath, the way it evened when Dex found his rhythm, the way his own breath matched without trying. When Dex tightened his grip and pressed the back of his head to Charlie's forehead, Charlie whispered I've got you, and Dex answered with the softest sound he'd ever made—a surrender that felt like choosing, not falling.

After, they stood under the water until it ran cooler. Charlie reached behind him and drew a heart on the fogged glass—quick, unskilled—and inside it he printed CHARLIE + DEX, block letters that looked like a kid's handwriting—and not like a kid's at all.

Dex huffed a laugh that broke off in the middle. "You're so corny."

"Extremely."

He traced the plus sign with a fingertip. "Leave it."

"Even if it looks like a middle-school locker?"

"Especially then."

"Why?"

"This way we won't forget," Dex said. "Even if the world tries to erase us."

Charlie nodded like he was agreeing to a tactical plan. "Then we'll rewrite it," he said, kissing him again with brevity and surety.

They toweled off and pulled on soft clothes that smelled of detergent and a life unchanged. In the bedroom, the lamp threw that same golden wash across the wall. They didn't turn it off. They slid into bed and found the shape of each other like it was a place they'd kept keys to for years.

Sleep came easier than expected. Sometime in the night the power hiccupped, a clock reset, and the heart on the glass softened at the edges as the bathroom cooled. It held anyway.

When the first gray light pushed into the room, Charlie was already awake. He watched Dex the way he had on the sofa, inventorying small, ordinary miracles: the flutter at the throat, the way his mouth softened when he dreamed, the way he reached for Charlie without waking. *Lucky*, he thought again, and didn't flinch at the word.

Dex opened his eyes to find Charlie watching him. He smiled like a sunrise—slight, inevitable. "Coffee?" he asked, voice thick.

"Always," Charlie said.

Dex swung his legs over the side of the bed and stood. He paused long enough to lean down and press a kiss into Charlie's hair. "Together," he whispered like a prayer.

"Together," Charlie echoed, and the day began.

Though their next shift wasn't until Friday, Dex's restlessness boiled over. After breakfast, he and Charlie headed to the precinct in search of answers from the Chief.

The precinct was half-lit, half-staffed, and thick with silence despite the stir of commotion. The usual rhythm of calls, dispatch chatter, and click-clack of typing had been replaced by something more stifling—compliance.

Dex clocked it immediately.

One of the senior sergeants—Caldwell—stood behind the front desk, not in uniform but in a dark suit with a lapel pin Dex recognized instantly: an ouroboros. When he saw them enter, he stiffened, then forced a smile that didn't reach his eyes.

"You two should be home," Caldwell said.

Dex ignored him. "Where's Chief Ramirez?"

Caldwell hesitated. "Took a leave of absence. Family emergency."

Charlie's brow furrowed. "Ramirez doesn't have any family."

Caldwell didn't blink. "That's what we were told."

Dex felt his pulse quicken. "Who's in charge now?"

"Command's been... reassigned. Interim authority's being coordinated through the—" Caldwell stopped himself, recalibrated. "Through emergency management channels."

"The Order," Dex said quietly.

Caldwell's mouth twitched.

From the bullpen, a laugh cut through the hush. "Well, look who finally showed." O'Hara leaned against the corner of a desk, arms folded. His nose was still swollen and crooked, a strip of medical tape strapped clumsily across it. His grin spread slow and ugly.

"Guess you two don't bother with duty rosters anymore—must be nice to clock in only when it suits you. Or maybe you've been too busy fucking each other to remember you even wear a badge." His voice pitched louder, making sure more of the room heard. "Guess it's official then—our golden boys are fags after all."

A couple of younger officers shifted uncomfortably, eyes dropping to their keyboards. Nobody spoke. The silence was worse than laughter.

Charlie didn't hesitate. He stepped forward, squared his shoulders, and raised his voice so it carried across every cubicle, every corner of the dimmed room. "We're not even scheduled today, fuckwad. And yeah, it's official," he said. "I know you're probably jealous, O'Hara, since your ball-and-chain hasn't fucked you in years, but Dex and I *are fucking*. Anybody here have a problem with that?"

He turned, grabbed Dex by the collar, and kissed him full on the mouth. Not a peck, not a whisper of affection, but deep and hungry, a claim and a dare all at once. The sound of it, the audacity, snapped like a gunshot through the silence.

When he pulled back, Charlie looked around the room, eyes hard, daring. "So? Who's got something to say?"

O'Hara's mouth twitched like he wanted to, but the swelling in his nose and the memory of Charlie's fist kept him silent.

Someone in the back clapped, followed by two others; soon whole room was full of people on their feet applauding Charlie. O'Hara sat back down, jaw tight, and the applauding stopped. The quiet that followed was heavier than before, but different. Charged.

“You’re not scheduled until tomorrow,” Caldwell repeated, voice clipped. “Go home.”

“Like hell,” Dex snapped. “Tell me who’s giving the orders now. Who’s pulling the strings? Because it sure as shit isn’t the law anymore.”

A second figure appeared in the hallway behind Caldwell. Someone Dex didn’t recognize—clean-cut, bland, forgettable in a way that made his skin crawl. The figure wore a long black coat and dark gloves despite the summer heat.

“You’re not needed here anymore,” the man said, tone calm but unmistakably final.

Dex looked at Charlie. They didn’t need to say it out loud. Neither was about to turn over their gun and badge in the middle of militia control, but they weren’t coming back.

Back at Dex’s place, they packed in silence. Just the essentials—the stuff they’d swiped from his mom’s stash, medical kits, canned food, two water filters, ammo. Charlie grabbed Dex’s second sidearm and slipped it into his belt.

“North?” Charlie asked.

Dex nodded. “Casey’s lake house is outside the Curtain. If she can’t host us—as awkward as it may be—perhaps Jake can. If we move fast enough, we might be able to find a breach in the construction.”

“We could always go south to my place in Stockbridge,” Charlie suggested.

"I thought about that, at first, but then remembered how much of the southern part of the wall was already built—probably expedited that section because of the airport."

"Fuck, you're right." Charlie cursed. "What if we go east first, then venture south once we're past the Curtain?"

"Their other base of operations is at Stone Mountain, so I am guessing they've fortified the eastern perimeter already, too."

"Damn it!" Charlie knew he was right. "Both vehicles, or..?"

Dex suggested them just taking one—their vow of *'together, remember?'* echoing in his logic. They loaded his Jeep with precise efficiency, every movement taut with purpose. They rolled maps flat across the hood, tracing the grid of the city and the arc of the Curtain as best as they could recall. It wasn't finished yet—Dex knew that. But parts of it were already armed. Patrolled.

Charlie ran a finger along a stretch just south of Peachtree Industrial. "Here. There's a maintenance road, one of those forgotten back roads. If we're lucky..."

"If we're lucky," Dex echoed, "no one's watching."

They didn't linger.

The checkpoint wasn't on any map.

The makeshift barrier appeared like a trapdoor flipped open in the road—squat floodlights illuminating razorwire and two armed men with no insignia. One stood ahead, waving them down; the other lingered back with a scope trained on the windshield.

"Shit," Charlie muttered.

"Stay calm," Dex said, easing the Jeep to a stop. He tried to sound steady, but his hand brushed the gearshift like a fighter flexing before the punch.

The man approached slowly, scanning the interior. "Where you headed?"

"Family. Out near Buford," Dex lied. "Emergency run."

"You got papers?"

Dex offered his police ID. The man took it, glanced, sneered. "Doesn't mean much anymore."

Someone behind the barrier laughed—sharp, deliberate. "Cops think they're still special."

Charlie's jaw flexed. Dex pressed a hand briefly to his thigh to calm him.

As the man handed back the ID, his eye snagged on the glint of Charlie's holstered pistol.

"What's that?"

"It's mine," Charlie said, voice low.

"You're not authorized."

"I'm a cop."

"You were." And just like that, the man raised his weapon.

Everything slowed. Charlie drew first. Two shots rang out—one struck the man in the shoulder, the other in his head. But he fired back before the second shot hit. The round tore into Charlie's stomach. He doubled over, gasping.

Dex didn't think. He slammed the Jeep into reverse, tires screeching as they pulled back from the barricade. The second soldier opened fire. Dex swerved, barely dodging the burst of bullets.

Charlie, pale and hunched in the passenger seat, fumbled with the rifle between his knees. "Window," he rasped.

Dex rolled it down further.

Charlie leaned out, aimed, and fired a single shot.

The pursuing vehicle's tire exploded, sending it tumbling into the ditch with a sickening crunch of metal and fire.

Dex didn't look back.

Charlie slumped against the window, breath shallow, "I think I'm hit... bad."

Dex looked at the wound and lied. "You're gonna be fine."

Charlie forced a laugh—a quiet, wet cough. "Don't bullshit me."

Dex kept one hand on the wheel, the other pressed hard to Charlie's stomach, blood soaking through his fingers.

"I should've said something sooner," Charlie whispered.

"Said what?"

"That I never stopped feeling it. Since the academy. You were always the only one that made me feel... like home."

"Charlie—"

"I wasted so much time trying to be someone I wasn't. All I really wanted was to be someone you wanted," he said, blinking slowly. "I just—God, Dex, these last three nights... they were the best of my life."

Dex's chest tightened. "You're not dying."

"Maybe not, but drive faster anyway," Charlie murmured, fading.

The hospital was barely operational.

Generators powered only the surgical wing and life support systems. Most of the staff had been reassigned to med-centers controlled by the Order. Dex burst through the emergency entrance with Charlie in his arms, blood slicking them both.

"Help!" he shouted.

A nurse snapped to attention, waving for a gurney. Two orderlies rushed forward, metal wheels shrieking against the tile.

"What happened?"

"Gunshot," Dex said. "He's lost a lot of blood."

The orderlies attempted to pull Charlie from his arms, but Charlie's grip clamped weakly on his sleeve. Charlie's lips parted like he wanted to say something—then his head rolled back, body going limp against Dex's chest. In one breathless instant, Charlie was gone.

"You need to let go!" the nurse yelled. "We need to get him to a bed."

Hands seized Charlie, rolling him onto the gurney, already cutting his shirt open, pressing gauze to the wound.

Dex stumbled after them, blood dripping from his hands, reaching for Charlie's arm until the swinging doors snapped shut between them.

He felt powerless as he stood alone in the corridor, chest heaving, crimson to the elbows. Charlie's slack body haunted the crook of his arms, the phantom weight refusing to leave even after the gurney was gone. His knees buckled, but the wall caught him.

He cursed himself for not echoing Charlie's words before—the ones now pounding in his heart and in his head, the ones he'd swallowed every time Charlie had spoken them.

Hope was all he had to hold onto, but the sobs came without stopping. Between chest heaves and lost breath, a painful proclamation slipped past his trembling lips: *"I love you, too."*

July 31, 2026

"He has walled me in so I cannot escape; he has
weighed me down with chains."

~ Lamentations 3:7

16
LAMENTATIONS

THE WALLS WERE the color of old teeth—not white, not yellow, just worn, with a patina of years no cleaning products could erase. Every chip in the paint caught his attention, darker spots of plaster forming constellations if he stared long enough.

The air smelled like a tired cocktail of iodine and burnt coffee. Occasionally, the scent of bleach drifted in from the corridor, always half-hearted, as if even disinfectant was rationed. Somewhere down the hall, a cough barked and wheezed until it dissolved into silence.

Outside his window, branches scraped the glass in the wind. Beyond them lay a parking lot mottled with more rust than paint. He'd watched the same blue pickup roll in and out twice that morning, each time with a different patient in the passenger seat—a rotation that spoke to the scarcity of transport as much as to the scarcity of care.

Overhead, the heating pipes groaned—metal on metal—before settling back into the steady hiss of circulation.

David shifted against the thin hospital pillow, the paper slip beneath his head crinkling like old parchment. He'd been here long enough to know the rhythms—the squeak of the med cart at dawn, the sharp tap of the night nurse's shoes on the floor, the radiators clicking to life with a sigh before sputtering out.

What he didn't know—what gnawed at him harder than the headaches—was what lay beyond the fog in his head. He could remember faces—his mother, a dog with shaggy ears—but not the lives they belonged to. And every time he tried to follow a thread back to its source, it unraveled into nothing.

A cart rattled past his door, followed by the faint beep of a scanner and the low murmur of a nurse's voice. He closed his eyes, willing the sounds to drag up some matching memory from before the accident, but all that came was static.

The door opened without a knock.

"You're awake," his mother said, smiling like she'd been holding her breath.

"I couldn't sleep." His voice sounded wrong in his own ears—scratchy, distant, as if the air had to travel farther to reach it.

She stepped in with a foam cup, the smell of coffee preceding her. "It's swill," she said, setting it on the tray table, "but at least it's hot."

He managed a faint smile. "Could be worse."

She sat in the chair by his bed and looked at him the way only a mother could—taking inventory without saying a word. He noticed faint lines at the corners of her eyes, carved not just by age but strain.

"I talked to Marianne again this morning," she said, folding her hands in her lap.

He frowned. "Marianne?"

"My friend—lives inside the Curtain. We went to school together. You met her one Christmas dinner—back when you still..." She stopped, her expression going as blank as his memory.

"I don't remember," David said quietly.

"I didn't think you would." She smoothed a crease in her jeans with her palm. "She's not the same anymore."

David leaned forward slightly, his fingers curling in the blanket. "Not the same—how?"

"She used to be a firecracker—quick laugh, quicker temper. She organized neighborhood dinners, bake sales, farmer's markets, little protest marches. People listened to her. She had that kind of pull."

He tried to picture her—maybe tall, dark hair pulled back, eyes catching the light. But every shape dissolved before it sharpened, leaving only the stale light of the hospital room.

"What's she like now?"

She saw the question behind his eyes before he asked it.

Part of her was almost glad he didn't remember. Glad he couldn't recall the sharp edges of their last fight—the words she'd thrown in frustration, the way she'd kicked him out and let the silence stretch for weeks.

When the hospital first called, panic was her only thought. The drive had been a blur of white knuckles and worst-case scenarios. But once the worst of it passed and she knew he would live, another feeling had crept in—relief. Relief that the accident had carved away the memory of how badly they'd left things.

She hated herself for that. Hated that she'd sat in this chair and thanked whatever power there was for his memory loss.

It wasn't that she wanted him to forget forever. She just wanted a clean slate. A chance to start without the weight of that fight. To see him look at her without the shadow of resentment she'd grown used to.

Now, when his eyes met hers, there was only curiosity. And that was something she could work with.

She thought about all the conversations they'd never had because pride got in the way. The birthdays marked only by terse phone calls. The last time she saw him—her words so sharp they seemed to slice the air between them. This—here, now—was a chance she wouldn't waste.

"Flat," his mother said. "She talks like she's reading from a script. Says she's happy, healthy, safe. But there's no heat in it. Last week I asked if she remembered the block party she hosted—the one with the lanterns in the trees—and she acted like I'd made it up. She even said maybe I was thinking of someone else."

"She really forgot?"

"She really changed," his mother said. "The Marianne I knew would've told me which wine was served and how many paper lanterns we strung. Now she just changes the subject."

David felt a cold pulse in his chest. "You think it's the injections you mentioned?"

"I *know* it is," she said. "Others with family inside say the same. They call it Serexin. Makes people compliant. Polite. Quiet."

Even though he wasn't the one to say it, the word *compliant* tasted bitter on his tongue. He tried to recall his own life inside—his street, his neighbors, anything—but what surfaced was a fragment: a hallway with sunlight spilling across a hardwood floor, the faint scent of citrus. He reached for it, but the image shattered like glass, leaving only the antiseptic sting of the present.

"Was I—" he stopped, throat tight. "Did I live inside?"

"You did."

"Then why am I here?"

Her eyes softened, but her tone was steady. "Because your accident was out here. They brought you to the nearest hospital. You've been here ever since."

"And I can't go back."

She shook her head. "Not without their approval. And they don't open the gates for just anyone—even residents. Especially not if you've been treated outside their system."

The radiator kicked on with a rattle, filling the pause.

He tried again to summon a memory—not Marianne, but someone else. A voice laughing in a kitchen. The clink of ice in a glass. For a heartbeat, it felt close enough to touch, then it dissolved, leaving him empty-handed.

"Maybe it's better this way," his mother said softly.

He looked at her, sharp. "Better?"

"If they're changing people in there, maybe the best thing for you is to stay who you are right now."

It was meant as comfort, but it landed like an insult. He wanted the memories—even if they hurt. Maybe especially if they hurt.

"What's it like out here—outside of the Curtain?" he asked finally.

She exhaled, her gaze shifting toward the window. "Harder than it used to be. Fuel costs more than most people make in a week. Power cuts without warning. We trade more—food, clothes, labor—because money doesn't stretch far enough.

"There's crime, sure, but it's honestly desperation. Petty stuff. But we've still got air you can breathe, stars you can see at night, and the ability to feel. That's more than I can say for inside the Curtain."

He pictured the Curtain his mother had described in a previous visit—a wall thirty feet high, steel and concrete, cutting off the horizon.

He tried to imagine his own apartment somewhere beyond it but found only blankness.

"You ever think about trying to get inside?" he asked.

Her laugh was small and humorless. "Not since it went up. The people inside aren't the same anymore. Marianne's proof of that."

"What did she say the last time you talked?"

His mother's mouth tightened. "She told me I shouldn't waste my energy worrying about things beyond my control. That's not her. The old Marianne would have told me to fight harder. She would've sent me flyers for another march."

A nurse passed in the hall, humming tunelessly. The sound made David's head throb—of all the things he wanted to forget, her singing was high on that list.

They spoke for a while about smaller things— the winter market shifting to avoid patrols, the neighbor's dog digging under her fence again. But the air between them was thick with the unspoken: that his life inside the Curtain was as unreachable as the parts of his own mind locked in the fog.

When the nurse finally appeared in the doorway, clipboard in hand, his mother let out a sigh. "They'll want to run your scans again," she said as she stood.

"Leaving already?"

"I should get going before the weather turns. They're saying some storms are coming in from the west."

He wanted to ask her to stay, but the words felt too much like a plea.

"Don't forget me," he said instead.

Her smile was quick and fragile. "They'd have to build a bigger wall."

She kissed his forehead, lingering as if memorizing him, then left. Her footsteps faded down the corridor until they vanished, leaving only the hum of the radiator and the faint, bitter smell of the coffee she'd brought him, now cold.

David closed his eyes, chasing the last trace of sunlight on a hardwood floor. But like everything else, it slipped away before he could hold it. In its place came flickers—unsteady broken frames. A man in his kitchen moving as though he belonged there, as if he was a part of that space. The image refused to sharpen, the face a shadowed blur where features should have been.

Other fragments pressed in. A body against his—perhaps the same man—heat moving in rhythm, the muffled sound of breath tangled with his own. He tried to grasp the details—the curve of a mouth, the lines and edges, the shape of hands on his skin—but each time he reached for them, the memory dissolved like smoke. All that remained was the ache of knowing it happened, and the hollow terror of not remembering who.

17
SONG OF SONGS

THE SILENCE IN the bungalow was worse than any nuisance noise he'd ever complained about.

Dex sat on the shower floor, steam curling around his shoulders like the breath of death, staring at the love letter Charlie had left on the glass through his flooded eyes. The water had long since gone lukewarm, but he didn't move—couldn't—fingers pruned, skin reddened, soul blackened by grief.

Charlie's toothbrush was still in the holder. His towel was still on the hook on the back of the door. The left-side pillow had become a cotton cross Dex crucified himself against the last two nights, hoping to catch his fading scent—haunted by a memory far too soon. He'd stopped sleeping. Stopped eating. Sometimes he stopped breathing, remembering halfway through the dizzy descent that his body hadn't given up yet.

Not on its own.

Charlie's ashes rested on the mantle, but there'd been no ceremony. There were no more funerals. No more songs. No more prayers. Only the echo of his own failure rang out—louder than the gunshot that was the beginning of the end.

He hadn't protected him. Should've kept him closer. Should've insisted they leave Atlanta sooner. Should've gone south to Stockbridge. Should've done... something. Instead, Charlie had all but died in his arms—wide-eyed, lips parted— the faintest light in those kind eyes before being wheeled away for nothing.

He hadn't said goodbye, hadn't told him how much he loved him—at least not in words. The ache inside Dex was not sharp. It didn't burn or sting. It just... was. A dull vacancy. An evacuated soul.

He scrubbed his face and turned off the water. He didn't bother drying off. Just stepped out— water pooling beneath his feet—and stared at his reflection: beard overgrown in coarse patches, purplish hollows under his eyes, skin almost gray.

He didn't remember turning it on, but the TV ricocheted through the emptiness of the house, an emptiness echoed within his body.

"...as we've previously reported, neurotoxicity from post-strike fallout continues to rise in vulnerable sectors," a plastic-faced anchor was saying, her teeth a little too white, her smile a little too fake.

"Thanks to swift action from the Department of Health, citizens can now receive preemptive neuro-serenity boosters, called Serexin, at all designated clinics."

A graphic slid onscreen:

SEREXIN means SERENITY

Dex stared, unblinking. The footage cut to bodycam clips—edited, degraded, looped: a woman hurling herself against an electrified, chain-link fence, blood smeared across her shirt; a man clutching his head, screaming nonsense; a young boy seeming to levitate three inches off a detention-cell floor, eyes rolled back, the frame glitching like a corrupted file.

The voiceover returned over more footage, but Dex had looked away: "Unchecked Tangents can exhibit dangerous and irrational behaviors. Hallucinations, violence, emotional contagion. Serexin helps you stay grounded. Helps keep *them* contained."

Another video flashed—this one, per the caption, supposedly leaked from a rogue Tangent encampment: shaky firelight, laughter curdling into sobbing, then static. A jump cut to a young man curled in the fetal position, mumbling, "I see it—I see everything—" before the screen feed returned to the anchor's practiced concern.

"In compliance with Order SRX-Seven," she said, "all citizens within the Curtain must report for the mandatory Serexin inoculation by Monday at eighteen-hundred hours."

Dex didn't flinch. Not at the familiar screams of Tangents rounded up and tagged like livestock. Not even when their warped cut of a young woman's final moments as she begged for her life. He just sat, towel around his waist, watching the Order propagandize lies while scrubbing the truth.

The clinic smelled like a mix of sterile plastic and lemon cleaner. Everything inside was achromatic—white tiles, white walls, white scrubs on the nurses. The kind of color that made you forget you were human.

At least fifty people waited ahead of him, each marked by a glowing ID strip at the inner wrist. Dex's own buzzed softly under the scanner as he stepped through the second checkpoint—a forced implant that felt like mutilation.

"Lane Four," the coordinator muttered without looking up. "Shirt off. Arm out."

Dex complied. There was no protest left in him. No more songs to sing. No anger. Only muscle memory and vacancy. He sat on the vinyl chair as the injector hissed.

"You might feel some dizziness," the female tech said, almost bored. "Or euphoria. That's normal. Drink plenty of fluids. If you experience hallucinations, report them immediately."

The liquid hit his bloodstream like a shiver—cold, quick, clean.

The room swayed—but not the way they'd warned.

The back of his skull bloomed open—at least it felt that way—something soft and writhing unfurling from his spine to wrap around his thoughts. He gasped, but no sound came out.

The lights changed—just slightly. More detail. More definition. He saw tension pulse behind the technician's temple. Smelled sour stress leaking from the man two chairs down. Tasted grief trapped behind a woman's stoic face as she cradled a child already gone numb.

Dex blinked, fingers twitching. The fluorescent lights whined at a pitch he hadn't noticed before. Or maybe it had always been there and it was inaudible before now.

Color shifted. Breath shifted. As if the world had taken off its mask—and underneath was everything he'd never seen.

It was overwhelming.

And yet... it didn't break through the numbness.

Grief swallowed it. Blunted it. Made the shift feel like a fever dream barely worth noting. Nothing—not visions, not revelations, not empathy dialed up to eleven—could compete with the silent void Charlie left behind.

Aside from the initial effects from the Serexin shot, his full transformation went unnoticed— even by him.

Later that night, Dex stood in his hallway, staring at the closed bathroom door, thinking of the night Charlie had rushed inside in a drunken dash.

He wept—not loud, not cathartic. A slow, dry unraveling that left his body limp with absence. He didn't sleep that night either, but he made a decision.

The hiring office was three blocks from the train depot. Dex wore a plain black tee over long sleeves despite the August heat. He didn't want to talk, didn't want to explain the tattoos.

But he knew what he was doing.

He hadn't been there for Charlie, hadn't stopped the bleeding, hadn't even known where to begin beyond a rudimentary CPR class at the precinct. He couldn't have saved him, but maybe he could pay penance by saving someone else.

"Experience?" the intake clerk asked, flipping through a battered tablet.

"Cop for more than a dozen years," Dex said. "Before the Curtain went up. Before the Order created chaos."

The man narrowed his eyes. "We're not Order-affiliated. Private response only. No pick-ups, just damage control and injury assessment. Minor treatments so victims don't bleed out."

"I'm aware," Dex said. "That's why I'm here."

The man looked him up and down. "You'll need a psych eval. New regs."

"Fine."

"You been dosed?"

Dex nodded. "Yesterday."

The man scanned his wrist. "Serexin administered. No anomalies. Guess you're one of the lucky ones. Most folks feel like they've been gutted for a week."

Dex didn't answer. Maybe having *already* been gutted is why he passed.

"You'll ride as secondary for two weeks," the man said, scribbling something on a clipboard. "Then you're on your own."

The first shift was mostly quiet: a heat stroke in Grant Park; a diabetic seizure in an alley near Decatur. Dex rode beside an older woman named Shayna who didn't ask too many questions, chain-smoked Black and Milds, and kept a beat-up copy of *As I Lay Dying* in the glove box.

How dark, Dex thought.

By the fourth call, a jumper—young, mid-twenties—sprawled across the tracks like spilled paint.

Dex crouched beside the body, checking pulse. None.

But something shifted in his gut.

His vision fluttered—just for a second—and he *felt* it: the echo of the man's final thought. Not words or images. Just raw panic and a burst of shame.

Shayna noticed him stagger back, clutching his temples.

"You okay, kid?" she asked.

He nodded. "Just... adrenaline."

She grunted. "It'll pass."

But it didn't.

The next call, he touched a woman's wrist and felt her heartbreak like a static shock. The one after that, he tasted the cancer in a man's blood— acrid, metallic—like shrapnel in the back of his throat.

By night's end, he was shaking.

He didn't understand it. Not fully. But the world was louder now. And somehow, he could hear it.

Back home, Dex stood in front of the mirror again.

He stripped off his shirt and stared. The barcode on his wrist blinked red once, then green. But his reflection didn't match. Not quite.

His pupils dilated differently now. His veins traced strange constellations beneath the surface of his skin. His body felt too full and too hollow at the same time.

He reached into the nightstand drawer and pulled out Charlie's tee again—the one he'd vomited on that first night. It didn't smell like him—Dex's detergent had done its work with that—but it felt like him, presence imprinted in the threads.

And for the first time since the injection—since leaving the funeral home with Charlie's ashes—he whispered, "I love you."

With the words—words he'd been too scared and stupid to say when he had the chance—came a flood of tears. When Charlie had said them to him, it felt improbable—too soon—but the truth was he already loved Charlie. It was the kind of love that originated slowly, first from proximity, then routine turned into mutual respect and trust, ultimately forming a friendship—almost familial—that flourished into forbidden desire.

In that moment, amidst the salt-soaked sobbing, he wished the Serexin worked as promise instead of making him feel everything—especially his grief in this moment—even stronger. He wished for release, to leave the corrupt world that took Charlie from him; he wished to join him, wherever he'd gone.

Together.

He glanced back at the open drawer and stared at the pistol he'd never relinquished when he left the force. Like a siren calling a sailor to certain death, its cold black surface called out to him, tugged at him like a tether, until it was in his hand.

The weight in his hand matched the weight in his heart. He had never felt anything so heavy, so crushing. In a flare of rage at the world, he closed his eyes and set his lips around the barrel.

As soon as the metal touched his mouth, his phone—purposely always silenced—erupted with a song at full volume, pulling his focus from the trigger.

It'd had been years since he'd heard it, but the unforgettable melody and lyrics instantly transported him—to the patrol car, a meth-lab stakeout, the first moment the song meant something.

"I love this song!" Charlie said, cranking the volume a bit too loud.

"Me, too," Dex admitted, "but we should turn it down some before we blow our cover."

Dex melted once Charlie belted the star-filled lyrics in near unison with the lead singer, even using his drink can as a mic.

Before that, Charlie had never once hummed— let alone sung—a single song from the radio. It felt like an olive branch, an apology for all the shit he'd put Dex through during their first year and a half as partners. It felt like walls being lowered enough to let Dex in, even if just a little.

Dex joined him for the last two verses and chorus—an answer to his apology, a release of the tension between them. From that moment, it was their song.

Dex thumbed the safety and let the gun fall to the floor, succumbing to a fresh onslaught of tears. As the lyrics echoed through the emptiness, he sang them back in a ragged whisper, the prophetic poignancy of one line punching him in the chest: *I wanna die in your arms...*

It felt like Charlie had reached across time to stop him—and to remind him how long those feelings spanned. That first night in bed, Charlie had admitted he'd kept them secret; maybe the patrol-car duet had been an attempt to tell him. Dex would never know the full story—their story had ended.

He grabbed Charlie's pillow, buried his face and sadness into its depths, and let sleep pull him from the pain.

At first, Dex thought the work might save him.

Each call blurred—bodies on sidewalks, collapsed in shelters, curled in alleyways or heat-locked apartments. Most had no one. Many didn't make it. Those he kept breathing were often returned to the system broken, tagged, or worse.

But some... *he saved.*

A man with third-degree burns with a daughter refusing to leave his side. Dex took his hand and *felt* the pain scream in his bones—and the stubborn love beneath it. The man would've let himself burn again just to keep the girl safe. He medicated, bandaged, cooled. When the man opened his eyes two days later, Dex stepped outside to cry.

Not for the pain. But because this time, someone lived.

Then an elderly woman in Capitol View, trembling on her porch, confused and half-dehydrated. Her husband had died three weeks prior; she hadn't left her rocking chair since.

Dex approached carefully, her wrist tissue-thin in his hand.

"I don't want to go," she whispered, even as the IV slipped under her skin. "It's the only place I can still feel him."

Dex said nothing. But he *felt* it—her grief, soft and wild, clinging to the air like a song only he could hear.

He didn't make her leave. He fixed the water line, left some protein pouches, sat with her until she smiled, and wrote the call as "non-critical dehydration, stabilized on site."

Shayna didn't ask questions—just lit a cigarette and passed Dex the clipboard.

By week three, Dex knew something was changing.

It wasn't just the senses—the way voices pulled different colors, how he could taste someone's anxiety before they opened their mouth. It was how he *reacted.* How he *felt.*

The numbness had begun to thaw, just barely, and what it left behind wasn't peace. It was something messier.

Connection.

He couldn't touch a patient without absorbing their emotions; he couldn't kneel beside a dying body without seeing their last memory; worst of all: he couldn't see someone in need without remembering Charlie.

Every overdose. Every lost kid. Every person clinging to life with nothing but hope and stubbornness—they all looked like him, sounded like him, smelled like the damn cedar soap Dex had used for years but only reminded him of Charlie now.

Dex slept even less, snapped at Shayna, and reached for bourbon again. And then came the call that finally cracked him.

It was supposed to be a simple assist—a child with a broken arm, domestic dispute, routine extraction. But at the housing block they found a boy, no older than eight, curled in a closet, glass in his hair, blood on his shirt.

His mother was unconscious on the floor. His stepfather—already cuffed—still screamed through the hallway walls.

Dex could tell the boy was neurodivergent; he'd grown up looking out for a neighbor like him, protected him when others were cruel. He crouched low, hands open. "Hey. I'm not gonna hurt you."

The boy didn't move. Didn't blink. Amber eyes hollowed by something Dex recognized too well: detachment.

Dex reached, and the moment their skin met, the flood came.

Terror. Shame. Pain—like teeth buried in skin. It stole Dex's breath to feel it. And beneath it... love. Fragile, buried. A mother's lullaby when the man wasn't home. A crayon drawing tucked under the floorboard. A hope that someone—*anyone*—might save him and his mother from the abuse.

Dex swallowed the sob threatening to rise, lifted the boy, and carried him to the ambulance— hands shaking for hours after.

He visited the kid in the recovery wing three days later. The child didn't say anything, just stared at him like he was a ghost. Then, quietly, "You felt it too, didn't you?"

Dex nodded.

The boy grabbed Dex's hand. "I'm sorry about Charlie."

Dex didn't understand how, but the boy had seen inside of him as easily as he had into the boy.

That night, Dex sat alone on the edge of the cot in the EMT locker room, staring at his hands.

He hadn't saved Charlie.

But this boy... he'd saved Dex just as much as Dex had saved him. Not in the literal sense, but the boy knew his secret, his pain, his loss, without even having to put words to it. Maybe that was enough to hold the pieces together.

The work got harder. Gloves dulled the edge but never silenced it. A wrist would slip, or a pulse would drag too deep, and suddenly the connection would split wide open again.

On one shift, a woman coded mid-transit. Dex felt her flatline like a vacuum imploding in his chest—so total, so violent, he nearly vomited in the rig. The paramedic beside him barked orders, but Dex heard only the absence, the cavernous nothing swallowing her last spark.

And yet not every impression was grief. Once, in the chaos of a pile-up, his fingers grazed a woman's shoulder. Instead of terror, what poured through him was defiance—a flash of paint against brick, a circle half-finished, and voices murmuring beneath the sirens: *Chaos, Persephone.* The names hushed but urgent, carried like contraband between breaths. He pulled back, shaken. For a moment, he thought he'd imagined it. But the resonance clung to him, sharper than death, like the world itself whispering secrets of salvation.

Another call: a collapsed apartment building. The dust was thick with fear and crushed potential, grief hanging heavier than the concrete slabs. Dex brushed a man's ankle protruding from the rubble and was hit with a memory—an unopened birthday cake, still boxed, waiting for candles that would never be lit. The sweetness of it seared him worse than the loss.

He didn't cry on scene. Couldn't. But when they got back to the depot, he stayed in the rig until Shayna drove off, climbed into the back, pulled the curtain shut, and let the grief shake him apart. He pressed his fists against his eyes as if he could squeeze the visions out, but they kept returning: the unopened cake, the painted circle, the names whispered like a secret liturgy.

After a three-shift bender—thirty-six hours without eating or sleeping—he found himself back at the clinic. Not for patients this time, but for himself.

The waiting room smelled of bleach and resignation. Someone had scrawled something faint on the backside of the plastic chair beside him, the curve of a circle nearly rubbed away by use. He traced it absently with his thumb and wondered if it was nothing...or if it was the same mark he'd felt in the wreckage.

Symbols, pamphlets, whispers of Persephone— he'd brushed against them all, but they were fragments without shape, signs he wasn't ready to read. The only thing clear was the weight breaking him apart, and the truth that he couldn't keep carrying it alone.

He told the intake nurse he was dizzy, hallucinating.

She scanned his vitals. Logged his Serexin dose.

"Looks like the booster's working just fine," she said.

Dex stared at her. "Then why am I still feeling *everything?*"

She frowned. "You're not."

He realized then—she couldn't see it. Wouldn't. The Order had written it off. Tangents who slipped through were ignored unless they became a problem. The "Serenity" reading was their shield. Their excuse.

Dex left without speaking.

That night he stood in front of the bathroom mirror, peeled off his shirt, and stared at the barcode on his wrist. He pressed his thumb to it. Held. Waited.

The red light blinked once. Then steadied.

Active. Registered. Serene.

It was a lie. He wasn't serene. He was haunted.

November 1, 2026

"Blessed are those who find wisdom,
those who gain understanding,
for she is more profitable than silver
and yields better returns than gold.
She is more precious than rubies;
nothing you desire can compare with her.
Long life is in her right hand;
in her left hand are riches and honor.
Her ways are pleasant ways,
and all her paths are peace.
She is a tree of life to those who take hold of her;
those who hold her fast will be blessed."

~ Proverbs 3:13-18

18
PROVERBS

T HE LAKE HOUSE didn't look like a place where people plotted to put a broken world back together. It had the beauty of weekends and quiet evenings—cedar deck turned toward a sheet of water, floor-to-ceiling windows, shelves of books that looked read (some more than once).

Everywhere upstairs showed a life curated over years: framed maps, a brass telescope near the glass, a record player with vinyl sleeves stacked beneath it. The table by the stairs had a dish of smooth stones, each labeled in Asa's small, neat hand. Everything said: a scholar lives here.

Downstairs, the place changed its mind. The basement had been a recreation space once—carpet, a faded ping-pong table, a rack of mismatched dumbbells. Now it was a lab. White benches stood where the sectional used to be. Two centrifuges gleamed under LED strips; a laminar-flow hood hummed softly in the corner. The concrete was sealed and leveled; cable trays ran like silver vines overhead. Along the far wall, a server cage breathed steady heat. A laminated card on the cage read, simply: MIRROR. University of Georgia equipment tags dotted monitors and microscopes—discreet stickers that would never appear on any official inventory. Other machines bore the names of companies that had "lost" them in transit to research hospitals. It didn't feel makeshift. It felt deliberate.

Asa Whitby kept a hand on the back of the central chair, watching the three younger scientists take their positions as naturally as a trio tuning before the first movement.

Priyanka Patel settled at the primary terminal—spine straight, hair pulled into a neat knot, glasses pushed up the bridge of her nose—as lines of recovered text scrolled past.

Emily Spaulding half-leaned against a support post, arms folded, gaze tracking the room with the practiced suspicion of someone who expected the world to disappoint her. Her twin brother, Derek, perched on a lab stool, one foot hooked on the lower rung, twirling a pen between and tapping out an off-beat rhythm against his knee.

"I will never get over the fact you mirrored the Emory lab to your lake house," Emily said, scanning the room like the place offended her on principle. "It's... obscene. And it could've been compromised."

"You mean like the *actual* lab was?" Derek pointed out.

She scoffed.

"It was insurance," Asa said. His voice always sounded like it had learned restraint the hard way. "Institutions fail. Hard drives become corrupted. If a truth matters, you don't leave it in one place waiting for a fire or flood to erase it."

Derek flashed a grin without looking up. "Paranoid old man saves civilization. Story at eleven."

"Paranoia preserved our work," Priyanka said calmly, still typing. "Let's not malign tools that keep us alive."

On the main display, the phantom code of Emory's research assembled itself into legible shape: Corazamine schematics re-stitched from backups; trial notes with corrupted margins; tables coaxed back into meaning. The annotations had survived, too: a half-dozen hands in different colors arguing in the margins about dose windows, receptor crosstalk, whether stress priming was a nuisance or a necessary feature.

Emily pushed off the post. "Where are we, honestly?"

Priyanka exhaled. "Structure's right. Binding affinity is on target in vitro. But stability is still a mess. We can keep the compound adherent for hours if we treat it like spun glass. The second we move it out of ideal conditions it starts to degrade."

"How fast?" Derek asked, pen still dancing.

"Half-life falls off a cliff with temperature shifts. The pH variance makes it tantrum. We need a carrier that keeps it honest," Priyanka said. "Liposomes helped just a little. Microencapsulation's promising but finicky at our molecular weight." She tapped a line of notes. "And we still don't know if the code that made early batches succeed is input or artifact."

"Even a couple of hours would be something," Emily said. "If it works, that's hours of being human for someone who hasn't felt anything in months. We can deal with perfection later."

"A cure without restraint is another toxin," Priyanka replied. "Especially one that alters how a person feels and connects. We don't get to be cavalier because our intentions are good."

"Sometimes good enough is enough," Derek said. "War medicine—you stop the bleeding first, worry about scar tissue after."

Asa lifted a hand without raising his voice. "We do both. We don't hand the world an unstable tool and hope virtue keeps it safe, and we don't polish so long that people drown while we admire our principles. Wisdom is knowing which way not to fall."

The pen slowed in Derek's fingers. Emily let out a breath she hadn't fully inhaled. Priyanka turned back to the terminal.

They worked, and the place listened. The server's hum was steady and grounding, anchoring the lab to something bigger than any one of them. Priyanka called out adjustments; Derek translated them into simulations with shortcuts that would have scandalized Emory's compliance people; Emily stood sentry, stabbing holes in assumptions before they hardened into doctrine. Asa moved among them like a silent conductor, keeping the arguments useful.

A phone buzzed on the bench—that small modern sound that broke the spell. Four heads turned at once. Emily reached, thumbed open the group thread without needing to ask whose number could cut through.

"Gabriella," she said, and the room added a layer of attention.

She read: "The hollow forget. The restless lash out. The awakened... harder to hide."

No one spoke right away, pondering the three sentences.

Priyanka found words first. "She's seeing the anomalies again; it's divergence, not destabilization."

"Or she's seeing noise," Emily said, the edge in her voice more self-defense against hope than conviction.

"Noise doesn't keep texting us," Derek said. He turned the phone around to look at the thread like it might say more if he stared. "*Hollow*—those are our calm clinics. *Restless*—those are the ones who punch walls. *Awakened* isn't a word you choose lightly."

Asa's expression barely changed, but something in his posture settled, as though a thought he'd carried once returned in a new language. "It's the same fracture Gabriella witnessed before the Curtain when Serexin was rushed to scale. It doesn't level people—it splits them. Most drown in numbness. Some thrash. A few... open."

"Anomalies won't win wars," Emily said.

"They don't have to," Asa replied. "They prove possibilities. Possibility is the one thing tyrants can't kill."

The phone stayed facedown after that, as if that could keep it from choosing the next moment to break in. They went back to work with the text sitting silent between them like a stone dropped into a deep well, echoes still traveling.

The lab's rhythm changed, subtly, after the message. Priyanka narrated a little more than usual—drawing lines between Emory's raw notes and their rebuilt protocols: why dosing after sleep deprivation changed outcomes; why hydration seemed trivial until it wasn't; why cortisol baselines mattered for reasons beyond convenience. Derek—who had made a private religion of improvisation—gritted his teeth and built the stress simulations she asked for, layering sleep debt, dehydration, and tight temperature variations into runs that made the server cage breathe harder. Emily kept watch, mind organized like a grid of possible failure points, questions coming fast and surgical.

"If we amplify empathy, what stops the Order—or anyone—from turning it into leverage?" Emily asked. "Serexin was born from Corazamine's notes, deconstructed then restructured. If we put this back in the world, we can't pretend it won't be twisted again."

Priyanka nodded, eyes on the screen. "We build in failure—delivery vectors that collapse outside narrow conditions. Protocols that demand consent at every stage and degrade if coerced."

"That's ideal," Derek said. "Ideal looks lovely on paper. On the ground, people take the path that gets results—and they lie about how they got there if the result is good."

"And?" Emily asked.

"And we design the path so lying breaks it," Derek said, surprising himself with the seriousness of it.

Asa watched them like a gardener pleased to see strong plants crowd the space. "Every tool teaches the person holding it something about themselves," he said. "Corazamine won't be the exception. We can choose what it rewards."

Another batch finished spinning. The centrifuge beeped—a gentle, domestic sound out of place in a room trying to save people. Priyanka uncapped the tube, pipetted with extreme care, having learned the hard way that variables had their own stubborn personalities. Derek adjusted the scope without being asked.

"Stable pH," Priyanka said. "Temperature within half a degree of the sweet spot. Try the carrier adjustment."

Derek logged it, eyes flicking across numbers. Emily stepped closer, arms unfolding—intent outweighing skepticism for a moment.

The phone buzzed again, as if whatever decided timing for these things had a sense of theater. Priyanka picked it up this time and read before anyone asked: "Clinics full. Hollow calm spreading. Restless violence worse. Two new awakenings. One elder says touch hurts and heals. Chaos grows."

"Chaos?" Derek said, setting his pen down for the first time in an hour. "That's not a description. That's a name."

Emily swallowed. "Open rebellion gets people killed."

"Whispers get people killed, too," Asa said— not arguing, just naming the world as it was. He leaned in and read the text for himself. "If Gabriella is capitalizing a word, the rebellion has learned to call itself something and answer to it."

Priyanka read it again, softer, as if pronouncing the lines would make them settle into place more cleanly. "Touch hurts and heals," she repeated. "That's exactly what we were trying—turn disconnection back into connection, even if it stung on the way."

"She's telling us what it feels like from the inside," Emily said. "Not just numbers."

"They'll try to sever it," Derek said. "If Vexley can't make Serexin uniform, he'll cut off the people who won't go flat from each other. You kill a network by isolating the nodes, then the hubs—make resistance impossible to build."

"Then we design redundancy they can't map," Priyanka said—and for a second the tired basement lab felt taller than the house above it. "We teach people to replicate it, not just distribute it. A single lab can be raided. A dozen small labs, each able to restart the work—that's harder to kill."

Asa gave a thin smile and pointed to the mirror server. "Life survives by redundancy. So will we."

They didn't talk for a while after that. They worked. The hum of equipment made its own music—the centrifuge downshifting, the server fans rising and falling, the faint hiss of the hood.

The next batch made the room remember what hope felt like. Priyanka lifted a small vial into the light; the liquid looked ordinary, hiding the possible miracle in plain glass. Then it didn't. A faint blue bloomed from within—not an LED or a reflection, but something alive waking up. Silver threaded through it—fine as breath, quick as thought. It held. A second. Two. Five. Ten. Long enough for their bodies to remember the muscles that make room for joy and terror at once.

Derek's voice came out louder than intended. "You see it?"

"Not long enough," Priyanka said—her caution more stewardship than dismissal.

"Long enough to prove this isn't a ghost we're chasing," Emily said, eyes doing that strange thing where possibility pushes suspicion aside. "Long enough to tell someone we aren't lying."

Asa rested two fingers lightly on the bench, as if touching something would steady the moment. "Proof the cure isn't lost."

The blue dimmed; the silver settled back into nothing you could point to. They didn't mourn its passing. They let themselves feel what it had given them.

"What happens when this leaves the room?" Emily asked softer than usual. "When it's not us controlling the conditions—or when someone decides the condition is fear?"

"Then we test our failsafes until we hate them," Priyanka said, still looking at the vial as if meeting a person's eyes. "Carriers that degrade outside narrow windows. Dosing protocols that require two separate consents. Biochemical tripwires that collapse the structure if forced."

Derek picked up his pen and spun it once. "Distribution has to be cell-based," he said. "Not centralized manufacturing. Protocols simple enough that any small lab with a clean hood can make it. Five labs that don't know about each other can't all be arrested the same day. That way, if one's raided, another still has the compound and the recipe."

"Rules only matter if people follow them," Emily said, surprising herself. "If someone's going to break them, they will. Better to write them so breaking them backfires."

Asa listened, quiet, while the three of them shaped something that sounded less like protocols and more like a way to live. He thought of Gabriella, sending texts that spoke like carvings—because stones survive floods. He thought of Sanjay, killed the night the Order raided Emory. Five of the six were still alive, and four were still in a room together, still working toward a future that might exist.

"Let's keep it simple," Emily continued. "Failsafes. Consent built in, not tacked on. Small batches that can vanish and return. Nothing the Order can grab in one strike."

"And a promise," Priyanka added. "We never put this into anyone who doesn't understand what it means. Not even if we think it'll save them. Especially not then."

Derek nodded. "And a story." At their sideways looks, he added, "Something bigger than protocols. People follow a story."

"We're not making fairytales," Emily said.

"Not fairytales," Derek replied. "Names. Words that stick. If Gabriella says, 'Chaos grows,' and people feel the rise of a rebellion, then it's not just us anymore. The story carries itself."

The phone stayed quiet. The vial sat between them—just glass again, just liquid. It had still changed the room.

Asa straightened. "We should write the distribution protocol as if someone we don't trust will read it," he said. "Teach it to people we do trust without paper."

Priyanka fingers were back on the keys. "I'll draft the biochemical guardrails."

"I'll break them," Derek said.

"You'll try," Priyanka said—and something like a smile flashed between them.

"I'll write the model," Emily said. "What moves where, who needs what, how to make it disappear without destroying it."

"I'll keep the light bill paid," Asa said, "and the neighbors thinking that I'm retired."

They laughed—quiet, tired.

Upstairs, if anyone had looked, the lake lay still enough to pass for peace. In the basement, peace was motors, minds, and a stubborn commitment to not look away.

They cycled one more run—momentum has its own kind of grace. The vial glowed again—a breath shorter than the last time—which none of them took as failure. They cleaned the bench and capped the tubes. Priyanka labeled vials in a handwriting that made even chaos legible. Derek shut down simulations.

They stood a moment longer than they needed, none of them wanting to break the shape the night had taken.

They turned lights off in stages—not because it mattered to the work but because ritual had a way of steadying people. Emily checked the deadbolt on the way up; Derek turned back once to be sure the hood was really off; Priyanka hovered by the server cage until the fans settled into their night hum; Asa paused at the top to look back at the lab—the hood, the centrifuges, the vial that had glowed long enough to change something he couldn't name.

In the living room, the place returned to what strangers would read it as—a scholar's refuge, nothing more. The lake held the last bit of orange of the fading sky.

The phone on the bench downstairs would rest until the next buzz broke the quiet. Somewhere on the other side of a line they hadn't drawn, Gabriella would choose her words with the caution of someone who understood the cost. Somewhere under streets the Order thought it owned, a rebellion had begun to call itself Chaos.

Inside the house truth lived under comfort, like a proverb you carry in your pocket. Beautiful above, hidden below. The seed had been planted, and seeds—as the old line goes—find their way around fences.

Inside the lab that had no business existing, the four stood at the threshold as custodians of their choice—their promise—to pursue and find it. The cure wasn't whole, but it was hope enough to keep going.

And sometimes hope saves people, too.

Part VI
CHAOS

December 21, 2026

"Growth comes from chaos, not order."

~ Rakesh Jhunjhunwala

19
HERETIC

THE CHAMBER SMELLED faintly of antiseptic and ozone—one of HALCION's clinical debriefing rooms designed to look neutral, harmless. White walls, white table, a single overhead strip of lighting that left no shadows—a neat contradiction to the darkness that existed within its walls. Regina sat across from Charlotte Moss with her usual precise stillness, hands folded neatly, eyes sharp as glass.

Charlotte mirrored the stillness, but hers was practiced from years of being watched. She didn't fidget or bite her lip. She just asked questions, voice steady. "Why do some of us feel more instead of less after the injection?"

Regina blinked once, slow. "Serexin doesn't fail. Variation is expected."

Charlotte tilted her head, a braid slipping loose of her headband. "If variation is expected, then why so many guards outside the dormitories?"

"Precaution," Regina said flatly. "Security protocols aren't yours to question."

Charlotte let the silence stretch. Then she asked, "And the Tangents who don't come back from assignments? What happens to them?"

Regina's jaw tightened. "They are reassigned."

"To where?" Charlotte pressed. Her tone wasn't loud or insubordinate—it was worse: curious.

Regina leaned forward just slightly, and her voice took on a cool edge. "Your task is to perform, not to postulate."

Charlotte held her gaze. "If empathy is such a sickness, why study it so closely instead of curing it?"

For the first time, Regina's composure cracked—just a flicker. She stood, smoothed her jacket, and gave a nod toward the camera dome in the corner.

"Interview concluded," she said. Her voice was low, final. "This one is a liability."

Charlotte sat very still, heart pounding. She understood what those words meant.

Charlotte didn't know how long she sat after Regina left, staring at the white table under the humming strip light. The words *this one is a liability* echoed in her skull like a verdict. She expected two guards, hands on her shoulders, a quiet transfer to a place she'd never leave.

Instead, a technician appeared—mid-level, badge crooked—a face she'd seen but never spoken to. He paused at the threshold, weighing something, and muttered, "Walk with me."

She didn't move. He glanced at the camera, then back at her, his tone a bit sharper, "Now!"

Charlotte rose. Her pulse thundered but her steps were steady. He led her down a service corridor she'd never seen—white walls giving way to exposed conduit, air shifting from clinical chill to the warm breath of boilers and generators. They passed two security nodes; each time he keyed them too fast for protocol, as if rehearsed.

At a dark junction he pressed a card into her hand. "Northbound access," he whispered. "Follow the red line. Don't stop."

She wanted to ask why, but he was already gone, back toward the light. Charlotte slid the card and the door clicked. She stepped into a tunnel system linked to HALCION. After a few turns, the wall tiles changed and she realized she was no longer underneath HALCION.

She was in the bowels of MARTA, Atlanta's transit system. The smell hit first—rusted iron, old oil, damp concrete—and the MARTA logo affixed to the locked doors appearing every so often. The tunnels were half-lit, bulbs swinging slightly from an unseen draft. She followed the red line, shoes scuffing gravel where tile had crumbled. Far above, the city throbbed with order and surveillance; but down here, the world belonged to no one.

She passed abandoned platforms where graffiti sprawled like murals—slogans, sigils, names remembered only here. A generator rattled in the distance, feeding light strings looped along the ceiling. Quick silhouettes vanished when she looked full-on—scouts, sentries, or ghosts; she couldn't tell.

Finally, the tunnel opened into a larger chamber where an old maintenance station had been transformed into something else. Cables crossed the floor like veins. Folding tables bristled with laptops, patched routers, radios cannibalized from police bands. A half-dozen people bent over equipment, screen-glow painting their faces.

The sound of typing, murmured code, the low thrum of patched-in power—it all sang of defiance. Charlotte exhaled for what seemed like the first time since Regina's threat. Perhaps she hadn't escaped execution into complete safety, but she had stumbled into something that felt real, felt safer.

The chamber buzzed with quiet intensity. No one wasted motion. A wiry man hunched over a gutted server tower, the tip of his soldering iron sparking. Two coders traded murmured instructions while their screens flooded with green text. A corner generator droned, feeding strings of lights overhead that turned the graffiti-scrawled walls into a canvas of dancing shadows.

A tall figure in a patched jacket stepped forward, voice carrying across the room. "New arrival. Northbound entry."

Heads turned; work paused. Charlotte stayed near the doorway, feeling the heat of watchful eyes.

From the back, a woman rose. She wasn't tall, but every eye followed her. Closed-cropped hair, with a red blazer that sharply contrasted the concrete room. When she spoke, her voice was steel edged with velvet.

"You survived HALCION," she said, measuring Charlotte in a glance. "That tells me you've got sense."

The others murmured assent. Charlotte didn't need an introduction to know she was in charge.

"This is Imani Cade," the man beside her offered.

"Why did you come?" Imani asked Charlotte directly.

Charlotte steadied her voice. "Because Regina Roth tried to make sure I never left."

A ripple ran through the chamber—anger, recognition, maybe even respect.

Imani nodded once. "Then you understand. You're not alone anymore."

The next night Charlotte stood against a wall, watching the rebellion bare its teeth. A long table was cleared, wires spilling across it like arteries of anarchy. Laptops glowed with lines of code. Someone manned a salvaged switchboard from an old broadcast truck, knobs worn smooth.

"This isn't an attack," Imani said, pacing behind them. "It's defensive, reminding them that the city is ours. It was never theirs."

"Ready," a coder called.

"Send it," Imani ordered, crisp and certain.

With a single key pressed, the feed on the monitor stuttered, garbled, then dissolved into static. For three heartbeats Charlotte thought they'd crashed the system. Then the feed stuttered and burned through to black. From the darkness, a symbol bled into view.

A letter C within a circle of fire, its edges tangled with barbed wire. From its crown rose a phoenix—wings flared, head angled in defiance—rendered in raw, burning red against the void. It looked less like a logo and more like a brand seared into the screen, pulsing faintly.

A voice followed—filtered through layers, corrupted, and distorted—neither man nor woman, only urgent.

> "People of Atlanta. The Order calls us Heretics, but they are the ones who speak with corruption and heresy. They twist medicine into poison and call it safety. They disappear your neighbors and call it protection. But truth survives. Empathy survives. We are not anomalies but advanced; not diseased but cured; not broken—we are woke."

Charlotte inhaled sharply before the voice continued.

> "You are not alone. If you feel more instead of less—if the injections burn but do not bind—there are others like you. The Order will brand us defectors. So be it. We will, too, name them as they are—fascists who betrayed their own cure. Chaos grows, and with it, hope."

The symbol pulsed once more, then the feed snapped back. The HALCION anchor stumbled, then resumed the script.

The room exhaled. Coders grinned. Imani's face stayed sharp, unreadable, but her voice carried. "Every time we cut through, they lose ground. And every time they call us Heretics, we will own the name more."

"To Chaos!" the room called out in near unison.

"To Chaos," Charlotte echoed under her breath thinking no one heard—until a woman's glance slid from the screen to her face.

"The Order will find us if we're not careful," the woman said, eyes and tone emotionless.

"How haven't they found this place already? I mean... I found it easily enough."

"You were able to find this place because you came in from the Northbound entry—it's a direct path from HALCION," explained the woman. "Toby— the tech who handed you the card that gave you access—is one of us. An implant at HALCION. He watches, listens, waits for Tangents like you."

"How did you know I was a Tangent?"

The woman shifted her eyes to Charlotte's gloves, then offered her hand, "My name is Gabriella... Spencer."

"Gabriella Spencer... as in?"

"That's me," Gabriella confirmed. "The only one of my team stuck behind the Curtain because I was caring for my sick mother."

Tired eyes, steady gaze—this woman knew more about the Order's toxins than anyone. "Charlotte Moss," she said. "Nice to meet you."

Emerald City was half-lit, its mirrors catching the warm gold and green bar lights, stretching them into something dreamlike. Dex worked his usual rhythm—pour, shake, slide— keeping one ear tuned to the room and the other to the jukebox's low hum. It was a steady night: not loud enough to get sloppy, not quiet enough to get restless.

The door squeaked open and a woman Dex recognized stepped inside— shoulders hunched in a coat too heavy for the season, as if chilled deeper, by more than the weather. She looked different tonight—careful, eyes scanning the room before settling on a stool halfway down the bar. Not too close to anyone. Not too far, either.

Dex drifted over, polishing a glass. "Your usual?"

Her voice was quiet but sure. "Yes, please."

Dex had still yet to catch her name—she always paid with cash. "You've got it."

He worked the drink with muscle memory— bourbon over ice, grapefruit, honey syrup, a quick shake. As he slid the glass across, her hands caught his attention more than the drink itself. She wore gloves—thin, fitted, not for warmth—something he wasn't sure he noticed during her previous patronages. Nobody wore gloves inside unless they had a reason. Dex didn't linger, didn't let her see he'd noticed, but the detail stayed.

She took a slow sip, nodded once. "Thanks."

That was it. No chatter, no opening. She drank in silence, her gloved fingers steady on the glass. Dex moved on to other customers, but each time he glanced back she was still there—watching, listening, taking in the room while giving nothing.

When she finally rose to leave, she set her glass neatly on the counter. Her cash sat atop a small stack of folded slips that she'd left in her place, edges damp from condensation on the bar. Dex frowned and reached for them. Pamphlets—cheap print, grainy ink, but bold in their message:

**CHAOS GROWS.
THE ORDER LIES.
YOU ARE NOT ALONE.**

The logo burned red against black—the letter C, encircled by a juxtaposition of flames and barbed wire, the semblance of a phoenix rising from the top.

Dex's jaw tightened. It wasn't the first time whispers of Chaos had brushed the edges of his world, but this was the first time one of their leaflets had landed on his bar. He gathered them quickly, sliding the stack under the counter before anyone else could notice.

For a long beat he stood there, weighing the risk. If the wrong eyes walked in and saw these, the place would be flagged—maybe shuttered, maybe worse. Emerald City survived because it looked like what it was: a bar, nothing more. Neutral ground.

He tucked one slip under his till. The rest he tore in half and fed into the trash. His hands moved without hesitation, but his chest tightened as he did it.

Later, when the night slowed and the last-call crowd filtered out, Dex leaned against the bar, staring at that single pamphlet he'd hidden away. He didn't know the woman's name—only the name of her usual drink—*Brown Derby.*

He had questions. More than he wanted.

The streets felt different after leaving the bar. Laughter spilled from neon-lit doorways, the clatter of late-night buses echoing—every sound set her on edge, as if it might cover the footstep of someone following. Charlotte kept her coat tight and her head down, one hand inside her pocket, fingers brushing the slim stack of pamphlets she hadn't left on the bar.

She moved like any other nightwalker in the city—purposeful, unspectacular. But every corner she turned felt like a choice. She slid one pamphlet under a stack of free papers outside a coffee shop; another pressed onto a bench at the bus stop where gum held it in place. Each drop felt both small and seismic.

The words glared back at her in block letters whenever she caught a glimpse. She knew the danger. One wrong set of eyes, one patrol sweeping too close, and she'd be marked. Yet leaving the slips behind felt necessary, almost ritual, proof that she hadn't been silenced in Regina's sterile little chamber.

Outside Five Points station, she paused. Patrols lingered at the entrance, helmets gleaming under harsh fluorescents. She folded a pamphlet into quarters and pressed it between two ads already stapled to a pole. Her pulse hammered. The paper looked louder than it should have.

A voice called out, sharp and official. Charlotte pulled her coat tighter and blended into a stream of commuters, head bowed, footsteps measured. She didn't look back until she'd reached the far corner and the crowd thinned again. No one followed.

By the time she slipped down into another service stairwell, the pamphlets in her pocket were gone, scattered across the city like seeds in cracked pavement. She didn't know who would pick them up, who would believe them, who would panic. That wasn't her concern anymore.

Her task was simple: carry the message forward. If only she could get a message to Tobias.

Back in the bunker, Charlotte borrowed a cracked phone from one of the coders. Her own had been abandoned in HALCION during the scramble— perhaps still glowing on that sterile white table like a breadcrumb she'd never retrieve.

She typed out the number from memory and thumbed out a message to Tobias, her fingers shaking as she typed:

They're watching you. Stay low. I'm safe. —C

Charlotte hit the send button.

The bubble appeared—then: *Message failed.*

She tried again. Another failure. The signal bled out against the thick concrete and miles of tunnel above.

"Reception's garbage down here," the coder muttered without looking up, "but the internet works just fine."

She switched tactics, moving to an open computer. She logged into the only social media she still had—thankful she'd set up the two-factor with her email instead of her phone. The laptop lagged but finally connected. She found Tobias and typed the same words from her text and hit send. This time the message went through—but the little icon beneath stayed hollow.

Unread.

She stared until her eyes blurred. Tobias had always answered—no matter how late, no matter how trivial. Even that thread felt severed now.

Charlotte closed the browser, the hollow mark still gnawing at her. She slid the phone back across the table, her gloves whispering against the plastic.

For now, she had to endure the silence.

February 5, 2027

"Three things cannot be long hidden:
the sun, the moon, and the truth."

~ Buddha

20
HIDDEN

*T*ANGENT.

Dex hated that word just as much as he hated the city's fear of it. Empathy and emotion had been reclassified as defects—something to suppress instead of something to spark.

His evening run was his moment to decompress and recharge—earbuds in to tune out the world and all the noise, especially the emotional static. The early February air felt good in his lungs even despite its iciness. His breath, rhythmic and focused, was in sync with his footfall on the pavement.

Dusk was his favorite time of day, especially once the sun slipped below the horizon, cloud bellies cast in copper and rose. The city came alive with light to mask the deadness within, the glow and warmth illuminating the night despite the deep darkness that plagued its denizens.

Seven months had passed since the Last Gleaming, a clean line between before and after, his life imploding as the bombs exploded across America. He felt heavier, burdened by loss. First David; his townhouse remained as empty as the void he'd left in Dex's life. And then Charlie.

Losing Charlie was the one outcome he'd never considered. Charlie's confession, the brief blazing after—carved him deep and left him unfilled.

They hadn't had enough time.

That was the thing that struck hardest in the quiet moments—how brief it had been. Just a few mornings of waking up tangled in each other, shared showers, meals cooked shirtless. Charlie's hand grazing his like touch alone could keep the world intact.

Dex had thought they'd have more time. Enough to figure out the shape of it. Enough to get comfortable. Enough to build something beyond just tension and timing and takeovers.

But death doesn't answer to time; it doesn't ask—it just takes.

And when it took Charlie, it took the part of Dex that still believed in anything like *later*.

He remembered the sound Charlie made—a single, sharp gasp, then nothing. No scream. No final words. Just the sudden slackness of a body surrendering to what it shouldn't have had to endure. Dex was holding him, one hand pressed against the wound, the other gripped the back of Charlie's neck, like proximity could anchor a soul.

There'd been so much blood.

He could still smell it; still feel its heat soaking through his shirt into skin. It dried sticky on his forearms, in Charlie's beard, in the creases of his palms where he'd cradled Charlie's jaw and whispered, "Stay with me, please, just stay…"

But Charlie didn't stay.

And Dex hadn't saved him.

He relived it often—at night, in the stillness, when his body was too tired to fight sleep but mind refused to go under. The memory didn't fade like people said it would. It sharpened. Got clearer. More vivid. Like trauma had etched it into the inside of his skull and turned it into a film reel that wouldn't stop playing.

He saw Charlie's eyes, wide and confused, searching his face as if Dex were the one dying—like he wanted to memorize details, like Dex was the last thing he wanted to see.

That haunted him. So did the little things.

The day after he died, Dex stripped those sheets off the bed and sat on the floor with them over his face, breathing until dizzy. He didn't cry at first. A slow rock as he held the sheets, like motion made it bearable and staying still gave it permanence.

The crying came later. Hard. Ugly. Alone.

There was no one to call. And if there *had* been—how could he explain they'd become more? That Charlie was the only person Dex had ever *truly* let in, long before he admitted it. That his death had broken something fundamental and unfixable.

Charlie had loved him, even said it out loud that last night, voice quiet and a bit uncertain, like maybe he was afraid of how intense things were becoming in the short span of time. "You don't have to say it back," he'd whispered, head on Dex's chest. "But I needed you to know."

Dex had wanted to say it. He *felt* it. God, did he feel it. But he hadn't said it, kissing him instead. A long, slow kiss meant to carry everything he didn't yet know how to put into words.

Now it wasn't enough. The silence he'd offered to Charlie's courage haunted him—heavy in his chest and gut, in the spaces between his ribs, and in the rift of his heartbreak.

Sometimes, mid-run, the city lights made him wonder if leaving it sooner would've saved him. But what did wondering change?

Charlie was gone. All Dex could do now was carry him forward—in memory, in grief, in the ache of hands that still remembered the shape of his body and the feel of hair between fingers. Dex didn't try to scrub those things away. He *couldn't*. It was all he had left.

The Order's grip on Atlanta ran deeper than Dex could've imagined. The mandatory Serexin shot had left the city numb, a city he once loved but now hated because its pulse had flatlined.

He'd left the force—partly because the Order had infiltrated it, mostly because wearing a police badge after losing his partner felt like lying, betrayal even. His need to help people had always run deeper than duty, so becoming an EMT after losing Charlie felt like a natural shift. Same city, different sirens. He traded cuffs for chest compressions, de-escalation for defibrillators. In that role, feeling his patients' pain helped—not just them, but him.

He could *feel* again, even when the people around him couldn't. But trauma settled like ash in his lungs. The screams, the silences, the vacant stares of overdose victims too sedated to cry. He walked away. He might not have regretted it if walking away hadn't cost him his cover.

Dex went back to bartending—a trade he'd done for a few years before joining the force—disappearing into a half-forgotten pocket of the city where he served drinks, scanned faces, and listened more than he spoke. Sometimes a knuckle brushed his, or a gaze held too long, and he felt them. He remembered what he was: a human who still felt.

Not an aberration. Not dangerous.

No one even knew—all too numb to notice—until he touched *him*...

Tobias Sloane had never asked to feel more; he already felt too much long before Serexin. In a world flattened by numbness, emotional hypersensitivity was far more curse than gift—the Order thought so, too. Feeling was dangerous, so when the initial tetherings began—accidental slips revealed he was one of the anomalies, a Tangent, as described by the Order—he learned quickly that carrying other's emotions on top of his own was often an unbearable weight.

It hurt. Constantly.

In the early days—before the camps, before the Curtain, before Corazamine was corrupted into control—he tried to end it. Alone in his room, he rigged a length of rope to the exposed beam above his bed. He'd never tied a noose before, and doubted he did it correctly, so as he launched himself from the top of his dresser at the side of his bed, he wasn't sure what to expect.

The rope bit deeper than he expected, but not enough. It didn't snap his neck. It just tightened, cutting off air until panic replaced despair. He realized too late—he didn't want to die, only to stop feeling—and the botched noose had trapped him between both, prolonging his pain.

Charlotte Moss found him. Moments before the asphyxiation set in and the world turned to black, she clambered onto the bed, braced herself, and lifted Tobias' weight while screaming for help, for a knife, for someone to cut him down.

The scar around his throat was a reminder of that moment—and of her. He called Charlotte his angel; she joked back that he was the one who tried to fly and—pointing to his scar— was the one with the halo. She was his best friend. Only after her disappearance a month ago did he admit to himself it had always been more—that he loved her—and realized it too late.

She'd vanished without a real explanation, "reassigned" to some covert program that didn't officially exist, which had him thinking the worst. His sleepless paranoia only sharpened the suspicion. He knew better than to ask too many questions—or the wrong people.

Tobias kept his head down, wary of eyes on him, as he slipped into one of downtown's long-forgotten corners. It still carried old Atlanta charm—he missed the world before the war. The alley bricks turned from weathered red to a bright, yellow gold, catching the glow of a neon sign ahead. It buzzed faintly, the kelly-green script: Emerald City. This was the place.

A smaller neon sign just above the double doors glared in gold with a bold promise: "Come Enjoy Our Tasty Cock….." Further inspection revealed that "tails" had burned out. Tobias smiled—barely—wondering if the owner had left it that way on purpose. It was a gay bar, after all.

He tugged the scarf a bit tighter to cover his scar and stepped inside. Dim lights, empty stools. Too early. He quickly pivoted on his left foot, already turning to leave.

A voice called out from behind him just as he pulled open the door. "Change your mind, did ya?"

Tobias turned back and saw the source of the voice standing behind the bar. He lied, "I thought you were closed."

"Nonsense," the bartender replied casually. "You got in, didn't you? Now, what can I pour for you?"

"I… uh, I don't really drink," Tobias admitted.

"At all? Or just not that much?"

Tobias stepped toward the bar.

"C'mon, have a seat."

Tobias slid onto a stool. "Not lately. Though recent occurrences have made me wish drinking had any effect on calming my troubles."

He'd said too much already—and hadn't had a sip.

I should go, he thought—then heard himself say it aloud.

"Stay," the bartender said, studying him. "A drink'll do you good."

Dex studied his lone patron. A bit ahead of the crowd today, for sure, though typically the bar should've been filling up by now. Sandy-brown hair, tousled to match his unkempt beard, eyes that remained downcast despite Dex's attempt to look at them.

"I should probably go," the man repeated.

Dex set two shot glasses on the bar, filled a shaker tin with ice, and poured tequila. A quick, hard shake; he strained the liquid from the tin into both glasses evenly.

"A shot," Dex said, "for your troubles."

The man hesitated, then lifted his glass toward Dex's. "To Order."

Their eyes met, even if briefly—hazel flecked with gold, catching the light like they glowed—and Dex smiled. "To Chaos. The Order can go fuck itself."

Their glasses clinked; Dex tipped the contents back with ease while the patron choked a bit on his.

"Disgusting."

"Oh, c'mon—it's not that bad," Dex rebutted. "Makes the pecker stiff."

"I've as much use for a stiff pecker as I do for another shot."

Dex smirked. "So, anoth—?"

"No!" the man cut in. "I'm good."

"Fair enough," Dex replied, cleared the glasses, and cleaned his tin. "Name's Dex. And you are?"

"Someone who shouldn't be here."

"You keep saying that, yet here you sit. What brought you in?"

"I was hoping to ask around about my missing friend," the man said. "But clearly I missed the crowd."

"Well, you found me," Dex replied. "I know most who enter those doors—once they bother to introduce themselves."

"Tobias," he said at last, offering a gloved hand.

Dex shook it without hesitation, "If it weren't cold outside, I'd have guessed you for a Tangent in gloves like those. We don't get many in here."

"Lucky for me, it's February," Tobias replied cheekily, hoping it was enough to stifle any further questioning. He tightened the garment around his neck again. "They're saying snow. It's got me chilled to the bone."

"Another shot'll warm you up."

"Thanks, but I'll pass," Tobias replied with a smile.

"Something else then... something that won't choke you."

Tobias reached under his scarf and rubbed his neck instinctively. Dex didn't know choking the way he did.

He should have left already. No one here but the bartender. Charming as Dex was, Tobias doubted he knew anything about Charlotte's disappearance— that was the only reason he'd come. But still he stayed, something holding him tighter than his excuses to leave.

Three more patrons slipped in, and before the door even shut, Dex had three glasses filled with ice and waiting.

"About time you made it," Dex called across the room. "The usual?"

"Yup," the oldest answered. "A round."

Dex poured without pause, three drinks exact, Tobias watching. Given that he recalled the three drinks without missing a beat, maybe he was wrong about him. Maybe Dex knew more than he let on—or maybe the men were just that regular.

"One for you, Tobias?" Dex smiled, the same look he'd given him when he first sat down.

"Sure. Bartender's choice... just no tequila."

"I think I know just the thing," Dex said, chuckling. A few shakes later, a cocktail slid across to Tobias.

Tobias stared, disbelief flickering. A Brown Derby. Charlotte's drink. "I don't understand... how did you know?"

"Know..?"

"Charlie's drink."

"Charlie?" Dex swallowed hard. Hearing that name, even after all this time, jarred him.

"Charlotte," Tobias clarified. "I was the only one she let call her Charlie."

"Strange as it sounds... I lost someone named Charlie, too," Dex said, the words weighted with real grief.

Tobias winced inwardly—he'd said too much again. But maybe destiny had landed him in this very spot for a reason. "Well... you don't know everyone who ventures into your bar then... she was a regular. That's why I came."

"Ah, yes... the patron I know," Dex elaborated, "but the name I never caught."

"Why this drink?" Tobias asked, confusion shaking him as hard as the cocktail had. His eyes narrowed as he peeled off his gloves and sank into thought...

Was Dex a Tangent? Did he tether without touch? Only one way to know—though dangerous. If he touched him, the feed would go straight to the Order. They'd know he'd found an unregistered Tangent. Maybe they'd reward him. Maybe they'd tell him where Charlotte was. Or maybe he should wait— see what Dex knew—before alerting anyone and losing the chance forever.

"It's a popular drink here," Dex lied smoothly, interrupting Tobias' thoughts. The truth was, he'd picked up on Tobias thinking about the drink and decided to make it. "Figured you might be a bourbon man—that's all, nothing more."

Tobias took a large drink from his cocktail and a deep breath. "Tell me about her—the woman who ordered this drink? She frequented here often. Did she come here with anyone else?"

"Listen, Tobias..." Dex glanced around, checking the other three patrons. Satisfied they weren't eavesdropping, he continued. "Brown Derby—that's all I ever knew her by—hasn't been in here for months. When she was here, it was always solo."

Tobias chuckle despite himself. "You called her Brown Derby? Sounds like something a racist asshole would say."

"It wasn't like that," Dex recovered quickly. "It was her drink. More of a shorthand—verifying her order. That's all I ever knew of her. She kept her head down and stayed silent. The last time she came in, she wore gloves—kept them on the whole time. Winter or not, it stuck with me."

Tobias caught Dex's glance at his bare hands. "Yeah, too warm for gloves once you're inside."

"She's a Tangent, isn't she?"

Dex's bluntness caught Tobias off guard. He bought time with another sip.

"Are you friend or foe?" Dex asked flatly, wondering if Tobias was Order, hunting her because of the Chaos leaflets. He shook another Brown Derby and strained its contents into Tobias' glass. Perhaps she was in trouble.

"Charlotte was—is—my best friend," Tobias said. "She saved me once, during a dark time in my life—right after the Last Gleaming."

Dex re-cleaned his tin while he listened in silence.

"It was all just too much... the war, the cruelty, the apathy, even before the Order..." Tobias leaned closer, lifted his scarf, revealed the scar. "I tried to end it. I no longer wanted to live in what the world had become. Charlotte saved me. She was my anchor, my reason to keep breathing. And now she's gone."

Dex's eyes lingered on the scar, recognition flickering—like he knew the weight of that edge. Tobias didn't need to tether to feel it: Dex had stood there too.

“When I lost Charlie,” Dex began, “I tried to end it, too. Charlotte may have been your anchor, but Charlie was my angel. I still don’t understand how, but the moment I was going to pull the trigger, he reached across the ether and my phone started blaring with our song.”

Perhaps it was the shared trauma of wanting to end it, but Tobias felt Dex was trustworthy. “Charlotte liked coming here because the guys didn’t hit on her—a Tangent, as you guessed. The Order says that she was reassigned to a covert program beyond the Curtain, but I have my suspicions of something more nefarious.”

“Did Charlotte say she was in trouble before she went missing?”

“No. But I looked up the program, and it doesn’t exist.”

“That would be the covert part, wouldn’t it? I doubt they would keep it on any sort of record if they were trying to hide it.”

“You don’t understand,” Tobias said, “I work at HALCION as a Facilities Support Technician.”

“Fancy title for a maintenance worker?”

“You joke, but my keys get me into a lot of restricted areas without being suspected,” Tobias explained. “And trust me—there’s no Project Resonance.”

Dex remembered the leaflet under his till, grabbed it, and handed it to Tobias. “The last time she was here she left a stack of these—I threw away all but this one.”

Tobias stared at the leaflet. He wasn't paying attention when Dex reached for his empty glass—his ungloved hand resting to the side of it—and the back of Dex's hand brushed against his knuckles.

He regretted taking his gloves off the moment their skin touched, not just because the flood of information from Dex was intense, but because he realized in that initial contact that Dex, too, was a Tangent. And unregistered. His neurosync reporting would reveal the unauthorized tether, so if he didn't pre-emptively report the discovery, he'd face harsher punishment.

"I have to go," Tobias announced as he stood, pulled some money from his pocket, grabbed the leaflet, and—just before turning toward the door—announced, "I'm so sorry, Dex. If you see Charlie, can you tell her that Tobias was looking for her."

21
HALCION

THE SKY OVER Midtown Atlanta sagged beneath the winter drizzle, the afternoon sun choked by dull, gray clouds that promised only precipitation and no silver linings.

HALCION—Headquarters of Administrative Leadership Command and Intelligence of Ordo Novus—loomed where Georgia Tech and WarnerDiscovery once stood, the rebranded buildings—stripped of warmth—now cold and sterile. What had once been complexes of innovation and media had become the brainstem of the Order's southeastern command.

Since the Last Gleaming—the night the bombs fell—the Order metastasized like a virus. Technocrat funding, quietly siphoned from the remaining corporate elite, fueled HALCION's evolution into a multi-tiered operations center: military-grade communications hub, advanced broadcasting capabilities, AI-driven facial recognition surveillance, biotech research, and tether analytics all housed in one sprawling, fortified complex.

Tobias Sloane adjusted the collar of his black-and-silver uniform, the Order's insignia stitched over his chest. It still felt wrong, wearing the mark of the very system that had swallowed his city whole—but since the siege, compliance was currency. And Tobias was nearly broke.

He scanned his badge at the outer gate. The retinal scanner blinked once, then clicked him through.

Inside, the campus was unrecognizable. New scaffolds stretched skyward at angles too precise for architectural chance. Overhead, drone swarms buzzed like bees protecting a hive. What remained of the Tech Green was now a paved security checkpoint the size of stadium. The past, Tobias thought, had been erased.

IN ORDINE, PAX.

His eyes read the inscription etched into steel above the entry arch, but he whispered the translation to himself, "In Order, Peace."

Sector C—formerly the VanLeer Building—had been repurposed into the GEIST Integration Center. Tobias stepped into the atrium, the air dense with the hum of server cores and the sharp tang of sterilized circuitry. He moved through the corridor like a ghost of the old world, though his ID badge insisted otherwise. He was here on a mission, even if unofficial. He needed access. He needed Charlie.

Charlotte Moss, a Tangent like Tobias, had been missing for two months. One day she was here, wiped from record the next. Tobias had trawled the backend archives, probed blackout folders, even risked pinging colleagues who responded with nothing but sidelong glances and silence. All he managed to uncover was a thin, damning note: pulled into questioning for an unauthorized tether.

He knew the night they meant. They had been off duty, cutting across Peachtree when they spotted the girl standing on the ledge of a midrise balcony, arms slack, eyes empty. Protocol dictated they walk away, call it in, let the numb and the broken vanish like so many others. Tobias had whispered *don't,* had even reached for her arm, but Charlotte stepped forward anyway. She touched the girl's hand, let her tether flare open, and poured raw, reckless joy into the void—bright bursts of laughter, warmth, the electric rush of being alive. The girl's body jolted like a wire catching current. Tears spilled. Her knees buckled.

Together they coaxed her down, carried her through the cold air, and brought her to the emergency ward until the staff took her. Tobias still remembered the way Charlotte's grin cut through the fluorescent wash of the hospital lights, defiant even as the system closed in around them.

"Worth it," she told Tobias when he warned her it was unauthorized. To the Order, a life meant nothing; as long as the city stayed docile and the money kept flowing, the broken, the desperate, and the dying were expendable. But the girl—and Tobias—weren't the only ones Charlotte had rescued, and no protocol would ever stop her from saving the next.

Tobias met with Dr. Regina Roth, Lead Neuro-Infrastructure Architect, in the GEIST central lab. Tall, ash-gray hair pulled back so tightly it made her face look carved from bone.

"You're late," she said without turning.

"Security is tighter. Ever since the Meridian Break."

She glanced back. "Everything changed after that."

"Did you see it?" Tobias offered. "Potential unregistered Tangent—Dex Truitt. No entry in standard logs. Facial match with archived public records."

Regina's thin lips twitched in interest. "Who authorized the field detection?"

"I was off shift—noticed him at a bar," Tobias explained. He hated turning Dex over to the Order, but he had to protect himself or risk being disappeared like Charlotte. "There was slippage in his response. Emotional feedback didn't align with normal Serexin behavior."

She stared at Tobias long enough to make him sweat. Then: "You'll testify to this?"

He nodded. "In exchange for info about Charlotte."

His temerity deepened her glare—sharp, bloodless. "Everyone wants something these days, but I've already told you that Charlotte was reassigned."

Tobias leaned forward, refusing to let it drop. "Reassigned where? Which division? If she's still in play, I want to be posted with her. We worked well together. You know that."

Regina's lips barely moved, but the temperature in her tone dropped. "Requests aren't yours to make, Sloane."

He pressed on, voice rising before he could temper it. "She's not just another Tangent. She saved lives—she saved *mine.* If she's out there, I deserve to know where. If she's not, then I deserve to know that, too."

Her hand flattened on the desk, a gesture quiet but final. "What you deserve," she said evenly, "is continued placement in this program. And that placement depends on restraint, not sentiment."

Something in him snapped. He drew back, shaking his head. "Then forget my testimony. If you won't give me answers, I'm not giving you anything."

Her eyes narrowed, a flicker of amusement curling at the corner of her mouth. "Testimony?" She leaned in slightly, voice silk over steel. "We don't need your words, Tobias. Your GEIST port uploaded every second of the tether. The data is already ours."

Tobias felt the weight of the implant beneath his skin, heavy as a shackle.

Regina straightened, already reaching for the next file. "Your cooperation is optional. Your compliance is not."

Tobias held her gaze, throat tight, but she'd already shifted her attention. Her dismissal wasn't spoken, but it was absolute.

"Close the door on your way out."

The door clicked shut behind him, and for a moment Tobias just stood in the hallway, fists clenched at his sides. The air smelled recycled, manufactured, processed, suffocating.

He replayed Regina's words in his head, every syllable sharpened by that thin smile. *Your GEIST port uploaded every second… your cooperation is optional.* It was a leash, welded under his skin, feeding them everything the instant he tethered. He'd thought he had choices left—testify, refuse, bargain—but there were no choices. Only illusions.

Every step down the corridor echoed too loud, like the building itself was listening. He wanted to rip the port out, smash it against the wall, run until he was far beyond the Curtain. But he didn't. He walked on, head down, fury caged tight in his chest.

Because in this place, anger was just another thing they'd measure, record, and use against him.

Emerald City was never truly quiet. Even on its slowest nights, the air thrummed with the ghosts of basslines past and the slick scent of sweat, leather, bourbon, and tequila—the two spirits seemed permanently soaked into the wood and walls.

But tonight, it felt hollow. Echoing. Like a stage set no one bothered to strike after the actors left.

Dex wiped down the bar with slow, meditative strokes, dragging a rag across the lacquered wood in a tired rhythm. It was barely midnight, but the crowd had already thinned to a sad scattering—two regulars nursing watery vodkas, a pair of fresh-faced newbies too nervous to flirt, and a drag queen still in full make-up flicking aimlessly at the phone screen in their hand.

The drinks weren't flowing like they should've been. Thursdays were usually decent—a soft prelude to the weekend. But this week, the city felt choked. Like it was holding its breath. Even the regulars had their heads on swivels.

Dex blamed it on the broadcasts. The so-called mandates. The ever-growing sense that freedom was becoming more of a rumor than a right.

What made it even more absurd was the fact that bars like Emerald City were still allowed to operate. Technically, they were among the last legally sanctioned gathering spots, thanks to the exorbitant taxes levied on alcohol sales. Booze had become a quiet benefactor of the Order's machine, funding their surveillance tech and stability ops one overpriced cocktail at a time.

"Sanctioned sin," Dex muttered to himself as he unloaded and reshelved rocks glasses. "Praise the fucking state."

He clocked the movement before he fully registered it—three figures slipping in from the back corner entrance. Not regulars. Not even close.

They moved like shadows, scanning the room with surgical detachment. Dex pegged them immediately—not for what they were, but for what they weren't. No drinks ordered. No casual glance at the drag show flyer. No pretense of fun. They took a booth near the back and sat in silence, but their eyes—especially the one on the left—kept drifting to the bar.

To him.

Dex kept working, but he adjusted his stance subtly, angling so the mirror behind the bar gave him a better view. They weren't cops. At least, not in any official way. But they had that posture—controlled stillness that reeked of training.

He made it a point not to look directly at them.

A fourth man joined them briefly. Whispered something, nodded toward Dex, causing the one on the left to smile. They left at last call. No drinks. No interaction. Just players taking their exits, stage left.

The silence that followed felt even heavier than before.

By half-past one, the place was cleared out. Dex kicked the doors shut and locked them behind the last lingering patron, then killed the house lights, letting the neon of the 'Emerald City' sign outside spill green and gold shadows across the floor.

He poured himself a double shot of bourbon, slumped against the back bar, and let the burn of the first swig carve its way down.

"Wouldn't believe the kind of day I had, Charlie," he said into the dark, the words punching the quiet like a fist.

Charlie wasn't here. Hadn't been. Not since Dex held him during his dying breath and watched the light fade from his eyes. But memory is a tenacious bastard, and sometimes Dex found solace in an uninterrupted soliloquy. And tonight, when one of the bar's first customers had casually voiced *Charlie*—unrelated to his Charlie but felt like a kick in the mouth just the same—it had taken everything in Dex not to break down into tears.

"Should've known better than to think I could keep going," he muttered, downing the rest of the glass. "This whole act—slinging drinks, pretending I'm not looking over my shoulder every second, trying to forget that none of it makes sense anymore."

The tears came fast. Hot. Uninvited. But he welcomed the catharsis once they started flowing. He slid to the floor, back against the cooler, and let the sobs claw their way out. No one to hear him. No one to judge. Just the crippling weight of grief pressing him down against the sticky floor mat like gravity gone rabid.

He missed Charlie. Not just the man, but the *might-have-beens*—the taste of something real that flared up like lightning and vanished just as quickly. Their time had been short. Fragile. But God, it had felt true.

And now it was all thunder and echo—and apparently rain—without the flashes to light the darkness.

He finally dragged himself up, wiped his eyes on the hem of his shirt, and poured one more shot for the road.

As he stepped out the back door into the cold night, any icy breeze brushed his neck. He didn't even hear the footsteps over the wintry whistle of the wind, just the sharp sting of cloth against his nose and mouth, soaked with the acrid bite of chemicals.

Just before the lights faded and darkness swallowed him whole, a low voice whispered, "Got you."

22
HAVOC

THE FIRST THING Dex noticed was the light—too bright, too clean—pressing against his eyelids before he even opened them. When he finally did, the glare cut like glass. White walls. White ceiling. A steady mechanical hum vibrating through the floor.

He tried to move. His wrists clinked against metal—cold cuffs anchoring him to the chair. His ankles too. He tested the restraints twice, but there was no give.

Memory bled back in fragments—the bourbon, the back door, the cloth that stole his breath and scorched his throat, and the voice before everything went black: *Got you.*

The door hissed open.

The edges of a woman began to shift into focus—two dark curls framed her pale face, but the rest of her hair was pulled tight, amplifying the intensity of her verdant stare.

"You are at HALCION, Mr. Truitt, the Order's Atlanta and Southeastern Headquarters."

"And why am I here?"

"You were flagged earlier this evening as an unregistered Tangent." Her voice was cold, unemotional. "You were apprehended to stand trial against said accusation—unless you admit to the charge now."

"Admit to being a Tangent?" Dex asked nervously. "And if I do… what then?"

"You will be registered and processed, sent to a holding cell for the night," she answered. "In the morning, you'll undergo surgery for our latest GEIST port implant. Afterward, your memories will be scrubbed for intel, and you'll be placed into one of our programs."

"And if I deny it?"

"Then the trial proceeds," she said evenly. "And when you're found guilty, we continue as scheduled—cell, surgery, and so on."

"And I get no say in the matter?" Dex blurted. "I didn't realize that being Tangent was now a crime."

"Only being an unregistered one," she snapped back without much pause.

"And who are you… exactly?"

"How rude of me," she said with a mock-earnest smile, her tone still laced with condescension. "I am Dr. Regina Roth, one of the lead architects of the GEIST program."

Dex gave a thin, uncomfortable smile.

"I would encourage you to skip the formality of a trial, Mr. Truitt," Regina said smoothly. "It only postpones the inevitable—we already have proof of your Tangent abilities, recorded by another Tangent."

Tobias, Dex thought immediately. He'd felt the telltale pull when their hands had brushed, the memory of Tobias' attempt to fly flashing briefly. *Was it all a setup?*

"Don't blame Tobias," Regina added, as if reading his mind. "He had to report the unregistered tether. Protocol."

"Once Tangents are implanted with this port… they're at your beck and call? No privacy of their own, everything recorded?"

"Not everything," Regina replied. "Only the tethers."

"You say that like we can actually control when a tether happens."

"We?" Regina's mouth curled into a thin smile. "Sounds like a confession?"

"A confession never truly mattered, according to your evidence," Dex met her stare head-on. "So go ahead—escort me to my cell now."

Regina gestured, and a guard uncuffed Dex from the chair and re-secured his wrists before leading them down a secured corridor. She spoke lightly, almost conversationally: "The port's not so bad, Dex. Most forget it's even there—unless we connect it for a download session."

"Download session?"

"Each tether is recorded automatically," Regina explained. "The data is uploaded to HALCION's servers. The old models glitched occasionally, the newer ones less so; when that happens, the port lets us pull the session data directly."

"How did you figure all of this out?" Dex asked. "How did you even know where to begin?"

"You know what Plato said about necessity…" Regina's voice trailed, leaving the quote unfinished. "When the Serexin trials began, the first team was blindsided by the anomalies. They didn't know the cause, nor how to handle the outliers.

"I wasn't with the Order then, during the trials," she lied smoothly, Dex none the wiser. "What they did to the first anomalies was revolting. An embarrassment to the creed they claim to uphold."

Dex let out a sharp, bitter laugh. "Creed? The Order is a cult with, at worst, Nazi and nationalist roots and, at best, ties of Evangelical corruption. They're not bound by faith—only by their fear. Fear of wokeness. Fear of empathy. Fear of compassion."

Regina said nothing. Only their footsteps echoed off the corridor walls. Finally, she stopped, forcing Dex and the guard to a halt. She turned, her tone quieter, measured. "Not all of the Order is bad, Dex."

Whatever warmth she'd shown before vanished, her tone now as icy as the winter air outside. Dex didn't like her, and his patience dissolved just as quickly as her warmth.

"Save your misguided dogma," he barked. "You've got my hands in chains, but you'll never shackle my mind or heart to your twisted sense of purpose. How dare you defend terrorism while whitewashing history in the name of patriotism—false patriotism."

Regina started to reply, but Dex cut her off, his voice rising, sharp with fury. "The Order didn't do this out of love for America—it was because the Order loathed that America had become the melting pot we once embraced with pride. Having the audacity to speak hate and call it free speech, but that does not make you brave—or powerful. It makes you weak. People afraid of strangers, afraid of difference, of change, of progress, of letting love rule instead of fear—those people are (and always will be) cowards. The Order may have murdered the president and gutted the government, but his twisted ideology, hate, and corruption still surge through every vein of your organization."

"Yes, there are less-than-honorable members in the Order," Regina said, seizing a chance to speak, "but we're not all the same."

"A table with even one Nazi is a table full of Nazis," Dex shot back. "Sit in silence, and you share the guilt. If you won't speak against injustice, you're just as guilty for what follows."

"My, my..." Regina cut in, her tone scolding, dripping with condescension. "For a lowly, stupid bartender, you certainly have a lot to say about things you don't understand."

A low, feral growl rose in Dex's chest before he even knew it was there. In a sudden blur of motion, he snapped his cuffed hands upward with startling force, the edge of it cracking against the guard's temple, dropping him hard into the wall before he crumpled, unconscious, to the floor.

Before Regina could even draw a breath, Dex lunged forward. She gasped as he drove her back into the corridor wall. The chain of the cuffs pressed against her throat—not crushing, but biting just enough to choke her breath and force silence.

She clawed at his wrists on instinct, but Dex didn't flinch.

"Don't you fucking dare reduce me to a bartender," Dex snarled, his voice a low rasp just inches from her face. "You don't know *shit* about who I am."

Her eyes flared, but she didn't speak.

"I returned to bartending after the Order dug its claws into Atlanta—because the *work* was mindless—not *me*. Before that, I was a cop. Then an EMT. I'm neither a doctor nor a neurotech architect like you, but I am *far* from stupid! I've got a bachelor's in criminology and a master's in psychology. I joined the force to *serve and protect*, like the goddamn oath demanded. I believed in it. Believed I could change it from the inside."

He leaned closer, breath hot against her cheek. "Then Charlie died in my arms. My partner on the force, my lover off the clock."

A muscle twitched in Regina's jaw.

"Shot by one of your jackbooted militia thugs at a fucking checkpoint in a wall nobody asked for or wanted. I watched him bleed out, begging me not to let go. He died choking on his own blood—a moment I still see when I close my eyes."

Dex's voice cracked—not weakness, just history breaking through.

"I never even turned in my badge. I walked away—not because I stopped caring, but because once the Order had its claws in the APD, I knew I couldn't change it from the inside. Hell, I couldn't even save the man I loved... and I *had* to find some way to make that right. I became an EMT instead. Pulled overdose victims out of alleys. Patched up kids caught in the crossfire. Made peace with the blood—because at least it wasn't *his*."

Her eyes flicked toward the unconscious guard, but Dex tightened the cuffs enough to snap her gaze back to him.

"So no, Regina, don't *ever* mistake what I *do* for who I *am*. I've built strength in a world that branded me its enemy just for who I love. My whole life I've been underestimated, beaten, spat on, treated like a threat for the crime of *existing*. And every time, I came back stronger."

He exhaled hard, words spilling through clenched teeth. "The next time you look at me like I'm beneath you, remember this: I've been forged in fires hotter than anything your Order's ever lit."

Dex held tense, bristling, silent—but unable to ease the pressure on Regina's throat. And that's when the tether snapped open—uninvited, unwelcome, and undeniable. He didn't know why it'd taken so long.

It hit him like a riptide, dragging him under with no escape.

He saw a child—Regina, maybe six or seven— watching helplessly as her mother was dragged out of a house by a man, maybe her father. Regina screamed for him to stop before a backhand sent her sprawling. He saw Regina, pregnant, then a flood of rushing water and mud. Then flashes: a bunker.

Indoctrination marked as survival. Fear curdled into belief. Belief hardened into loyalty. And somewhere in it, the hollow space where empathy had been amputated was filled with doctrine and darkness.

She wasn't evil. She was empty.

And Dex could feel it—her craving to matter to a purpose greater than herself, even if that purpose had poisoned her from within.

He released her suddenly, stepping back. A baton came down hard across the side of his skull. His body seized, staggered.

The world fractured.

He crumpled to his knees, the corridor spinning, the cold tile rushing up to meet him. Darkness claimed him before he could brace for the fall.

Regina, breathless and red-throated, just stood there.

Except—she *stared* at him. Not with contempt now, but confusion, her expression twitching like a malfunction.

She had felt it.

More than that—*she had received something.*

Unwittingly, Dex had passed his pain to her. A flash flood of memory—hot, raw, soaked in trauma and grief. She saw him as a child in the schoolyard, surrounded by boys taking turns punching him until he fell, the blows turning into kicks. She felt his bruises and broken bones, tasted the blood as it seeped past swollen lips onto his tongue.

Then it jumped to Charlie's final gasps—the helpless rage, the stab of pain in the chest, the broken heart and failing breath as Dex realized Charlie had taken his last.

Regina's chest heaved once. Then again. She looked like she might vomit—or cry—but did neither. But for the first time, she had *felt* the true cost of what her allegiance demanded.

Not abstract. Not in theory. But through him.

And it shattered something in her that she hadn't realized was intact.

23

HAUNTED

WHEN MALIK RENSHAW was recruited by Isabella Merrick, he had been the top of his class at MIT; that's what initially got her attention, but it was Malik's hacker notoriety that held it. She'd needed someone willing to take the paths others wouldn't. She'd also needed someone who knew how to find out information when normal routes proved ineffective.

When he spliced HALCION's security feed to his private server, it was out of protection. Not for his, but for hers; she'd whispered that she felt watched and followed, both inside and outside the complex.

Unfortunately, for Isabella, the feed showed nothing to corroborate her suspicions—at least not within HALCION—and a few months after asking for Malik's eyes and help, she died.

They called it an accident, of course, but he never doubted it was an inside job. A malfunction in one of the service elevators—faulty brakes, the engineers claimed. The internal investigation produced the usual, carefully-crafted reports— vague apologies, meaningless accountability. HALCION sent her husband flowers and a settlement.

But Malik knew.

Isabella wasn't clumsy. She wasn't reckless. She'd been smart—*too* smart—and far too cautious to be claimed by something as mundane as an elevator failure since she almost always took the stairs. She'd gotten close to something. Close enough to see it, but not enough to name it—or finish it.

And now she was dead.

From that moment on, Malik became obsessed. He rotated the feeds daily, scanning for patterns. Watched who entered and exited the executive levels. Studied the guards' shifts. Tracked inconsistencies in faces, body language, the energy in the room.

What began as a gesture of loyalty hardened into liturgy. A ritual of watching those that watched—*they just didn't know it yet.*

Malik was sipping lukewarm tea when Dex Truitt appeared on-screen—flanked by Regina and a guard, eyes squinting under the fluorescents, bottom lip split open like he'd just come from a prize fight.

Malik's mug froze halfway to his lips.

There was something about the way Dex moved— deliberate, grounded. Even cuffed, even surrounded, he walked unafraid.

Goddamn, Malik thought at first, *he's beautiful.* And then... *Wait, what?*

Malik leaned forward, brow furrowing as Dex went head-to-head with Regina.

There was no fear in his eyes. Only anger. Maybe something deeper. Something older.

When Dex slammed the guard against the wall, Malik's eyes widened. The suddenness of the motion. The raw force. But that wasn't what caught him most.

What pinned Malik in place—what made the hairs on his neck rise—was the speech that followed.

The rage. The conviction.

Dex spoke like a man with nothing left to lose and everything left to say. Like he hadn't just discovered who he was but had *fought* for it. *Earned* it. Like he might survive this place—if it didn't swallow him first.

"Where the fuck did you come from, Truitt?" Malik whispered, half-enamored.

He clicked back through the feed, flagged the timestamp, and scanned the drive for Dex's intake file. *Unregistered Tangent. Former cop. EMT. Bartender.*

Malik's fingers hovered over the keyboard, his mind already pulling pieces together—something not fully formed yet, but urgent and alive.

Dex wasn't just another detainee. He was an anomaly among anomalies. Maybe even a disruption.

And Malik had learned to pay attention to disruptions. Sometimes they were dangerous. But sometimes—*just sometimes*—they were exactly what the system needed.

He stood and crossed to the far wall, unlocking a narrow drawer hidden beneath the molding. Inside lay a matte-black journal. He opened to a blank page, then scribbled words in tight, slanted ink:

Ghost in the machine. Beneath it, a question: *What if he was the kind of anomaly Isabella was seeking?*

He tapped the pen twice against the paper, a small smirk tugging at the edge of his mouth.

The Order, he wrote, *just detained their own destruction.*

But that part would come later. For now, he rewound the feed over and over, each time freezing the frame on Dex's face—cuffed, defiant, unbroken—an expression Malik hadn't seen in a long time.

The holding cell's blue-tinted light hummed, underscored by the mechanical buzz of perpetual surveillance. Dex stirred on the uncomfortable cot, pain and disorientation blooming behind his eyes like slow thunder—a reminder of the baton's brutal kiss. His wrists throbbed where the restraints had bitten skin, and his throat was so dry enough it felt ready to splinter.

The door hissed open: Regina.

She stepped inside carrying a tray—water and something that might pass for broth. Her eyes were rimmed red, and her tone held a brittle edge, as if trying not to appear shaken.

"You're awake," she said, her tone like tempered steel.

Dex blinked against the light. "And still cuffed. How hospitable."

She ignored the barb, setting the tray down on a recessed ledge near the cot. "You cracked Collins' orbital bone. He'll live, but he won't forget *you* anytime soon."

Dex gave a bitter, lopsided grin. "Send him my regards."

She lingered a spell too long before finally exhaling. "They've scheduled your implant surgery."

His brow furrowed. "Already?"

"You're slated for integration by morning. Full GEIST sync within twelve hours."

He sat up slowly, his body sore but not broken. "And you're telling me this out of... courtesy?"

"I'm telling you because you deserve to know." She hesitated. "Whether you believe it or not, I don't enjoy seeing pain."

Dex let his silence be answer enough.

Dex's ass felt like ice against the frigid surgical table, his thin gown doing little to keep the cold from his exposed backside. At least they'd managed to secure him one. The operating chamber wasn't sterile in the conventional sense. This wasn't a hospital—it was a repurposed lab, buried deep in the bowels of HALCION. Everything was dim-lit steel and backlit instruments, the overhead lights muted to keep the patient calm. He was already half-sedated, muscles slack, breath slow but steady.

Malik stood over him, masked in surgical white layered with tactical gray. The mask hid the lower half of his face, but his eyes—dark, deliberate, sharp—tracked Dex's vitals with clinical precision. He tapped the console near Dex's head. "Vitals are steady. Neural conductivity shows minimal lag."

"Put him under now?" asked an unseen voice.

"Yes but have him to turn over first—it'll be much easier with his help," Malik replied.

Without prompting, Dex turned himself over, the split at the back of the gown revealing everything.

Malik paused—just a moment—long enough to take in the ink winding across Dex's right shoulder blade, the faint tan lines at the small of his back, the trail of fur crowning an even furrier ass—perfect, rounded, and firm—sculpted by sweat, strength, and intention.

"Mr. Truitt, I've just injected your IV with propofol," a technician said. "Can you count backwards from one hundred for me?"

Dex was out by the time he'd reached ninety-three.

Malik supervised as his team made a clean lateral incision at the base of Dex's neck, exposing the interspace between the C3 and C4 vertebrae. With micro-forceps and dermal retractors, they carefully parted the semispinalis capitis and underlying fascia, revealing the cervical spine with deliberate precision. A cauterizing sheath minimized capillary seepage, leaving the field dry and unmarred.

Once the vertebral landmarks were fully exposed, the surgeon guided the GEIST port into place—a matte-black hub no larger than a thumbprint, laced with bio-reactive alloys and neuromimetic filaments. The base seated flush against the bone, its microspikes anchoring into the cortical layer with a soft, audible *click*. Its filament array unfurled like a sea anemone, threading into the neural canal with autonomous accuracy, aligning with Dex's spinal relay points. As the implant synced, a shimmer of blue underlit the exposed tissue, bonding with the central nervous system without disrupting signal continuity.

"Full relay achieved," the tech confirmed, eyes on the diagnostic HUD.

"Begin closure," Malik ordered.

From a sterile tray, the tech retrieved a cartridge of the Order's proprietary cyberskin, a semi-translucent membrane suspended in temperature-controlled biogel, and handed it to the surgeon. They flexible graft was applied across the incision. On contact with Dex's dermis, it metamorphosed—shifting hue, temperature, and texture until it mimicked the surrounding skin seamlessly.

Capillary mapping initiated instantly, the graft pulsing faintly as it bonded at the cellular level. No sutures were needed. No scar would remain.

"Interface concealment?" Malik asked, voice low.

"Initiating now," the tech replied as a soft chime marked system sync.

As the cyberskin settled, its surface normalized, hiding all evidence of the port beneath. Only when a tether interface cord came near it would the port respond, activating a subdermal ripple and revealing its access point.

Until then, Dex's neck looked untouched.

Normal. Human.

But inside, the system was already listening.

Dex woke to a strange hum in his spine.

He blinked against the filtered light overhead, slow and disoriented. For a moment he stayed still, listening—to the room, to his own breath, to the eerie stillness inside.

And then he felt it. Not pain. Presence. He reached for his neck, fingers grazing the skin just below the occipital ridge.

GEIST, **G**lobal **E**xtraction Interface for **S**urveillance and Telemetry, was the Order's crowning achievement. A biotech neural interface, the GEIST port allowed full emotional and sensory tracking during a Tangent's tether session. What began as empathic research had become data-mined obedience.

It felt unnatural and unyielding—yet undeniably alive. His fingers circled it once, then again, tracing the subtle curve beneath the surface. No scar. No stitches. No heat. Only a humming awareness. The more he focused, the more he could feel it—not physically, but neurologically. A vibration at the edge of perception, like a second heartbeat buried deep in his spine. Not rhythmic, not organic, but patterned. Designed.

Dex sat up slowly, every vertebra seeming to respond. The movement tugged at something invisible, filaments woven into muscle and nerve. It didn't hurt, but it wasn't silent either.

There was also memory, but not his.

Regulation code. The edge of static that felt like language but wasn't. Blips of internal diagnostics whispered beneath his awareness—security phrases, sleep cycles, standby status. Like someone else's thoughts brushing against his own.

"This is how they enslave us," he muttered.

Dex rose from the cot, bare feet padding against the sterile tile. Every step pulled faintly at the interface, the subtle vibration responding to movement, to balance. He swore he could feel the port calibrating in real time.

A chime interrupted the moment. Soft. Musical. Wrong in context. Dex turned, startled. His phone. It sat on the stainless-steel tray across the room—screen lit, unlocked, and freshly loaded with an unfamiliar icon: a silver eye set against a black background.

A pop-up appeared: New Assignment Pending. Tap to Acknowledge.

He lifted the phone with reluctant fingers. It was still his—same worn case, same slight hairline crack across the top corner—but now it felt... compromised. New permissions had appeared. The SENSATE app was installed without his authorization.

He tried holding it down to delete it. Nothing happened.

Long press. Swipe. System settings. Nothing. It wasn't just an app—it was root-level, part of the operating system itself now. A command node with control privileges.

"Jesus," he whispered.

A second chime. This one sharper, more urgent.

Welcome, Tangent Truitt. You have been successfully integrated into the SENSATE system. Your compliance ensures continued autonomy and privilege. Tether assignments will dispatch directly through this interface. Refusal to acknowledge will be considered a breach of civic duty.

No **AGREE** and **DISAGREE** buttons.

Only: **ACKNOWLEDGE.**

Dex stared at the word. Tapping it meant surrender. But ignoring it could mean something worse.

He set the phone down, backing away as if it might burn him. His stomach churned. He crossed to the small wall mirror near the sink, leaned in close, and turned his head just enough to glimpse the base of his neck. Nothing. The skin was perfect. Flawless.

But he could *feel* it.

Beneath the façade, something was watching. Waiting.

Surveillance and surrender—his body and his phone. A closed loop.

He splashed water over his face, letting the cold shock him out of the spiral. The worst part wasn't the implant. Not even knowing that he'd been wired into the very system he despised. The worst part was the fractured voice whispering in the back of his mind: *Now you're useful again.*

Not aimless. Not adrift. Just... directed.

Exactly as they wanted.

He straightened slowly, watching his reflection steady in the glass. He thought of Charlie—of the blood, of the gunshot echo that still haunted the folds of his memory like a trapped ghost. He'd sworn to dismantle everything the Order stood for. To never be their tool. To fight from the margins, from the cracks.

And now he was a vessel.

His breath trembled with disgust—at himself, at them, at the world that let this become normal.

He turned back to the tray, to the blinking phone. The silver eye stared back.

He tapped the word: **ACKNOWLEDGE.**

The screen went dark, then lit again: Tether Assignment #1190 scheduled. Briefing will arrive at 0600.

The app closed itself, leaving Dex staring at the screen. No notifications. No alerts. No messages from others checking in. Nothing.

He felt utterly alone—doubly isolated within the imposed isolation of the Curtain.

"What am I going to do now, Charlie?" he asked his reflection. "How do I fight the machine now that they've turned me into one?"

February 19, 2027

"Shape without form, shade without color.
Paralyzed force, gesture without motion;
Those who have crossed
With direct eyes, to death's other Kingdom
Remember us—if at all—not as lost
Violent souls, but only
As the hollow men."

~ T.S. Elliott, *The Hollow Men*

24
HOLLOW

DEX WAS EXPECTING a sterile room—white walls, observation mirrors, maybe a gurney. Instead, the apartment door in front of him looked lifted from a realtor's brochure: matte wood finish, brushed-nickel handle, even a welcome mat in front of it that read *hello, sunshine* in lowercase, gray font.

Regina's voice buzzed in his earpiece.

"You'll be monitored the whole time. No spoken briefing first—we want a clean tether. You'll learn what you need to afterward."

Dex glanced up at the ceiling vent. Cameras. He could feel the heat of them already and hear the mechanical shift as they locked onto him.

The door opened with a soft click.

Inside it felt strange and painfully familiar. A two-bedroom apartment dressed in emotional taxidermy: family photos in frames on the wall, a throw draped over a worn sofa, the kind of lived-in clutter only time creates. But none of it was real—no dust, no scuff marks on the floor, no mismatched mugs or out-of-place papers. It was a perfect simulation, a curated echo of somebody's life.

In the center of it, behind the coffee table, stood a man so still he looked as if he hadn't moved in hours.

"Say his name," Regina's voice sounded in his earpiece.

"Gus Loring?" Dex asked.

The man nodded. Late forties, white shirt tucked into dark slacks. His skin was pale, thin, his face sunken, like a hand-carved wax skull, eyes as hollow as empty sockets. His aesthetic reminded Dex of the Catrin and Catrina collection his mom would set out for Día de Los Muertos.

Dex stepped inside; his chest tightened as the door sealed with a hiss.

"You ready?" he asked.

No answer—just the nod again.

Dex sat on the sofa; the cushions didn't give under him. A prop, like everything else. He steadied his breath, letting his posture settle as much as possible on the false pretenses.

The back of Dex's neck prickled as Gus slid into the seat beside him, as if anticipating the tether. Gus sat rigid—face slack, spine perfectly straight, hands folded in his lap like a man awaiting judgment.

Dex exhaled and opened the tether.

At first, there was nothing—no resistance, no emotion, no memory.

Just silence.

Dex waited. Training had taught him not all connections ignite immediately—some are sluggish, some shy, some buried beneath trauma like bedrock.

But this felt like a void.

He pressed gently into the tether—not forcing, merely inviting, like a hand reaching through fog.

Still nothing. No pulse of emotion. No flicker of recognition. It was like tethering to a photograph.

And then—just barely—something. The tether tightened like a taut string pulled across distance. Dex leaned closer.

A sliver. A flicker. A name.

Zoë.

He saw a girl—seven, maybe nine at most— auburn curls and a soft laugh. Chocolate frosting smudged her cheeks; a paper crown sat in her hands. She turned toward the window, light catching the freckles across her nose.

Then it was gone, wiped clean like a shaken Etch A Sketch.

Dex recoiled.

He steadied himself, then reached again— slower this time.

Fragments surfaced, not even full memories: a music box, a red backpack, hands held too tightly, the warmth of a porch swing in the sunlight.

All tied to her. All blurred.

Beneath them all lay one core emotion: Hope.

Not joy. Not longing. Not grief. Hope—sharpened to a blade's edge.

Dex pushed further.

Images blurred—not memories now, but extractions: rooms, wires, repetition. Dex saw Gus in stages—hooked to monitors, surrounded by technicians, sometimes slumped, sometimes screaming.

The Order tethered him repeatedly. Used him. Pulled at every thread in his psyche like a bloodless vivisection. They hadn't been searching for information; they were trying to erase it—erase him.

Dex saw the trials, the early Serexin injections, the clinical notations on cognitive response. They thought they had the perfect test case—someone with something to forget but refused. As Dex pulled at what remained, he realized Gus had once been one of theirs.

Gus had joined the Corazamine project at Emory as a junior researcher in its development, hoping to unlock empathy before the world tore itself apart. But then the rebellion began he learned of Project Last Gleaming—learned where the bombs would fall—one of the target cities was where half his family lived.

He'd changed his mind, wanted out after learning the truth. But when they kidnapped Zoë to force his compliance, he went on as ordered.

They told him she was dead. But they never let him go.

Dex felt the moment when Gus stopped fighting—not out of surrender, but necessity. His compliance turned mechanical. His cooperation, a mask.

But beneath the sedation, the tethering, the years of psychological excavation, one thing never moved.

Zoë.

The memory refused to be pulled.

Dex's hands trembled. His eyes stung. He blinked hard, but the image stayed: a man hollowed out by every hand that ever touched him, still clinging to the last thread of fatherhood. The tether peaked. The port pulsed. Dex could feel his own memories brushing Gus's now—not sharing, just observing. And then—

Cut. The tether ended abruptly.

Dex opened his eyes, breath hitching and chest heaving.

Across from him, Gus sat exactly as he had at the beginning. Unmoving. Empty. But now Dex saw the toll.

His eyes weren't blank. They were hollow, unguarded. Like a door that had been broken down so many times, it stopped bothering to lock.

Dex stood up slowly. "Thank you."

Gus didn't respond.

The lab was warm despite the oversaturation of cold, eerie light.

Dex sat in the observation chair, electrodes cuffed to his temples, wrists, and spine. His jaw stayed clenched; his muscles still buzzed with aftershock. The technician to his left clicked through the scan as if cataloguing groceries.

Regina stood by the monitor, arms crossed, lips pursed as data streamed in. Her annoyance that the port's failure to transmit the tether data to HALCION's cloud showed in her furrowed brow. "Why didn't the data transmit?"

"I'm not sure, ma'am," the tech replied. "But that's what the port is for—back-up. Everything is downloaded from the Tangent and filed."

"And the read out?"

"Nothing," the tech said. "Emotive signature reads flat. No primary memory imprints. No central trauma tied to familial anchors. Suggests we've finally neutralized the Zoë imprint."

Regina exhaled slowly, almost laughing. "Took long enough."

Dex said nothing. He looked at the floor. The port at the back of his neck still hummed—still warm.

"You did good, Truitt," she said, her voice softer than usual. "You helped end a very expensive... distraction."

He felt the words echo inside his chest. A very expensive distraction.

His mouth opened.

I saw her, he nearly said. *I saw the way she smiled. I saw the frosting on her cheeks. I saw the way he never stopped hoping.*

But he didn't say it. He only nodded coldly.

Regina turned back to the screen.

The download ended. The data was clean. No mention of Zoë. No trace of her in the session log.

She was invisible. Erased.

Except Dex knew different. He stood and walked out of the room without a word.

Just before the door closed, he caught a glimpse of a man in the corridor—arms crossed, eyes calm and familiar, though from where Dex couldn't remember.

Their eyes met.

The man's expression stayed still, but the faintest smile edged his lip. Not smug. Not mocking. Just there.

Knowing.

Dex looked away. The elevator carried him down in silence, steel walls reflecting fragments of his face: tired eyes, clenched jaw, a faint redness at the corner of one eye that hadn't been there before.

He rubbed at it, but it didn't go away.

The elevator finally deposited him onto his assigned level without ceremony. The hallway was empty—gray walls and motion-triggered lights buzzing softly overhead as he walked. Every door looked the same. Every step echoed too loud.

Everything in HALCION felt like too much, and he needed to get out.

Dex entered his apartment without thinking, let the lock seal behind him, and leaned back against the cold door. He didn't move for a long time.

He stared across the room at the television screen, black and cold since the last newscast; then at the half-folded blanket draped over the corner of the sofa, discarded there by Charlie after their post-breakfast cuddle; then to the kitchen, unused since it had last smelled of bacon and blueberry pancakes.

He pushed off the door, walked to the bathroom, ran the sink, and splashed his face. His reflection looked tired—not just from the tether, but from everything.

The tether had left a residue in him. Not memory. Not energy. Just... vacancy. Gus' emptiness had seeped into his bones like cold through concrete. And it felt familiar.

Too familiar.

He didn't realize he was still gripping the edge of the sink until his knuckles whitened. The first time he'd felt like this—truly hollow—was the night Charlie died.

The checkpoint. The confusion. The shooting. The muzzle flash. The way Charlie slipped away so quickly Dex couldn't even process it for fear of slowing, of not making it to the hospital in time.

He had been holding Charlie's wound, applying pressure, whispering reassurances he didn't believe.

Dex hadn't cried that night after leaving the hospital. Not in the Jeep. Not even in the empty house where he'd gone afterward, where he laid on the floor with the blood still on his hands.

He had shut down. The grief hadn't come in waves. It had come in a vacuum—one day he woke up and there was nothing inside him. Not pain. Not rage. Just the absence of Charlie's laugh and his scent in the sheets—absence that howled like wind through a broken pane.

The only thing that kept him tethered to reality was the memory of someone else lingering in the back of mind with a flame of hope.

David.

The last time Dex saw David was the night the bombs burst. He'd left the lake house early, needing to get back to get to his mother. He'd kissed Dex in the kitchen, hard and certain, and said, "I'll text when I get in."

The text never came, but that wasn't David's fault. Dex had mistyped the number he'd given without time to confirm it before David was gone.

Just failed messages and silence.

A different kind of hollow. Different than Charlie's death. Charlie had *ended* in Dex's arms. David had *vanished* from them.

Even now, there were nights, when Dex dreamed of a knock at the door. He'd open it, and David would be standing there—dirty, tired. His voice would crack when he said, "I thought you were dead."

Those dreams weren't comfort. They were torture. But he clung to them anyway.

Because somewhere deep in the same place where Gus kept Zoë—buried beneath layers of grief, and logic, and survival—Dex, too, had stored a seed of hope.

It was the only thing that had survived the bombs.

And now he wasn't sure if that hope was a strength... or just another cruelty the world hadn't stolen yet.

He left the bathroom and moved back to the kitchen. His phone sat on the counter, screen black. He tapped it.

The SENSATE app blinked to life: Session Complete. Data Received. No Anomalies Detected.

Dex stared at the message. No anomalies.

He laughed under his breath. Bitter. Quiet.

Zoë had been an anomaly. Love was an anomaly. And yet the machine read clean. It didn't matter that he'd seen her—that Gus's entire being had coiled around the memory of her like roots in frozen soil.

The GEIST port hadn't picked it up. Or worse— it had and filtered it out.

He wondered, briefly, if that would happen to him one day. If someone tried to tether with *him* and found nothing but a blank wall and an empty room, would they call it progress? Would they call it peace?

Dex pressed his fingers to the back of his neck.

Still warm. Still listening.

Later, he lay in bed, staring at the ceiling. His thoughts drifted—not by choice, but by inertia.

He thought about Gus sitting alone in that apartment replica, day after day, waiting for a daughter who might not even be alive. A man imprisoned inside his own memories, clinging to the one thread that kept him human.

And Dex realized he wasn't any different.

Both survivors in cages made to feel like homes. Both still holding onto ghosts.

And yet... Dex didn't want to forget. Not Charlie. Not David. Not even the pain. Because pain was proof.

Proof that they were real. That they mattered. That once, he had loved hard enough to leave a hollow behind.

He rolled onto his side and closed his eyes. And in the darkness, he saw her again.

Zoë.

Smiling. Turning toward the window. And this time, behind her, a familiar silhouette started to manifest.

Not Gus. Not even real. But standing in the soft light of that memory was David.

Just far enough away to make Dex sit up, breath caught. But when he opened his eyes, the room was still and empty. The only sound was the faint, steady hum of the port beneath his skin.

Still whirring. Still waiting.

Part VII
PERDITION

February 20, 2027

"Science without conscience
is the soul's perdition."

~ François Rabelais

25
UNDERTOW

MOST TETHERS HURT. The good ones burned. Dex had learned to breathe through the heat of a stranger's grief or pain and remain himself, to let joy pass through him without trying to claim it. Those sessions left him wrung out—but clean— rinsed by feeling. Like the subject the night before, tonight's had also been polished down to a nub by Serexin. Dex had leaned in for something to grip onto and found only nothing. His biotech spiked right before the tether ended, a single breadcrumb captured by the telemetry.

The feed uploaded information of a congregation of unregistered Tangents in one of the eastside neighborhoods of Atlanta. Not much more was parsed through the data, just a symbol—a butterfly—that Dex recognized as an icon of Inman Park but kept it to himself. He figured with most of the Order's leadership not being from Atlanta, it might take them a while to figure out, and he sure as hell wasn't about to give them any more help in hollowing others.

Dex left HALCION without looking up, the guard's bored nod skimming off him like light off glass. He pressed his wrist to the plate and waited for the door to slide open. Outside, the city moved around him as if he weren't there. Voices slid together in a blurred cacophony. The glow from storefronts spread across the sidewalk, lighting his walk toward his Jeep. He kept walking, hands deep in his pockets, feeling the hollowness like the pull of an undertow—an invisible drag beneath the surface, always there, always tugging at the edges of him.

He found his Jeep where he'd left it, the windshield freckled with condensation, the hood carrying the day's grime. Sliding behind the wheel felt less like going somewhere and more like lowering himself into a water tank.

The passenger seat waited, the dark stain on the fabric still visible even in the dim light. He had never tried to clean it. The thought of scrubbing Charlie away, of turning the fabric back into something ordinary, felt like betrayal. The stain was proof, as permanent as any scar, that Charlie had been here—that he had mattered. Keeping it was a way Dex could hold on.

The half-full streets were the usual mix of end-of-shift and nowhere-to-be. Dex sat rigid at red lights, staring past the world. Inside, he felt empty. His reflection in the windshield showed him a face he'd stopped recognizing—unkempt beard framing lips that no longer smiled, eyes dulled of the light that once shone behind them.

The Jeep rocked over potholes, swaying with the camber of the road. Every time a streetlight passed overhead, the stain beside him seemed to gather the shadows. Dex drove on autopilot, eyes open but unseeing, until he was already turning onto the narrow street leading to Emerald City's parking.

Emerald City, the one place where his motions still felt like choices, greeted him in its usual way—neon sign buzzing faintly overhead, mirrors catching light and throwing it back warmer than it had arrived, bottles lined like patient jewels, the bruised velvet of the booth seats.

Dex ran a palm across the bar top, the grain smooth from years of wiped spills and bent elbows. He unlocked the back room, checked the safe with its stubborn hinge, then came back to stand behind the counter—as if manning his post might give his life meaning in a world that now felt meaningless.

When the first regulars wandered in, he poured without thinking. The rhythm of it was a language older than the work he did for HALCION: glass, ice, liquor, the exact number of shakes that made a sound like sleet, the wrist flick that landed a drink with precision. When people thanked him, he nodded. When they joked, he smiled enough to be polite, not enough to commit. Once or twice someone almost grazed his hand in passing, but he'd learned to avoid touch since receiving the Ghostjack.

Around eleven, a regular slid onto a stool and said, "You look wrecked, man."

Dex fixed another drink for someone else and said, "Long day." The guy waited like there might be more, then gave up and turned to the ballgame. Dex felt the apology rise and vanish before reaching his mouth.

When the last table emptied, he flipped the chairs onto it, wiped until the rag went from damp to nearly dry, then dimmed the lights low enough to keep his reflection from catching in the mirrors. He listened to the bolt sliding into place as he locked up, then stepped into the parking lot with his hands in his pockets, letting the night's damp darkness swallow him whole.

David Gibson sat stiff in the passenger seat of his mother's car; hospital discharge papers still folded like a verdict in his jacket pocket. Seven months in a rehab facility had gotten him mobile again—walking with the help of a cane—but only in short bursts before dizziness threatened to drag him under.

His long-term memories—the ones he'd spent most of his adult life trying to forget—had mostly returned, but everything after college graduation blurred into flashing fragments that taunted him with the life he was desperate to remember.

The ride was quiet, save the metronome click of the turn signal and the sweep of the wipers. His body still ached from the crash, but the deeper ache came from knowing exactly where they were headed. He couldn't go back to Atlanta—everything behind the Curtain was lost to him now. There was only this house, the woman beside him, and the memories he had spent years trying to outrun.

When they pulled into the drive, the porch light spilled across the familiar blue door. His mother cut the engine. Neither of them moved for a long moment, both frozen with words that needed to be said but stayed locked within them.

She unbuckled first, circled to his side, and steadied him with a hand on his arm as he climbed out. He walked ahead, unable to assist her as she grabbed some groceries from the trunk.

The key rattled as he slid it into the lock. The door stuck the way it always had if you didn't lift as you turned. The spark of muscle memory overrode like instinct, remembering even if his mind had not. When it finally gave, the smell of lemon pledge and linseed oil hit him like a wall of memory.

He stepped inside, and the flood began. The entry rug was the same one he'd tracked mud across in second grade, earning a lecture promptly after. The hat rack held the straw hat his father had once received as a gift—worn for two minutes before he declared it made him look like an idiot. On the hall table sat a photo of all three at a church picnic, their smiles stretched bright enough to pass for believable happiness.

Each detail triggered another: the sofa sagging in the middle, the crocheted throw slung over its arm, the lamp still tilted from a fall no one ever fixed, and the shelf of books no one had read. His muscles tightened as the house flipped every buried switch at once.

He heard his father immediately—the voice that treated tenderness as a trap and affection as a weakness to be beaten out. *Be a man*—barked like an order designed for him to fail, the belt slung over the chair as warning of what would come when he did. The mocking corrections about the way he held a pencil, the way he spoke, the way he dressed.

David remembered the day his father smashed the cheap guitar he had saved for—not because he played badly, but because the sight and sound of his son singing made him cringe and encouraged his cruelty. The crack of splintering wood carried a finality that lodged itself deep, truths he had spent years trying to forget.

Then the funeral—delayed while his mother recovered from the accident—strangers gripped his hand in this very room, calling his father a pillar. They praised his strength, his discipline, his faith. David had tasted bile with every word. To them he was a good man. To David, he was a drunk who despised him, who twisted his sexuality into shame, wielding violence as proof of his authority.

And his mother—her silence had cut almost worse. *Why didn't you stop him? Why did you take his side?* He remembered demanding answers, trembling with fury, desperate for her to be the one adult who would finally protect him. Instead, she had folded her arms and told him he was exaggerating—that his father only wanted to "make a man" of him. She'd turned bruises into lessons, humiliation into discipline, cruelty into a kind of love she expected him to swallow.

He remembered the last fight most of all, when he told her he was leaving. His voice had been sharp with disgust, anger writhing underneath every word. The community's saint had been his tormentor, and he couldn't bear to breathe in the house where that lie was allowed to live any longer after his death.

And then her words—hurled like a curse that burned hotter than anything his father ever said: *If you leave, don't bother coming back. You're dead to me, and I never want to see you again.*

The memory yanked him hard, like an undertow pulling him down, until her voice in the present cut through.

"David?" Her voice trembled from the threshold as she noticed him struggling. "Are you okay"

He wanted to meet her with the speech he had rehearsed a hundred times in his head before the accident—knife-clean words that might cut the pain into something understandable. Though he'd memorized them, the words were now gone. The crash had stolen them—or maybe the house had. All that remained were fragments breaking loose inside him, too jagged to hold.

When he finally spoke, the words were clumsy, stripped of the weight he had meant them to carry. "It feels weird to be home."

They stood with a coffee table between them like a treaty no one had signed. She looked at his hands—the scar under his thumb from a childhood fall—and he watched her recalibrate.

The anger she had spoken in this very spot was gone now, replaced by regret and grief—not for his father, but for him. Her eyes glistened as she fixed on his hands, as if to say:

Yes, these are the same hands that once gripped the stair rail and slammed the door too hard the day he left. But these were once the hands that held mine tightly while crossing the road; that helped me shell peas in our kitchen; that once crafted crayon drawings—of suns and happy stick figure families—that hung on our fridge; that carried his father's coffin as a pallbearer, even after those same hands had been struck too many times by that father's anger.

"I shouldn't have said it," she breathed at last. "Not those words. They were meant for your father, and I threw them at you because he wasn't there to take them. It was ugly of me."

There it was: the simple truth that mattered, wrapped in something more complicated. David had believed he would need more—a ceremony of atonement, a litany. But the softness of the admission undid him.

"You were drowning," he said, bracing his emotions like a dam holding back floodwaters.

"So were you," she replied softly.

They moved at the same time, stepping around the coffee table. When they met, it wasn't cinematic, just human—awkward, too tight at first, then looser, the hug of people who had forgotten the mechanics and had to figure them out again.

For a long minute they held on. The undertow didn't reverse, but it shifted—maybe its direction, maybe his relation to it. He felt it carrying them both toward something safe, something other than a breaker where everything shattered.

When they let go, she did what she had always done after storms: she went to the kitchen and put water on. He followed—because you follow a ritual that part of you recognizes, even if the other part of you doesn't, even if a part of you resents it. The kettle rattled on the burner. The two mugs waiting felt like peace, and not simply because they matched.

They sat at the small table where he had once done homework. She set coffee in front of him, and he wrapped his hands around it, grateful for the heat.

"I don't remember it all," he admitted. "Pieces are missing. It's like this house has the whole file and I only have the summary."

"That might be mercy," she said—and he could not argue.

They talked in the sideways way people talk when the center is too bright—about the neighbor's dog that used to dig under the fence, about the church ladies who still brought casseroles several months past the funeral because no one had told them to stop, about the old tree out back that had lost a limb in a storm and now looked lopsided.

Between those braided the short, brave lines that mattered. *I was afraid. I was angry. I didn't know how to forgive a dead man, so I hurt the living. I left because I thought that was the only way to breathe.*

At some point she reached across and brushed her fingers over the back of his hand. He flinched, not because it hurt, but because some part of him had trained itself to prepare for pain.

"I can do better," she said. "If you'll let me."

He nodded. He didn't draft a speech about conditions. Forgiveness was not a contract he wanted to write; it was a choice he could keep making until it felt real.

The evening settled around them and his mother returned to the kitchen; David followed, unsure what else to do. The clatter of pans and the sharp scent of onions drew him in. He leaned against the counter, watching her in motions he realized he had never really studied before.

A flicker from a distant morning rose unbidden—a man stood beside him browning sausage while David joked that he was hopeless in the kitchen; it faded as quickly as it came, but its weight lingered differently now. He swallowed, then asked quietly, "Can you teach me?"

His mother glanced at him, surprised at first, then softened. "Of course," she said, sliding a cutting board toward him, placing a knife in his hand. He gripped it awkwardly, and for the first time that day, a faint smile tugged at the corners of his mouth.

After dinner, he paused at the doorway of his old room. He chuckled at the buffalo plaid bedspread—a pattern his father once insisted was rugged and masculine, though now it only gave the room a butch, gay cabin aesthetic. The walls still bore faint shadows where posters once clung. He moved to the middle of the room, letting memory press in around him. This wasn't a place he could visit and leave behind anymore. It was home again—for better or worse.

He sat on the edge of the bed and let the thought settle: maybe being here didn't have to mean becoming that boy again. Maybe it could mean introducing his mother to the man he'd become— though now his memory failed to remind him exactly who that man was.

Dex checked his phone and found nothing he wanted to answer. His feet had taken him back to the bar because he had to get out of his bungalow, still haunted by the last days with Charlie. He unlocked, turned on the top-lighted shelves, and watched the liquid within the bottles seemingly glow, filling the space with warmth.

He sat on the floor with his back to the cabinets, letting his head tip against the wood. He closed his eyes, but he did not fall asleep. Every time he drifted close, his body startled itself awake.

At some point, without asking himself for permission, Dex thought of David. The worry came sharp, uninvited—the echo of Charlie's warning gnawing at him: an accident, a hospital bed, something broken he couldn't reach. He cursed that he didn't even know David's last name—no way to search, no way to prove or disprove the fear.

Just as suddenly as he'd cursed, an image formed: David standing in a small bedroom, walls marked by the faint shadows of posters long gone, a campy plaid bedspread pulled tight across a sagging mattress. The vision clung with such clarity it unsettled him. He shook it off with a muttered scold—*don't be ridiculous*—never realizing that what flickered through him wasn't imagination at all, but the edge of a tether pulling across distance.

He pushed himself up from the floor—getting up was the only proof he hadn't gone completely under. Behind the bar, he poured himself a drink—measured carefully, no ritual this time beyond the slow tilt of the glass. He carried it to the stool at the far end, the one he never offered to anyone else—and sat in silence.

The first swallow burned, but he welcomed the fire. He let the warmth spread through his chest—slow, heavy, a counterfeit comfort. He drank the rest slower, savoring each mouthful until the glass was empty—until the heat dulled the edges inside him the way nothing else could.

When he finally stepped outside, the rain had thickened, slanting across the street in sheets. It wrapped around him, tugging at his coat, dragging at his shoes. He let it. The downpour was cathartic—steady, unrelenting—carrying him through the parking lot where his Jeep waited.

By the time he reached it, he was soaked through, hair plastered to his forehead, hands slick on the handle. He slid into the driver's seat and glanced at the passenger side lit by the dim glow of the streetlamp. For a moment, he just sat there, listening to the water drum against the roof, the world outside dissolved into liquid blur.

Then he started the engine. The wipers swept furiously, barely keeping up. The tires hissed as they cut through standing water. He let the Jeep carry him into the storm, the city rising and falling in neon reflections across the windshield. The rain pressed on, an undertow aboveground, pulling him forward whether he wanted it or not.

Tonight, at least, it carried him home.

March 13, 2027

"The god of love lives in a state of need.
It is a need. It is an urge.
It is a homoeostatic imbalance.
Like hunger and thirst,
it's almost impossible to stamp out."

~ Plato

26
URGE

T HE ELEVATOR CARRYING Dex to the Langston tower penthouse rose without sound. Not the low hum of regulated lifts or the mechanical sighs of those at HALCION—nothing. Just stillness and upward motion, as though gravity had been suspended in deference to money.

He adjusted his collar as the skyline unfolded behind him—Buckhead's glittering skyscrapers, sharpened into clean vertical spires. This part of the city didn't just survive; it flourished. Families like the Langstons made sure of that.

Dex had seen the name once before, back when he was on the force; more recently, it had appeared linked to the Order somehow. Now he understood. Families like this didn't bankroll the machine. They built it.

The elevator opened into a private vestibule lit like a boutique—muted golds, brushed concrete, with the faint woody spice of expensive fragrance. A single interface scanned him.

A voice, calm and amused, floated in from the main room: "Come in. I'm almost decent."

Dex stepped inside.

The penthouse stretched across the entire top floor. Floor-to-ceiling windows framed the city in severe geometry. The furniture looked untouched—too elegant to be lived in. The air was filtered and pristine. Music—orchestral but unfamiliar—played softly from somewhere.

Beau Langston stood by the window in a silk robe, barefoot, drink in hand. Younger than Dex expected—late twenties, maybe—slender, toned, groomed with the effortless polish only the ultra-privileged could buy.

"They said you'd be quiet," Beau said. "They didn't say you'd be handsome."

Dex said nothing. He scanned the room for surveillance, but nothing obvious.

"I don't get many house calls," Beau continued. "Not like this. Usually they send the cold ones— the men who look like they haven't fucked or cried in years."

"I'm not here to entertain you."

"No? That's funny," Beau smirked, swirling his glass. "I hired you. You're on loan to me today to show me if I'm still capable of feeling."

Dex almost laughed at the absurdity. *Hired.* That wasn't how this worked. The Order didn't let clients buy men like him—they assigned targets, collected data, and called it service. Whatever Beau thought this was, Dex knew better: an interrogation wrapped in silk sheets. He was here to extract, not indulge.

Beau crossed the room, stopping inches away. Nearly the same height. Gray-blue eyes that flirted without words. Then, without ceremony, he smoothed a hand along Dex's chest, fingertips testing the shape beneath the fabric. The touch lingered—curious, hungry—then Beau leaned in and kissed him.

Dex stiffened, instinct snapping him back into protocol. This was an assignment, not a dalliance. He was supposed to hold the line, extract what the Order needed, and walk away untouched.

But the kiss was warm, unhurried, and unarmored—no performance, no trick. Just the soft press of lips after too many numb nights. Dex hadn't let anyone close since Charlie; he hadn't trusted his body to remember how to want.

The resistance in him cracked. The ache of absence roared up, and before he could stop it, he leaned into the kiss. His mouth parted, answering Beau's with a hunger that had been waiting in silence for far too long.

For the first time in months, Dex didn't feel like the Order's instrument. He felt like a man being touched.

The tether ignited with a shiver.

Not sharp. Not violent. Just... alive.

Beau's mind was like polished glass—smooth and fragmentary, casting back images Dex didn't expect in a sensory overload: heat, bodies, champagne on a rooftop at dusk, sex in a half-lit gallery, kisses with no names attached. Then static. All of it interrupted by long blank stretches. Emotional silence.

Amid the hungry kisses, Dex steadied the tether and pulled gently. Then something else came through.

Beau, on a train—alone, staring at his reflection in the window. Not crying, not even sad. Just empty: a stillness threaded with silent screams. Beau at six, hiding under a table during a party, watching adults drink and dance. The world moved past him like a piece of art no one noticed.

Dex let the memory pass, pressed deeper, and found another flash.

Beau at thirteen, reaching for another boy's hand on a park bench—tentative, desperate, altogether natural and innocent—until his father's voice thundered across the memory. *"Don't you ever shame me like that again. You want to be a fag? You'll do it where no one can see you."*

The hand withdrew. Beau's face burned with humiliation, the ache of desire colliding with the terror of being seen.

Dex felt the cut of it—sharp as glass—before the memory dissolved.

Then, a car interior at night—the city lights sliding by. Beau, nearly his current age, sat rigid in the back seat. His father beside him, a presence stern and foreboding.

The car slowed near the Curtain. Guards in dark armor, floodlights cutting across steel. And there—a break. A recessed checkpoint, a gate nearly swallowed by shadow.

His father's voice, low and fierce: *"If anything happens to me, you go here. Do you understand? This is where you get out. I know I've been hard on you in the past, but these people... Beau, these people will make sure they ruin you. They'll beat you into submission."*

Beau only nodded once, eyes fixed on the steel.

The image wavered, broke apart into static. Letters bled through—DECAT—then it was gone.

Dex gasped; the tether recoiled like a live wire.

Beau flinched, breaking contact for a heartbeat—lips trembling, not from arousal but fear.

"You weren't meant to see that," he whispered, voice muffled against Dex's skin.

The telemetry stream didn't flag—Dex felt the absence of a spike. Whatever slipped through distorted, unreadable. Protected by the static that clouded the visions.

But Dex had seen enough to know it mattered.

Beau's eyes met his, suddenly hard. *Not a word.* The warning pulsed louder than speech.

Then Beau kissed him again—messy, hungry— and the tether swung back into flesh and heat.

Their mouths met, slow and tentative—not a test, not a play for power. Just contact. Warm, human. Beau tasted faintly herbal, citrus edged with heat. Dex parted his lips and let the tether thrum between them like a second heartbeat.

Beau leaned into him, fingers brushing Dex's ribs, then his waist. Dex didn't stop him— couldn't. The tether amplified everything. Touch became echo. Breath became resonance.

When Beau's hand slid beneath his shirt and flattened against his chest, Dex felt it like a memory—like Charlie. He felt every ache that had been locked away since the injection. His skin lit beneath it—not fireworks, not fire, something sharper and more dangerous: recognition.

Dex's shirt was yanked over his head and tossed aside.

Beau's robe slid from his shoulders with quiet drama, exposing a body that was as curated as it was inherited. He was lean, almost delicate, but not weak. Everything about him had the softness of money—not gym-hardened bulk of men who built their strength, but the elegant tone of someone maintained. Sculpted by privilege more than work.

His skin was pale and warm, faint freckles scattered along his shoulders and arms like stardust across porcelain. His back curved with a dancer's grace. His ass was perfect—full, smooth, a little high (but not exaggerated).

His cock was—Dex thought the word before he could stop it—pretty. Not monstrous or threatening or imposing. Resting against his thigh, cut, naturally curved, pale shaft flushed at the head. Not huge, but proportionate. It twitched slightly as Dex's gaze lingered, already thickening.

Every inch of him seemed alive with desire—not polished into perfection for someone else's gaze, but restless. Dex saw it in the quickening of his breath, the way his chest rose a little sharper now, in the faint tremor along his abdomen. The symmetry was there, yes—the careful grooming, the effortless privilege—but beneath it ran something raw. A body kept like an heirloom, now straining, aching for touch it had dared to pay for.

Dex didn't see it in Beau's cock or the curve of his spine, but in the small tells: the tremble of his breath under Dex's gaze; the flush blooming behind his ears, on his cheeks; the slight arch of his foot against the tile, grounding himself for what he didn't know how to demand.

This wasn't just exhibition. It was a plea.

Beau straddled his lap, shifting chest to chest, hips aligning, hands threading his hair. The kiss deepened—open, slow, but hungry—and Dex grew harder with every gasp for breath.

The tether flickered behind Dex's eyes. He had forgotten how to want something that wasn't numbed at the source. Emotional bleed pushed through the connection—not images, just feelings.

Hunger. Abandonment.

Beau rocked forward. Their cocks slid together, hot and urgent, and Dex groaned, surprising himself.

"Let me," Beau whispered, dropping to his knees, Dex leaning back against the lounge and watching.

Beau's mouth wrapped around him with shocking ease—wet, slow, skilled. He worked Dex like he wanted it, not like he'd been taught to perform. His tongue traced along the underside, lips tight and open all at once.

The tether shimmered.

Dex felt the feedback again—Beau's pleasure at giving. Dex's own arousal reflected and returned.

This was what he had missed. Not the act, but the acknowledgement.

He whispered Charlie's name without realizing it.

Beau looked up—eyes glassy, pupils wide—then climbed back into Dex's lap, kissing him again, messy this time. Their erections pressed together.

When Dex grabbed his ass, squeezing hard, Beau gasped, grinding into him. Dex flipped him, pressed him back against the cushions, then reached for a small tube of lube on the end table he'd only just noticed. Warm to the touch—undoubtedly preheated.

He slicked his fingers with it, kissed Beau hard, then slipped one inside.

Beau moaned into his mouth, overcome with pleasure.

Dex added a second, then a third—slow, careful—until Beau pushed down into him and whispered, "Please."

Dex lined up and entered slowly, the heat and pressure nearly undoing him.

Beau arched beneath him, mouth open, eyes fluttering. Dex gripped his hips, held still, letting it settle—letting the tether hold them like suspension wire.

Then they moved. Slow at first, measured.

Then faster.

Dex thrusted, hips rolling, nerves screaming. Beau matched him, hands clawing down his back. The tether pulsed—not with pain, not with data—with grief, need, craving.

This wasn't sex.

It was solace; something almost whole but still broken.

Dex felt the coil snap just before release, spilling deep, mouth buried in Beau's neck to stifle the cry. Beau clenched around him and followed moments later, his breath stuttering silent and a stream of hot cum pooling on the floor at Dex's feet as release took him.

Dex flipped them again. Beau collapsed against him there, cheek on his chest, heartbeat slowing.

Dex stared at the ceiling, body trembling.

For a long time, neither spoke. Then Beau shifted, tracing an idle line down Dex's arm before pulling away, making sure their skin no longer touched.

"Everything okay?"

Beau's voice was low, fragile. "Whatever you think you saw… you didn't. It wasn't meant for you."

Dex tilted his head, studying him. "Then why did it come through at all?"

Beau's mouth tightened. He shook his head, refusing the question. But Dex cupped his jaw, thumb brushing the faint stubble there, and pressed a slow kiss to his lips—gentle, coaxing.

The resistance in Beau's body softened. His eyes closed, and when he spoke again, once their kiss broke, once he stood and re-donned his robe, the words slipped out like something stolen. "My father... before the injection, before any of this... he showed me a place in the Curtain. A breach no one talks about. He said if anything ever happened to him, I was to go there. Escape. Live."

He swallowed, eyes wet but not breaking. "I never went. Never even thought to. Serexin made it easy not to feel the fear, easier not to want survival more than obedience. Even after he died, I stayed. I told myself there was nothing outside worth the risk."

Dex brushed his thumb across Beau's lip, holding him steady, but Beau pushed it away.

"We can't touch—can't be tethered—or it will record," Beau explained.

"But there is a way out?" Dex asked, searching Beau's eyes for the answers his abilities were forbidden to discover.

Beau hesitated; his eyes locked on Dex's as if weighing the danger of saying more. Then he exhaled, and the words came in a whisper. "East side. Near Decatur. A service gate recessed into the Curtain. Guards rotate every twelve hours. My father said it was weaker construction. It's the only place he believed could be breached."

Dex felt the weight of Beau's response settle into him—there was a fracture in the wall of their prison. A way to escape.

Beau's eyes flicked down, almost ashamed. "You have it now. What he never really meant me to keep. Maybe it was fate. Maybe that's why you are here."

Dex kissed him again—firmer this time. Beau let himself yield in a way that felt deeper than the sex. Something shared, something unguarded.

For once, Dex thought, Beau wasn't curated or polished or numb. He was just a man, finally giving into the desires his father had forbidden him to feel, finally revealing what the Order had tried to bury inside him.

He looked down at the boy.

Beautiful. Bare. Hollow.

This was what survival looked like under the Order—polished numbness. Curated luxury and loneliness. And if Dex kept obeying—kept burying his own memories for the safety of protocol—he'd end up the same.

He looked out the window at the city glowing below, knowing full well that he couldn't go back to the numbness he'd let himself feel since losing Charlie.

March 14, 2027

“I have been all things unholy.
If God can work through me,
he can work through anyone.”

~ St. Francis of Assisi

27
UNHOLY

THE CORRIDOR TO the lower cells smelled like damp iron. The walls here weren't whitewashed like the rest of HALCION; they were raw cement, streaked with mineral stains and scored with age. Overhead, industrial fixtures bolted into steel beams buzzed a faint orange overhead. This wasn't where they kept ordinary detainees. This was where they buried the ones they feared.

Dex's escort stopped at a reinforced door. A sliver of glass ran down its center—no bigger than an eye. The guard keyed in a code, and the locks gave with a groan.

Inside, Aurelio Alameida waited.

He sat cross-legged on the cement floor; a gold robe pooled around his waist. His skin was a warm bronze, the kind that held light even in the gloom. His chest was mapped with geometric tattoos—equations, star charts, constellations spiraling across ribs and sternum. Thick black curls had grown wild during confinement, tied back in a loose knot at the nape of his neck. Dark-amber eyes—almost black—watched Dex with a glint that was equal parts mischievous and unholy.

The room was bare except for a single cot, leaned and unused against a wall that bore faint smudges of chalk: circles, triangles, starbursts scratched into the concrete like a prayer.

Watching from the corner, arms folded, was Thomas Gallows.

Dex stiffened. He'd seen the man from the broadcast once at HALCION, but he had never met him—a part of him had hoped he never would. Gallows carried presence like a blade—square jaw; shaved head; pale, sharp eyes. He wore no insignia—no need. Everyone knew who he was.

"You know why you're here," Gallows said, more statement than question. His voice was quiet, but it filled the cell. "This one's been a problem. Blocks every Tangent we throw at him. Shows us what he wants, nothing else. Even feeds us false memories. If you can't pull him open, he's worthless."

Aurelio smiled faintly, as if the insult were a compliment. "Worthless is still freer than Ghostjacked."

Gallows' boot slammed into his ribs, knocking him sideways across the floor. Aurelio coughed but didn't cry out.

Dex forced his features into stillness, contempt burning behind the mask. He refused Gallows' gaze, saving his eyes for Aurelio—a glance carrying the apology he wasn't allowed to speak.

"Well?" Gallows barked, snapping to Dex. "Aren't you going to do your job?"

Dex bit the inside of his cheek, willing himself to keep silent. But the words pushed out anyway. "I could do my job if you weren't busy breaking him apart. Do you really expect him to comply by beating him?"

Gallows' eyes narrowed. "Mind your tongue, boy."

Dex's jaw tightened. "If you wanted a corpse, I wouldn't be here."

Gallows stepped closer, looming—air heavy with iron and sweat. "Careful, Truitt. You're not half as indispensable as you think."

"I know exactly how dispensable I am," Dex said evenly. "But if you want results, let me work without you kicking the target."

For a long moment, silence pressed in, thick as the concrete walls around them. Gallows studied him, jaw flexing, the veins in his neck taut. Then his mouth twisted in something between disdain and amusement.

"Fine," Gallows said, voice like grit. "Do it your way. But if he doesn't give me what I want, it's your ribs next."

He stepped back, the command in his presence no less suffocating. Dex released the breath he'd been holding and turned toward Aurelio, hand extended.

Aurelio looked up from the floor, robe falling open at his chest, and then he reached his hand toward Dex's.

The tether ignited.

Dex felt something between their clasped hands, but ignored it as heat ran through his arm, up his spine, into the back of his throat. Images rose like smoke in his mind:

A warehouse bathed in candlelight. Dozens of figures, masked, pressing foreheads together, clasping hands. Their bodies trembled with the relief of contact. Across the back wall, painted in white letters: SENSATE. Beneath, a phrase: *to feel is to fight.*

Aurelio's wordless whisper brushed through the link: *They call us Tangents. But we call ourselves Sensates. Because no one can name us.*

The scene shifted: a butterfly, stenciled on brick, wings dripping yellow. Another painted on cracked pavement. The symbol pulsed, faint but insistent.

"You'll know where to go," Aurelio murmured aloud; then, only in Dex's mind: *"Just follow the stone."*

Dex pushed deeper, reaching for faces, names, locations—but Aurelio's mind was velvet-slick, curated, refusing.

From the corner, Gallows' voice cut in. "Pathetic. He's toying with you, just like the rest, isn't he?"

The tether wavered. Aurelio's grip tightened. His other hand shot out, seizing Gallows' wrist.

For a heartbeat, everything changed.

Gallows froze—rigid, every muscle drawn tight as if invisible cords lashed him to the floor.

His jaw locked, his eyes wide and furious, breath rasping through clenched teeth. He strained against it, but Aurelio held fast, using Dex's hand as an anchor.

The tether surged into a triad—Aurelio the conduit, bridging Gallows and Dex together.

Dex fell inward.

Images detonated: Stone Mountain under floodlights, soldiers drilling; HALCION corridors full of rows of servers humming with data; schematics of the Curtain, choke points circled in red. A blurred photo of a hooded woman, the name *Persephone* scrawled beneath.

Aurelio's ragged voice bled through: *"See him. See what he hides."*

Dex's pulse hammered. Aurelio had scrambled the Ghostjack, the overload frying the relay. None of this was being recorded—it was Dex's alone to keep.

Then Gallows bellowed, veins bulging in his neck, and with brute force he tore free of Aurelio's psychic clamp. The conduit shattered like glass under a hammer. He lunged, clasping Aurelio's throat and hoisting him off the floor.

The tether severed instantly, leaving Dex gasping in its absence.

Gallows' eyes burned. "How dare you use your Tangent voodoo on me."

Aurelio, choking, still managed a defiant snarl through split, bloody lips. "I'm not a fucking Tangent. I'm a Sensate."

Gallows sneered, then twisted hard. The crack was final.

Aurelio's body went slack in his grip, Gallows let him drop like refuse, and guards rushed in to drag the corpse away—the robe trailing like a fallen banner.

Gallows wiped his hands on his trousers, casual, as if he'd only crushed a cup. He turned to Dex. "If you don't want to end the same way, you'll learn to pull harder. Do you understand?"

Dex swallowed. "Yes, sir."

Gallows studied him a moment longer, then left the cell without another word.

Only then did Dex unclench his fist.

A stone was there, what he'd felt between them during the tether and clenched hard when Aurelio was pulled from his grasp. Black, smooth, etched with a sigil—circle, triangle, open hand with an eye. Warm against his skin, though the cell was cold.

You'll know where to go. Just follow the stone.

Dex didn't go home.

Instead, he steered east, the stone heavy in his pocket and Aurelio's words circling in his mind. Traffic was light, the streets quiet, giving him too much room to think as the skyline thinned into older neighborhoods. Inman Park looked the same as it always had—porches with swings, gardens tucked behind wrought-iron fences, oak trees arching overhead in green tunnels.

Dex slowed near a corner café, parked, and chose to walk the rest of the way. If Aurelio's clue meant anything, undoubtedly he'd find it on foot, hidden in the details.

The butterfly lingered in his thoughts—Inman Park had claimed it decades ago, long before bombs and walls. Murals still clung to businesses; cast-iron plaques on lampposts bore the symbol; banners, faded but visible on the corners.

But it wasn't butterflies guiding him. It was the sigil.

Etched into a fence post. Chalked discreetly at the base of a stairwell. Scratched onto a brick wall in a narrow alley. The same mark—circle, triangle, open hand with the eye—as the stone in his pocket.

He followed.

The marks pulled him deeper—away from the main avenues, past half-wild gardens and fences rusted with time. At last, the trail converged.

The Inman Revival Theatre loomed before him. Its marquee was blackened, its letters half-gone. The ticket booth was boarded, the façade scorched. To anyone else, it was ruin. To Dex, it felt like it was waiting for him.

The corridor inside breathed heat and perfume, sage and bergamot trying—and failing—to mask rot. Red-orange sconces lit the hall, their melted glass like warped jellyfish. Two guards stood at the end, shoulders squared, eyes unblinking.

Dex pulled the stone from his pocket and held it up.

Recognition flickered in their gaze. One stepped aside, gesturing toward a velvet curtain.

Dex moved through.

The theatre's bones were still visible, but its soul had been reborn.

The orchestra pit was gone—filled and leveled into a broad floor where velvet pads and battered chairs were scattered in circles. Bodies occupied them—men and women in varying stages of undress, heads bowed together, hands entwined, some wept, some whispered, some simply breathed in unison. The seats had been replaced with rows of beds and chaises, most filled with naked, writhing bodies engaged in acts of touch and solace.

Above, chandeliers flickered with dim red filaments, their light throbbing like a pulse. Sculptures of twisted brass caught the glow, bending it into strange, unholy shapes. The air hummed, not with Order surveillance, but with something cobbled together, hacked, raw and alive.

A woman stepped forward from the shadows. Her dark skin shimmered as though brushed with gold leaf. Her head was bald, golden rings coiled tight around her throat. Her eyes swept over Dex, then landed on the stone in his palm.

"You carry the mark," she said. "I'm Nyssa."

Dex's throat tightened. "Aurelio gave it to me."

Her smile was sharp, almost pitying. "Then you're either one of us—or the knife sent to cut us open."

"I'm here for answers," Dex said honestly.

That seemed to satisfy her. She gestured him forward.

She led him deeper, past circles of tethered bodies. The air grew thick, electric with emotion unshackled. Dex felt threads brush against him— grief, desire, relief—raw currents leaking across the room.

In the center of the stage, nine Sensates sat cross-legged in a ring, their hands linked, eyes closed. Their breaths rose and fell together like tides.

One of them, a man with hollow cheeks, opened his eyes and fixed Dex with a steady look. "The Order calls us Tangents," he said. "Mistakes. Deviations. But we call ourselves Sensates. Because we stole the name back."

Dex turned the stone over in his palm. "Why show me this?"

"Because Aurelio trusted you. Because you've seen the Unholy."

"Unholy?" Dex asked.

"The Unholy is the hollow left by Serexin," explained Nyssa.

Dex's chest tightened. He had no name for it before, but the emptiness he felt in tether sessions, that numbing void—of course it had a name.

"You tether into it," the man continued. "Let it swallow you. And then you push back. That's how you break Serexin. Not forever. Not yet. But long enough to feel. Long enough to remember what they stole."

Nyssa leaned closer, her voice hushed. "She taught us how."

Dex's voice dropped. "Who?"

They exchanged glances—a pause, breath held. Then the man whispered: "Persephone."

The name crawled over Dex's skin—he'd seen it in Gallows memories.

"She walked into the underworld and returned with fire in her hands," Nyssa began. "She showed us where the seams are, how to slip past the Unholy. With breath. With touch. With enough hands tethered together, Serexin gives way. For a moment, you feel again. Some nights it nearly kills us, but we'd rather burn on our own terms than stay hollow."

Dex didn't understand—not that part. He still felt—more than he wanted to.

A second man spoke, "One day, she says, we won't need tethering at all. We'll break free forever."

Another voice—a woman reclined on the velvet pads behind them—chimed in, "Chaos uses what we've learned. Not all of us joined them, but most.

They fight the Order's machine; we fight the poison in our blood and brain. Same sides of the war.

"Two sides of the same rebellion," the hollow-cheeked man corrected. His eyes stayed on Dex. "But Persephone says one day there won't be two sides."

Dex looked around the theatre—at the bodies pressed together, at the flickering chandeliers, at the sigil chalked across the floorboards beneath them.

The stone pulsed once more in his palm, warm as blood. Aurelio had died to put it there. And Dex realized, for the first time, that the tether wasn't just a leash.

It might be a weapon.

Dex looked at the man with the hollow-cheeked man. "Can you teach me?"

"No. But Persephone can."

March 17, 2027

"If you shut up truth, and bury it
underground, it will but grow."

~ Emile Zola

28
UNDERGROUND

DEX HAD BEEN underground before. He'd walked sewer tunnels during patrols; he'd moved through busted transit corridors during calls to investigate noises or check on the homeless that often sought refuge within them. But HALCION was different. This place didn't hide what it was. It celebrated it—every wall seam, every pressure-locked corridor, every light panel flickering just a fraction too long.

It was a cathedral built for fascism.

Sublevel Three was colder than the rest of the compound. Not just in temperature, but also in tone. The elevators that reached it were unmarked. So were the guards posted outside it—faces smooth behind mirrored visors, standing motionless like mannequins dressed for tactical performance art. No questions. No acknowledgement. Just a scan.

Even the slate he carried—normally bloated with target data and session prep—showed only a single line of amber text:

VOSS, HALINA – SUBLEVEL 3 – DOOR A

No summary. No dossier. No handlers. Nothing more.

He walked the corridor slowly, boots soft against the composite floor. The deeper he went, the more the silence expanded—a silence that felt engineered. No surveillance domes. No interface terminals. No plaques. Just seamless metal, architecture without any corners, and the creeping sense he was trespassing in someone's mind.

This part of HALCION wasn't the system that ran the city—it was the digestive tract. The place the Order sent people they couldn't process or purge. Where things were broken down, classified, and quietly forgotten.

He reached the final panel—a black square blinking faint green—and raised his wrist. A silent scan swept his forearm. A retinal check followed to verify. A low hiss, then a seam in the wall split open and he stepped inside.

The room beyond was clinically simple. A bench. A standing cabinet. A sealed terminal mounted into the wall behind a sheet of reinforced glass. And at its center, seated at ease with one leg crossed over the other, was Dr. Halina Voss.

Her white coat looked worn thin, the insignia at the shoulder scrubbed to a blurred gray. Her sleeves were rolled past the elbow, revealing dark mesh beneath—remnants of a neural interface once threaded into both arms. Her left wrist bore the telltale crescent scar of a subdermal extraction.

She looked up but didn't rise. "You're not like the ones they usually send."

"I get that a lot." Dex remained by the door. "They've stopped telling me what I'm supposed to be."

That earned him a faint smirk. "Smart."

He took a few slow, measured steps forward, scanning the space with both instinct and habit for possible weapons, recording units, or even the residue of recent emotion. There was nothing.

"You're not restrained," he finally said.

"No need," she replied, rising fluidly. "If I were going to run, I would've done it before they locked down my access and erased my name."

Dex didn't reply.

Voss stood and walked to the cabinet. She removed a steel canister from within, unscrewed the lid, and poured herself a half-glass of water. "Do they still say I helped her?"

"Isabella?"

She sipped. "They don't say her first name down here. Just Merrick. Like she's a system fault, not a person."

"That's not an answer."

She set the glass down. "No. It's a question in disguise."

He stepped closer. "You're flagged. That's all I know."

"Then you're better off than most." Her posture didn't shift. Neither did her voice. But there was something behind her eyes—not panic, not anger. Readiness. Like she'd expected this for a long time. She held out her hand, "Let's begin."

He hesitated, just for a breath, then he took it.

The tether surged like cold rain—sudden but clean. Not invasive. Not violent. Just deep.

A rush of clarity that nearly disguised how deep it dropped. Dex had been through all kinds: bitter conspirators; the spiked emotional mines of traumatized targets; the oily slick of people so eroded by heavy Serexin doses they barely had thoughts of their own left.

Halina Voss was different.

Her surface was clockwork, order masking the chaos. Memory loops, test protocols, numeric architecture. Dex skimmed across lines of code, schematics, metadata—all filed, labeled, encrypted.

But deeper down, the order of things began to unravel.

A lab, late evening. Isabella stood at a projection interface, looping a neural signature on repeat. Each time it collapsed into static every time.

"She wanted the relay to adapt," Halina whispered over her own memory. "Not reject. Not block. *Absorb.*"

Another layer emerged: Isabella again, voice sharp but soft, "Emotion is the only thing we still own. If we don't learn how to protect it, they'll find a way to own that, too."

Dex pushed further.

A conference room, unlit. Isabella seated alone across from Halina, murmuring to herself as she activated a schematic: three linked nodes, rotating in sequence, then blinking out of phase.

“Not believable enough,” she said. “It’ll get flagged, discovered.”

Dex felt Halina’s hesitation—even now, in memory. She had tried to warn her, talk her out of it, reroute her logic.

“They’ll call treason, what you’re building,” she said in the memory.

“I’m building something they won’t understand,” Isabella corrected her.

Then… a gloved hand reached into the frame and adjusted one of the node calibrations. The entirely of the face attached to it was never shown. But the frame of his shoulders, the angle of his movement—Dex knew it in his gut it was the same man from the operating room when he was fitted with the GEIST port.

Never named. Never acknowledged. Just *there.*

Halina had hidden him even in memory.

Dex pushed further, and with his push came the fear.

Halina’s memory shifted. A sterile room, standing alone. Smoke clung to her coat. A case opened to reveal a half-melted drive, tagged: TEST 7A — ABORTED.

A new scene flickered—brief, indistinct. Isabella in a sunlit conference room, standing beside a man Dex didn’t immediately recognize. Tall, composed. Older. Well-dressed in a way that suggested generational wealth rather than fashion. His voice didn’t come through the tether—just the soft cadence of conversation blurred by distance.

But his eyes—Dex saw them clearly. Striking blue. Familiar.

They hit him like a pulse. Not from the man, but from memory—something inside Dex twitched. Those eyes reminded him of David's. That same intensity. Kindness cut with gravity. Eyes that looked at you like they could see who you were, even if you couldn't.

The memory collapsed before he could follow it. But the imprint lingered.

Another memory, this time brighter: Isabella smiling, handing Halina a velvet-lined case.

"If anything happens to me," Isabella said, "don't give it to them. It's gotta be given to someone who's still able to feel."

Halina's hands trembled.

The tether quivered, and Dex released it gently, retreating just before a final memory could rise—one that pulsed with grief too hard to touch.

They broke contact.

Halina didn't move, but her shoulders lowered slightly.

Dex exhaled and took a slow step back.

"You saw it," she said.

"Enough."

She turned, walked to the bench, and pulled a slim, hard case from beneath it. She set it on the table between them and unlocked it with a worn brass key.

"She trusted you," Dex said quietly.

"She trusted that I'd hold onto this long enough to give it to someone who could still make use of it."

Dex leaned closer. "What is it?"

"A drive," Halina said. "Encrypted. It holds a short video she recorded. Not instructions—a memory. Her face, a few words, and a single image. A clue. You'll know it when you see it again."

He lifted it, weighing it in his palm. It was heavier than it looked. Warm, as though it answered to his touch. "Why me?"

"Because you're still feeling things you shouldn't," Halina said. "To them, that makes you dangerous. To Isabella, it made you necessary."

He slipped the drive into his coat. It settled against his chest.

"Won't they see the tampering?" he asked.

"I've malformed the upload," she answered. "Small disturbances in the suit data. Enough to make the session look like a corrupted sequence. A glitch. We can't keep that from forensics forever— but it buys time."

Dex nodded, the drive a weight and a promise.

Halina's voice softened. "She used to call tethering sacred."

Dex turned toward the door.

"A sacrament," Halina added. "A secret shared so deeply it could never be owned from above. That's why they'll never understand it. They think tethering is control. It was always connection."

He paused in the doorway, her words heavy in his chest. Then he left.

They downloaded him before release. The tether data had failed to upload into HALCION's cloud again—almost certainly due to Halina's tampering.

Standard protocol followed: a full pulse scan and digital extraction of the tether log. Dex sat in silence, staring at the static bloom on the monitor as the GEIST interface tried—and failed—to make sense of the session with Halina Voss.

The tech asked no questions.

He just frowned, logged the sync, and muttered something about another "corrupted data sequence" and that "someone better figure out why these sessions keep logging as ghosts."

Dex kept his face still. Nodded when expected. And left.

His bungalow greeted him with the familiar sound of air cycling through vents, the hum of the lights warming overhead, and the subtle ache behind his ribs that always showed up when he left HALCION, that always grew stronger once he slid his key in and turned the polished knob.

He kicked off his boots but didn't bother changing clothes. Instead, he dropped into the chair by the kitchen window, reached into the breast pocket of his shirt, and pulled out the drive.

Still there. Still warm. Still humming.

He turned it over in his palm. Just a matte-black surface that caught the light wrong, like it absorbed it instead of reflecting it. It reminded him of something dead. Or sleeping.

They'd already pulled the file. Saw the null read. Blank. No usable data, no digestible transcript. The session had technically occurred—the biometric record confirmed it—but the output was noise. Distorted. Not all of it, just enough to hide the existence of the object in his hand and the plan surrounding it.

He replayed the last thirty seconds before the disconnect in his mind. The shift in Halina's body. The slight stutter in her breath. The way the tether itself had... flattened, like it hit a pressure wall.

She did it on purpose.

Not by fighting the session—that would've triggered resistance markers—but by embedding disruption into the session. A neural decoy. Subtle enough to slip past GEIST's detection, strong enough to foul the record.

They won't find anything, he thought.

He was the only one who knew what had happened. That scared him more than he expected.

He moved to the window, pulled the shade halfway, and leaned his forehead against the cool pane.

You're still feeling things you shouldn't, she'd said.

Maybe. Or maybe he was finally starting to feel what he'd spent the last few months trying not to.

The problem now was Malik.

If Malik had helped Isabella with the project—and Dex was nearly certain he had—he might be the only one left who knew how to figure out what was on the drive. Or why it mattered. But reaching him would be suicide. Malik wasn't someone you requested. He was unreachable.

Dex closed his eyes.

If he asked the wrong question too openly, they'd audit his previous sessions. If he waited too long, it might be too late.

He needed to find a thread. A glitch. A coincidence. Something Malik might see without Dex ever needing to say his name.

He turned the drive over in his hand again. It was inert. But it felt like a key. The question was: to what? And how long could he keep it before someone came looking?

The tunnels beneath the city were never still. Air moaned through forgotten ducts, water dripped from broken pipes, and somewhere deeper a generator thrummed like a pulse. Charlotte crouched beside fresh graffiti, the word SENSATE still wet, jagged strokes bleeding into the brick.

Around her, half a dozen members of Chaos shifted in the lantern glow. Faces sharp with hunger, eyes wide with sleepless fire. They weren't just survivors anymore. They were insurgents waiting for the first real break.

"Aurelio's gone," one of them murmured, voice almost too low to carry.

Charlotte's expression shifted to anger. "Not gone. Murdered. That's worse. He'll have left us clues, though. Persephone, too."

Her gaze was fixed on the map scratched across the concrete wall—an old sewer schematic overlaid with chalk marks from weeks of scouting. Lines crossed and recrossed, dead ends marked in red, collapsed corridors notated with yellow. But one section was circled in green.

"We checked again tonight," said Liam, the youngest of the group, his fingers still stained with chalk. "The Order poured concrete down most of the feeder tunnels, but they missed a spur here." He tapped the circle with a dirty, oil-stained fingernail. "Old storm drain. Rusted grate, half-sheared already. Wide enough to slip two—maybe three—at a time."

Another, Elias, shook his head. "They'll have sensors aboveground. You step out, you trip a grid."

"Not here," Liam insisted. "We rigged a voltmeter. Nothing—no current, no pulse. It's like they forgot it was there."

Charlotte stepped closer, her palm pressed against the wall where the chalk circled. She could feel the chill seeping through the stone. She remembered the day the Curtain went up, how the air itself had seemed to shiver with finality. But here was proof: even walls built to last had cracks.

"If they missed one," she said, "they missed others. We map this. We test it. We see if it runs beyond their line."

"And if it doesn't?" Elias asked.

"Then we widen it," Charlotte assured. "We turn one weakness into ten. The Curtain isn't invincible. Neither are they."

The crew exchanged glances, tension sparking like a live wire. For months they had been scavengers, ghosts in the ruins. Now Charlotte was asking them to become something else—saboteurs, infiltrators, a blade against the Order's armor.

She crouched again, wiping her fingers through the wet graffiti, smearing the word until her palm came away black with paint. "They wanted us underground," she said, her voice steady and sharp. "But the earth isn't a prison. It's a foundation. We only have one direction to go—so we rise."

Silence followed, raw and electric.

The lantern guttered, shadows fluttering like moth wings across the walls. Above them, the city was oblivious. But down here, beneath Atlanta's skin, Charlotte and her crew had found something that mattered more than survival.

Not just a way out. Not just a way in. A way forward.

Part VIII
PROVIDENCE

May 24, 2027

"When good befalls a man he calls it
providence; when evil, fate."

~ Knut Hamsun

<h1 style="text-align:center">29</h1>

<h1 style="text-align:center">UNSPOKEN</h1>

TOBIAS TURNED THE leaflet over in his hands again, the paper already worn soft from nights of study. Charlotte had left it behind at Emerald City. He hadn't seen her since she vanished, but the leaflet was proof she was alive. Proof she was with them.

Chaos.

The Order spat the name like poison, branding them heretics, traitors, liars. But Tobias had read the words on the page until they felt like scripture: *The Order lies. The Curtain is a cage. Empathy is not a sickness. You are not alone.*

He knew propaganda when he saw it, but this was different. It wasn't only rhetoric. It felt like a message meant for someone who could listen close enough to hear what pulsed beneath the surface.

He sat at his desk, the city humming low through the walls, and spread the leaflet open under the lamplight. He had memorized every sentence, every jagged flourish of the phoenix logo, but his eyes still traced it, searching.

The trouble with Chaos was that no one would say where they were. People whispered about them in alleyways, rumors traded like contraband—but the headquarters was always *elsewhere*, never marked, never mapped. Silence protected them better than walls.

And yet Charlotte had left this for him; he could feel it somehow. She must have known he'd look deeper.

Tobias leaned closer, squinting at the fine print along the top border. It wasn't quite even. A handful of letters looked shifted—almost imperceptibly—and bolded. At first he thought it was a flaw. Now he wrote them down on the pad by his left hand: **E, V, I, F.**

His pulse quickened as he scanned again and found another small cluster along the bottom border: **S, I, N, P, O, T.**

The letters had to mean something, but what? Thinking they must be an anagram, he began writing them in different arrangements until he finally solved it.

FIVE POINTS.

The city's oldest crossroads, the knot of tunnels where every artery seemed to converge. It was unspoken—never written outright—but there it was, hidden in the text like a whisper between the words.

He sat back hard in his chair. He'd passed through Five Points a hundred times, walking the bright, camera-patrolled concourses where commuters shuffled without looking up. But below those polished floors were levels the public never saw anymore—sealed stairwells, forgotten maintenance tunnels, old rail lines swallowed by the Curtain's construction.

The more he thought about it, the clearer it became. Where better for Chaos to root itself than in the city's own veins? A place everyone passed through daily, but no one ever really saw.

His fingers traced the jagged logo again. The phoenix's wings weren't symmetrical. On the left side, one feather bent at too sharp an angle to be decorative. On the right margin of the page, a line of text tilted to match it: *The way out is under.*

Coded instructions, meant for anyone desperate enough to notice.

Tobias set his palm flat on the leaflet—not to steady himself but to prove it was real. This wasn't a private message Charlotte had left just for him. It was a trail left in plain sight, waiting for the desperate, the watchful, the ones ready to flee. He just happened to be one of them.

Still, fear crawled close. If the Order caught him with this in hand, it would be enough to end him. They didn't need proof of allegiance to Chaos—only suspicion. Silence was Chaos' shield, and here he sat holding a paper that hummed with quiet instructions each time he looked at it.

He whispered into the silence of his apartment, "You wanted to be found."

The city outside his open window seemed to answer in stillness—the pause between trains, the low thrum of power lines, the rare absence of sirens. Secrets lived in those spaces between sounds.

Tobias pulled out an old transit map from his desk drawer. He spread it beside the leaflet, aligning lines, marking points where the tunnels crossed. Five Points glowed in his imagination, the heart of a web. The leaflet's coded letters fit the map like teeth in a lock.

It was all there, if you looked hard enough for what wasn't said.

He let out a shaky laugh, half disbelief, half relief. He'd been chasing shadows for weeks, convinced the search was impossible—yet the answer had been here all along, hidden in the leaflet's design.

Charlotte was there. He knew it as surely as he knew his own name.

He folded the leaflet carefully, tucking it into the false bottom of the desk drawer where he kept his other dangerous secrets. His resolve sharpened with the motion. Tomorrow he would find an excuse to reroute his shift toward Five Points. He'd take the maintenance stairwell the public never noticed—the one he'd passed a dozen times without question.

It terrified him. But the thought of doing nothing terrified him more.

He sat back in his chair, staring at the shadows pooling in the corners of his apartment. The city outside slept, unaware of the battle growing in its veins. And in that quiet—in that hidden silence—Tobias felt his decision settle.

He would find Chaos. He would find Charlotte.

Vaughn Merrick had walked the same block three times already, his polished shoes slick with rain, his breath fogging in the cold spring air. Downtown had changed since the days when he knew every shopkeeper by name—glass towers rising like sterile sentinels, most of the diners gone, most of the bookstores shuttered—but Emerald City still glowed stubbornly, its neon sign spilling warm color across the pavement. Each time he told himself he'd keep walking, yet each time he circled back, orbiting the door as if pulled in by its gravity.

He told himself it was only curiosity, but the lie was thin. The truth was harder, heavier. He was restless, unmoored, and something unspoken had been lodged behind his ribs for years.

He thought of Isabella, as he always did when his steps grew uncertain. She had been his partner in every sense—they had shared everything from boardroom battles to Sunday mornings tangled in bed. Their sex life had been good—better than good. And Isabella had known from the beginning about the shadow in him, the desire that bent differently than the world expected. She hadn't shamed him for it; she met it with honesty. Over the years they found ways to navigate it together: a handful of carefully arranged nights where he was allowed to step outside their marriage to scratch the itch he could not ignore. Those nights had never broken them; they were part of the trust that bound them.

A year before her death, she told him she wanted to separate. She said it without cruelty or anger— just clarity. She was tired of compromise, tired of bending her life around the shadow he never let fully into the light. They stayed under the same roof—for appearances, for habit, for the strange comfort of each other's company. But their intimacy shifted; their laughter softened into quiet conversations; their touches grew rarer.

Despite the separation, she remained the center of his world, and when she died, the center collapsed.

Her absence made the house even emptier now, every room echoing with what they had been and what they hadn't. And here he was, circling a bar like a man rehearsing a decision, knowing full well this door wasn't only about whiskey or want. It was about the part of himself she had always recognized, accepted, and finally set him free to face on his own.

Vaughn slowed his steps the fourth time he passed the entrance. The glow of the sign washed against his face, softening the few lines age had carved there, and for a moment he almost let himself believe he belonged in its light. Then the old instincts snapped back—the ones that kept him polished and careful, unshakable no matter what the room required of him.

He stopped just shy of the door, pretending to check his watch though he had nowhere else to be. The sidewalk stretched quiet, damp with the last of the rain. Through the door he heard the hum of conversation, scatter of laughter, the low clink of glass. Ordinary and safe, yet to him it felt like a border, a line more dangerous than any courtroom or boardroom he had ever faced.

For decades, he had lived by what he didn't say. His career, his marriage, his friendships—all carefully tended gardens where silence did the work words never could. He learned early that desire was something to be dammed, denied, and buried beneath obligation. Even when Isabella gave him permission to unearth urges, it was always in carefully measured increments—never fully, never without secrecy.

Now no one was left to make excuses for him, no one to arrange the boundaries. The decision was his alone, and the weight of it pressed down on him heavily.

He imagined being recognized—the respectable widower, still invited to fundraisers and council dinners, caught stepping into a bar that made no pretense of being anything but what it was. The shame tightened his throat—absurd, misplaced but relentless.

He lingered long enough to feel the old reflex—turn, walk away, swallow the hunger until it quieted. He had done it a thousand times. But tonight the hunger growled; it prowled the edges of him, restless, insistent. The unspoken part of himself pressed harder, no longer content to be dismissed.

He stood with his hand almost at the handle, close enough to feel the chill of metal. The door was only wood and hinges, but to him it might as well have been a confessional. He wasn't sure which terrified him more—that someone inside might see him, or that no one would.

Rain began again, soft at first, drumming lightly on the awning above the door. Vaughn lingered there, collar turned up, telling himself he'd wait out the weather before heading home. But when he glanced sideways through the narrow pane of glass, the lie unraveled.

Inside, the bar glowed with warmth no weather could touch. Bottles gleamed amber under soft lights, laughter rippled easily through the air. Some patrons just mingled while others danced under the mirrorball in the back—all inside without any care of being seen. Vaughn's gaze shifted from the patrons to the man behind the bar.

He moved with a steadiness Vaughn recognized instantly, though he couldn't have said why—something in the set of his shoulders, the unhurried way he wiped down the counter before pouring another drink. He wasn't trying to charm the room or command it; he was simply present. And that presence charmed, commanded without effort. Vaughn glanced at the patrons around the bar and realized he wasn't the only one watching him.

Vaughn felt it hit—sudden and undeniable. Attraction, yes—but more than that. A pull, as if the restlessness that had been pacing inside him all night had finally spotted its quarry. He didn't even know the man's name. That didn't matter. For the first time in years, something in him stopped circling and leaned forward.

He looked away quickly, embarrassed by the sharpness of it, like someone had caught him staring at something he had no right to want. But the image stayed with him—stubborn. The cut-off sleeves. The strong, quiet hands. The unspoken invitation in his smile.

Vaughn's chest tightened. He had stood at thresholds before—hundreds of them—and always chosen the safety of silence. Tonight, silence felt heavier than stepping through.

He stayed with his hand near the door but not yet on it, pulse ticking faster than the rain. Through the glass, he glimpsed again at the bartender—steady at his post, moving with the calm of someone who had all the time in the world. Vaughn envied that kind of ease. His own life had been built out of polish and posture, always careful, always deliberate. Calm had never felt natural to him—a bit of chaos was the perfect armor. This man wore his calmness like a second skin, as tightly as the jeans clinging to his ass and thighs.

The urge to turn away rose again. He could imagine it so easily—slipping back into the anonymity of the wet street, retreating to his house with its curated silence, pouring a drink alone, convincing himself tonight had only been a test. It would be safer. Cleaner. The kind of choice Vaughn Merrick had made his entire life.

Yet the thought of that empty return felt unbearable. The house without Isabella was no refuge—it was a mausoleum. He had spent too many evenings there replaying her absence, listening to the echo of his own footsteps in rooms once alive with her laughter. He couldn't face another night of sitting in the dark mourning her while pretending he hadn't wanted to explore the shadows of his urges for decades.

His fingers brushed the handle at last, the cold metal startling in its simplicity. How many years had he been stopped by fear of this moment? He thought of Isabella—not in anger, not in guilt, but with the strange gratitude grief sharpens. She had known who he was. She had given him space, even permission, to name it. And in the end, she had left him with the truth: she could not live his silence for him.

The rain drummed harder, sliding off the awning in sheets. Vaughn's reflection looked back at him in the glass of the door—gray at the temples, lines carved by time, eyes darker than he remembered. A man still standing, yes, but one who had lived too long with everything important unsaid. For the first time, he didn't feel shame at that reflection. He felt... tired of it. Tired of carrying the unspoken truths like it was duty instead of the weight it truly was.

The handle turned easily under his grip, a quiet click. He closed his eyes for a breath, letting the air out slowly. All the words he had never said—the confessions, the wants, the truths—crowded his mouth, eager to spill. But he didn't speak—didn't need to. He stepped inside, leaving the silence, the fear, and the rain behind him.

30
UNINHIBITED

MOST NIGHTS AT the bar, Dex wore a fitted black tank with chest fur spilling from its top, layered under an open, sleeveless flannel, that hung just to the waist of his jeans—hugging him in all the right places. The look did nothing to conceal the thick hair under his arms or the tattoos that climbed his forearms like vines— mixed with others inked with intention, symbols of memory, connection, and protection... and a few he no longer cared to explain.

Tonight was no different; his red-and-black flannel stood out in the crowd.

The room buzzed with soft bass, low light, and bodies thirsty for distilled distraction. Loneliness drifted between tables like fog. Not desperation—just a low, steady ache everyone had learned to carry. A thirst no liquor could quite touch.

Lately, though, something had shifted. Patrons seemed... livelier. Over the last few weeks more faces had started to thaw, some more than others. Dex moved among them with ease—pouring, nodding, filtering the noise like straining ice in a shaker. He'd memorized the rhythms: who wanted two limes, who tipped, who flirted but never tipped, who always came with their friend but left with a stranger. The regulars were part of the heartbeat of the bar.

"Hey Daddy," a bright, teasing voice called from the lower corner of the bar.

Dex glanced up without turning fully. Kevin—baby-faced, artfully tousled hair, tight pants—licked his lips whenever he ordered.

"What's it gonna be tonight?" Dex asked, already reaching for the well vodka.

"You already know," Kevin purred. "You're the reason I keep showing up."

"You sure it's not for the free popcorn?" Dex teased as Kevin grabbed a handful from the bowl on the bar.

"Daddy, please." Kevin grinned, then leaned in. "If I said I was ready to be corrupted, would you at least consider it?"

"You're already corrupted." Dex said, sliding a vodka soda across the bar. "I'm just here to hydrate you."

"You do nothing of the sort," Kevin said, winking. "I always leave this place parched."

Dex smirked and kept walking. The world outside had shifted, but boys like that never did. They craved danger in safe portions—enough to feel alive, never enough to bleed. The upside of pouring drinks for them was knowing the liquor did more than lower inhibitions. Alcohol dulled Serexin's grip, blurring the chemical chokehold the Order had forced on everyone. Most of them just thought it made the night brighter. The Order, for all its surveillance and science, still hadn't put that together.

He moved past a table of older men playing cards with fierce focus, beers barely touched. Near the jukebox a couple of regulars argued about whose song would play next. Familiar sounds wrapped around him like muscle memory—proof the world outside still didn't entirely matter here.

He slid under the hinged section of the bar just as a voice called out from the far end.

"Dex!"

Dex glanced up and grinned. Diego waved a salt-rimmed margarita glass like he'd won something.

"You gonna make me beg for a refill, Daddy?" Diego teased.

Dex raised an eyebrow. "Aren't you already on your third?"

"Irrelevant."

Dex reached for the tequila. "Calling me Daddy again?"

"Only because it's accurate."

Kevin chimed from down the bar, "Hey—he's my Daddy."

"Correction," Dex said dryly, sliding the drink over. "I'm nobody's Daddy. Y'all call me that because it makes your drinks feel earned."

Laughter followed—easy, warm. These were his people in the way only bar families get to be. They didn't know his past and didn't ask; they showed up and took whatever presence—and poison—he offered.

He was finishing a tab when a voice beside him said, "That crowd's rowdier than usual."

Dex turned.

Marcus—his manager and unofficial keeper of calm—stood there with a bottle of Ketel in one hand and a tablet tucked under his arm. "I thought Javier was helping you handle the rush tonight."

"He was," Dex said. "Called out sick about an hour ago. I didn't have time to grab someone else."

Marcus blinked. "And you handled it alone?"

Dex shrugged. "Routine at this point. Lots of memorized orders from regulars makes it a bit easier."

Marcus let out a low whistle. "I'll make sure you're tipped out extra. Don't want you burning out and feeling shorted."

Dex gave a lopsided smile. "Don't worry—I recharge with bourbon."

Marcus chuckled, saluted half-heartedly, and headed back toward the office with his vodka.

Dex grabbed Diego's empty glass and wiped the salt off the bar, catching sight of the door just as a man entered. For a moment the room leaned toward him—fresh meat whose arrival pulled hungry eyes from every corner.

Dex wasn't immune to his charm. Not because he tried to be noticed, but because he didn't. There was a steadiness to his walk, and you could tell he was used to commanding in spaces that bent to him. The fact that he was alone made him stand out even more.

He sat at the far end of the bar—tall, wide shoulders, dressed in a charcoal suit cut to his frame rather than off a rack. Dark brown hair with a few gray streaks, neatly combed; beard trimmed, but not too close. His eyes—striking blue, piercing, sharp—hit Dex like a chord and reminded him of David's; his stomach tightened at the thought of him. He pretended to adjust a bottle on the shelf above and watched.

That recognition again. Not of the face, necessarily—but of the *energy*. Like a tuning fork vibrating against memory.

A flash from Halina's tether session surfaced— this man, briefly seen beside Isabella Merrick in a memory not meant for him.

Dex finished with the tab he was closing, took a breath, and moved to the man's side of the bar— figuring he wanted something classic versus a basic alcohol and mixer.

Sure enough, the man said, "An Old Fashioned— Maker's if you've got it."

The voice matched the frame: low, confident, just enough drawl to suggest Georgia roots, refined with an educated, businessman polish. Even that reminded him of David.

Dex nodded without a word and reached for the bottle. Angostura, muddled sugar, Maker's, twirling the spoon so the contents swirled around a single ice sphere. The scent of toasted port filled the air between them. The man watched him work, faintly amused. Dex expressed an orange peel with fire, tossed it in the glass with a candied cherry, and slid it across.

Their hands brushed.

SHIT.

A spark—not deep, not overwhelming, just a flicker—a jolt beneath the skin like a quiet and unspoken resonance that almost went unnoticed.

Dex felt the man's tension, the walls he kept up. And something else beneath it—*curiosity.* Maybe hunger. But not just physical.

The man blinked once. Dex didn't react; he'd learned not to.

The man eyes sharpened for a second. Dex stayed composed—professionally casual—but inside he clocked the reaction too.

Interesting.

The man lifted the drink to his lips, sipped, and exhaled softly through his nose like he'd discovered something he'd been missing.

By the time Dex finished the next two orders, the gentlemen flagged him again with a lift of his glass.

"You pour with confidence," he said, lifting his glass, the amber liquid glowing under the captured light. "And skill. Rare these days— nobody puts love into the craft."

"Love is a commodity these days." Dex smirked, perhaps with a bit more cheekiness than he intended.

"Touché."

"Besides," Dex added with a wink, "confidence comes easy when you're good at what you do."

The man chuckled low, like he wanted Dex to feel the vibrations. "The question is... are you only good behind the bar?"

Dex laughed under his breath. "Well, that bourbon seems to be doing a number on your inhibitions."

"You've been watching me," the man said, leaning in just enough for Dex to catch the spice of his cologne. "Since I walked in."

Dex didn't deny it. "You were hard to miss. Figured you were straight and lost. Still not sure that you're not."

The man rested both elbows on the bar now, hands folded loosely, eyes even more captivating up close. "I'm not here to define myself for your comfort."

Dex tipped his head. "You do know you're in a gay bar, right?"

"Figured it out pretty fast."

"And you stayed."

"The music's good." The corner of his mouth tugged. "And so's the view."

Dex slid a coaster toward him. "Smooth."

"Honest," the man countered. He let the word sit there, then added, "You've got a tell, you know. You watch people's eyes, like you're looking for a story."

Dex blinked at him, caught off guard. "Do I?"

"You do," the man assured, tracing the rim of his glass. "It's disarming."

Dex smiled faintly, sliding a fresh cocktail in his direction. "I guess I like stories."

"I've got a few," the man murmured.

"I bet you do."

They held each other's eyes for a moment too long, static humming in the air between them.

"I've been with men before."

Dex didn't flinch, but the room shifted.

"Years ago," the man continued, almost clarifying for himself. "When I was younger. Before I married. And a few times after that."

Dex poured slowly, giving him space to say it. "You don't strike me as the type to follow a traditional path."

"I didn't marry for tradition," the man said. "It was natural. Convenient. Practical. There was loyalty. And we had children almost immediately, all grown up now and moved away." He stopped, thumb brushing his glass. "I haven't heard from them since..." his voice trailed off, the thought unfinished. "We built a beautiful family and a beautiful life. But after they left, nothing remained between us—not physically, not for years—except the kind of love you can't erase, even if you try."

"Still," Dex said with a slow nod, careful not to reveal too much, "you don't look like you're here for closure of that relationship."

"Maybe I'm here for distraction," he replied.

"Distraction doesn't usually come in a glass."

"No," the man said, eyes catching the light, "But sometimes it starts there."

"Trying to drown something?" Dex asked, his gaze narrowing.

"Grief," the man admitted. "Though not the fresh kind."

Dex went quiet. Then, carefully: "You lose someone?"

"A friend," the man said. "Someone brilliant. Someone the world didn't deserve."

Dex's throat tightened. He knew "friend" meant Isabella. He felt the hair on his arms rise.

"She'd hate that I'm here wallowing," the man said, voice lower now. "But she'd commend me for finally letting go of some demons."

"She might appreciate the bourbon."

A soft laugh. "She'd certainly appreciate your pour."

Dex smiled faintly. "I lost someone, too. It's definitely been a hard thing to overcome."

"Sorry for your loss, handsome."

"For yours as well."

Their eyes met and held. The man let the moment stretch, the hum of the bar receding around them.

"You got a name?" he asked finally.

Dex tilted his head, a small smile curling his lips. "Do you?"

The man leaned closer, voice like velvet. "You can call me Daddy."

Dex laughed, full and unfiltered. "Funny."

"What's so funny about that—I definitely could be."

"What's funny is that's what *most* here call me," Dex replied with a wink. "You're not old enough to be mine... but I'm bold enough to be yours."

"I'll call you whatever you want, Daddy," he said smoothly, his smile deepening, "if it means you might come home with me tonight."

Dex didn't blink, but his breath hitched slightly. The banter had been a game until now; this sounded like a promise.

Between orders, the man stayed at the bar, the conversation sliding between teasing and confessional. He asked about the music, Dex's tattoos, even his favorite drink to make. Dex avoided questions he didn't have to answer but found himself giving small pieces away anyway—his laugh, a glance held too long, a hand almost brushing closer than it should.

Last call bled into clean-up. Marcus flipped chairs onto tables. The house lights flickered to amber. Dex untied his apron, aware of the man's eyes tracking every move.

The gentleman drained his glass, pulled on his tailored suit coat, and stepped up to the bar's edge.

"So, Daddy..." he said, pausing just long enough for it to matter. "Am I taking you home?"

Dex couldn't name the feeling, only that it had been stirring since the moment the man walked in—something that wound tighter with every glance, every word. He rinsed the glass clean, set it carefully on the rack, and dragged the towel across the counter more to steady himself than to dry it.

Then he met the man's eyes, a smile tugging at his mouth. "Sure, handsome. Lead the way."

May 25, 2027

"The only way to get rid of
temptation is to yield to it...
I can resist everything but temptation."

~ Oscar Wilde

<h1 style="text-align:center">31
YIELD</h1>

DEX HADN'T PLANNED to drive tonight, let alone steer a luxury sedan through Midtown, but his companion was in no shape to—leaning against the passenger window, one eye closed, held up by nothing but trust and residual charm.

"Nice BMW."

"Thanks," Vaughn murmured. "You're a careful driver."

"Habit," Dex said, keeping his eyes on the road. The leather wheel was warm beneath his palms, the console glowed amber in the soft dark.

"That from your past life?"

Dex paused. "Something like that. I used to drive these streets, almost daily on patrol, before the Order..."

The silence that followed wasn't awkward—just measured. They passed an empty greenspace within Ansley Park, the statue in its center lit like a marble ghost while the city slept around it.

Then he said, "I'm Vaughn Merrick."

Not a boast—more like a confession.

Dex glanced warmly at his passenger. "Dex Truitt."

"Dex," Vaughn repeated, like he liked the taste of it. "Short for something?"

"Nope."

Vaughn looked out the window again. "I felt it."

Dex didn't answer right away, waiting until he completed his turn onto Vaughn's street. "Felt what?"

"The spark," Vaughn said softly. "When our hands brushed at the bar."

Dex swallowed hard.

"I've never felt anything like that before," Vaughn continued. "Like something moved through me. Or maybe into me."

"You were drinking."

"I was," he agreed. "And still a bit drunk. But don't insult me by pretending I imagined it."

Dex said nothing.

Despite the address he'd selected from the navigation, Vaughn's house was much grander than Dex had expected—a sleek, modern home nestled within a mix of the typical Tudor and Craftsman style homes for which Ansley Park was known.

Dex stepped into understated elegance—dark wood floors, tall ceilings, a wall of glass framing a backyard featuring a softly-lit pool and scattered glimpses of the skyline beyond.

And art—real art—the kind that carried history, weight, and depth in its brushstrokes.

Vaughn set his coat over the arm of a leather chair. "Make yourself at home."

But Dex didn't move.

Vaughn turned, eyes softer now. He stepped in close and kissed him without hesitation.

Dex melted into it, surprised by how soft Vaughn's mouth was, how warm. Their lips moved slowly at first, then deeper. Vaughn's tongue teased the edge of his, asking for more; Dex gave it, heart stuttering in his chest.

When Vaughn pulled back, his smile was faint. "I can tell by that kiss you're used to having control."

"And I can tell by yours," Dex said, a bit breathless, "you're accustomed to stealing it."

Vaughn laughed.

Dex blinked. "You need something to soak up the bourbon."

"Planning to feed me?"

"Unless you'd rather pass out on the floor."

"You know that's not what I meant," Vaughn replied, flirting in earnest.

"I know," Dex countered, "but let's eat something heavier before we get to... dessert."

Ten minutes later, Dex was barefoot in Vaughn's open kitchen, flipping grilled cheese sandwiches in a hot skillet. Vaughn leaned on the counter, sipping water to dilute the whiskey.

"Apparently, you *are* good behind more than just the bar," Vaughn said, voice smooth.

"You haven't even tasted the sandwich yet."

"I wasn't talking about the sandwich."

Dex smirked. "You're bold when you're buzzed."

"I'm bold when I'm interested."

Vaughn took a bite of the sandwich and let out a groan. "Jesus. That's not fair. How did you turn such a boring sandwich into something gourmet."

"Grilled cheese is *not* boring," Dex replied. "It's sacred."

"I stand corrected."

They ate in the hush of shared appetite—and something hungrier. Dex hadn't cooked for anyone in months. Not since Charlie.

When the plates were empty, Vaughn stood. "You smell like bourbon, butter, and trouble."

Dex raised a brow. "That a compliment?"

"Well, I like all three, so I suppose it is."

Dex smelled himself, "I smell like more than that—I'm actually quite ripe and could probably use a shower."

"I could use one, too." Vaughn reached out, touched Dex's wrist. "There's a guest room down the hall. You can shower in there. Clean towels on the shelf. Or actually—"

"I'll take the guest room," Dex said quickly.

Vaughn's mouth twitched, but he said nothing.

Dex stepped into the guest room and immediately knew.

The books. The faint scent of neroli and vetiver. A framed photo on the desk—Isabella posed in front of a granite façade with a teenage boy in a Yale hoodie, likely her son, both smiling beneath the canopy of autumn's red leaves. This had been her room.

He touched nothing.

Instead, he stripped quickly and stepped into the ensuite shower—matte black tile, rainfall steam. Dex stood beneath it until his skin flushed pink, letting the hot water drum against his chest until his thoughts stilled into nothing but heat and breath.

He towel-dried, wrapped it around his waist, and stepped out barefoot.

The house was dim now, only the patio lights outside painting shadows across the floor.

Vaughn waited in the living room, seated on the sofa, robe open and loose around his shoulders. His posture was relaxed, open, unapologetic. He was thick and stunning—broad chest covered with silver-sprinkled dark fur that matched his hair, soft stomach, strong thighs. A bear in the best sense: muscle built under softness; power wrapped in comfort. His cock hung thick and veined, heavy between his legs; his balls hung lower, bull-like and full.

Dex froze.

Vaughn looked up.

"You took your time," he said.

"I didn't think you'd be waiting like that."

"You didn't think I'd want you?"

Dex didn't answer, just walked forward. Vaughn met him halfway.

Their mouths found each other again—slower, deeper. Dex moaned, breath shuddering. Vaughn's hands cupped his jaw, then slid down his neck, over his shoulders, tracing his outline.

Dex had shared amazing kisses with several men before, but kissing Vaughn wasn't the same as with other men. Vaughn kissed like he was listening— every shift of his lips and swirl of his tongue a question, and Dex's movements were the answers. He bit gently at Dex's bottom lip, soothed it with his tongue, hand cradling the back of Dex's head, fingers moving through damp hair, pulling him closer.

Dex hesitated slightly but let him lead.

Vaughn pressed him back toward the wall, hands roaming now, palming his chest, exploring every edge of muscle and scar like he had the right.

"You're rock solid," Vaughn whispered, reaching for Dex's cock. "Everywhere."

Dex moaned gratitude into Vaughn's mouth.

Vaughn kissed his Adam's apple, down his throat, traced the path to his collarbone with lips and tongue, bit gently, then sank to his knees.

He looked up, eyes weighted with want.

Dex's breath grew shallow, staggered.

Vaughn mouthed him through the towel first— slow, insistent, playful.

Dex shivered. Although he'd recently been intimate with Beau, the connection here was different—tender, intense, reminiscent of his first night with David. He thought of Charlie, too, but pushed the thought away.

"You okay?" Vaughn asked.

"Yeah," Dex breathed. "Just... haven't done this in a while."

Vaughn kissed him again along the waist. "Then let me."

The towel dropped.

He took Dex into his mouth with practiced ease, beard brushing Dex's thighs and balls, tongue tracing every contour. Dex gasped, one hand braced on the wall, the other buried in Vaughn's hair.

It was slow. Patient. Worshipful.

Dex yielded. For once, he didn't try to take control.

When he came, it was with a shudder and a sound he didn't mean to make—something between a growl and a whimper.

Vaughn stood, kissed him again—tasting of cinnamon and semen—and collapsed gently onto the sofa.

Dex sank to his knees, taking Vaughn in his hands. He licked up the length of his cock, kissed along the underside, savoring its weight and heat. His tongue curled around the head before he slid him into his mouth.

Vaughn groaned, fingers finding Dex's damp hair again. "Fuck," he hissed.

Dex bobbed slowly, sucking him deep, dragging his tongue on the pullback. He could feel Vaughn getting close—hips twitching, breath uneven.

But Vaughn pulled him off gently. "I don't want to come like that."

Dex looked up, surprised.

"I want to be inside you," Vaughn said, voice hoarse.

Dex stood, heart pounding, and glanced back down at Vaughn's dick. "Be gentle."

Vaughn rose too, turning him slowly. He kissed Dex's shoulder, the nape of his neck, the space between his shoulder blades. Dex melted into it, goosebumps rippling across his shoulders and arms.

Vaughn bent Dex forward, hands sliding to grip his ass.

"You're—" he whispered into Dex's left ear, kissing the space behind it before adding, "fucking beautiful."

He leaned forward fully, kissed down Dex's spine, then paused at the base before kneeling completely.

Dex gasped as Vaughn parted his cheeks and kissed him there—gently yet greedily. His tongue circled, teased, coaxed. Dex's knees buckled.

Vaughn took his time, working Dex open with his tongue, stretching the muscle loose, and slicking his hole with spit. When he was satisfied Dex could take him, he stood, hands steady on Dex's waist, and pressed against him with gentle intent.

The stretch was slow, deliberate.

Dex groaned, both hands braced on the back of the sofa.

Vaughn filled him slowly, running his hands over Dex's chest, pulling him upright as he leaned forward until their torsos pressed together. He whispered into his ear again. "You took me so well."

The motion was so slow and delicate that Dex shuddered.

Vaughn moved in deep, deliberate thrusts, his chest brushing Dex's back. Sweat formed along their bodies. Dex could feel Vaughn's breath on his neck, the way he groaned into the curve of his shoulder.

"Look at me," Vaughn said, turning his face gently.

Dex did, and their eyes locked as Vaughn's rhythm quickened, grip tightening. Dex had already come, but feeling Vaughn inside him made his dick hard again. He reached down, stroking himself in time with Vaughn's thrusts.

When Dex came for the second time, it was hard and shot across the leather sofa cushion.

Vaughn followed seconds later with a grunt, collapsing against him, holding him tight.

They cleaned up in the dim light, laughing softly at the mess they'd made.

"You're trouble," Dex muttered.

"You like it."

Vaughn led him into the bedroom.

The sheets were soft. The bed, firm.

They lay tangled—Dex's head on Vaughn's chest, one arm draped over his stomach. Vaughn's hand never left his back. He held Dex like a man starved of touch, and Dex fell asleep there, safely in his arms.

The smell of sausage woke him.

Dex blinked into the early light slanting across the bedroom. The sheets were still warm beside him, but Vaughn was gone.

He rolled out of bed slowly, bare feet striking the cold, wood floor as he followed the smell.

Vaughn was in the kitchen, back turned, wearing absolutely nothing—except newfound confidence. He stood at the stove stirring a skillet of potatoes, crumbled sausage, and eggs, muscles flexing as he worked. Toast popped behind him, and two mimosas already sparkled next to mugs of black coffee.

Dex leaned against the doorframe, arms crossed, just watching for a moment.

"Impressed?" Vaughn asked without turning.

"Terrified," Dex deadpanned.

"Don't be. I'm good with breakfast," Vaughn chuckled. He turned to Dex and gave him a show, dick swinging. "Also good with naked cooking—so long as the grease behaves."

"I see that," Dex laughed as he added some cream and sugar to one of the coffees, moving into the open living space. He slid onto the sofa and stretched out.

Vaughn plated the food, brought it over with the mimosas and his own coffee on a tray, and set it on the coffee table. He sat beside Dex, thighs brushing. They ate with their legs tangled—bare skin pressed together, warmth layered over warmth.

Conversation came easy.

They talked about food, the weather, a book Vaughn had been reading. No pressure. No assumptions. Just comfort. Every now and then their fingers brushed, or their knees nudged under the plates, and Dex felt something deep inside him unwind.

When they finished, Vaughn leaned back with a satisfied groan. "Goddamn. I forgot how good it feels to just... be with someone."

Dex turned, laid a hand lightly on his chest, palm over heartbeat. "You're easy to be with."

Vaughn blinked, surprised. "You think so?"

Dex nodded. "Comfortable. Uncomplicated."

Vaughn smiled, reaching for Dex's hand and lacing their fingers.

They sat like that for a while, morning light soft across their bodies, city sounds just a faint hush beyond the glass.

Eventually, Dex leaned in and kissed him—slow and soft, their mouths barely moving. It was less about hunger this time and more about grounding.

Vaughn pulled away first, lips still parted. "What was that for?"

Dex brushed his thumb along Vaughn's jaw. "Go take a shower."

Vaughn narrowed his eyes. "Yeah?"

"Yeah," Dex said quietly. "I want to be inside you this time."

Vaughn hesitated. He didn't smile. Didn't joke. Just... looked at Dex. There was vulnerability in his expression—real and unhidden. A flicker of something Dex hadn't seen in him before: nerves.

But behind it, trust.

"You sure?" Vaughn asked.

"Never been more so."

Vaughn nodded once, then he stood and walked to the bathroom without another word.

Dex cleaned up the plates, ran soapy water over the pan. He wasn't rushing—he wanted Vaughn to take his time. He needed the space and time, too, to steady himself.

When Vaughn returned, he wore nothing but a towel around his waist. His hair was damp, beard combed neatly. His posture was open—but Dex could still sense the tightness beneath it.

Dex stepped in close, and Vaughn's breath caught.

"You don't have to be anyone here," Dex said. "Not strong. Not in control. Just yield to me, like I did with you."

Vaughn nodded again, eyes shining.

Dex kissed him gently, hands gliding down his sides. He walked Vaughn backward toward the bedroom, pausing only to peel the towel from his hips and let it fall to the floor.

When they reached the bed, Dex guided him down with care, kissing his chest, his stomach, every inch he could reach.

Dex took his time and explored every part of Vaughn's body with desire—the arch of his back, the curve of his hips, the thick muscle beneath softness. He stroked, licked, kissed—listening to every reaction.

He spent extra time on Vaughn's hairy hole, lapping and darting his tongue all around the edges and inside—hunger growing with each curse and moan that escaped his feast. When Dex finished, he flipped Vaughn onto his back, staring ravenously at the man who had reawakened his humanity while stirring something feral and unrestrained.

Vaughn's hole was saturated, naturally relaxed, but Dex still lubed his cock and gave him time to respond to the pressure of his head pushing gently against it. Dex entered slowly, patiently, tenderly, watching every reaction. Vaughn gasped, groaned—his hand gripping Dex's arm like an anchor—keeping him close, keeping him deep.

Dex pressed kisses to Vaughn's lips, his shoulders, his throat, anywhere his mouth could reach—while whispering, "You okay?"

Vaughn nodded, biting his lip. "Yeah... you feel so good. Keep going."

Dex obeyed, his rhythm gentle at first—slow and measured—then turning more primal as his pace quickened. He watched Vaughn's face, every breath, every flicker of tension and release. He wanted him to feel held. Opened. Worshipped.

They moved together until the thrusts deepened, sweat glistening between them, breath stretching into gasps.

Vaughn came hands-free, burying his face into the pillow to stifle the sounds of pure ecstasy; he clutched Dex's arm, pulling him downward, wanting him closer.

Dex followed seconds later, embracing Vaughn tightly, spilling his seed with a moan that felt like a confession.

Afterward, they curled together beneath sticky sheets, Vaughn's head rising and falling with Dex's breath, his fingers tracing quiet paths along his ribs, while Dex sealed the moment with a scattering of tender kisses against his temple.

"Thank you," Vaughn blurted after some silence.

"For what?"

"If it weren't for seeing you behind the bar that night, I never would have stepped foot in Emerald City."

"Does that make me Dorothy for leading you, or does it make me the Wizard for giving you courage?"

"Well, the Wizard... aside from him being an asshole," Vaughn chuckled. "You also gave this Tin Man heart palpitations and this Scarecrow enough brains not to leave."

"I guess I *am* the Wizard," Dex said with a cheesy grin. "I even brought a drunk Dorothy home in her ruby red BMW."

Vaughn kissed him deeply. "There's no place like home."

Dex couldn't deny how at home he felt with Vaughn, especially after the past few months of feeling more like a house had fallen on him.

They fell asleep like that—wrapped in each other, tethered not by protocol but by intimacy. The connection wasn't a search into the past but an anchor into the present, resonating with hope for something beyond it.

32
CLUTCH

VAUGHN DROVE DEX home later that morning, once they woke from their nap. At the curb, he put the car in park and looked over.

"I want to see you again," he said.

"Yeah, I'd like that." Dex looked at him for a long moment, then grabbed his phone from the cradle. "I am putting my number in your phone."

"That's probably more practical—and less cheesy—than the business card I almost handed you," Vaughn said with a breathy laugh.

Dex handed the phone back and leaned in for a kiss—an opportunity Vaughn seized with fervor. Their mouths met with a firmness that left no room for second-guessing, Vaughn tasting faintly of the coffee he finished before leaving. His hand slid to the back of Dex's neck, warm fingers threading his hair, anchoring him.

His other hand found Dex's chest, pulling him closer across the console, knuckles pressing into muscle. The kiss deepened—tongues tangling, breaths mingling, each flicker of contact a demand for more. The air in the car thickened, leaving their breaths shallow and charged. Vaughn's thumb traced slow circles at Dex's jaw, grounding him even as the kiss threatened to sweep him away.

Dex had been kissed with lust and kissed with affection, but this was something else—something that pulled at the base of his spine, that wove into muscle and marrow, electric whispers telling him to stay in that moment forever.

The connection felt older than the single night they'd spent together, familiar and comfortable. He could feel Vaughn's pulse against his wrist, steady but strong, matching his own heartbeat until it was hard to tell where one ended and the other began.

When they broke apart, Vaughn kept his forehead pressed to Dex's, noses almost touching. Neither spoke. The silence was full, but not awkward—heavy with everything unspoken. Dex eased back, fingers lingering a moment too long on Vaughn's arm before he slipped out of the car. Vaughn's gaze held, something raw flickering in his expression, and Dex felt it: possibility—the dangerous kind, the echo of David, the resonance of what he shared with Charlie before the world collapsed.

The morning air cut against his skin, jolting him back into the here and now. He walked up the path to his door without looking back, though he felt Vaughn's eyes on him the whole way. Inside, the space was dim, holding the stale scent of absence. He shut the door and leaned against it, torso flat to the wood, his pulse still running high.

Then, as if pulled from a locked drawer in his mind, the last morning with Charlie unfolded: beard scraping against Dex's shoulder; the sharp inhale when Dex kissed his neck; years of professional partnership bleeding into the bedroom with an intensity almost too much to hold. They'd only had four days and three nights—and then it was gone.

Dex pressed the heel of his hands to his eyes to stop the tears, but they came anyway. He slumped to the floor under the weight of everything pushing him down, chest heaving in full sobs as he tried to catch his breath. He felt torn. Vaughn's kiss still clung to his lips, warm and present. The thought cut both ways: that it might be the start of something... or just another thing he would have to survive losing.

Two and a half days. That was all Dex managed before the pull of Vaughn's presence overcame the walls he'd built out of habit and fear.

In that time, Vaughn sent three texts—each warmer and sweeter than the last.

The first:

Enjoyed the other night. You have a way with grilled cheese.

The second:

I've kept my porch light on in case you need help finding your way back home.

The latest one that sent Dex over the edge:

I still want to see you again. I haven't stopped thinking about you.

Dex hadn't stopped thinking about him either. Forty-five minutes later he was on Vaughn's front step, the late-afternoon light fading around him, the porch lamp already burning—lit for him, waiting, a quiet promise that he was wanted.

The Prado breathed small sounds—the clack of a cyclist's chain, a dog's collar chiming as its owner led it on a stroll, leaves rustling together like a quiet applause. Behind the door: jazz, low and warm; the soft clink of glass; Vaughn moving somewhere close.

The door opened. Vaughn stood barefoot, sleeves shoved to his forearms, hair a little mussed, smile tugging. That smile unknotted something in Dex, an old tension surrendering in a fraction of a second.

"I was starting to think you'd make me wait all week," Vaughn said, stepping aside.

Dex crossed the threshold into a cool breath of citrus, clean linen, and a whisper of rosemary. "Couldn't stay away."

Vaughn kissed him, then drifted toward the kitchen as Dex walked in further. The house wore its elegance without trying—tall windows, warm floors, a few soft scuffs that hinted at lived-in late nights filled with laughter. Through the French doors, the patio glowed; string lights hung like constellations above the turquoise pool. Evening edged toward itself—darkening, softening, air cooling just enough.

Vaughn returned from the kitchen with a glass. "Old Fashioned. Not your level, but I took notes."

Dex sipped, letting the sugar and bourbon's burn bloom on his tongue. "It's good."

"It's almost embarrassing how much I enjoyed proving that to you—I couldn't stop watching you behind the bar the night we met."

"The proof's in the details. Well done," Dex said, watching pleasure flicker in Vaughn's eyes.

Even though Dex had been there before, Vaughn gave a short, impromptu tour of the house: the study with a desk too neat to be useful; a library with a ladder and shelves peppered with dog-eared paperbacks and pretentious hardbacks in equal measure; then back to the kitchen, its familiar butcher block stained by meals and memories. Photos existed, but not many. None of Isabella were on display. Vaughn wasn't hiding his grief—he'd simply chosen where it was allowed to live.

Back on the patio, they claimed lounge chairs in the perfumed air beneath the jasmine-covered pergola. The first sip's burn softened into sweetness. Conversation opened: music they loved, concerts attended before the Curtain, Dex's old habit of reading people by their drink order, Vaughn's dinner parties.

"One night we dressed like midsummer fairies," he confessed.

Dex choked on bourbon laughing. Vaughn's return laughter lived low and generous, and Dex found himself eager to earn it again.

A lull came easily—the kind built by two people comfortable with silence. Dex watched the light dance on the pool's surface, felt the bourbon warm his mouth, and said, "I haven't felt like this in months."

Vaughn turned his head. "Like what?"

"Like I'm not on guard." Dex let the pause breathe. "The last time I let myself care was with Charlie. He was my partner on the force—strong, smart, stubborn as hell. He'd walk into danger first just so I had a way out."

The memory broke something gentle in Dex's face, then settled. "I used to think that he was always trying to prove himself—the better cop, the bigger man—only to discover later he was doing it to protect me."

Vaughn could see the ache but didn't try to fix it. He reached and rested his fingers on the back of Dex's hand. Warm. Steady. Present. "He sounds like a good man."

"Turns out, better than I once thought," Dex said, head hanging heavy with regret. "He spent years wanting to be more than just my partner on the force, but he never found the courage to step outside his comfort until after the Order had taken over Atlanta..."

Dex's voice faded out, prompting Vaughn to squeeze his hand a bit harder.

Dex squeezed back. "Losing him hollowed me out. I don't give that kind of trust to anyone."

Vaughn's thumb traced once along Dex's knuckles. That small, human gesture sharpened a quiet knowing in Dex—something he'd noticed and ignored since the first night. The range in Vaughn's face—the bright, unmuted way he felt— wasn't how people moved anymore.

"You never got the Serexin," Dex said— surprised by how certain his voice sounded.

Vaughn stilled. Not flinching—choosing. He lifted his glass for a sip, set it down again, and met Dex's eyes. "No. Isabella arranged my 'processing' at her tent. She swapped the vial. Placebo. Timing and paperwork made it look proper." He exhaled softly. "I'm not proud of the lie, but I am grateful for it."

Gratitude curled warm and rough in Dex's chest also. *Of course,* he thought. *Of course it was Isabella.*

Vaughn's face still showed the weight and wear of emotion. *No wonder you feel like a person, feel real,* he thought, the realization not exactly relief, but something adjacent and more dangerous.

"Why?" Dex asked.

"She asked me to stay awake," Vaughn said. "Not for her—for myself."

That landed hard and heavy. How he missed the world when people felt things and gave a damn—about each other, about anything at all.

"We should run away together—Isabella and I talked about it before the accident," Vaughn interjected.

Dex pulled his gaze from Vaughn's for a moment, hiding the moisture in it. "Charlie and I tried, before the Curtain was even completed, and it killed him. I don't think I could live with myself if I attempted it again and something happened to you."

Vaughn lifted Dex's chin. "I am sorry, Daddy, I didn't know."

It had begun as playfulness, but something about Vaughn calling him Daddy in that moment triggered a memory of Charlie. Dex could no longer hold back the tears in his eyes with Vaughn staring into their depths.

They drifted from the chairs to the pool's edge without deciding aloud, shoulders nearly touching. The stone tile still held the day's heat; the air carried a sweetness from the cut hedges and grass lingering in the humidity. Somewhere a timer clicked—underwater lights flared, and the pool glowed like an invitation.

Vaughn tipped his chin toward the water and smiled. "Care for a swim?"

Dex's mouth curled mischievously. "There are easier ways to get me wet."

"True, but only one way to skinny dip."

The words jolted in the best way—no game, no theatrics, just a clean slide into yes. Vaughn stripped with confident grace: shirt, shorts, underwear—devoid of any shyness. Warm light ran the plane of his chest, the hard angle of hip bone, the curve of muscle along thigh.

Dex looked openly, felt the desire rise and let it. He pulled off his own shirt, then jeans, then briefs. The tile was warm under his soles, but the cool night air swept over him like icy hands, lifting hair along his arms. Vaughn's gaze shifted from appreciation to hunger—restrained but clear—and Dex's breath shortened in a hunger of its own.

They stepped together and slid into the pool. Water closed around Dex's shoulders—soft, warm, giving. Chlorine stung faintly, but jasmine quickly threaded through it like a reminder that the world still knew how to be pretty amidst the ugliness. They swam loose arcs that narrowed— ten, six, four feet—until they shared a breath in the center, knees brushing as they treaded close.

"You're dangerous," Vaughn murmured, voice half-swallowed by water.

"Not half as dangerous as you," Dex returned. And the space vanished.

The kiss came slowly by design. Vaughn's hand rose to the back of Dex's neck; Dex's palms found the slope of Vaughn's back and drew him close until chest met chest and heat replaced thought. Water lapped softly against the tile. Beyond the fence, the city exhaled.

They drifted toward the shallow end, feet finding purchase. Vaughn pressed Dex to the wall; Dex turned them, pinning Vaughn instead, savoring the little sound that slipped from Vaughn's throat when he yielded control. Lips slid to jaw, to the soft place below the ear, to the hollow where his pulse flickered and quickened. Vaughn tasted like bourbon and cherry, cut clean with chlorine.

"Bed?" Vaughn breathed.

Dex's mouth curved against his throat. "Here," he said, voice rough. "Now."

Vaughn's laugh hitched, which was as good as a yes. Dex lifted him by the hips; Vaughn's legs gripped his waist with easy strength. They half- walked, half-floated to the steps and then Dex lifted them onto the deck, water sheeting off in quicksilver, hair dripping trails down spine and ribs. Dex found the large, round rattan daybed—fairy lights twinkling from its canopy—and laid Vaughn back on the towel he'd dragged over with a fumbling hand.

The night pressed closer—the chirp of crickets, a distant car door, leaves whispering secrets overhead.

Dex kissed down Vaughn's chest, sternum to navel, mapping with mouth and palms. He learned quickly: Vaughn gasped when thumbs circled nipples, went still and quiet when Dex licked lower, arched hips not to escape but to meet. Vaughn gave in without passivity—open, alert, answering with hands and mouth and a low curse when Dex sucked him slower. Fingers tangled in Dex's hair, palms sliding over the ink on his arms, memorizing patterns for later.

Dex leaned up and kissed Vaughn, letting him savor his own taste upon tongue. "Tell me what you want."

Vaughn held his gaze, pupils blown, voice wrecked and sure. "I want to feel you inside me."

"Then breathe," Dex murmured, slicking spit over his fingers. "And trust me."

They didn't rush. Dex worked him open slowly, two fingers easing inside, whispering steady, filthy encouragement as Vaughn's body adjusted. Vaughn shivered, thighs trembling; Dex kissed the inside of his knee, waited through the tense flutter, stroked until breath evened again. When Vaughn's hand rose to Dex's cheek, thumb tracing water from his beard, Dex slid in and pressed forward—inch by inch—watching micro-expressions bloom and fade across Vaughn's face.

The first push stole air from Vaughn's lungs; the second pulled a sound from deep inside that Dex felt more than heard. Dex stilled, kissed him, asked "Good?"—and waited for the nod, the yes, the tightened flex around him that said: *more.*

He rocked shallowly at first, letting Vaughn's body take him instead of forcing a tempo, breathing with him. Vaughn's hands gripped his back, nails scoring the skin lightly; his mouth found Dex's shoulder; he said Dex's name in a way that felt like a plea. Dex framed his face, bent to kiss him and swallowed the sounds they made together—desire in a language they both understood.

Stars pricked through the lattice. Vaughn arched; Dex adjusted; found the angle that carved a breathless moan out of Vaughn every time he pushed deeper. Dex wrapped a hand around Vaughn's cock, stroking to match the pace. Curses changed into chants, moans into melody.

Dex told Vaughn he was safe; Vaughn told Dex he was perfect. Vaughn came first—a sharp, unguarded shout and spill of heat slicking Dex's fist and abdomen. Dex was seconds later, a guttural sound tearing loose as release throbbed through him. He pressed his body to Vaughn's, riding the last shudder, breath stuttering on the edge of relief—and something close to joy.

Silence followed—not empty, but full. Earned. They lay side by side, chests heaving beneath the string lights that flickered softly overhead. Vaughn's fingers, still trembling faintly, traced idle shapes through Dex's chest hair, down to the notch of his ribs.

"Stay with me tonight," Vaughn said—quiet but unambiguous.

"I'm not going anywhere," Dex answered, surprised at how easy it was to mean it.

May 28, 2027

if we move too fast,
we'll break things.
if we move too slow,
we'll miss things.
and if we don't move at all,
we won't see things for how
beautiful they truly are.

~ r.m. drake

33
ACCELERATE

THE NIGHT AIR cooled their damp skin. Cicadas sang from the cypress trees lining the backyard. Vaughn slipped inside, returned with a flannel throw and a chilled bottle of sauvignon blanc. Wrapped together, they sipped—Vaughn nestled between Dex's legs, shoulders pressed to his chest, hand entwined with his, both gazing at the glowing blue of the pool beyond their feet.

"I need you to know that I loved her," Vaughn said after a long stillness, eyes on the slice of moon hanging above the oaks. "Isabella, I mean."

Dex drew a slow breath. "I felt it—not just during the tethers. Tell me something about Isabella."

"She hated fundraisers," Vaughn offered. "Said all that money turns brains to garbage. But she wanted funding, so she ate canapés and pretended to laugh. She was brilliant—and insufferably certain when she knew she was right." Fondness softened his mouth; then it thinned. "The Order says it was an elevator that malfunctioned, but the story doesn't hold."

"It doesn't make sense to me either."

"My gate cameras pinged her forty-eight hours after the supposed accident," Vaughn said, taking a sip of wine. "Then that log vanished from the cloud upload. I keep an offline mirror of the recordings, and her appearance on that backup is still there."

"She showed up on your cameras here?" Dex asked, puzzled.

"Yup. She also had an appointment blocked off two days after the supposed accident," Vaughn said, his tone hardening. "And it wasn't old or automated. It was updated about an hour after the elevator malfunction was logged. Just one word in the subject line: Persephone. Three o'clock. Then— her entire calendar was scrubbed. Every entry. Dead women don't erase their calendars."

The name slammed into Dex. *Persephone.* Not a myth, not a coincidence, but the whispered moniker of the figure everyone in the theater spoke of and no one claimed to have seen. The one some Sensates treated like a ghost, others like a leader. Persephone had reach—long enough to cross into Isabella's private life. His thoughts spun: was Isabella meeting her? Reporting to her? Or hiding under her protection?

Vaughn's jaw tightened, the anger in his face etched clean. "Her car never even made it to campus, but the GPS tag showed her keys did. And the condolence call I got? Scripted. Same three sentences, word for word, from three different administrators—like sympathy should be standardized."

Dex's chest tightened, a prickle of unease at the base of his spine. If Isabella herself had typed Persephone—after she was supposed to be dead— then the accident wasn't an accident at all. It was a cover, and someone had gone to meticulous lengths to erase the trail.

Vaughn stared at the moon as if it might confess something. "She wasn't reckless. If something had gone wrong, at least half a dozen people would've reached out. No one did. Not one."

Dex slid his palm across Vaughn's sternum, pulling him back tighter against his body, grounding him.

Vaughn's next breath shuddered, then steadied. "She asked me to stay awake, so I did, but never told me exactly why. That's the beginning and end of it, as far as I'm willing to say aloud."

"Hence the placebo," Dex murmured. But even as the words left him, a cold realization crawled up his spine. The tether had been recording. Every word, every tremor of Vaughn's confession, already siphoned off through the Ghostjack, streaming to HALCION's cloud.

His pulse kicked. He thought—just for a savage, irrational second—about tearing the port out of his neck, ripping the damn thing free before it could bleed him any further. But it was too late. He knew it. The data was gone, packaged and stored, beyond his reach. And the more he thought about who would parse it, who would be waiting to dissect every syllable, the more the air seemed to thin.

Dex forced his touch to remain steady against Vaughn's chest, not daring to let the panic in his head ripple outward. Vaughn couldn't know. Not now.

Vaughn looked up, head tilted back, completely unguarded. Dex didn't say he knew pieces of

Isabella from other angles—he didn't need to. This moment was about Vaughn's loss, his certainty, his refusal to let the world rewrite her.

A breeze stirred the jasmine; laughter rose and ebbed somewhere down the block. Vaughn turned slightly and let his head rest on Dex's shoulder, both comforting and confessional, like an unspoken vow.

"Tell me something about Charlie," Vaughn said—not a command, just an invitation.

Dex's smile was slow, almost reluctant, but real. "He used to be an ass to me—loud, homophobic, the kind of guy who'd make a joke just to watch me bite back. Until the day I finally put him on his naked ass in the locker room, pinned him to the ground, and straddled him in nothing but a towel with my fist aimed at his face.

"I remember my towel came apart, so our bodies were pressed skin to skin. My ass and cock were pressed against his torso, and though I wasn't hard, the tip of it had slapped him in the face when I first straddled him. After that, he looked at me differently... and slowly, he treated me differently. He admitted later that is was that moment that changed something in him."

Dex paused, the faint flicker of pain in his eyes soon overwhelmed by a building flood at their edges. "The first time we kissed, I discovered that he made these little noises when I reached his neck... like he was trying so hard not to give himself away. We'd been partners for years, so we already knew how to move around each other, trusted each other without speaking. When it turned physical, it was... intense. Like all that history boiled over into something neither of us saw coming."

Dex blinked away the water in his eyes as his voice faltered at the end. The burn in his throat swelled until it was impossible to swallow. He turned his face away, but Vaughn caught his jaw, guiding him back. The first tear slipped before Dex could stop it, then another, until they fell in a steady, silent stream.

Vaughn pulled him in without hesitation, wrapping around him like he could hold the grief still. "It's all right," he murmured, though his voice was breaking too. When Dex finally looked up, he saw Vaughn's own tears spilling over, saw the way his mouth trembled as he tried to keep control and failed. They stayed like that—lying in an embrace, breath shared, the air between them thick with everything they'd lost and couldn't get back.

For a moment there were no words, no lines between past and present—just two men holding the weight of ghosts together, one with the ache of love that hadn't been given enough time, the other with the ache of losing the love of a best friend. And in that fragile space, something between them rooted deeper—as if grief itself had braided them tighter.

"She'd like that you're here," Vaughn said.

Dex swallowed. "Yeah. I think Charlie would approve of you, too... in his absence, of course."

Near midnight, they migrated inside— nakedness wrapped in the throw, damp towels abandoned on the pool deck like molted skins.

In the kitchen, wine warmed them as Vaughn sliced peaches and set them beside prosciutto and a soft wedge of cheese. They ate standing at the counter, sharing bites from fingers. Dex watched

Vaughn's throat move when he swallowed, the quick dart of tongue when he licked juice from his thumb; desire rose again, easy and inevitable.

"Shower?" Vaughn asked, eyebrow up.

"Together this time," Dex said, already moving. As much as he'd wanted to hold tightly to the memory of the last shared shower with Charlie, the past had now collided with the present, lines blurring and shifting.

Steam clouded the mirror while citrus soap slid over shoulders, spines, the cut of hips. They searched each other again—slower now, bolder now—because once wasn't enough and repetition felt overdue. Vaughn dropped to his knees and took Dex into his mouth, this time with a patient hunger; nothing withheld, just attention and heat and a low rumbling sound from somewhere deep that made Dex brace one hand on tile while the other gripped Vaughn's shoulder.

Vaughn choked a bit from an eager swallow but opened wider, sliding Dex deeper. His skills were impressive, especially for a novice, but Dex tugged him upward, kissed him hard, and pulled him tight.

After another intense kiss, Vaughn turned Dex to the wall, palm low on his back, lips at his shoulders. He leaned across Dex's left shoulder and whispered, his tone more question than statement. "My turn."

Dex managed only a moan of consent before Vaughn's lips traced down his back, following the line of his spine. He tugged Dex slightly out of the spray, just enough to avoid the deluge of water cascading between Dex's cheeks so that he wouldn't drown while eating his hole.

Vaughn ate his ass with the same eagerness as before—teasing, tonguing, thrusting deeply toward the finish before returning to his feet. "I'll be right back—I forgot to put the lube in the shower."

"No, stay; spit'll work just fine," Dex said, grabbing Vaughn's arm, tugging him farther from the spray, then dropping to his knees to coat his cock in a viscous layer of spit. "That, plus the amount you left in my hole, should be enough."

Vaughn was slower this time, pushing gently with the slightest pressure, waiting for Dex to open and accept him. Steam curled around them as they drew close—close enough that Vaughn could wrap an arm around Dex's waist and pull him back while he pushed in. Dex's right hand flattened on the tile; his left found Vaughn's and laced their fingers. Their rhythm pulsed like the tide—ebb, flow, ebb—retreating and surging just deep enough that Vaughn's voice wore rough from his constant purring.

They came together—Dex painting the wall in thick ropes while Vaughn filled him in pulsing waves—both braced hard against the tile. Their breath tangled in a ragged chorus until heartbeats eased and steam thinned. With a slow swipe of his left hand, Vaughn shut off the water, pressed a lingering kiss to the back of Dex's neck, then pulled free and turned him—bringing them face to face.

"That was even more intense than the first time," Vaughn admitted, "I didn't expect that."

"A deeper connection always means deeper intimacy," Dex declared.

Vaughn lifted Dex onto his hips and carried him into the bedroom. They tumbled onto the bed, barely dry. Cool sheets, low lights, bodies finding the shape of each other—chests pressed, calves tangled, fingers searched, finding, but never settling as their explorations continued for some time. Sleep came in stitched pieces of dream and desire.

Dex woke to Vaughn watching him—studying him like a problem he couldn't solve—and whispered, "What?"

"Just making sure you're real," Vaughn said with a small smile.

Dex kissed his smile. "I'm here."

Rain tapped against the window, soft at first, then harder. The smell of wet earth drifted in under the sash. Vaughn's breathing slowed, his mouth parted slightly. Dex watched him in thin light—the cut of cheekbone, the shadow of lashes—and marveled at the luck of finding this man on the far side of the worst year of his life, someone untouched by the hollow of Serexin.

Unwanted thoughts pressed hard: the Order, the work, the way *feeling* always cost more than it gave. Another thought rose beside them—clear and quiet: *He's worth the risk.*

The room ticked, shifted, then stilled. Dex's hand traced the curve of Vaughn's ribs, following the slow rise and fall. Breath by breath, he synced to Vaughn's rhythm until it was instinct.

In the quiet, Charlie's voice surfaced as a whisper in his head: *Atta boy. Take the good when it shows up.*

The ache it stirred was no longer a wound but a release—a marker of something rare. What had been was giving way to the unguarded, raw beauty of now.

Dawn scraped pale along the blinds' edges, flooding the room with more light than Dex was used to.

Vaughn stirred and blinked. "Coffee?"

"Please," Dex murmured.

They moved around each other with an ease that felt older than it was—Vaughn at the coffee grinder, Dex at the stove. Bread and eggs sat beside a sprig of rosemary; a ripe tomato waited on the sill. Vaughn sliced it while Dex browned sausage and whisked eggs, the skillet hissing in greeting. Soon, sausage and cheese omelets filled their plates—alongside toast slicked in too much butter and tomato slices sweet enough to cut the savory pairings.

Rain freckled the glass as they ate at the small table by the window. Vaughn set his mug down, elbows resting on the table, gaze lingering. "You always cook like this?"

Dex glanced up, one brow raised. "Like what?"

"Like every dish has an ulterior motive," Vaughn said with a slow grin. "Like you're trying to seduce someone with rosemary and sausage."

Dex's mouth curved. "Maybe I am."

Vaughn chuckled low and warm. "Dangerous man." He tapped the side of his mug. "My dad used to say you can tell a lot about someone by how they feed you. Problem was, he could ruin toast in three minutes flat."

Dex laughed. "Burnt offerings?"

"Every time," Vaughn said. "But he meant it—effort mattered more than outcome. People remember the care." His voice softened, eyes never leaving Dex's. "I think he was right."

Dex held his gaze, something unspoken stretching in the space between them. "Then I guess I'm just making sure I'm memorable."

Vaughn's grin widened, slow and certain. "Are you kidding? A dementia patient couldn't forget you."

Dex barked out a laugh, shaking his head. "Wow. Romantic *and* cynical. You really know how to flatter a guy."

"Hey," Vaughn said, hands raised in mock surrender, "I'm just speaking the truth." He leaned back in his chair, but the smile stayed, a quiet undercurrent of warmth beneath the humor.

The rain outside deepened its rhythm against the glass, the quiet folding in around them like it had been waiting for this exact moment.

They cleaned up, side by side—Dex washing, Vaughn drying—until the kitchen shed the happy wreckage of a good meal and resumed its shape. In the doorway, Dex leaned, watching Vaughn rack the last plate.

"Have a great day, handsome," he called, smile wide, barely held back.

"I meant the text," Vaughn said. "About the porch light. I've not turned it off since our first night together. Think of it as a symbol of the light you've brought back into my life."

Dex turned back toward Vaughn, "You've given light to mine, too—a place once drowning in darkness."

Vaughn shuffled toward the door, and they kissed—not grand, not small, but with enough of a promise for more to come.

Shoes in hand by the front door, Dex hesitated. Outside, the rain softened—a lull like held breath. He didn't want to leave, but he knew he had to. Something in him had shifted—not a collapse, just a slow alignment toward a new center.

"Tonight?" Vaughn asked—easy on the surface, not beneath.

Dex let himself feel the choosing. "Tonight."

He stepped onto the porch, the light glowing against the misty air, the world smelling new. He tucked his hands in his pockets and walked into the street like a man who had remembered how it felt to want—and for the first time in months, he didn't want to run from it.

34
MERGE

T HAT MORNING, RAIN had chased him off Vaughn's porch; this evening, it welcomed him back. The drizzle kept time against the windows—soft percussion that slowed the world to a hush. Ansley Park blurred into watercolor: inky oaks against a pewter sky, porch lights bleeding into halos, azaleas drooping in pink and crimson. Dex lingered beneath the portico, breathing petrichor and cut grass, letting the quiet settle. The city felt as though it were holding its breath.

Vaughn opened the door before Dex could knock—barefoot, shirt unbuttoned one notch lower than usual, collar damp where wet hair had soaked through. For a moment neither spoke; the small smile that found them both said enough.

"Come in," Vaughn murmured, voice a half-step lower than usual. "You're exactly on time."

"For what?"

"For this." Vaughn took Dex's coat, shook off a few beads of rain, and hung it with practiced diligence. He stepped close and pressed his mouth to Dex's—slow and certain—like a promise he had no intention of breaking. The kiss tasted like the fresh-cut lime sitting on counter mixed with the rain Dex had walked through to get to the door.

Inside smelled like citrus and smoke from the candles scattered about the room. The house lights were dimmed, rooms defined by pools of glow—under-cabinet in the kitchen, a single lamp near the sofa, a garland of warm bulbs strung outside the back windows. The jazz tonight wasn't background; it had bones, a heartbeat—more Parisian than Orleans. Its bass line calmed, making it easy to breathe.

"I was going to offer you a drink," Vaughn said against Dex's jaw, not stepping away, "but let's pretend I already did."

"We can circle back." Dexter's hands settled at Vaughn's hips, the edges of the day sliding off him like his now-absent coat.

Vaughn led him into the living room, sat him on the sofa and studied him—cataloguing what the light did to his eyes and the sharp lines of his face. Rain whispered against the glass doors to the patio; beyond them the pool shimmered like a spill of diamonds falling in the dark.

"Let's change it up tonight," Vaughn said, a spark curling through his voice. "No script. No patterns. Just see where it goes."

Before Dex could answer, Vaughn moved in one fluid, deliberate motion—climbing onto his lap, knees bracketing his thighs, palms resting hot on his shoulders, heat and hunger bleeding straight through.

Dex's breath shuddered. His hands traced the sweep of Vaughn's back beneath the open shirt, then plunged them deep to grip his ass, thumbs circling low at his waist. Vaughn bent to kiss him again, deeper. The slow roll of his hips cauterized the last of Dex's pretense; the world narrowed to the give and take of motion and the low sound Vaughn made when Dex answered him.

They didn't rush. Vaughn unbuttoned Dex's shirt slowly, alike turning pages, pausing to taste the hollow at his throat, the edge of a collarbone, the place where ink disappeared under fabric. Dex sank back and let himself be moved—worshipped. Leather creaked softly under their shifting weight, rain thrummed the time, and the bass of their beating hearts threaded everything.

"Look at me," Vaughn said.

And Dex did. He saw the want, yes—but something steadier beneath it, changing the temperature of the room and his own skin.

Vaughn rocked over him, finding a rhythm that belonged only to tonight—deliberate, unhurried. He set his hands over Dex's, laced their fingers, pressed Dex's palms flat to his body, and held them there like a vow. Each lean forward was welcomed; each retreat pulled a quiet sound from Dex he didn't bother to swallow. They breathed together, the music a forcefield that framed them as the rest of the world blurred away.

When Vaughn eased back, it wasn't to stop. He slid off Dex's lap and stood, still close enough that Dex could feel the heat in the space they'd made. Without breaking eye contact, he stripped—then helped Dex out of the rest of his clothes.

Dex closed his eyes as Vaughn took him to the base and one swift motion, each bob deeper, letting saliva string and coat him—mirroring what Dex had done to him in the shower a few nights before.

Once satisfied he was slick enough, Vaughn straddled Dex once again, lowering himself slowly, gently, until Dex was buried deep within him.

Dex moaned upon feeling the heat of Vaughn's ass. "I-I'm... impressed," he stuttered, trying to steady himself.

Vaughn hushed him with a finger his lips, followed by a deep kiss. "Just lie back and enjoy it."

Vaughn's tempo quickened, like a jockey coaxing its horse to the front of the race, moaning softly with each thrust deeper. And Dex could feel the tension—the push and the pull of contractions—as Vaughn's eyes rolled back in ecstasy, sweat beading on his forehead as he drew closer to the finish line, no longer concerned if the steed beneath crossed it with him.

Vaughn's climax tore through him—hands-free—his release spilling in milky arcs that caught even him off guard, streaking Dex's chest and beard with unexpected heat.

Dex hadn't come. He let Vaughn catch his breath, then offered his hand and led him backward toward the bedroom—a slow retreat, a seduction that felt deliberate in every step.

The room was dim; rain hushed against the open window. Vaughn fell back onto the mattress with a thud of surrender, propping himself up on his elbows as Dex stripped his socks, the lamplight running over muscle and ink. Vaughn's lips parted at the sight; his cock stirred again, still slick from his recent load.

"I want to remember this exactly," Vaughn said, voice breaking on the edge of need.

Dex crawled up the bed like a predator savoring his catch. He kissed Vaughn hard, tasting salt, sweat, the faint tang of semen on his skin. His mouth moved down—jaw, throat, sternum—leaving wet trails until he reached Vaughn's cock. He stroked it once, twice, then bent and took him whole, swallowing greedily. Vaughn's back arched; his hands clutched at Dex's shoulders.

"You're going to kill me," Vaughn groaned, hips trembling as Dex worked him—slow, obscene pulls of tongue and throat, punctuated by the scrape of teeth just enough to make him jolt.

Dex released him with a slick pop, stroking his length while licking lower, mouthing his balls before pushing his tongue between Vaughn's cheeks. Vaughn shuddered violently, half-laugh, half-curse, legs thrown wide in invitation. Dex feasted there until Vaughn's voice turned to raw, broken syllables.

"Please—fuck, Dex, please."

Dex slicked his cock with spit and pressed forward, spreading Vaughn open inch by inch until he was buried to the root. Vaughn's cry stuttered into a moan, body clenching around him. Dex held still, forcing Vaughn to feel every deliberate throb, then pulled back and drove in again—harder, deeper.

The rhythm built—long strokes, rougher thrusts, hips meeting hips with wet, slapping sounds that filled the dark. Vaughn clung to him, nails raking across his back, breath a litany of curses and praise—*yes, harder, don't stop, fuck, you feel so good.*

Dex angled his hips until Vaughn broke, crying out with each thrust as Dex hit the place that made him shake. Dex made use of the precum glistening on Vaughn's cock, wrapping a fist around the girth, and stroked in time with his thrusts.

Vaughn shattered first, spilling between them. The tight clench of his body dragged Dex over with him—one last punishing thrust before he emptied inside, forehead pressed to Vaughn's, teeth bared with the force of it.

They collapsed together—gasping, slick, and shaking. Dex stayed buried in him, unwilling to lose the connection just yet. Vaughn stroked his beard with trembling fingers, pulling him into another kiss—messy, grateful, greedy.

"Again," Vaughn whispered against his lips. "I don't care if it kills me."

Dex laughed, breathless, and kissed him harder. "Then let's make sure you remember every second."

He eased out of Vaughn, slow and wet, and rolled onto his back. Vaughn simply stared for a moment— at Dex's sweat-slick chest rising and falling, the heavy throb of his cock still flushed and glistening, the tattoos mapped across muscle. Vaughn's pupils widened as he dragged his gaze over him like he was memorizing every line, every shadow.

"You're beautiful—I'm taking it all in," Vaughn said hoarsely, hand sliding up Dex's thigh to grip him at the root, stroking once.

Dex smirked, voice low. "Yours for the taking."

Vaughn didn't hesitate. He climbed back over him, kissing his mouth, his jaw, the salt-slick hollow of his throat, before flipping Dex onto his stomach. He slapped his hard cock against Dex's ass.

"How are you still hard?"

"Little blue pill," Vaughn admitted.

Dex's groan melted into the pillow as Vaughn spread him wide, lined up, and pushed in with one long, steady thrust.

"Fuck—" Dex growled, gripping the sheets, his back arching as Vaughn filled him to the hilt.

This time Vaughn set the pace—hard, grinding thrusts that had Dex bracing himself, moaning low as the bed rocked beneath them. Vaughn's chest pressed to his back, his teeth catching Dex's ear, breath hot as he drove deeper.

When Dex turned his head, Vaughn caught his mouth in a sideways kiss, tongues colliding, the rhythm of their bodies synced and relentless. Vaughn's hand clamped to his thigh, dragging him back with every thrust until Dex thought he might come again.

But Vaughn pulled out suddenly, flipped him again onto his back, throwing Dex's legs over his shoulders. Dex's chest heaved, cock already hard again and leaking across his stomach. Vaughn slid back in, pinning him to the mattress, sweat dripping from his hair and beard onto Dex's skin.

Every thrust tore a cry from Dex's throat— louder now, unrestrained. "Yes, fuck yes, don't stop—"

Dex wrapped a hand around his cock, stroking in time. The double assault ripped him open with sensation—body trembling, begging for release but refusing to let go of the moment.

"I want to feel you tighten around me as you come again," Vaughn rasped, voice breaking. "Make me feel you."

Dex clenched down on him and stroked faster, and Vaughn lost it—coming with a shout that filled the room, spilling into him in pulsing waves. Dex's stroking dragged him over the edge seconds later; he painted both their stomachs, groaning through the aftershocks as Vaughn pounded him through it.

They stayed locked together, gasping, clinging, Dex kissing him like he needed to commit the taste into memory.

Finally, Vaughn eased out and collapsed at his side. Dex pulled him close, chest to chest, Vaughn's head finding its place above his heartbeat, leg hooked over his hip, keeping them tangled.

The rain softened outside, steady and constant, like it was etching their rhythm into the night. Vaughn's hand slid down Dex's ribs and back again, fingertips tracing him lazily.

When he finally spoke, it was quiet. "Stay with me."

"I'm not going anywhere," Dex murmured, kissing his damp hair.

The second afterglow was lazier. Vaughn dozed with his mouth against Dex's shoulder while Dex watched the rain thin to mist, then gather itself again. When Vaughn stirred, he reached blindly for Dex's hand, brought it to his chest, and held it there, teaching him the song of his heart.

"I wish we had more time," Vaughn said, not wanting Dex to leave.

Dex didn't lie. "Me, too."

Hours passed and they still hadn't found sleep. Every time Vaughn shifted, Dex pulled him back in, hands hungry, mouths colliding, cocks grinding until the need built all over again. When Vaughn finally rolled off the bed, sweat-slick and panting, he jerked his thumb toward the bathroom.

"Shower. Or I'll drown in your scent before morning."

Dex smirked. "And you say that like it's a bad thing."

The bathroom steamed within minutes, grapefruit soap thick in the air. Vaughn pressed Dex to the tile, water cascading over their bodies, tracing tattoos and scars, making every line slick and gleaming. Vaughn's hands spread across Dex's chest, fingers teasing his nipples before sliding lower, wrapping his cock and stroking until Dex groaned, head thudding back against the wall.

"Fuck, you're heavy in my hand," Vaughn said, pumping him slow, water mixing with pre-cum, making every slide obscene.

Dex gripped his wrist, voice rough. "On your knees."

"Yes, Daddy," Vaughn joked, but he obeyed without protest. Water rained over him as he swallowed Dex down, jaw straining, beard scraping in ways that made Dex buck hard against his throat. Vaughn opened wider, steadied, his hands braced on Dex's thighs.

"Goddamn, Vaughn, your mouth is..." Dex growled.

Vaughn pulled back with a grin, spit and water slicking his beard. He stood, kissed him hard, then turned and braced his palms to the wall, glancing back with a dare in his eyes.

Dex didn't hesitate. He spit in his hand, stroked his cock until it was dripping, and pressed in, slow but insistent. Vaughn groaned, forehead to tile, ass pushing back to take him deeper. The water made everything hotter, slicker, Dex's hips driving harder until the slap of skin echoed through the steam.

"More," Vaughn gasped. "Give me everything."

Dex gritted his teeth, slamming into him, one hand clamping Vaughn's hip, the other snaring his wrist and pinning it to the tile above his head. Vaughn's moans broke into curses, his cock swinging, untouched, dripping pre-cum onto the wet floor as Dex fucked him mercilessly.

Dex buried himself deep and spilled hot inside, grunting into Vaughn's wet neck as they both trembled through it. They stood under the spray for long minutes after, chests heaving, Dex holding Vaughn against the tile until his legs stopped shaking.

The house was dark but for the soft glow under the kitchen soffit. It had been hours since their shower, the morning spent curled together on the couch, in and out dozing.

Vaughn leaned against the counter, shirt hanging open, breath uneven. Dex closed the distance, dragging his teeth along Vaughn's throat until a groan slipped out. He caught Vaughn's wrist, pressed it to the counter, and kissed along Vaughn's neck, tongue circling slow and indecent. Vaughn's laugh cracked into something lower, needier.

"You like that sound?" Vaughn teased, voice still hoarse.

"I'm storing it for later," Dex replied, biting gently at his knuckles.

Vaughn pulled him close by the waistband, their mouths colliding, playful and filthy. The air was lighter now—still hungry but threaded with laughter. Their bare feet squeaked on cold tile as they circled each other, trading kisses that turned from teasing to demanding, rain pattering against the glass like a steady drumbeat urging them on.

They left the kitchen flushed and laughing, Dex shoving Vaughn against the hallway wall, kissing him rough, beard scraping beard, before dragging him backward to the bedroom.

The bed welcomed them with the scent of their last session, sheets wrinkled and still damp with sweat. Vaughn sprawled face-down first, ass high, presenting himself like an offering. Dex didn't hesitate—he grabbed Vaughn's hips, lined up, and slid inside with one fierce, claiming thrust.

Vaughn's cry broke against the pillow, muffled and wild, his back arching as Dex's chest pressed down hard against him. Dex growled into his ear, words guttural, unformed—just breath and possession. He slammed into him repeatedly, hips snapping, the slap of skin sharp beneath the low roll of thunder outside. Vaughn clutched at the sheets, body clenching tight around him, giving back every ounce of force.

"Fuck—you're mine right now," Dex rasped, pounding him deeper, dragging his beard across the slope of Vaughn's shoulder.

"Yes," Vaughn gasped, raw and wrecked, "don't stop—don't you dare—"

Dex didn't. He gripped harder, fucking him with a brutal rhythm until Vaughn's body milked him mercilessly. The moment broke him open; he thrust deep, stayed buried, and emptied himself with a roar, pulsing until his whole frame shook.

Dex pulled out and flipped Vaughn onto his back, eyes blazing. Vaughn's cock was hard again, slick against his stomach. Dex straddled his thighs, grabbed hold of him, and pressed the blunt head against his own entrance.

Vaughn's eyes went wide. "Dex—"

"I want to ride you," Dex growled, voice feral, "and I want you to wreck me."

Before Vaughn could answer, Dex lowered himself slow, then all at once, impaling himself with a sharp cry that blurred pain into ecstasy. His nails raked Vaughn's chest as he took the full length, body shuddering, head thrown back.

Vaughn's hands flew to his thighs, steadying him, but Dex didn't need steady—he needed wild. He rode hard, bouncing with reckless rhythm, every thrust driving Vaughn deeper, every slam pulling groans from both their throats. Sweat dripped from Dex's beard, smearing Vaughn's skin as he bent low to kiss him—sloppy, desperate, feral.

"Fuck, Dex—" Vaughn's voice broke, his hips rising to meet every brutal descent.

Dex moaned loud, unrestrained, slamming down faster, chasing that raw edge until his body seized. He stroked himself furiously as he rode, and with a guttural cry he came again, ropes splattering Vaughn's chest. Vaughn followed seconds later, slamming up into him, filling him deep, his shout ragged with release.

They collapsed together, wrecked and trembling, Dex sprawled heavy across Vaughn's chest, mess smeared between them. Vaughn held him there, arms tight, both panting like they'd outrun the storm outside.

They lay face-to-face, noses brushing. Vaughn traced Dex's mouth with a fingertip, the scar at his temple, then the hollow of his throat.

"If you could keep one thing from tonight exactly as it is," Vaughn whispered, "what would it be?"

Dex thought, then smiled faintly. "The way you looked at me when you climbed into my lap. Like I was everything you wanted. Like you chose me."

Vaughn's eyes softened, unguarded. "I don't think I could have chosen better. And I'd choose you—over and over again."

Dex kissed him and returned the question.

Vaughn was quiet for a long moment, thumb making circles at top of Dex's ass. "The way you don't flinch. At anything. You don't doubt, you don't question. I know what grief can do, and how much room it can occupy in your mind. You never made me smaller to fit your world—you just made more room."

Something inside Dex loosened at those words, a tension he hadn't even realized he'd been holding. He pulled Vaughn close, kissed him gently, and let himself breathe into the rare truth of it: this was more than sex, more than heat. This was layered with a tether, allowing him to feel exactly what Vaughn was feeling at the same time without pretenses, doubling the intensity.

They slept for a few hours, until the rain thinned and the afternoon's eager light probed the blinds. Vaughn stirred first. Dex lay heavy beside him, beard shadowing his jaw, lips parted in unguarded sleep. For a long moment, Vaughn just looked—committing the shape of his body to memory. He hadn't expected this kind of presence again, not after Isabella, not after years of emptiness had taught him to expect nothing. But Dex had arrived anyway, shaking loose a part of him he thought long buried.

He slipped quietly from the bed, padded to the bathroom, and let the shower wash over him. Steam blurred the mirror; water ran hot across his chest. He tilted his head back and considered the future—something he hadn't dared picture in years. What would it look like to have Dex in his life beyond these nights? Could he hold onto someone like him when the world outside was still broken and cruel? Vaughn didn't know, but the thought alone steadied him in a way nothing else had.

When he finished, he toweled dry, padded barefoot back to the kitchen, and ground fresh beans. He let the aroma rise before pouring two mugs, one black, one fixed the way Dex liked. Returning to the bedroom, he set the mug on the nightstand and brushed a hand through Dex's hair.

"Coffee," Vaughn said softly.

Dex blinked awake, groggy, smile tugging. "That's the right way to wake a man." He sat up, took the mug, and let the heat bloom in his hands. Vaughn kissed the top of his head, then left him to shower.

Alone under the water, Dex let his thoughts expand. Charlie came first—his memory always did. The laughter, the loss, the weight of what he hadn't said in time. Then HALCION and the Order, their grip tightening by the day. The whispers of Persephone and the Sensates—Chaos rising underground, cracks in the Curtain. Maybe there was a way out. Maybe Vaughn could be part of that escape. The thought scared him, because it felt like wanting something bigger than survival, and he hadn't allowed himself that in a while.

By the time he dressed and stepped back into the kitchen, Vaughn was at the stove, plating eggs and toast, the air warm with butter and bacon. Vaughn turned, greeted him with a kiss—soft, certain, lips lingering as though they'd already shared years together.

The tether snapped open without warning.

Dex saw another morning: Isabella in the same kitchen, robe belted, hair damp from a shower, leaning up to kiss Vaughn with the kind of easy intimacy that only time could build. The scene shifted—another kiss, hurried, by the door as she left for work. Vaughn's hand on her cheek, her smile quick, her eyes bright. It was the last time. The kiss she never came back from.

Dex reeled silently, the flashes fading as quickly as they came. Vaughn didn't notice; or if he did, he said nothing, only pressed the plate into Dex's hands and smiled again, quiet and present.

"Eat," Vaughn said. "You'll need your strength."

Dex forced himself to breathe, to sit, to take in the warmth of food and company. The tether lingered in his chest like an echo, but instead of pushing it away, he let it anchor him to Vaughn— past and present braided together, alive in the same moment.

They lingered at the small table until the coffee cooled, their conversation tapering into silence. When the last bites were gone, Vaughn stood first, collecting plates.

"I should get headed back to my place so I can change before work," Dex said reluctantly.

Vaughn nodded, though his eyes dimmed just slightly. "I know."

At the door, Dex slipped on his jacket, rain-washed air pressing cool against the frame. Vaughn stepped in close, hand warm at the back of his neck, and kissed him.

The tether cracked open instantly. Dex felt the fear beneath Vaughn's lips—the tight edge of grief that still lived in his body. Not fear of Dex, but fear of goodbye. Fear of another kiss being the last. Isabella's ghost clung to it; Dex could feel the echo of her absence trembling just below Vaughn's surface.

Dex didn't pull away. He steadied the kiss, pressed back gently, pouring something Vaughn could hold into it: *I'll come back. I'm not gone.*

When they finally parted, Vaughn's breath hitched, but he managed a small smile. "See you tonight?"

"My place?" Dex suggested. "I'll text you the address."

"I'd like that." Vaughn gave a warm smile.

He stepped out onto the porch, the street gleaming silver from the last drizzle. The air smelled clean, new. Vaughn stayed framed in the doorway—bare feet on wood, shirt half-buttoned—watching him walk away like a man bracing against history repeating.

Dex felt the weight of it all the way down the street, the kiss still alive on his lips, thrumming with promise and with fear.

Part IX
PUNISHMENT

May 29, 2027

"The punishment suffered by the wise who refuse to take part in the government, is to live under the government of bad men."

~ Plato

35
SWERVE

T HE WALK DOWN the corridor was colder than usual. Dex kept his posture neutral, but the memory of Vaughn's body curled against him just hours earlier clung like phantom warmth. He'd slept—deeply, for the first time in weeks—but dread, not rest, was carrying him now.

Regina's summons came less than thirty minutes after he'd left Vaughn's house. She gave no reason; it felt more reprimand than routine—a feeling he hadn't felt since college, the last time he was called into the Dean's Office. Now the weight of it pressed with each echoing footstep.

The door at the end of the hall was open—Regina inside like a storm system waiting to collapse. The room was concrete and still; the overhead vent droned with a mechanical whirr that filled the silence too completely.

Dex stepped through, and the door hissed shut behind him.

Regina stood at its center, arms folded. Not a strand of hair out of place. Her mouth held its usual disapproval but sharper now. Beside her stood a new enforcer with a body meant for consequence not conversation—tall, heavy, eyes dead.

Dex kept his hands at his sides.

"No coffee? No donut? You're losing your bedside manner," he said, glancing around. "I'd almost think I was in trouble."

"Sit," Regina said.

"I'll stand."

"You tethered without authorization," she said.

Dex raised a brow. "Did I?"

"You engaged physically and emotionally with Vaughn Merrick. It showed in your GEIST relay—recorded, though distorted, like an EMP corruption."

Dex shrugged. "What can I say? The man is magnetic."

"You're not a comedian, Truitt."

"Shame you don't think so. It really is one of my best features."

The enforcer stepped forward.

Regina lifted her hand for him to stand down. "I'm not here for witty banter. I'm here to remind you of what you are."

Dex's jaw tightened.

"You think you've been clever," she said. "Circling beneath our notice. Meeting off the books. But you're always watched. Always."

He didn't respond.

Regina turned to the enforcer. "Trigger status."

The man tapped a button on the tablet . A buzz shot through Dex's neck. His GEIST port lit red—once, twice, three times—burning under the skin like dry fire. Dex inhaled sharply, hand reflexively seeking the pain; he didn't scream, but he staggered.

Regina's voice cut through the pulse. "That was only the pre-trigger sequence. The next one stops your heart."

Dex's hand dropped; his knuckles blanched.

"If you think I won't use it, you're mistaken," she said. "If you are ever compromised—if your loyalties wobble—we have contingencies."

"I'm not compromised."

Regina took a step forward. "You spent the night with him—several nights with him. You let him in."

"I'm allowed a night off."

"You're allowed nothing." Her words landed hard, final. "You're not a citizen. You're a Tangent. Owned. Enhanced at our expense. Deployed at our order and discretion. You don't get *privacy*, Truitt. You get assignments."

He stared at her, ice in his eyes, "I'm done working for you."

Her smile was slow. Cruel. The words twisted out of her mouth like inky ribbons of disdain. "No, you're not. You're just beginning to become useful."

Dex narrowed his eyes. "What's that supposed to mean?"

"There's a target. A high-value man we believe is not who he says, someone susceptible to emotional leverage."

Dex scoffed. "I'm bait now?"

"You've proven effective when properly motivated."

He stepped forward. "I'm not your fucking whore."

"No," Regina said. "But we both know you're more convincing when the target thinks you care."

"Vaughn and I already made plans tonight," he said, fists curling. "Am I just supposed to ghost him?"

"Yes."

"You want me to tell him it's over? Pretend he didn't matter—"

"Do what you have to," she said, clipping his thought. "But you're forbidden to see him again."

"The fuck I am!" Dex said as he lunged.

His hands found her throat, pushed her backward into the wall with a thud. The vent above them shuddered from the impact. Regina choked, her hands rising on instinct.

The enforcer acted fast. His tablet lit up red after engaging the program. Dex's GEIST port flared—a higher pulse this time. His spine seized.

Pain tore through his neck and down his back like a fuse being lit inside his bones.

Dex let go, gasping, falling to one knee, clutching at his neck.

Regina staggered forward, coughing, one hand pressed to her throat. "Try that again," she rasped, "and I'll end you on the spot."

Dex panted hard, fury hazing his vision. "Next time I'll take out your attack dog first... and then I won't fail to crush your damn windpipe, you fucking cunt!"

The enforcer raised his tablet again, ready to pounce.

"Stand down," Regina hissed, breath still ragged. Her glare could have cut steel.

She straightened slowly, smoothing her collar. "Is that language necessary, Truitt?"

He didn't answer. His pulse was still thudding in his chest and his head pounded, a surge of pain still throbbing at the back of his skull.

"If I didn't need you for another important tether," she said coolly, "I'd get rid of you now."

"Then stop wasting time," Dex said. "Who am I supposed to seduce."

She said nothing.

Dex took a step back toward the door, breath still shaking.

"You don't own me," he said again.

Regina tilted her head. "And yet... here you are."

The silence stretched long enough to leave something unfinished in the air between them.

"Malik Renshaw," she said finally. "You'll meet him tomorrow, here at HALCION. He thinks you're coming in for a replacement GEIST port—really you'll tether and uncover what he's been up to."

Dex didn't move right away but left without another word. The door hissed behind him, sealing tight. He walked down the corridor with the echo of her voice still ringing in his skull.

Dex went to work numb. He wanted to text Vaughn about Regina, to tell him what had happened, but decided against it, thinking it might spook him.

He went through his opening routine on autopilot: prepping the bar, breaking down bills for the register, tapping kegs, slicing limes into neat quarters, greeting the early regulars with a nod. It all felt hollow now, mechanical, as if his body were moving while his mind circled the trap Regina had sprung on him. She hadn't even bothered with subtlety—she'd made it clear the Ghostjack left him with no choice, that he was little more than property and he was required to deliver what they wanted.

And what they wanted was Malik Renshaw.

The thought twisted inside him. Dex had learned not to flinch at the names of strangers lined up on his assignment list, but Malik wasn't just another tether. There was something there—something vital, maybe even dangerous—in the way his name linked to Isabella, to Halina, to the thumb drive still burning a silent question in Dex's mind. Answers he needed, answers the Order would sooner bury than let him find.

He polished a glass longer than necessary, staring through the curve of it as if he could see the end of it all written in the distortion. What did Malik know that made the Order wary enough to push him into Dex's path? And what would happen when HALCION parsed through every shred of data the tether pulled?

Dex stood behind the bar, jaw tight. He wasn't afraid of failing the assignment. He was afraid of succeeding—of betraying the one man who might hold the key to unraveling the message Isabella had left behind. He had to figure out a way to mess with the transmission.

He texted Vaughn around midnight, during a quick break between crowd rushes. The text this afternoon with his address was marked as Delivered, Read, and even a heart Reaction attached to it, but no text had come through since. They'd made plans for Vaughn to meet him at his place after work, a change of scenery to help Dex face the emptiness he felt whenever he was home, a chance to make new memories in a space still haunted by his grief.

Still planning to swing by after close?

No reply.

He waited another hour then texted again.

Let me know if your schedule changed. I'll keep the lights on.

Still nothing.

Last call came and went. Dex closed the bar, wiped down the counter, dumped the tip jar, and checked his phone one more time.

No new messages.

He tried calling. No answer.

He called again. Voicemail.

Dex showered fast, soap and steam doing nothing to wash away the knot in his gut. In a hurry, he almost left the water running as he stepped out. He toweled off with one hand while scrolling with the other.

No new messages. No call. No Vaughn.

He stared intensely at the screen, as if willing it to vibrate, like maybe Vaughn was just late, distracted, or caught up in something trivial and forgettable. Maybe he fell asleep. Maybe he left his phone on silent. Maybe he changed his mind. Each excuse floated through his head, thin as smoke and just as impossible to hold onto.

None of them felt right.

At a quarter to four, Dex pulled on a hoodie over damp skin, shoved his feet into shoes without socks, and stepped into the night toward his Jeep.

Something was wrong. He could feel it. Not just in the way his chest tightened, but in the deeper place—the one that pulsed behind his ribs like a second heart. The city was too quiet for a Friday night. The lights too still. The silence too deep. He turned the corner onto the street facing Vaughn's house and stopped his car.

The flashing lights drew Dex before the smoke did.

He rounded the corner and saw Vaughn's street lit like a war zone—two engines parked crooked across the curb, hoses unspooled and hissing, red strobes slicing the dark. Flames licked from the second-story windows, black smoke boiling upward against the night.

Dex's pulse hammered. Vaughn's house—on fire.

Was Vaughn inside?

He scanned the scene, eyes sharp despite the panic clawing through him. Police had cordoned off the property with tape, their cruisers hemming in the fire trucks. Neighbors stood in clusters across the street, whispering, their faces bathed in strobing red.

He parked across the street and walked toward the driveway slowly. Deliberately. Like maybe if he took his time, the scene would rearrange itself, shift into something else—something less final.

Dex froze. His breath caught. And in that pause, the part of him that still hoped started to die. He pushed forward, but a firefighter in turnout gear threw an arm out across his chest.

"Sir, you can't be here."

"That's my—" He caught the word in his throat, swallowed it down. "I know the owner."

"Then you'll want to stand back." The firefighter's voice was muffled behind the mask, his tone flat with practiced distance. He shoved past Dex toward the yard, barking for pressure.

One of the officers by the driveway raised a hand. "Sorry, sir, this is a crime scene."

Dex didn't answer. Just kept walking, eyes on the house like it might open its mouth and swallow him, tears building in his eyes as he stared at the front door, at the porch light left lit, never glancing at the cop.

The officer stepped toward him, blocking him. "I am sorry about your friend, but you can't go past this point.

He moved back toward the edge of the sidewalk where he'd parked, pressed his palm flat against the door, and lowered his head, breathing hard.

The walls were closing in. The whole city felt rigged. Like everything inside the Curtain belonged to the Order. Everyone he touched. Every feeling he let himself feel.

Regina had warned him, but he hadn't listened, the words still ringing in his ears. Did she know that he had texted Vaughn, did she know he hadn't canceled their plans—their possibility of a future—like she had demanded.

And here it was. The price of disobedience.

He turned to get back in his Jeep and leave, and that's when he saw her. Blonde ponytail. Cargo uniform. EMS patch on the sleeve.

"Cami?" His voice cracked on her name. Though he didn't officially work with her, they'd met during his stint as an EMT.

She looked up from the back of the ambulance, surprised. "Dex? Shit. I didn't know you were still—"

"I'm not," he said quickly. "I'm just…"

Her face shifted, expression softening into sympathy. "You know the owner?"

He nodded, head sinking toward the sidewalk to hide his worry and watery eyes.

"I'm so sorry," she said, stepping toward him, voice low. "We got the call about twenty minutes ago. Neighbors called in gunshots, then saw flames in the windows. Report came through as a structure fire with possible victim inside—"

Dex flinched.

The fire crews pushed inside once the flames were doused. Dex strained against the line of tape, trying to catch a glimpse through the blackened doorway. Cami touched his arm but didn't tell him to step back. Maybe she saw something in his eyes that said it would be useless.

Minutes dragged, long and suffocating. Then Dex heard the call over Cami's radio: "Body located, first floor."

Cami's face seemed to be ripped away from his view, like a rapid zoom out from the scene. *Body?*

The firefighters emerged carrying a black body bag. The smell hit first—burned fabric, burned flesh—and Dex's stomach churned. He turned his head away and vomited.

Dex took a step toward the scene despite the nausea, but Cami grabbed him and held him back.

"Don't, Dex. You don't want to see that."

He tried to push past her anyway, but one glance inside the body bag stopped him. The charred outline was almost unrecognizable—skin and fabric fused; features melted into ruin. It didn't look like Vaughn. It didn't look like anyone.

Cami touched his sleeve again. "I'm sorry, Dex. The medical examiner is on their way, so we have to go—you should go, too."

Dex stared through her, past her, to the dark windows of the house. The reflection of red and blue still flickering in the glass panes like dying stars.

He felt hollowed out. Like the air had been punched out of him already, but the blows never stopped.

First David. Then Charlie. Now Vaughn.

The universe had a sick rhythm, a cruel pattern. Every time he reached out, let himself feel—really feel—something ripped it away.

Dex took a shaky breath. "Thanks."

He turned from her and disappeared into the shadows of a nearby tree. He didn't want pity. He didn't want condolences. He wanted answers.

The ambulance pulled away, silent and slow. The cruisers left one by one. By a quarter past four, the street was empty.

But Dex stayed. Crouched low. Watching. Breathing. Boiling.

The streetlights flickered. A breeze cut down the pavement, tossing an empty water bottle along the curb. Down the street, a light came on in the upper floor of a neighbor's house. Life moving on. Like nothing had happened. Like Vaughn hadn't mattered.

Dex clenched his fists, his nails biting into his palms, and let out a scream he was sure the entirety of Atlanta heard; it wasn't just this, it was everything—the pain, the loss, the apathy of the world around him.

He remembered the kiss on the sofa, the way Vaughn tasted—like whiskey and hope and grilled cheese; he remembered the feel of the sweat-soaked sheets twisted beneath them, the smell of rain and citrus and sex; the sound of soft jazz and Vaughn's moans reverberated in his ears and core. The way Vaughn had looked at him, quiet but certain, saying: *I want to see you again.*

And now—just hours after an unforgettable night together, never realizing it'd be their last—Vaughn was dead.

Just like that.

Dex stared up at the wind-stirred leaves, whispering as his own head screamed and heart turned to stone.

This wasn't an accident.

Not after those nights together—he'd felt him through the tethers. Not after Regina's warning. Not after everything Dex had dared to defy.

This was a fucking message.

We see you. We own you. We can take whatever you love.

He pulled in a ragged breath to focus, but it didn't help. There was no calming down. Not this time. Not after the Order stole *another* person from him.

He thought of David, who'd vanished without a trace. He thought of Charlie, taken by the Order's untrained goons so quick to pull a trigger without asking questions first. And now Vaughn, who despite only meeting a few nights before, was the first person in months—the first person since Charlie—that he'd let himself get close to. Perhaps it was the initial tether, or perhaps it was the intensity of the sex during the others, but Vaughn had made him feel like he mattered, like he was seen, desired, and real.

Now gone.

Because Dex let himself care, let his guard down, broke the rules.

He slammed his fist into the tree trunk behind him, hard enough to draw blood. He welcomed the pain. It sharpened the fire coiling in his gut.

The Order didn't want obedience. They wanted complete submission. Total emotional silence. They wanted him *empty.* But they'd failed. Because what Dex felt in that moment wasn't grief. It wasn't sadness. It was rage.

Pure, seething, sovereign rage.

He stared up the driveway one last time, to the half-charred house, to the porchlight, his jaw tightening as he made a quiet vow to himself. No more fear. No more silence. No more obedience. They wanted him to be their weapon. Fine. But they'd forgotten the other side of a blade.

He slipped back into the night, shadows swallowing him whole as he made his way back to his Jeep.

The fuse had been lit, and Dex was the bomb.

May 30, 2027

"But to surrender who you are and to live
without belief is more terrible than dying—
even more terrible than dying young."

~ Ste. Jeanne D'Arc

36
DETOUR

THE MORNING WAS too perfect. A pale blue sky stretched cloudless above Ansley Park like a canvas begging to be ruined. Pollen shimmered in the air with the scent of early magnolia blooms. Mourning doves cooed lazily from the branches overhead. Lawn sprinklers ticked like metronomes. Everything felt quiet.

Too quiet.

Dex stood on the opposite side of The Prado, half-shadowed beneath the twisted limbs of a live oak. His hoodie felt too warm, clinging to his back where sweat gathered between his shoulder blades. The coffee in his hand had long gone cold, but he still brought it to his lips out of habit. It tasted like ash now, bitter and metallic on his tongue. Still, he sipped, like some part of him believed routine could anchor him, like he was hoping the caffeine would wake him from his current nightmare.

His mind was a frayed cable—sparking and raw, dancing somewhere between fury and disbelief— his body moving on autopilot. A phantom pressure lingered in his chest, a heavy ache behind his ribs. His pulse beat unevenly, reacting to things more felt but unseen.

Across the street, Vaughn's house was blackened on its southern side, the huge magnolia trees flanking either side obscured most of the damage. What wasn't blocked by the trees, was hidden by the thick crepe myrtles lining the wrought-iron fence at the perimeter. Ivy on the southern and eastern walls was singed black at the edges. Several upstairs windows were spider-webbed and soot-streaked. Yellow tape crisscrossed the property in warning.

Dex crossed when traffic thinned—a lull between joggers and dogwalkers—but a cyclist from out of nowhere passed too close, wind slicing across Dex's face as the tires hissed against the pavement. Someone's golden retriever barked from across the greenspace. No one noticed him slip through the wrought-iron gate. No one looked twice.

The front path's rock chips crunched beneath his boots, the sound too sharp in the quiet morning. The grass was damp, still saturated from last night's deluge. The flower beds destroyed, full of mud and disheveled mulch. The azaleas wore a dusting of ash. The air still held the stench of smoke and something chemical beneath it.

Dex avoided the blistered front door, its paint bubbling and peeling. Instead, he followed the garden path around the side where the shingles had gone matte with soot. A rusted spigot dripped into an already-flooded flower bed, its rosemary and lavender bushes scorched at the tips. The glass of the windows above the beds had been punched out by heat and high-powered water. He stopped where the path bent behind the hedgerow and crouched low.

The soil had been disturbed. Faint churn marks scarred the ash—boot tracks overlaid by fire crew treads. On the brick wall, a bloom pattern arced upward. He leaned closer, brushing aside a flattened fern with his knuckles. Fresh gasoline—a dark, oily sheen clung to the mulch where runoff had failed to wash it clean.

He reached toward it, then froze at the sound of soft, deliberate steps sounding from behind. Dex rose fast, breath catching in his throat like a fishhook.

Malik Renshaw stood behind him dressed in fitted black with black gloves that matched, no insignia or security marker. He felt out of place in the daylight, looking instead like he belonged in the shadows.

"You followed me."

"No," Malik replied. His voice was quiet—low enough not to carry, but sharp enough to command attention. "I knew you'd come back. You seemed like the type to not let things—"

"You've been watching?"

"I've been listening," Malik corrected. "I arrived here last night right before you screamed."

Dex's jaw tightened. "That explains the outfit. You'd better not be playing games with me."

"I'm not." Malik glanced up at the balcony. "I'm here for the same reason you are. To prove what they tried to cover up."

"You think he was killed."

"I know he was."

Malik stepped lightly through the ash, avoiding the clearer prints. "Neighbors called in gunshots before the flames. Then the fire went up fast—too fast for an accident. This was staged."

Dex looked toward the blackened doorway. "They must have torched it."

"Doused it, too, by the smell," Malik said. "Lit it to wipe the scene."

Dex looked. "They failed... and left enough evidence to follow the trail."

Malik shook his head. "They erased it. Four hours after the call. No photos taken. No incident report filed." Malik's eyes met his. "I pulled the backend logs. This address was never tagged as a crime scene. Officially, nothing happened here."

The two stood in silence. Mourning doves cooed again, oblivious. Somewhere nearby, a child laughed. A lawnmower buzzed faintly from a street over. Life moved on. But Dex's hands balled into fists.

Then Malik reached into his coat and tossed something onto the stone path between them: a pair of slim, black gloves.

"Put those on."

Dex hesitated. "Why?"

"Because if you touch me—even by accident—I can't risk what you'll see. Or more importantly, what they will."

Dex crouched, picking up the gloves. "You think I want to tether right now?"

Malik raised an eyebrow. "You know it doesn't matter. Contact is all it takes."

"I should tell you," Dex began, "the Order assigned you as my next target. I'm supposed to extract information from you."

"I know," Malik smirked. "Why do you think I gave you the gloves?"

"But how?"

"I spliced into HALCION's security feed ages ago—not much gets past me."

Once gloved, they moved in parallel—but never close. Malik studied the burn pattern along the hedges and foundation. Dex surveyed sightlines to the street from the side entrance, the way someone could come and go without being seen. The porch light above the back door hung blackened and melted, a glass teardrop fused to its base.

"What about his smart system?" Dex asked. "Camera feed?"

"Replaced by the time the medical examiner arrived," Malik said. "The hub's serial number is already logged at a warehouse in Decatur."

Dex stood slowly. His knees ached. His spine popped. "So, that's it? No record. No footage. No prints. Just a clean fire no one will ever investigate?"

Malik's voice was quieter than before. "Not fire. Spectacle."

"They wanted me to believe it. To think it was my fault. That caring has consequences."

Malik tilted his head. "Did it work?"

Dex shook his head. "Not enough."

They fell into a careful silence, listening for the ordinary noises of a city that refused to stop: a bus grumbling, a dog barking, a distant siren.

"With the mains cut, we can get inside without tripping anything that may have survived the fire," Dex said. "He didn't tell me where it was, but Vaughn mentioned a hidden server—told me that his cameras picked up footage of Isabella two days after he was told she died. If it lived through this, it's our only shot as seeing what really happened."

"Vaughn must have really trusted you to tell you about the server."

"Vaughn and I shared a lot of things in the short time we had together. Perhaps it was the tethers during..." Dex's voice trailed off as he lowered his gaze.

"I knew about Vaughn," Malik admitted. "Isabella shared a lot with me. I knew about the mirror server, too. Actually, I was the one who installed it."

"Then we need it—it will show us what they tried to erase."

"Follow me."

Malik led him to the back where the window had blown out near the living room. The frame was warped and wet, the floor inside dusted with ash. He slid in first, then offered Dex a forearm to balance—careful not to make any skin contact by mistake.

The house smelled like soaked drywall and smoke. Soot smeared beneath their boots. Dex barely registered the ruined cookware and blackened towels in the kitchen. His feet carried him down the hall, slower with each step, toward Vaughn's bedroom.

The door hung ajar, but the fire hadn't reached it. Smoke stains tracked along the ceiling like rain maps. Pillows still held the memory of heads. The faint musk of their night—citrus, sweat, Vaughn—clung stubbornly beneath the soot. Dex stepped forward and sank into the mattress. He buried his face in the sheets and inhaled, and the sobs took him—first silent, then shaking, then ragged and raw. He clutched at the bedding until his knuckles ached. The sound he made didn't sound like him.

Malik stood in the doorway, hands flexing, useless. He couldn't touch Dex; a touch could tether, and a tether could stream. He did the only thing he could, turning toward the study and leaving Dex to grieve alone, his footsteps echoing as they retreated down the hallway.

Dex stayed folded for a long time, breath tearing, until the smoke smell creeping in filled his lungs. He wiped his face with his sleeve, found Vaughn's shirt crumpled on the floor, and lifted it. The scent was immediate, intimate. He folded it carefully and tucked it beneath his arm. On the dresser, he spotted a framed photo of Vaughn—younger, carefree, laughing into sun. Dex wrapped Vaughn's shirt around it, slid both into his hoodie pocket like a secret, and forced himself from the room.

In the study, a filing cabinet had been dragged forward to reveal a hidden panel. Behind it, a fanless server sat squat and stubborn. Malik had already uncoupled the fiber, easing the chassis into a canvas duffel he'd found in the closet.

"Got the server," Malik announced when he noticed Dex. He glanced at the shirt tucked into the hoodie pocket and added, "Find everything you needed?"

"Yeah, let's get out of here before someone returns."

They rode in silence in Dex's Jeep—Malik's car left as a decoy to throw the Order off their trail—but they didn't go straight to Dex's place. They circled once, then again. On the second pass, two men in plain, dark clothes stood where no one should be: one leaning against the stoop rail with eyes on the street, the other on the porch scrolling a phone.

"Order," Malik said. "Or at least hired mercenaries."

Dex parked three blocks over. He popped the lockbox beneath the seat and grabbed his pistol. "Stay here," he said. "I won't be long."

"Be safe."

It ended quickly. The alley swallowed sound; training did the rest. When it was over, there was only the sting of cordite, heat lifting from asphalt, Dex's pulse pounding in his ears.

He moved through the apartment fast: clothes into a bag, Halina's thumb drive from its hiding place, the sealed metal urn with Charlie's ashes cradled like a living thing. Then he scrawled a letter. He paused at the kitchen and left the envelope, palms flat to the counter, breathing until his hands steadied, then locked the door and left.

Malik guided him east to Decatur, to a sagging-brick bungalow that looked like nothing. Outside, however, belied the completely renovated inside. Malik dropped the duffle in a state-of-the-art panic room that housed a wall of CPUs and monitors and the hum of concealed systems. "They think I live in the loft," he said. "I've kept this place off the records, no ties to me."

Once settled, he wired Vaughn's server to an isolated rig. Directories bloomed: archives, logs, untouched caches. Dex stood with Vaughn's shirt clutched to his chest.

"Start with Vaughn," he said.

The driveway feed rolled, grainy and merciless: a figure approaching the house; a muzzle flare at the door; a man's voice and a gunshot striking Vaughn, who staggered backward into the foyer before collapsing. Minutes later, flames pulsed across the entryway camera—accelerant catching, fire blooming fast. The kitchen cam showed smoke swallowing the room in a rush. Then sirens, uniforms, an ambulance closing around the scene like a curtain.

Dex turned away, walked down the hall, braced his hands against the wall and waited for breath to return. When he came back, his face was pale but set.

"I'm sorry you had to see that," Malik said, queuing the next clip.

He found it—timestamped forty-eight hours after the elevator "malfunction." Isabella appeared on the front porch—alive, cautious, scanning the street, unlocking the door, then slipping inside.

"She's alive," Dex breathed. "She has to be."

Malik slid Halina's drive into the reader. The video loaded: Isabella recorded days before she disappeared. Her face looked worn but resolute.

"If you're watching this," she said, "then the story you were told about me was one I wrote myself. I staged it to protect the work—and to protect myself. Only Halina knew. I hope it's you watching, Malik. If it is, know that I trusted you more than anyone else, but I needed to protect you."

Her gaze lifted, steady. "You know me as Isabella. But those in the underground now know me as Persephone—taken into the darkness, returning with seeds of power in her hand. I had to descend to vanish from their sight. But descent is not the end—it is only a passage."

She paused, exhaled. "The code for the CASPER project is safe—encrypted and hidden on the local server in my house. If you have this video, you have the drive with the encryption key. Use it to free yourselves, then free the others. Use it to blind them."

Her voice softened, resolve beneath it. "Follow the clues. They will lead you to Persephone. And if you reach me, it will mean the world is not yet lost."

The screen went dark. The quiet afterward felt like a held breath.

Dex swallowed. "She knew," he said, voice rough. "And Aurelio—he hinted at her. At Persephone. After I tethered with him, I went to Inman Park. It lines up. All of it."

"Then let's blind them." Malik was already loading the encryption key into the program on the server.

Dex watched Malik speed read the code for Isabella's CASPER program—a "wow" and a "holy fuck" escaping his mouth as he skimmed.

"What does CASPER do?"

"CASPER stands for Cloaked Adaptive Signal Pattern Encoding Relay," Malik explained. "Isabella told me she was working on something, but from what I can tell, it is supposed to scramble the GEIST relay before it is uploaded to HALCION— a *ghost* in the machine—blinding the Order from the tethers. It appears it creates a fake session altogether, so they're literally out of the loop."

"Doesn't really help, though," Dex said plainly.

"What do you mean?"

"It's still sending data to HALCION, which means the Order would still be tracking movements of every Tangent."

"You're not wrong—she should have known that," Malik said. "Then we tweak it and really blind them. I can probably rework the code to sever any connection to HALCION completely."

Despite the grief, the thought of being free from the Order's grip brought the hint of a smile to Dex's face. "Let's do that."

Vaughn woke to the sound of someone breathing. Not the mechanical hush of a hospital vent, not the metronome beep that makes grief polite—just breath. Human, close.

The ceiling above him was low and unpainted, boards strung with wiring and a single bare bulb. The air smelled like alcohol swabs and neroli. His shoulder lit like a struck match when he tried to sit up.

"Easy." A cool palm steadied him. "Don't tear it."

He turned his head and—*impossible*—she was there. Isabella. Framed in the low light, close enough for him to see the scar near her left temple, the familiar constellation of freckles at her cheekbone. For a breath, he forgot the word for breath.

"Either I'm dead," he whispered, "or you're—"

"Alive." Her mouth tilted, tender and pained at once. "Very much alive. And so are you."

The world stuttered into place in pieces: a cinderblock room draped with sheets to soften the corners; a row of repurposed metal trays turned into sterile tables; IV bags hanging from welded coat racks; an ancient heart monitor whose green line crept with stubborn composure. At the far wall, two figures dozed in folding chairs, boxes of gauze and gloves stacked between them.

Vaughn swallowed. The motion scraped. "Where—?"

"A clinic," she said. "Not ours, exactly. A borrowed space we keep when we can't use the regular one. It's safe."

He closed his eyes, opened them. She was still there. "You died," he said helplessly, hearing the old story in his voice. "They told us you died."

"They needed that story," she said. "I needed it, too."

Her hand didn't leave his shoulder. It steadied him as the room tilted. The night returned in shards: the front door, the muzzle flare, the punch of heat washing the hallway, then a cold so complete it had to be the absence of everything.

"Persephone," Isabella said softly, as if confessing. "That's what they call me now. Down here. And outside. It kept me alive—being someone the Order wasn't looking for."

He tried to smile, failed. "The Underworld suits you."

"I would've preferred a beach and better wine," she said. Her laugh was the same as it used to be— the one that turned late nights into mornings and made hard choices survivable.

"I should have told you," she said. "I wanted to, a hundred times. But if you knew, you'd have been a map. And they would have used you to get to me."

"You hid from me." No accusation, only the ache of it.

"I hid you by hiding from you," she said. "I'm sorry."

He let the apology sit between them until it warmed. Then he nodded once, not because it didn't hurt, but because it mattered that she said it.

"Tell me," he said. "What happened last night?"

She drew a slow breath, eyes dropping to the bandage at his shoulder, as if the wound were a transcript and she owed him a faithful reading.

"I walk your street every night I can," she began. "Different routes, different times. I'm never the same person twice if I can help it. Lately it's been... busy. More patrols. More strangers who aren't neighbors. I was two houses down when I heard the shot."

Her voice did not shake. It was the voice she used in labs, in meetings where the truth needed clean delivery.

"I cut through the side yard," she said. "Your door was open, the foyer lit. He was tall, careful— Order posture, even despite the civilian clothes. He'd clipped you, intended for your heart but missed. You were on the floor trying to stand. He didn't see me until I was two steps behind him. He turned, and I didn't give him a second shot."

Vaughn's fingers twitched against the blanket. "You killed him."

"I did." She didn't flinch. "Head, then face—to destroy the teeth. That's how they confirm a body. I made sure they couldn't confirm it wasn't you."

He was quiet. The monitor's green line traced their silence.

"Our people came fast when I made the call for help. We pulled you out the back, kept pressure on your shoulder, hit you with something for pain. You were fading but present. You asked me if I was real." The faint flicker of rue tugged at her mouth. "You asked me if you were in heaven."

He felt heat in his cheeks that wasn't fever. "I don't remember anything other than thinking I had died."

"You will," she said gently. "When it stops hurting."

"What about the house fire?" he asked.

"That was me," she said. "I doused him and lit it once you were out safely. Gas from the can he brought for the job. He was thorough, but I used his plan against him. I wanted it hot and fast at the entry—enough to eat the evidence I couldn't hide." A tiny, frustrated breath. "I meant to grab the mirror server but didn't have time. The engine sirens were already on the way."

He pictured her there in the foyer—calculating accelerant and time, watching two clocks at once: his pulse and the neighborhood's.

"I checked your study door," she said. "Closed. Heat hadn't reached the hall yet. If it survived—and I think it did—the server will be there. I had to choose. You, or the machine."

"I'm glad you chose me," he said, not knowing what to do with the size of that simple sentence.

Her eyes softened. "I'd do it again."

He turned his head toward her. His voice came quieter than before, stripped of pretense. "Isabella... I met someone."

"I know," she said, her mouth curving, almost teasing. "I've seen him. On my patrols. Dark features. Brooding. Handsome. He's definitely your type."

Vaughn blinked, caught between disbelief and relief. "You've been watching?"

"I've been watching over you," she corrected. "And yes, I saw him. The way you looked at him told me enough."

His throat tightened. "His name is Dex."

Her hand lingered on his. "Then hold onto that, Vaughn. Because the Order already knows you cared for him—that's why they came. Feeling is the one thing they can't afford to let survive."

Vaughn thought of Dex, the porch light, the warmth of his laugh, the quiet ferocity in his eyes. He thought of survival, of betrayal, of the cruel grace of second chances.

"Rest," Isabella said again, her voice steady but kind. "When you wake, we'll decide where to put you. And what story to hand the world next."

37
EXIT

T HE FREIGHT ELEVATOR rattled open, carrying Regina, Gallows, and a four-man tactical unit into Malik Renshaw's loft. The men fanned out without orders, rifles raised, boots whispering over the concrete floor. Their presence was overkill—but that was the point. If Malik resisted, the Order wanted him subdued quickly, quietly, even permanently.

The loft stretched wide and industrial: high ceilings, exposed steel beams, brick walls weathered by decades of neglect. Yet beneath the rough bones was a strange precision—books stacked in deliberate order, cables coiled neatly, screens glowing with restless light. A dozen monitors lined the far wall, each one splicing into feeds they had never meant Malik to see: checkpoints, HALCION corridors, even the stark white of interrogation rooms.

"He's been inside our eyes," Regina murmured, moving closer, fingers hovering over a keyboard she dared not touch. "Every lens, every channel—spliced clean."

"Son of a bitch!" Gallows growled. "No wonder he ran. He knew we wanted Truitt tethered to him."

The tactical men swept the side rooms and came back shaking their heads. "All clear. He's long gone, ma'am."

"I think you meant, 'sir'—" Gallows snapped, annoyed that the team view Regina as their superior and not him.

"Yes, sir. All clear, sir."

Regina's gaze shifted from the monitors to a shelf beside the desk. Frames leaned in quiet defiance against the wall. She lifted one, brushing the dust with her thumb. A photograph of Malik, Vaughn, and Isabella standing in front of a sunset on the beach. The second frame was smaller, more intimate: Malik and Vaughn alone, bodies pressed together, Malik's hand on Vaughn's back in a way that was too familiar, with a look between them too obvious to be explained away.

She felt Gallows' presence behind her. Before he could speak, she set the frame back down, face neutral, voice clipped. "He's probably watching us even now. Call in the clean-up crew and pack up everything. We should trace these IP addresses and figure out if he's accessed them from another location recently."

"If he's still in the city, we'll smoke him out." Gallows' jaw ticked, but he gave the signal. The tactical men began disconnecting cables, yanking drives, stripping the loft bare.

Regina let her eyes linger on the photographs one last time before turning toward the door. Malik hadn't just fled; he'd taken the truth with him. And truth, she knew, was far more dangerous than any weapon in their arsenal.

Dex's bungalow smelled of gunpowder and blood before they even crossed the threshold. Two men lay sprawled across the porch, shot clean through the chest. Inside, the house was unsettlingly neat—every glass on its shelf, every book squared. A single envelope sat dead center on the kitchen island, propped against a vase of hydrangeas. Scrawled across its front in black ink:

FUCK YOU.

Gallows tore it open and began to read aloud:

> *You hide behind your Curtain and your toxins and your lies, thinking if you hollow us out enough we'll stop resisting. But you're wrong. Every injection, every broadcast, every grave you dig only fuels the fire you're so desperate to drown.*
>
> *I will no longer be a part of your idea of order. I won't be subjecting others to invasive tactics to steal their secrets, their memories, their truths. I won't be your weapon anymore.*
>
> *From here on, I'm the shadow lurking in your streets, the crack in your Curtain, the voice you can't silence, the Chaos you meant to kill.*
>
> *You preach that empathy is rot, that compassion weakens the spine, that anyone who dares to care is diseased. You peddle fear of weakness the way zealots once sold sin. You've poisoned a*

> *generation into believing that numbness is virtue, that cruelty is clarity, that to feel is to fail. You brand it all as liberal agenda—call it woke, call it corrupt, call it anything but what it is: human.*

Gallows skimmed the rest, his jaw tightening, but Regina grabbed the letter, her eyes lingering. There, folded between the threats, were lines written sharper than the rest—seemingly meaningless, unless you'd lived it.

> *You tell the world that mercy is dangerous, that kindness must be purged, that those who are different must be erased.*

> *You demonize emotion, but empathy and kindness are what save you from being swallowed by the darkness. It's a neighbor's punch striking the face of a father about to strike their daughter for being raped. It's losing a child and wanting to end it all, but being saved by a stranger's hand pulling you from the rushing waters you hoped would drown you. It's what drives firefighters to rush into burning buildings even if all they find is a lifeless corpse they couldn't save.*

"Looks like Truitt may have been the one to kill our assassin and start the fire at Merrick's house," Regina said, biting back the anger at being told her weaker moments.

"Doubtful," Gallows countered. "Dmitriev wasn't answering his phone, so I went to Merrick's house to check on him only to find it up in flames. The trucks arrived shortly after, and Truitt arrived right before I left—didn't want him to recognize me."

"He mentioned the burned corpse in the letter. Maybe he was hoping no one would recognize that it *wasn't* Vaughn."

"He said a lot of things in that letter," Gallows scoffed, "but what does a fucking bartender know about anything?"

Regina remembered Dex's words to her the day he was brought to HALCION, not to mistake what he did for who he was, and something hit harder this time. She'd been underestimated all her life, reduced to her gender instead of her ability. Gallows respected her—though not at first—but he still underestimated her, just as she had done with Dex, a truth even more telling as she stood in his empty bungalow without a clue of where to look for him next.

While Malik worked on rewriting Isabella's code, Dex ventured to the kitchen to cook dinner with whatever he found in Malik's fridge and pantry, returning a half-hour later with two bowls.

"Smells good," Malik said as he walked in. "But don't forget to put your gloves back on. We don't need any accidental tethers."

"Right," Dex said, setting the bowls next to Malik and retreating to the kitchen. He returned with gloved hands, still taking a seat on the other side of the room to avoid contact.

"What is it?" Malik asked as he took a bite.

"You didn't have much in there, so I just added some ground beef and tomatoes to a couple boxes of mac and cheese."

"It's delicious," Malik said through a mouthful.

"How much longer on the code?"

"I already finished tweaking the original code actually," Malik said between bites. "Right now, I am embedding a virus into the code to destroy the uplink capability, which will take you offline permanently."

It took nearly another hour for Malik to finish the updates to the CASPER program. Dex had dozed on the sofa in the living room, but Malik was too excited to wait for him to wake up on his own.

"Wake up, sleeping beauty." Malik couldn't risk the tether, so he poked Dex with a broom handle. "Time to really stir up some Chaos."

Malik retreated to the office and waited for Dex to shuffle through the threshold.

"Let's do this," Dex said with a yawn.

"The program is all loaded," Malik said, cord in hand, "I just need to plug this into your port. Take a seat."

Malik's gloved touch at the base of his skull was precise. When the CASPER program slipped into the GEIST port, Dex felt an electric pulse—almost like a shock—radiate down his spine and up into his brain. In that moment he felt more machine than human.

"This severs the stream," Malik said quietly. "No more uploads. No more live tethers to HALCION. From now on, what you feel belongs to you."

Dex closed his eyes. In the dark behind them, he saw the porch light the way it had been—lit for him, foolish and true—and for the first time since it went out, something inside him rose.

The computer chimed when the program ended. Malik's shoulders loosened by a fraction. "Done."

"What now?"

"Unfortunately, we'll have to test it."

"And if it didn't work?"

"Then we're screwed," Malik said. "But I helped Isabella on the original coding for the GEIST interface, so I am pretty certain I did a good job with the self-destruct code."

"Only one way to find out, I suppose."

Malik swung a monitor around and typed in a long string. "This is your GEIST serial," he said. "If anything leaks, it'll light up here."

A bare status line waited on the screen.

"Okay," he added, softer. "Think about something that would set you off emotionally."

Dex let the memories come.

He thought of Vaughn—the porch light, the smell of sex still soaked in those sheets, the look on his face as he straddled his lap. He thought of David—the smell of sandalwood and sweat on his bush as his cock slid down Dex's throat, those piercing blue eyes that unraveled Dex from first glance. He thought of Charlie—the first kiss, the love letter on the shower glass, his last struggled breaths. Tears poured in earnest.

He felt his pulse climb. Heat rushed up his throat.

Malik refreshed, but still nothing registered. "Try once more."

Dex pushed harder, let the grief and the want surge like a tide.

The screen stayed blank.

They stared at it a breath longer.

"Time to test touch," Malik said.

"You sure about this?" asked Dex, receiving a nod in response.

They peeled off their gloves together. Caution tugged at their muscles, but they ignored it. Dex set his palm to Malik's wrist and held.

Hours had passed since they'd left Dex's bungalow, but Regina was already back at HALCION. She sat alone at her computer, Dex Truitt's file open, the kill protocol ready.

But her mind wasn't on the screen. It was on her father's disgust when she told him she'd been raped—the underlying accusatory glare, like it was her fault. She thought of the daughter she'd miscarried, a child she grew to love as it grew inside her even despite the circumstances of the conception. She thought of the riverbank only weeks after the miscarriage—mud cold on her hands, lungs choking, the current dragging her under. A hand she didn't know had seized her wrist, hauled her gasping into air. A stranger's empathy. That's what saved her life—and she, despite wanting to end it moments before—wanted to be saved.

Tears burned at the corners of her eyes. She blinked hard, furious at herself. Emotion was weakness. Empathy was weakness. Dex had no right to dig those memories out of her—she saw the irony, that the Order had no right to do the same to others, and it infuriated her even more.

Her hands slammed the console. With a snarl, she punched the command and executed the kill switch. The monitor flickered. A single red line appeared across the screen:

SYSTEM ERROR

Regina froze, her reflection staring back through the crimson glow. The tears she'd held back broke free, streaking her face. Rage surged hot and bitter, colliding with the grief she thought she'd long buried. The system had failed her. She had underestimated Dex Truitt, and worse—he had somehow reached into her and found her humanity, something she'd shoved down and swallowed once she caught her breath on that riverbank.

It was decided from the start—long before Project Last Gleaming, long before Corazamine had been twisted and corrupted for their agenda—that the Order's leadership team wouldn't receive the Serexin shot. Despite the preachings of Vexley and Gallows—'Serexin is serenity' and 'Empathy is weakness'—neither of them thought it wise to numb those in charge of seeing the project through.

But Regina, regardless of all her efforts to ever show emotion again, now ached with the memory of all the pain she had tried to forget. She wanted nothing more now than Serexin's promise of serenity.

Dex Truitt had unlocked something in her and fucked it all up. She wiped her eyes, gathered her composure, and grabbed the makeup in her purse to hide the puffy redness plaguing her eyes.

The Serexin labs were on the other side of HALCION's campus, but she'd made up her mind—she would take the Serexin shot. She couldn't risk feeling pain and showing weakness in front of those that looked to her to lead. She needed to be hollow again.

Regina only had to feign her stone-cold reputation once, placating Victoria, Vexley's wife, with mindless gossip about the fire at Isabella Merrick's house before continuing to the lab, relieved to find it empty. She went immediately to the Serexin storage fridges lining the eastern wall, opening one to find shelves filled with trays of syringes pre-loaded with the perfect dose.

She hated needles, but she took a deep breath, grabbed a syringe, and moved to the injection station. The needle bit as it slid into her shoulder, but she hoped the effects would be quick, relieving her of all pain. She felt a cooling sensation flood from the injection site, calming her enough to finally exhale the breath she'd been holding.

But that calm didn't last. A surge of heat radiated up her neck, seemingly firing every synapse in her brain, forcing her eyes shut. When she re-opened them, color flooded in brighter than she had ever seen before. The world had changed, and so had Regina.

The tether opened—quietly, like a door easing on its hinges—and Dex saw Vaughn's house from behind Malik's eyes: steam rising from a pot as Isabella stirred, Vaughn grating some fresh cheese at the island pretending not to steal glances of Malik. He was terrible at pretending—the glance kept sliding back, the unhidden flush when Malik met it. Isabella noticed too, unbothered, a smile catching the corners of her mouth.

The scene shifted, Isabella washing the dishes, Malik rinsing and drying, and Vaughn putting them away.

Isabella's shoulder brushed Malik's. Her voice came low, meant only for him. "I knew he'd like you."

Malik glanced over at Vaughn, then back at Isabella. "And you're okay with this?"

Isabella smiled warmly. "Why do you think I invited you to dinner? Vaughn has urges that I cannot fulfill. I'd rather them be filled by someone I can trust to keep his secret."

The scene shifted completely. Night air on a quiet street, Malik and Vaughn walking, hands almost touching but hesitant. Then Vaughn stopped, turned, and pulled Malik into a kiss. The kiss was tender, but full of torment and guilt.

Another flicker came like smoke. Malik's loft— book-lined shelves, candlelight, a record on low. The vision narrowed to hands and breath, hunger without hurry, warmth and want, release without apology.

Then morning light, Vaughn on the edge of the bed lacing a boot too slowly, eyes red from lack of sleep. "I care about her," he said, voice rough. "And I know she says she's okay with this, but I can see that it hurts her, too."

The images loosened and slipped away. Dex eased his hand back and stared at Malik but couldn't find the words.

Malik's breath came out shaking, then steadied as he refocused on the monitors. No whisper. No data. No blip. Just a flat line. "We did it!"

"And you're sure that nothing registered?

"Nothing."

Dex stared in silence at the monitor for a moment, then back over at Malik. "Why didn't you tell me about you and Vaughn?"

"I didn't think it was important," Malik said softly. "It was a long time ago, Dex—years before the bombs fell, when Isabella and I worked together at Neurvana."

"I think it was important," Dex countered. "It came through during the tether."

"I just didn't think it was the appropriate time—not when you are grieving," Malik explained.

Dex grabbed Malik's hand again—the tether blooming in the back of his mind—and pulled him into a tight hug, consoling him. "You're grieving, too."

Malik inhaled sharply, fighting back the emotion. For a moment they stayed rigid, then pretenses broke. Malik's face pressed into Dex's shoulder; Dex's hand tightened its grip on Malik's; the sound that came out of them wasn't pretty. It was wet and human and unguarded, grief that didn't need permission. The screen beside them stayed blank—no whisper, no uploaded theft—while they let the weight do what it needed to do.

When Malik finally drew a breath, he pulled back enough to see Dex's face. "I was going to tell you," he said, voice rough. "And I wanted you to hear it from me, from where I stood, not as a rumor. If we're going to live through this, you're right: we can't leave shadows between us."

Dex nodded. Oddly, relief moved through him. Malik had known Vaughn as he had known Vaughn. They were not alone inside it, the shared loss now binding them.

Charlie was now just ash in an urn. Vaughn was now just a photo and folded shirt in a bag. The Order had been efficient—tidy, practiced, convinced of its permanence. Regina's script.

Gallows' orders. The elevator story. The arson. He had watched them scrub lives and call it order. He had watched them mistake quiet for consent.

But CASPER worked. The digital tether they used to reach into him had been severed, had gone slack. The room inside his skull felt uninhabited for the first time since the Ghostjack was implanted. Hollow in a good way, ready for his own voice.

There was no returning to before. The bar, the practiced smiles, the soft-shoe around feeling—those belonged to a man who still believed he could live on the surface. The world had decided otherwise. So had he. Persephone wasn't just a rumor anymore—she was Isabella.

Persephone's existence meant following the clues; it meant learning the city's shadow routes—service tunnels, forgotten basements, the back ends of systems the Order thought were closed.

The work ahead was clear: find her and every Tangent with a Ghostjack and help them vanish from the Order's grip; free them until the GEIST network went dark.

The world above still bowed to the Order's illusion of control, but Dex had suffered too much to kneel. Charlie's blood. Vaughn's murder. Nights of sleepless silence where even grief was stolen from him. Yet here he stood—untethered, unbroken, and unafraid.

The Order's control was as good as ash. Chaos was no longer rumor or scattered embers of rebellion. It had shape and a pulse. It was flesh and fire, carried in his chest, in Malik's, in Persephone's. Together, they were proof the Order's power and permanence were a lie.

The war began years ago—Dex had watched the bombs fall and the Curtain rise—but the Order had made it personal. Dex took a deep breath and in it felt hope—for himself, for them all—that the Order could be broken, that the Curtain would soon fall.

EPILOGUE

JUNE 24, 2027

"Freedom is never voluntarily given by the oppressor; it must be demanded by the oppressed."

~ Dr. Martin Luther King, Jr.

IT HAD BEGUN as a gamble. One Tangent at a time, hidden away in safehouses and forgotten corners of the city, Dex would hold them steady with gloved hands while Malik slid CASPER's patch into their Ghostjack. The reaction was never dramatic—just a shift, a long exhale as the invisible connection broke and their tether to HALCION went dark. Quiet freedom, but freedom all the same.

Tonight, the gamble had grown bolder. Weeks of putting up cryptic flyers had turned out waves of

Tangents in this part of the city, giving Malik his first chance to test the switchboard he'd built.

The abandoned gas station reeked of rust and old oil. Wires sprawled like veins across the cracked floor, feeding into Malik's makeshift contraption. A single cord snaked up into the tablet balanced in his hands, its glow reflected in his dark eyes.

Twelve Tangents sat in a rough circle, chairs turned to the wall with their backs facing inward, Ghostjacks tethered to the switchboard. Dex moved around them, collecting clipboards they'd filled out for verification, noting the sheen of sweat on their brows, the way their gloved hands clenched to avoid an accidental tether.

A wiry kid couldn't stop bouncing his knee. Pale, hollow-eyed, maybe twenty at most. He whispered as if the walls themselves might be listening. "I just... I don't want them in my head anymore. I don't want them recording everything I touch."

Beside him, a heavyset man in a grease-stained work shirt sat stiff, jaw tense. "They told me my wife forgot me. Said she signed papers to move on. But I saw her—three weeks ago. She didn't forget. She's just scared." His hand tremble on his knee. "Please, cut me loose so I can find her again."

Four chairs down, a lean man with bronzed skin and a long scar running from temple to jaw sat rigid—soldier maybe—his gaze never resting. He hadn't spoken, but his eyes swept constantly—doors, shadows, every movement in the circle. This one hadn't come here by chance. He was here for the promised quiet.

Three seats over, two sat close together, gloved hands intertwined. Dex recognized them instantly.

"A bit of fate seeing you here, Tobias," Dex said, a genuine smile tugging at his mouth.

Tobias looked up from his clipboard, guilt written into his features but steadiness beneath it. "Dex... I'm so sorry for turning you in. I thought Regina might tell me more about Charlie's whereabouts, but she didn't."

Dex's tone softened. "Everything happens for a reason—at least that's what I am told. If you hadn't turned me in, you'd have been punished. Malik and I never would have crossed paths, I'd never have been given Isabella's video, and CASPER wouldn't be here tonight. Strange as it is, we're all standing here because of that."

"I suppose you're right," Tobias murmured, then gestured to the woman beside him. Forgetting that Dex and Charlotte were already acquainted, he said, "This is Charlie."

"Charlotte," she corrected gently, her eyes locking on Dex's—calm, assessing, as though she were already reading him untethered. "But Charlie works."

Dex gave a small nod, the nickname heavy on his chest. "I only knew you by your drink order. It's good to finally meet properly, Charlotte."

"Nice to formally meet you, too, Dex." She extended her gloved hand. "If it weren't for you slipping Tobias that pamphlet, he might not have found me."

Dex chuckled under his breath. "Funny thing is, I threw the whole stack away. But something told me to save one."

Charlotte tilted her head. "Does it work? CASPER, I mean…"

"I've been severed for three weeks," Dex assured. "Since then, Malik and I have freed more than two hundred. Slow work—nine or ten a day. But tonight, this will be our fourth switchboard session. Forty-eight severed in a single night."

"There's a mass of Tangents in the Chaos compound," Charlotte said. "Perhaps Malik can bring the switchboard there."

"That's not a bad idea," Dex agreed. "He and I have been meaning to venture underground, but this has kept us busy."

"Ready?" Malik asked from the circle's center

Dex swept the room, taking in the faces one last time, then he gave Malik a nod. "They're ready."

Malik's face twitched with hesitation, but his finger tapped the command.

The mirrored registry flickered on the tablet while the room seemed to hold its breath. Dex and Malik waited for the chime; when it sounded, Malik watched twelve names wink out in unison. Twelve more Ghostjacks severed.

The room exhaled. The wiry kid sagged with relief. The broad man rubbed at his neck with trembling fingers. Tobias squeezed Charlotte's ungloved hand, and she squeezed back. The scarred soldier gave the smallest nod, neck no longer swiveling, eyes softening for the first time.

Dex allowed himself one steady breath—then saw Malik's expression darken.

The tablet stuttered. Static bled across the feed. A trace window opened. The Order had noticed.

"Shit," Malik hissed, fingers darting across the glass. "Clusters this big leave footprints. Four in one night—that's enough to triangulate us."

Dex moved beside him, voice taut. "What do we do?"

Malik didn't look up. "We can't keep this up. Groups are too visible. They'll box us in sooner or later." Finally, his eyes rose, sharp with resolve. "The only way forward is inside HALCION. A breach. Delete the data and sever them from the core."

Dex studied him. "Aren't you hacked into HALCION? Can't you pull it from out here?"

Malik shook his head. "If I try to scale it, they'll cut power to the main server, spin up a new backup, and I will lose access completely. The only way to free everyone is from the source."

Dex nodded grimly. "Then that's the plan. But until we figure out how to get in, it's back to one at a time. Quiet. Careful. No clusters."

Malik powered down the tablet. Dex moved through the circle, unplugging leads one by one, each click echoing in the silence. The Tangents shifted, free but uncertain, their lives suddenly their own again.

At the far side, Tobias and Charlotte exchanged a look, then stepped closer. Tobias' voice was low but steady. "If you're going back in... you'll need all the help you can get."

Charlotte's eyes fixed on Malik, then Dex. "Come with us to the compound tonight. Persephone will know what to ."

Dex and Malik exchanged a startled glance, eyes brightening at the name.

"We've been following clues to find her for weeks," Malik said quickly. "Are you telling us Persephone's with you?"

"She arrived nine days ago," Tobias confirmed. "We'd never met her before, but she worked for the Order. She spoke of CASPER—said her backup code was stolen but hinted at another hidden inside HALCION. She's been trying to convince Imani to form a team to break in."

Malik dropped his gaze. "We're the ones who stole the code—but only because she wanted us to. She must've gone for it and thought the Order had found it."

"She said she had to choose her husband's life over grabbing the server," Charlotte added quietly. "She set the fire to cover her tracks, hoping the study wouldn't catch before the trucks arrived to extinguish the blaze."

Dex's breath caught. He met Malik's eyes.

"Vaughn's alive?" they asked in unison.

The words hung heavy in the air—a promise, a second chance, a new beginning.

ABOUT THE AUTHOR

ELIJAH STEELE is inventing a new genre—part erotica, part speculative fiction, all fire. His stories fuse unapologetic gay lust with the story scale of fantasy and sci-fi, proving that worldbuilding can be just as raw, carnal, and dangerous as life itself. Each story blends imaginative stories with unflinching eroticism, pulling readers into worlds where passion drives the plot and desire reshapes destiny.

Elijah writes with the sensitivity of an empath and the sexual appetite of a storyteller who refuses to hold back. When he isn't at the keyboard, you can usually find him in the kitchen cooking or just enjoying time with his husband and two mini schnauzers in Tampa, Florida—living life as boldly as the worlds he creates.

ACKNOWLEDGEMENTS

THIS BOOK COULD not have taken shape without the people who stood by me through every draft, detour, and shift.

Patrick—thank you for the initial push for me to venture into erotica.

Mike—thank you for your patience as the story evolved, for your feedback and keen eye. Most of all, for your friendship and support when I needed it most.

Bruce—your encouragement and belief in me helped carry this project forward, and I'm forever grateful for your friendship and kindness.

Rick—thank you for offering to be an alpha reader and for being willing to dive into the work at its roughest stages... though who doesn't like it rough?

And to everyone else who read excerpts or chapters along the way and shared your thoughts— your feedback mattered more than you know. Each of you helped make the story stronger, and I'm deeply grateful.